Voracity

Brian T. Seifrit

Published by
William Jenkins
2106-1200 Alberni Street
Vancouver BC V6E 1A6
Canada

williamhenryjenkins@gmail.com
http://www.williamjenkins.ca

Telephone: 1-778-953-6139

Edition 1
ISBN: 978-1928164128

Dedicated to:

Ruth Thompson, Debra Shiveley Welch, and all those who have waited patiently for this book's release.

"Voracity" was written during a time for my need to write something dark, something that could in reality happen, and with the outbreak of the Ebola virus proves that such a reality is not as farfetched as it may seem. It was conceived and written in the mid-Y2K, long before these events happened, but it does hit home. I thank all my present and future readers for their continued interest in my writing, and for letting me take them to places they have never been. Thank you."

"Live your life to the fullest- Reach out to your dreams."
BTS 2001.

Web Site & Social Media Links:

Web site: www.booksbybriant.com

*Fan email: tbseifrit@gmail.com

Face Book: www.facebook.com/btseifrit

Twitter: https://twitter.com/TBSeifrit

Blog: http://briantspov.blogspot.ca/

LinkedIn: search- Brian T. Seifrit

G+: search- Brian T. Seifrit

Kindle Mojo: search- Brian T. Seifrit

Special Acknowledgements to: William H. Jenkins for his editing suggestions and hard work. Thank you, Bill.

Chapter 1

In 1993, an elite agency called K.A.T. (Kuru Assault Team) was formed to stop the spread of a new virus, one derived from the once incurable disease Kuru, and given the name K-15. A young neurologist discovered it. Papers he wrote and submitted to medical magazines, government agencies, and health organizations were blatantly dismissed as fiction. The neurologist's name was Trent Sweet and he died for the cause in 1994. The circumstances of his death were gruesome and horrific, and would always haunt his brother Blain. The Agency, though, had a purpose and so Blain continued on, building up the Agency to what it was today.

The virus they were fighting was not like the Kuru of old. Those infected did not die from it. Instead, they went on murderous rampages and, in some cases, even cannibalizing their victims. How it spread from person to person was a mystery. There was speculation that it was hereditary. Bodies started showing up in the cities at first. Then the killings moved to the suburbs. No one was safe. It was like a plague spreading from east to west. There was only one answer: to kill those infected unless a cure could be found. Mutilated cadavers of young and old began showing up daily in back alleys, forest parks and mountain hiking trails as the virus continued to spread. The body count kept climbing, and by 2007 body parts from the dead victims began to go missing. It was then that the K.A.T. learned that those suffering from K-15 were not only killing their victims but also eating them.

The western region of British Columbia seemed to be the hot spot where the attacks and killings were taking place, and so the K.A.T. Agency fanned out its operatives to cover all western areas. To the east there were very few attacks and the Agency's presence in that corridor was minimal.

The K.A.T. agency was unknown and hidden from the world. Not Ottawa or the CSIS knew of its existence. Blain Sweet, Trent's older brother, was an original founder and one of the first members of the K.A.T. He was also the most efficient assassin the agency put in the field, with over fifty-five confirmed kills. This was the real world; this was his reality. His life outside of the agency was a cover-up for his true-identity. In the field, he went by one name Entity. In the field he was exactly that, unseen and deadly.

To his wife and everyone else, he held a job as a software developer, which kept him travelling and always on the move. His office, 'the dungeon' he liked to call it, was in the basement of the King Royal Hotel. It was a hotel he bought secretly fourteen years ago. In the early days, the hotel was a hangout for riffraff and the desolate. Today, it attracted the more elite and sophisticated. It was a good cover, and Blain meant to keep it that way.

Blain married his wife Rachel in 1995, two years after the K.A.T. formed. She knew only that he was a software developer. His small office boasted this lie, with what looked like developing software scattered about, whenever she visited him at work. He loved her like no other and she was never happier. Lately though, things were beginning to unravel at the seams.

He noticed the change himself a year earlier in 2006, after killing an entire family of five that suffered from K-15. He drew five vials of blood that day. Never had he killed so many carriers at once, and it haunted him. Their screams echoed in his mind and the scent of their torched corpses was as real to him today as the day in question. It blackened his heart and made his blood run cold, like all the vials of blood he drew from those he killed.

Rachel sat down at the kitchen table the Calimay Yellow pages in front of her. Tears welled up in her eyes as she turned to the lawyer section. Divorce was never going to be one of her options, but for the past year on and off again she thought about it. Their relationship was deteriorating faster than she wanted and there was no use in even trying to pick up the pieces. She ran her finger down the column of divorce lawyers, and wiping away her tears, she dialed a number in her mother's locale of New Kootenay.

"Whitfield & Angus law offices, can I help you?"

"Yes," she began to softly sob, "I would like to file divorce papers."

"Are you okay, ma'am?"

"Yes, yes, I'm fine. It is just so sad that I'm doing this."

"It is alright, ma'am. Perhaps you would like more time to contemplate it? Divorce should always be a last resort, unless of course you are in danger. Are you in danger, ma'am?"

"No not at all."

"If you leave me your name we will keep it on file, until you have made your final decision."

"My name is Rachel Sweet. I'm afraid if I wait too long, I might change my mind."

"Well, Mrs. Sweet, if you are sure this is what you would like to do, or if you would like to go over a few other options with us, I can book an appointment for you with Beverly Whitfield. She is our divorce lawyer."

"Thank you. When can I see her? And what will the first initial consultation cost?"

"The first consultation is free, but we do ask for a three thousand to five thousand dollar retainer should you decide to hire her. She will explain her fees to you. I can book the appointment for Tuesday morning, May 22nd at 9:00 a.m."

"Okay. I will see her then. Thank you."

"We'll see you then, Mrs. Sweet."

Rachel hung up the phone. She didn't know how to feel. Reaching for a pen, she scribbled out a note for Blain. Standing now, she headed to their bedroom where she packed some of her things. Grabbing her car keys, she exited and left behind twelve years of a once truly magnificent marriage.

He had a feeling in his gut the moment he stepped out of his office that something was wrong. The feeling may have been due to the fact that it was a Monday and he hated Mondays. What he didn't know was that Rachel was well on her way to her mother's house in upbeat New Kootenay, a three-hour drive away, but the note she left behind would explain that. Blain closed the door to his office and walked down the long corridor to a set of stairs that lead to a steel door and exited into the back alley of the hotel. The corridor walls were painted a pale orange and a few dim lights lit the way. Unlocking the outside door, he stepped out into a murky afternoon. The brief walk to his car at the underground parking lot across the street was filled with the chirping of early spring birds, yet he paid no heed. It meant nothing to him.

Oddly, years earlier he would have stopped and listened. Years earlier it would have meant something; today though, spring, summer, fall, or winter he found nothing appealing about the season. He was a machine, a killing machine, and there was nothing appealing about that either. What he did and how he did it mattered as much to him as the seasons. Fourteen years of killing K-15 carriers was indeed taking its toll. He didn't kill those infected out of hate. The operatives of K.A.T. killed the infectious carriers as a necessity to preserve the living.

He pulled into his driveway around 4:30 p.m. that Monday, May 21, 2007, to discover that Rachel's car was gone. The answer for this was in the note he spotted on the kitchen table as he set his briefcase down. He read it with a heavy heart, saddened at some of the things she wrote. Nevertheless, he understood. He indeed had been neglecting her over the past year. She didn't say for sure that divorce was what she wanted, but she certainly hinted at it, giving him a few ultimatums, none of which he could accept. Blain read the note a few times, inhaled deeply and tossed it back onto the table. *Sounds like a divorce is in my future,* he thought. Nothing could be done about it, not until the last K-15 carrier was either cured or a dead and burned corpse.

Blain could not know then that the answers the Agency were looking for came in the form of an ex-patient from the Calimay Mental Hospital. Nor could he know that the patient was a direct descendant of the first K-15 carrier in Canada. It was speculated that a first generation K-15 carrier had the ability to produce a prophylactic antidote for the disease. Under normal circumstances, the disease caused degenerative deterioration of the brain and eventually an unpleasant and painful death. The K.A.T. lab had countless blood samples from all the K-15 carriers who their agents killed. None of the samples to date identified first-generation carriers.

Chapter 2

Shane Brentwood spent most his life institutionalized; both his mother and father were unknown to him. His parents were doctors, psychologists, and the staff from the institutions he called home. Now twenty-one, he could look forward to a new beginning.

When the doors to the Calimay Mental Hospital buzzed opened that Monday, *Hell* stepped out. Looking back at the duty psychologist, he smiled. Then turning on his heel, he took his first steps into freedom and an unsuspecting world. A smile crossed his face as he decided in what direction he wanted to go. To the east or to the west didn't matter, he was free. He had fifteen hundred dollars in his pocket, his ID, and a phone number for a crisis line. Shane shook his head as he tossed the note with the phone number to the ground.

"I'll never need that," he whispered.

The wind tussled his blondish shoulder length hair. Looking in the direction it blew, his pale blue eyes watered slightly. The wind came from the east and he began to walk in that direction.

Calimay was a sleepy town and although Shane saw it only on the outings he was allowed, he knew it was too small for him. He desired the big city lights of some far off city, a place where he could live in anonymity. Making the distance across town to the Greyhound station, he bought a one-way ticket to New Kootenay. It was bigger than Calimay and the perfect place to kill. He didn't know why he wanted to kill except that it burned in him like the need for oxygen.

"That will be one hundred and twenty seven dollars sir," the woman behind the counter said. "New Kootenay is beautiful this time of year," she added as Shane handed her the money.

He cared little about the beauty of the place and cared less in idle conversation. Handing back his change and ticket, the woman smiled as Shane took them from her.

"The bus leaves in one hour. If you are hungry the cafeteria is open."

"Thanks."

Making his way through the swinging doors, he looked at the menu on the far wall. Deciding on fries and a coke, he placed his order and took the order number he was handed.

"It'll be a few minutes."

Shane walked over to a table and sat. His mind drifted to another time and another place. *He was a child again, and in his hand he held a knife. At his feet lay the body of an unknown woman who twitched and gasped in pain and horror as she looked into the pale blue eyes of her assailant. A pool of blood was now her bed. She exhaled her last breath then went silent.*

A little bell rang bringing Shane back to the here and now.

"Number seven, your order is up," the young woman behind the counter said as she looked over to where Shane sat.

Rising, he walked the few paces and took his order.

"Thank you," he said as he returned to his table.

He looked once more at the young woman who handed him his order. She was beautiful; her long blonde hair reached past her lower back. Her eyes were brown, clear, and aesthetic. She was a younger version of the woman he had killed years earlier.

Finishing the last of his fries and downing what was left of his coke, Shane stood and picked up his bag of belongings. He looked one last time at the young woman behind the counter and went into the Greyhound station. It would be only a few minutes until the bus to New Kootenay arrived. Sitting he waited anxiously. Noting the smiles he got from complete strangers, he smiled back. It was only a gesture. Shane's intent wasn't to be nice. Still, he offered conversation to the man sitting beside him.

"Where you off to?" he asked politely.

"Heading to my niece's wedding in New Kootenay, yourself?"

"I'm heading that way too, just rolled in from the coast," Shane smiled.

"Got family in New Kootenay?"

"If one can call a senile old aunt family, then I guess I do."

"She's got Alzheimer's, then?"

"Yep. Quite a shame too. She never had any kids of her own and has always looked to me to fill that gap. To be honest, I really don't like her."

"Family is family."

The man shrugged his shoulders.

"You're going to see her then?"

"Yeah, I suppose. Don't really want to, but, like you said, 'family is family'."

The sound of air brakes now sounded outside and Shane looked out the window.

"There's the bus now."

He slowly rose and picked up his bag.

"I guess I'll be seeing you inside."

"No use quitting our conversation; heck, we could sit together."

"I hate to be rude, but I'd rather sit alone, if possible. That way I can stretch out. I get motion sickness quite easily."

"Maybe we can have a coffee together at one of the stops on the way," the man replied solemnly as he took his place in line.

"Sure," Shane said as he stepped into the bus and walked to the back.

Finding an empty seat wasn't difficult, and he chose one on the left side. The bus was less than full. He set his bag next to him on the seat, sighed, and closed his eyes. The door to the bus closed and the driver put it in gear.

"Our first stop today will be at Cresbrook for a forty-five minute dinner break and pick up. Please remain in your seat at all times except to use the bus facilities. Thank you, and welcome on board Greyhound Lines," the driver announced on the PA as he turned the bus east in the direction of New Kootenay.

It was then that the voices from the few passengers chatting with one another became audible. To Shane, the voices sounded like murmurs, distant cries, and constant babbling. How so few people could make so much noise was beyond him. It was one of the reasons he disliked people. It mattered little their race, religion, sex, or their public position in life. Rich or poor, he hated them all. It was also one of the reasons why he chose to go to New Kootenay. The more people, the more he hated, and the stronger his desire to kill would grow. That had always been the case. For twelve years, he had held back the monster. He had learned how to tame it, how to keep it hidden. Now, it begged to be released.

Looking out the window as a car passed, he noticed the personalized plate that read 'SMOKIN' and he wondered if the driver was 'smoking hot', or simply 'smoking one'. Averting his eyes back to the passengers, he shook his head in disgust. Most were filthy and greasy as though they were unkempt. God he hated people. Years of living in sanitized institutions with all their white walls and linens made him feel that the outside world should be the same. However, it wasn't.

Instead, it was filled with filth, degenerates and people with bad breath. The more he thought about it, the stronger the smells of the people wafted towards him and it sickened him.

Closing his eyes he tried to sleep, but for whatever reason, he couldn't. He decided then that when the bus stopped in Cresbrook, he would see if he could get a refund on the partial ticket, and hitchhike the remaining distance to New Kootenay. Even if it took longer, at least he would be in the fresh air and wouldn't be forced to smell the human scent that permeated the entire bus.

Rachel pulled into a small gas station/liquor store that also had a restaurant on the outskirts of Cresbrook to get fuel. She still had another two hours of driving before she would get to New Kootenay. Tired, upset and completely disappointed on how her life for the past year had been going, she decided to pick up a six pack of Vodka Coolers, a little something to help make the remainder of the trip less agonizing. She hated having to run to her mother's place. She hated it even more because of the circumstances. Hopefully, Blain would read the letter she left and maybe see things her way. A divorce from him she knew would be difficult. She loved him too damn much; still, she wanted to know what her alternatives were.

Paying for the drink and fuel, Rachel exited into the cool evening. Pulling out onto the highway, the Greyhound bus she passed earlier pulled in. Shane once more noted the personalized plate 'SMOKIN' of the car as it headed east. The air brakes hissed as the PA came alive.

"Welcome to Cresbrook. I hope you have enjoyed the trip so far. We will be stopped here for forty-five minutes. For those of you who wish to have something to eat, the restaurant is open. Please refrain from bringing opened alcohol back on the bus. Thank you."

The driver stood and exited the bus, followed by a few passengers including Shane.

The evening air was cool and welcoming as Shane inhaled deeply. With his pack in hand, he entered the restaurant and walked to the counter.

"I'd like to know if I can get a refund for this partial ticket."

He handed it to the man on the other side of the counter.

"You sure can, but you have to do that at the Greyhound counter."

The man pointed to the adjacent building.

"Go through the glass doors, Betty will take care of you."

"Thanks."

Shane turned and made his way to the counter. A wind chime echoed as he opened the door. There were a couple of chairs, weigh scales and a counter, but no one seemed to be around. Walking to the counter, he rang the bell for service. An old woman appeared through another door.

"Hello there. Can I help you?"

"Yeah, I'd like to get a refund on this partial ticket. I decided I don't like bus travel."

The woman laughed.

"You wouldn't be the first."

Shane handed her the ticket. She looked at it briefly and subtracted something on a calculator, then punched a hole in the ticket.

"Your refund will be eighty two dollars."

She hit a few keys on the cash register and handed Shane his change.

"Thank you."

"You're welcome."

Shane nodded and exited. He picked up some things to eat and drink then walked to the other side of the road and towards New Kootenay sticking out his thumb every time someone drove by. He walked close to a mile before the bus passed him. He was glad not to be a passenger. Out here, he was alone, and out here, the air was clean.

Ahead of him less than two miles, Rachel was pulled off to the shoulder, wrestling with changing a tire and waiting for the car's overheated radiator to cool. *Things always happen in three's; what else might I expect before this fucking day is over,* she thought as she leaned up against the side of the car, her hands stained with black.

Only a few cars passed. That part of the highway was pretty desolate and lonely. Still, of those few, no one stopped or cared that she was having troubles. She felt like crying, but instead grabbed for a second Vodka Cooler and cracked it open. She poured some onto her hands to wash the dirt off, and then wiped them dry on her jeans. Her mind was full of emotion as she took a long swig from the bottle in her hand. *Wish I knew what I was doing,* she thought, as she bent down and worked the wheel nuts of the flat tire.

Finally able to loosen them off, she sighed in relief.

"There, now the fun part," she mumbled as she removed the spare tire and jack from the trunk.

She had to think back to a time when she watched Blain change a tire. It seemed simple then. Now though, with all she was going through, it was confusing and she was dreading it. Looking at her wristwatch; she reached for her pack of cigarettes. She rarely smoked anymore except when she felt stressed. She noted the time to be 6:45 p.m. *A couple more hours and it'll be getting dark, damn it,* she thought as she lit a smoke.

Inhaling deeply, she looked down at the spare tire and jack. She contemplated using her cell phone to call for help. The trouble was, because of her location, she knew she'd be able to get only 911. She really couldn't call this a 'dire' emergency. Taking the last drag from her cigarette, she tossed it on the ground and stepped on it.

With the jack now placed, she turned the crank. It was hard at first, but by the third revolution, it became easy. Removing the flat tire, she fitted the spare in place and tightened the wheel nuts finger tight then lowered the car. Tightening the wheel nuts once more with the tire iron, and finally satisfied, she sipped on the Vodka Cooler as she put the jack and flat tire away. Problem one was solved. Now she waited impatiently for the radiator to quit hissing. Wiping her brow with the back of her hand, she looked westerly in the direction she had come. In the distance, someone was walking toward her. A car passed and she realized it was a hitchhiker. Feeling a little uneasy, she grabbed the tire iron and closed the trunk. Moving to the front of the car, she opened the door and slipped in.

Shane began to smile as he drew close enough to make out the car. It was the one with the personalized plate. He knocked on the window.

"Everything okay ma'am?" he asked as he bent down and looked inside.

Rachel rolled down her window an inch or so.

"Yes, I'm waiting for the tow truck. It should be along shortly."

Shane smiled.

"I see. Mind if I look. You might not need a tow."

"Thank you, but that's not necessary. As I said, the tow truck should be here any minute," she replied hesitantly.

"Alright then."

Shane knew she was lying; he wasn't stupid, but then again, neither was she.

"I guess I'll be on my way."

"Thanks for stopping and offering your help," Rachel said as she watched him walk away.

Shane looked back at her, smiled, and nodded. How he hoped he would see her again; she was beautiful, foxy. Her shoulder length hair was dirty blonde and her blue-green eyes were that of an angel's. Her lips were full and cherry red, and her breasts were more than a handful. He could only imagine she had a body to go with her looks. The moment he looked into the car, he desired her in more ways than one. The longer he thought about her as he walked away, the deeper his desire to make her his plaything grew, and the more it grew the more vivid were the fantasies playing in his head. And like all his fantasies, even this one ended in death.

The sound of a car approaching brought him back to reality and he turned westerly and stuck out his thumb, but as with every car, it too passed by.

He stood and continued his gaze. He could make out the silhouette of the car and the beautiful woman behind the wheel from where he stood. He smiled as he looked toward the sky. Soon it would be dark. If he didn't get a ride before the sun completely set, he would walk back and in the darkness take possession of both the car and the woman. He stood where he was and continued to stick out his thumb every time a car drew close. He was not enthusiastic at all in getting a ride as long as the car and the women he was preying on remained where they were.

By now, Rachel took notice that the stranger who passed her by was standing stock-still in the distance, as though he were watching her, and indeed he was. She quickly turned the key in hopes that the car would sputter to life, and a smile crossed her face as it fired up.

"Thank God," she softly spoke as she stepped out to close the hood.

Jumping back in and locking her doors, she signaled and pulled off the shoulder. She didn't look the stranger in the eye as she drove past, but the stranger looked at her and he smiled. She looked back once in the rear view mirror and watched as the stranger disappeared from view. *That was creepy, creepy, creepy,* she thought as she shuddered.

Shane stood on the side of the road and an evil silence enveloped him. His mind raced and he became agitated as the visions in his mind flashed to the fantasy he was contriving and like a pile of bricks crashed to nothingness. Headlights in the distance shone brightly now and he stuck out his thumb. Surprised that the vehicle pulled over, he conjured a fake smile and approached the passenger side. Opening the door, he slid in.

"Thanks for stopping."

"No problem. Where are you heading?"

"New Kootenay."

"Looking for work or visiting?"

It seemed a little forward to Shane, still he responded.

"A little of both I guess," he spoke as the man pulled onto the highway.

"What kind of work do you do?"

"Whatever I can get. I'm just starting out."

"New Kootenay is as good as any place to start out. I own New Kootenay Rendering Plant."

"Really, I've heard of that place," Shane lied.

He wanted the man to shut up.

"If you're interested we could use a few good hands. The pay is decent. Here, here is my card."

The man reached into his pocket and handed his card to Shane.

"Thanks. I'll think about it."

The drive from that point on was boring but short and finally the city of New Kootenay came into view.

"Here we are. Any special place you want to be dropped off?"

"Nearest convenience store that is close to a motel, I guess."

"Alright, that would be the Clayton."

The man drove to a small motel that sat kitty corner from a 24-hour convenience store.

"Excellent. Thank you very much for the ride."

Shane opened the door and began to step out.

"By the way, if you decide to take my job offer, my name is Burgess, Nick Burgess."

Shane looked at the card the man handed him.

"Yep, that is what it says on the card too," Shane smiled. "My name is Shane. Thanks Nick, I'll contemplate it."

"Sure and good luck to you."

Shane closed the door and waved as he stepped onto the curb. *Rendering plant, hmmm,* he thought as his mind raced. He booked into room 17 of the Clayton Motel, ordered in a pizza, and sat back watching television. He looked at the card Nick had given him and he thought about what a great way to dispose of those he knew he would eventually kill. There was no hiding from that desire, and there was nothing he, nor anyone else, could do to change it.

Chapter 3

Blain rolled over for the tenth time. It was hard to sleep especially since Rachel wasn't lying beside him.

"Damn it, might as well get up."

He swung out of bed, slipped on a pair of jogging pants, and headed to the kitchen. He hoped that by now she would have called, but so far, nothing. He stared blankly out the kitchen window into the bleak, dark night. Shadows were cast by the streetlights as a cat darted across the street. He sat transfixed. Everything he had done, accomplished, or was going to do, had robbed him of any normalcy that he could expect out of life. Obscurity, lies, and deceptions were his life. He was tired of the killing, tired of the lies. The masquerade of what he called his life, he began to realize, took its toll on him, and left him with a cold black heart and no change in his pocket. The only benefit of that being that the killing he was expected to do and was trained to do were easier to commit than ever before. He began to rise from table as the phone rang. He reached for it quickly.

"Hello," he said in a quick breath.

"Blain, it is me, Rachel."

"I know."

"Did you by chance find the letter I left for you?"

"I did."

"Well, what..." she trailed off for a second, "what do you think of it?"

"To be honest, not much."

"Why are you so callous?"

"How do you want me to react?"

"Maybe with a bit of heart. Geez, I don't know, Blain. But this is exactly why I wrote that damn letter in the first place."

"Sorry you feel that way."

"I bet you are. Obviously, you have no intention to change anything do you?"

"For now, Rachel, you know I can't."

Blain stared into the evening; he wanted her to understand, but knew she was as hard-headed as he was. There was a long pause.

"Okay, just so you know, I'm at my mother's now. I think I'm going to stay here for a while. Maybe you'll realize what we once had if I'm not there."

"I already know Rachel. I already know."

She was the best thing that ever happened to him, and he knew that. He loved her unconditionally, and he did indeed already miss her. The conversation brought up valid points for both of them. When he hung up the phone, he knew nothing changed. There was no cul-de-sac that either one could turn around in, at least not yet. Killing is all he knew. Everything else he learned in life meant nothing today, and would probably mean nothing tomorrow.

He sighed as he rose from the table. It was all black and white to him. He knew that sometimes in life people got what they wanted and other times they chose it. For now, he had chosen his path. Making his way into the cool and lonely bedroom, he lay on top of the bed. No blanket covered him as he gazed to the ceiling. The radio played softly in the background, and he listened. There was a time, not long ago, that the blankets from their bed would have been strewn across the floor, and he and Rachel would be lying together with their arms entwined. That all ended though, and the flame burned out as he began to devote more and more time to the K.A.T. and its cause. Indeed the killing also helped put out the flame, but what could he do? Those infected with the K-15 virus needed to be exterminated one way or another. The survival of the entire world rested on the K.A.T.'s shoulders, especially if they wanted to keep the

Kuru virus contained.

They knew too much about the virus to let it spread. What they knew, they tried to share with the world, but the world was a stupid place run by bureaucracy and bullshit and no one listened. Hundreds were infected and his brother proved it repeatedly. However, the world remained deaf. Looking over to the clock, Blain yawned.

"Nine thirty p.m., already. I've got to get some sleep."

He fluffed up his pillow and put his hands to his side. Closing his eyes, he waited for sleep. The sound of the alarm going off jolted him awake. It felt as though he had been asleep for only minutes. *Wow, that seemed short,* he thought as he rolled out of bed.

The blue glow from the clock read 5:00 a.m. He made his way to the bathroom, brushed his teeth and took a shower. The sun shone dimly through the bathroom window and he knew it was going to be a nice day. He even felt good. The only downside to such a beautiful day was that Rachel wasn't around and chances were he wouldn't see her for at least a week, maybe longer. He sat down at the kitchen table and waited for his morning coffee. In the background the kitchen radio played softly. He thought about the letter once or twice, but honestly, that wasn't where his mind was. It was Tuesday and his answering service would forward any messages from his office regarding new victims or possible leads on K-15 carriers. So, today he wanted to reflect, and the best place to do that as far as he was concerned was at home, in his backyard relaxing in his hammock. As he waited for his coffee, he sat at the kitchen table reading the Calimay Post.

It wasn't a big newspaper. Calimay wasn't that big a place and the news was usually quite boring. He read a couple of the articles; then closed the paper and tossed it onto the table. By now his coffee was ready and he poured a cup. It had been three or four days since he had heard from the main office of the K.A.T., and he wondered why. Even then, there had been no new victims or new leads on the virus carriers. It seemed odd. Usually, they were getting a couple of hits a week. Was it possible that the carriers had gone dormant? Blain couldn't imagine that being the case. That dream was as unrealistic as some of the articles he had read in the Post that morning. There had to be another reason. Something else, he knew, was going on, but for now there were no answers. There hadn't even been any reports in other newspapers and news channels of any missing people, locally or otherwise.

One of the things the K.A.T learned over the years of being in operation was that when people went missing, it was another sign that maybe a carrier, or carriers of the K-15 virus were near. That wasn't always the case but there were enough cases, and so the K.A.T did a study on it. Their findings showed that 26% of the time, those lost were often found in a gruesome and mangled state. As of late, more times than not, that 26% were cannibalized. That was always an undeniable sign of what the victims endured before and after death. Although ME's and the police believed the missing parts and pieces of the dead that were found were simply explained to have been done by animals, the K.A.T. Agency knew better.

It was also one of the reasons that he rarely showed remorse for killing the carriers, and why he would continue to do so. Finishing his second cup of coffee that morning, he rose from the table and was about to go into the backyard and his awaiting hammock when his cell phone in his briefcase sounded. He contemplated letting it ring and ignoring it. He could always check the message later. Instead, he decided he would answer it.

"Hello. This is Entity."

"Entity, glad you answered," the sultry voice of K.A.T. neurology researcher and office clerk, Canbra Lexis answered.

"I almost didn't."

"I would have left a message in that case, and called you again in a few minutes."

"I know and would have likely pestered me all day."

Blain smirked and rolled his eyes, he knew that is exactly what she would have done. There was a chuckle on the other end.

"Perhaps. Anyway, I'll make this short and precise."

"Good, get on with it," Blain interrupted.

"You have noticed the decline in victims and carriers of the K-15 virus, yes?"

"Obviously. I thought you were going to make this short."

"I'm trying too, now please listen. I need you to do some research on a family name that seems to have an interesting gene in its DNA structure. The name is Brentwood."

"There could be a million Brentwoods. You also said you were going to be precise," Blain pointed out.

"That is as precise as I can be."

"What does this name have to do with anything, and what is so special about this gene?" he asked her flatly.

"As I said, the family name seems to be coming up a lot during certain tests. Their DNA structure is different from say yours or mine. They seem to have an acquired immunity to K-15. However, the Brentwoods we have located in the past few weeks and who agreed on DNA testing, don't harbor the critical DNA thread.

We're hoping your research will prove that the DNA samples I send you to research do have this gene."

"Why me? Why not another operative? I'm not much of a researcher. I hate that kind of work."

"The agency asks you for obvious reasons. Don't you have access to your brother's research?"

Blain sighed, "I do. Let me guess, that is where you want me to start?"

"Indeed it is. Perhaps his work may shed some light as well."

"Really," Blain replied in derision. "You know what that means don't you?"

"Yes, you need a flight ticket."

"That is correct."

"It has already been secured, both to Winnfield and Yellow Lake. You will be using the same cover as always, I'm presuming?"

"Of course, people know Mr. Todd in Yellow Lake, they don't know Entity, or Blain Sweet. Is it Monday? Because, that was a stupid question."

"It is not Monday, Entity, and yes perhaps it was a stupid question. I only want to be clear."

"Are you?"

"I am now."

"Very good," Blain teased.

"Okay, Entity. Your flight to Winnfield, Yukon leaves on Friday at 10:30 a.m. from the Calimay Regional. I will make sure you are equipped upon your arrival. Keep your eyes open for a box of test tubes and microscope slides. Those will contain a sample of the DNA as well as a slide of blood. There will also be a live K-15 virus sample. It will be covered with paraffin wax, same as with the DNA sample."

"Goodie, so I have to spend time looking through a microscope, playing with lab torches, reading, and cross-referencing Trent's research against this new research. How exciting," Blain said with little enthusiasm.

"Yes. That will be part of the research. The documents will explain it all. Is there anything else you'll need, other than the usual?"

"No, except why couldn't you have made the flight sooner? I don't know if I will have the same attitude by Friday," Blain badgered.

Anything he figured was better than sitting around home and sulking or waiting for some kind of action. Rachel, he knew, wouldn't call him for at least a week. That was the way it was, when she went off on her tiffs. Besides a fishing trip sounded good, not that he'd be fishing much, but he'd cast a hook while he was there. Yellow Lake was a serene mountain lake community, and he hadn't been there in almost two years, since the last time the agency requested him to do research. It was where his brother did most of his research. It was also where the documents and related material remained. Only Blain knew where.

Blain and his brother had bought a cabin on Mud Creek, a tributary that fed Yellow Lake. It was another secret he was forced to keep from Rachel due to his career. He wasn't happy about that, but to be honest he wasn't terribly upset about it either. Yellow Lake was a place he could go to in a heartbeat if he ever needed to get away. No one knew about it except the K.A.T. Agency. No one knew about them, so he could always disappear if he had to, and no one would be the wiser. Besides, up there, he was known, as Mr. Ben Todd. No one knew his true identity; he was a ghost whenever he was there.

The population of Yellow Lake on the whole may have been one hundred and fifty, give or take a few. Most were fishers and resort owners, and in the summer, the place might have an influx of about triple that. It was a peaceful and secluded lake community. Blain waited patiently for a response from the other end of the phone. Finally Canbra came back on.

"I have checked and we can get you a flight, Thursday at 12:45 p.m. But, you'd have to get yourself to New Kootenay. That flight doesn't arrive at your destination until late evening. However, there is another one leaving the Canupe International, and it arrives three hours earlier, at 5:00 p.m. They like to have the passengers there early. You'll have to get there by noon"

"Really? Okay, I'll head to Canupe first thing tomorrow, Wednesday. You'll assure me that my ticket will be there at Canupe?"

"Have I ever let you down, Entity?"

Blain smiled and nodded; she never had.

"Good. I will make contact with you once I arrive at Yellow Lake."

"Fair enough. Good bye, Entity."

"TTFN," Blain said as he turned off his phone.

Canbra's voice reminded him of Rachel, and for a minute, he contemplated phoning her at her mother's, but decided he'd leave her a note instead, in case she returned before he did from Yellow Lake. Closing his briefcase, he turned and walked outside. Leaning on the deck railing, he looked out across the Kentucky Bluegrass of the backyard, and to his hammock that gently blew in the breeze.

Nah, no use getting comfortable, I think I'll head for Canupe now, he thought as he turned and made his way back inside. It didn't take long to write the note to Rachel. He simply told her that he was called away on business. It was a lie that would put her mind at ease if she did return before he did. Packing a few things, he walked around making sure their house was locked and secured. Then he headed for Canupe. It was a four-hour drive, but it was a good day for it. He was in no rush and so took the scenic route. For one reason or another, the theme song from 'Littlest Hobo' began to play in his mind, and he hummed along, his mind adrift as he travelled. An hour later, he pulled into a gas station and filled the tank. It was an old gas station and the man running the place was as old as the gas station looked.

"How are you today?" the man questioned as he approached the car window.

"Pretty good. Fill her up and check the oil, please," Blain responded as he popped open the hood and stepped out.

"Sure thing. It's gonna be a lovely day today, I think."

"I hope so, got a few more hours of driving ahead of me. I'm heading to Canupe, and then onward, to the Yukon."

"The Yukon, eh? I bet it is as beautiful there this time of year as it is here."

"Great fishing too."

"You a fly fisherman?"

"I've dabbled in it, but no, I'm more of a spin caster," Blain responded.

"Yeah, a fellow needs to have a knack for fly fishing, which I ain't got either," the man said as he now checked the oil. "Yep, your oil is good."

"That's what I was hoping." Blain followed him inside to pay for the gas.

"That'll be forty-six seventy five," the man said as he rang up the sale.

"Gas isn't as cheap as it was a decade ago, is it."

He reached into his pocket and handed the man a $50 bill.

"Nope. It sure isn't. But, if you're gonna drive than you need to buy it," the man chuckled as he handed him his change.

"Have a good day, sir."

"I will, thank you. You have a good day too."

Blain made his way to the exit. He stopped only once after that to get a coffee and a bite to eat. By 3:00 p.m. he was resting on his bed in the posh and elaborate Heritage Hotel under his alias Mr. Ben Todd, which coincided with the only ID he now carried. Even the cell phone was registered under that name. The hotel really wasn't that posh nor was it elaborate. It was, in fact, the cheapest hotel in all of Canupe. Whenever he travelled and needed to stay in a hotel or motel, he always picked the cheapest. The Heritage was exactly that, cheap. It was good cover, and if it could save a penny then he was all for that.

He turned on the TV and propped up a couple pillows behind his head. Flipping through the channels, he decided to shut the damn thing off as there wasn't anything on at that time of day. Instead, he walked across the street to a convenience store and picked up a newspaper.

The Canupe News wasn't much bigger than the Calimay Post. Both towns were mid-sized and the news was local. Again, he found nothing interesting in it, just like the Calimay Post he tried to read that morning. Tossing the paper on the desk beside his bed, he closed his eyes. He was tired from the drive and since there wasn't much else he could do until the following day it seemed like some shut-eye was the best idea.

He woke around 7:00 p.m. that evening. The dreams he had during his nap were filled with Rachel, their life, his life, lies, deceit and, of course, death. Death was always in his dreams. It was what he did, it was who he was, and he was getting sick of it. What made things worse was that there was no lifejacket anyone could toss him to change that. Not yet, at least, but in time that would change, and in time he would also come clean with Rachel. He would leave behind the agency and the killing, if their marriage survived, that is. Until then, this was it; this was his life. There was a better one waiting for him he knew, but it was as out of reach as the stars themselves. Time was the essence. Could Rachel wait until they found a cure for K-15? That was the question. If not, then so be it; there was nothing he could do about that.

Making his way to a fast food restaurant, he ordered a couple of cheeseburgers, fries, and a coke. Back at his hotel room, he set the bag of burgers down on the desk and pulled up a chair. It wasn't the best supper in the world, but it wasn't the worst either. The burgers sat in the bottom of his stomach like a sack of rocks when he was finished with them, but he was full and that was all that mattered. Turning on the TV he listened to some documentary on aliens. Were they real or were they a hoax, was the gist of the program. He already knew the answer to that. *Of course they were fake.*

"What a load of crap, aliens, please," he said as he finished the last of his coke and tossed the empty cup into the wastebasket.

It was hard for him to believe such drivel, but then again, who would believe in people eating people, which is exactly what those infected with K-15 were doing. He shrugged his shoulders as he stood. *Maybe, aliens are real,* he thought as he went to the bathroom. Looking in the mirror, he shook his head, *yep, might as well hit the shower and have a shave. You aren't looking as good as you used to, old boy,* he thought as he ran his fingers across his face.

At 46, he didn't look terribly bad; he knew that. He was thinking about his younger days when his eyes were bright and there were no bags under them, and the damn grey streaks in his moderately short hair didn't exist. God he hated that. Turning the shower on, he removed his clothes and stepped in. The water pressure was nothing spectacular and it took a bit to clean up and rinse off. He hated that too. In fact, he began to realize that as of late he was really starting to hate a lot of things including his position with the K.A.T. Agency. The mess his marriage was in, the constant yarning, the smell of gunpowder and smoke, the sound his Glock made every time he needed to pull the trigger all bothered him. He was glad in a sense that he didn't have the Glock with him this time around; there was no need to be packing heat for a simple research assignment. Instead, he had left the Glock locked up in his office safe.

The more he thought about it, the more he realized how much he hated the life he was living. His brother Trent, however, would have wanted him to pursue and eliminate all K-15 carriers until either a cure was found, or the last living carrier was put to rest. He was torn in a sense. On one hand, he wanted to fulfill his brother's wish, and on the other, he wanted to live as normal a life as he could have. The one he was living was as far from normal as it was for humans to eat humans.

Finishing up with his shower and shave, he dressed, stepped out of the bathroom and sat down at the small desk supplied with the room. He wasn't thinking about anything particular and feeling bored. He once more turned on the TV. Again, there wasn't much on as he flipped through the channels. It was the sound outside his room that startled him. He looked over to the door and listened. There was indeed a ruckus going on out in the hallway. Standing, he made his way to the door and opened it slightly to look. On the other side of the hall a man and a woman were arguing. Her nose was bloody and the man had her by the throat.

Blain flung open the door and grabbed the man

by the top of his head then slammed him into the wall. The woman slumped to the floor gasping for air. She was trying to warn him about something, but it was too late. He felt the muzzle of a pistol against his gut and then the searing pain as the man pulled the trigger. The gun echoed with a loud clap and the bullet tore through his stomach and embedded itself in the wall of the hallway. The everlasting smell of gunpowder filled Blain's nasal cavity as he grabbed for his stomach and stooped over in pain. He looked in horror as the warm blood from the wound seeped through his fingers and ran down the front of his pants.

Using the wall, he steadied himself and watched as the man now turned the gun on the woman and pulled the trigger for a second time. The woman's expressionless body fell to the ground as blood spewed from the wound to her face. There was no doubt in his mind that she was dead before she hit the ground. In shock and agony, he watched as the man ran out the front doors. No longer able to stand, he slid down the wall to a sitting position, a smear of blood painting it behind him.

"Shit! Why did that have to happen?" he asked before passing out.

The next things he remembered were distant voices and the sound of sirens. Then, everything turned black again as though someone had turned off the light.

He awoke three days later in a hospital bed, surrounded by tubes and IVs. He was startled at first until the pain he was feeling snapped him out of it. It all came back to him like a flash from a camera. Looking around he noted that he was in a private room and sitting at the door was a very official looking man.

"Ah, you are finally awake. Hello Mr. Todd, I'm Tyler O'Brien."

The man pulled out an official badge and

credentials, letting him know that he was a private investigator.

"I'm here on official business, and am relieved that you are alive. That was quite a wound you suffered."

The man stepped closer and pulled up a chair next to Blain's bed.

Blain didn't say two words and instead waited to see what else this O'Brien fellow was up to, or why he was there. Besides, he didn't feel like talking yet anyway.

"I don't imagine you can give us a description of the man who shot you, could you?" the investigator asked as he made himself comfortable and pulled out a small digital recorder.

Blain shook his head. He knew the face alright, but now wasn't the time to get into details; he was in too much pain to care. Closing his eyes he fell in and out of consciousness as the man named Tyler continued to talk. He listened when he was able, but he didn't respond.

"It is important, Mr. Todd, that we find this man. We need to confirm that he is who we believe he is... Mr. Todd," O'Brien trailed off and ended it there noting that Blain was no longer responsive.

Rising, from the bedside he made his way back to the door, sat down and waited. There was no way he was going to leave. The information Blain had was vital to a murder and rape case that he was working on. Tyler O'Brien worked for the 'Henderson & Co., Private Investigation Agency', a private investigation firm that catered to the rich and not so rich. A Mr. Jonas Vanderhott, whose wife of forty-two years was brutally attacked, raped, and murdered six months earlier, hired the agency to speed up the investigation. The police, according to him, were lagging. That however was far from truth.

The police were as close to finding the responsible party as was O'Brien. It was a matter of time only, before one or the other collared the "perp". O'Brien had been tracking down leads for a week already, and he was that much closer to finding the perpetrator with this newest one. He got the word that the bullet pulled out of the wall at the Heritage Hotel that ripped through Blain's gut and took the life of another matched the bullets that were dug out of Mrs. Vanderhott's skull. The information that he received came from an acquaintance of his who worked at the mortuary. It would only be a matter of time, he knew, before the police received the same information, and they and the newspaper reporters began showing up. O'Brien's hope was that he'd be the first to talk to Mr. Todd before the chaos.

It was the sound of a cell phone ringing that caught his attention. It rang for a bit then stopped, then rang for a bit and again stopped. Finally, after the third time, he walked over to the hospital closet where Mr. Todd's belongings hung, reached into a shirt pocket and answered.

"Hello" he began.

There was a short pause and then finally a woman replied in a somewhat cautious voice.

"Entity?" the voice questioned.

"Ah, who?" O'Brien responded as he looked around confusedly.

The phone went dead. He looked at the screen to see if there was a number where the call came from. The screen, however, was completely blank. *That is odd,* he thought as he put the phone back.

"Entity," he repeated softly as he made his way back to the chair, and patiently waited.

Back at the K.A.T. Agency, Canbra Lexis, was putting in a warning call to the head of the Agency,

Dwayne Gonsite, letting him know that something was wrong, and that, 'Entity' had somehow been compromised. It was a simple first alert procedure with a mild warning to be on the lookout for anything conspicuous that might jeopardize the agency and its operatives. With the call made, she proceeded with downloading all of 'Entity's' history, his contact numbers, and related data from the K.A.T. database. The only thing to remain was his current aka, *'Mr. Ben Todd'*. That way the agency would be able to monitor his credit cards, cell phone, and co-ordinance, in case there was only a mere mishap and 'Entity' was in fact en-route to his destination - Yellow Lake. It took a mere five minutes to erase his name from the closely guarded database and to upload it all to a USB flash-drive. From there it travelled to Dwayne Gonsite's hands.

Gonsite worked closely with both Blain and Trent before Trent's reported death in the field. The K.A.T. was in all actuality Trent's baby. Blain hadn't had much business sense about him, and so the clerical, financing, research and planning were obviously left up to Trent. The only other person with as much knowledge on the K-15 virus and the ability to do all that Trent did was Gonsite, so he was the obvious choice. He had received flash-drives before, but this one was special. Never in all the years that the agency had been in operation had 'Entity' ever lost contact or not followed through with an objective. His rules of engagement were implacable, yet by now he was supposed to have made contact and receive the documents pertaining to the research he was expected to be doing at Yellow Lake.

There was something the agency was missing and Gonsite knew that. For now, he would follow the rule and wait the allotted *'five days to report'*, after losing contact. If 'Entity' hadn't made contact by then, they would move to a level two alert. The contents on the flash-drive that Gonsite now held in his hands would be permanently destroyed, as would Blain's current aka, "Mr. Ben Todd".

Chapter 4

Still immobile and in excruciating pain, Blain once more opened his eyes. Focusing, he could make out that the same man who introduced himself as a private investigator sat next to the door, his legs outstretched and his own eyes closed; he was obviously sleeping. Blain took a moment to look around undisturbed. The clock on the wall read 1:00 p.m. He was unsure of the day or date. As far as he knew, he could have been laid up in that bed for days already. He gently closed his eyes as the pain from the wound he received shot up his back and ripped at his gut. The sound of something heavy falling caused him to move slightly and his eyes sprung open. Looking toward the sound, he watched as O'Brien jumped up from the floor and brushed himself off. He had obviously slid off the chair. It was quite comical in a sense and he gently chuckled until the pain brought tears to his eyes.

"You're awake."

He grew flush with embarrassment as he approached Blain's bedside.

Blain managed a few words.

"You are too," he said as he smiled and tried not to laugh anymore at the detectives blunder.

"Yeah, well, been here a while. I guess I dozed off. How are you feeling, Mr. Todd? Are you able to talk?"

"What day is it?" Blain asked as he winced in pain and tried to get comfortable.

"Friday, May 25th. You've been here since late Tuesday evening, and I've been here since yesterday."

"I see. What did you say your name was again?"

"Tyler O'Brien. I work for Henderson & Co Private Investigation Agency."

"No kidding, so you are an investigator?"

"Correct."

"And why are you here?"

"To have a talk with you and to see if you can describe the man who shot you."

"Uhuh, well, he was about your height, with salt and pepper hair..." Blain sucked on an eye-tooth as he inhaled deeply at the pain he was in from simply talking.

O'Brien raised his hand.

"That's okay, Mr. Todd. Take your time. I'm in no rush."

Blain nodded his appreciation.

"Thanks, give me a minute."

"You don't mind if I record our conversation do you? You only have to nod, 'yes' or 'no'," O'Brien said as he reached into his pocket and pulled out his digital recorder.

Blain nodded that he didn't mind.

"Good, I don't want to get anything wrong. Taking notes isn't one of my stronger points. Whenever you are ready to continue, Mr. Todd, feel free."

He watched as Blain squirmed to a more comfortable position. He didn't want to force the man to talk if he couldn't, but the information on and description of his assailant were quite relevant, and so he waited.

"Is there anything I can help you with, prop up the pillows or something?" O'Brien asked.

Blain shook his head, no. A few minutes later he was able to continue now that he was finally comfortable.

"The man had salt and pepper hair, he was about your height, was wearing a black leather vest over a long-sleeved light blue shirt. From what I recall, he was wearing brown pants and wearing some kind of dress shoe; maybe they were sneakers even."

Pausing for a moment, he corrected his

composure.

"I didn't get a look at his eyes because he was wearing dark glasses. I can tell you also, that he had a tattoo of something black, like a raven or crow, on his right hand, with perhaps a church steeple in the background. That is all I can honestly remember."

"You say, 'may have been wearing' some kind of dress shoes, or maybe sneakers. Can you elaborate?"

Blain knew that question was coming. If O'Brien did his job properly, he would be probing every one of the descriptions that Blain offered, even a measly pair of shoes. Regardless though, he wasn't sure he could continue with the conversation. His gut wretched with pain and he felt nauseous. Talking made it all seem worse.

O'Brien, noticing this, raised his hand.

"That's okay, Mr. Todd. I think you should rest some more. I'll stay near."

O'Brien rose from where he sat and made his way out into the hallway. He needed to stretch and maybe find some coffee. It was 1:15 p.m., and knowing that Mr. Todd would not likely talk anymore that day, he left the hospital and headed for a hotel and some much needed sleep. He would head back to the hospital in the morning and with luck once more go over Mr. Todd's description of the man.

Chapter 5

It was an ordinary Friday in New Kootenay as Rachel sat on the back deck at her mother's house. She hadn't yet told her mother her real reason for being there. She missed her first appointment with the divorce lawyer that Tuesday and her second was later that day at 3:00 p.m. She wasn't sure divorce was an answer or for that matter a remedy. Her marriage to Blain had always been so fulfilling. Picking up the phone, she dialed Whitfield & Angus to cancel her appointment for the final time. Speaking with the secretary, she explained that she had reconsidered. There was an encouraging chuckle on the other end as the secretary responded.

"Good, I'm glad for that. I wish you luck, Mrs. Sweet. Bye for now."

"Thank you. Good bye."

Rachel hung up the phone in relief and smiled. Rising from the table, she entered her mom's kitchen with a completely new outlook on her marriage and the determination to fulfill her vows to Blain.

"Till death do us part," she said quietly to herself.

Her mother who was a late sleeper was finally awake, and Rachel could hear the shower running. Walking to the bathroom door, she knocked.

"Mom, I'm going to go shopping. Is there anything you need?"

"Not today, Rachel. Nevertheless, thanks for asking. Will you be long?"

"No, I'll likely be back within the hour. Talk to you then."

Rachel stepped away from the door and picked up her handbag. She looked herself over in the hallway mirror and gave her hair a quick brush. Satisfied, she stepped out into a warm spring day. The birds chirped and whistled and she inhaled deeply the clean spring air. She felt good today; better than she had in sometime. Perhaps it was the spring air or the fact that she decided not to pursue a divorce. Whatever the reason, today she felt like a new person. Putting on her sunglasses, she started her car and slowly backed out of the driveway.

It was only by coincidence that Shane was walking by on the other side of the street. Rachel didn't notice him, but he certainly noticed her. It was her car that gave her away and the personalized plate that read 'SMOKIN'. Shane smiled as he took note of the house number 1252 Yorkwood St. It was one block away from the rental flat he had secured the day after he arrived in New Kootenay.

"How convenient," he whispered as he picked up his pace and continued.

He was on his way to meet with Nick Burgress, the owner of New Kootenay Rendering Plant, in regards to a job. He thought about the job offer for almost a week finally deciding that indeed a rendering plant was as good a place to work as any.

He had called Nick the night before, curious to know if the offer of employment was still open after being unable to find work elsewhere. He was pleased when Nick said yes and that they should meet to discuss it further. They agreed to meet at a local coffee shop called the 'Koffee House.' It was not far from Shane's apartment and a place Nick frequented. Shane was the first to arrive and he sat nearest the window that looked out toward the parking lot. The smell of hazelnut, French vanilla, and regular coffee filled the café. The server approached as he sat there vigilantly looking out the window.

She smiled at him when their eyes locked.

"Welcome to the Koffee House. Would you like a coffee, a menu or both?" she asked.

Shane smiled back.

"A regular coffee, please."

"You don't want to try one of our famous other flavors?" she asked with a return smile.

She was a beautiful girl. Her dark brown hair was short and well kept, and her eyes were as blue as any blue he had ever seen, almost turquoise. The nametag on her Koffee House garb read Sapphire. He didn't need to guess why she was named that.

"No thanks. They're too sweet, unnatural."

He wrinkled up his nose.

Sapphire chuckled, "I hear you there. I'll be right back with your coffee," she said as she turned and walked away.

He couldn't keep his eyes off her and wished that he had heard of the Koffee House sooner. He would have been a regular customer by now and may even have had the nerve to ask her out in a ploy to kill her, just for practice. She would make a delicious first kill; there was no doubt about that. He smiled at the thought of the things he would have her do before killing her. Never having the chance to be intimate with a woman because of being institutionalized since the age of 10, his desire to kill was as great as his desire to have sex. Of all the women he had seen since his release, there were only two he desired sexually: this one named Sapphire and the woman with the personalized plate that read 'SMOKIN'.

Sapphire returned with his coffee and set it down in front of him.

"Thanks," he said as added his condiments.

"You're welcome. Is there anything else I can get you?" she cheerfully asked.

"No. I'm good."

Shane turned his glance to the parking lot as he watched Nick pull in. Noticing him, Nick waved as he parked his truck, and Shane returned the gesture. He watched Nick as he entered and walked over to Sapphire and gave her a kiss on the cheek.

"Afternoon, honey. How has your day been so far?"

"Afternoon, Dad. How come you didn't tell me you were coming in today?" she asked.

Shane's heart sped up as he listened in on their conversation.

"Only here to do a job interview. Are you going to be home tonight or are you staying at Rebecca's again?"

"I'll be home tonight."

"Good. I'll see you then."

Nick walked over to the table where Shane was sitting.

"Good afternoon, Shane."

"Afternoon, Nick. How have you been?"

Shane reached out his hand to shake Nick's.

"Pretty good, how about yourself?"

"Surviving I guess."

"That's good to hear. Decided you might want to give the rendering plant try?"

"I've been unlucky getting employment anywhere else. Everyone is looking for experienced personnel. I thought about moving on, further East, but I like it here."

Nick chuckled.

"Yeah, it is a beautiful place. You are right, though. Most people around here expect new employees to be experienced. I don't operate like that. I don't mind training people. I do want my employees to be long term though. They have to be able to handle the early hours, the squealing, and of course, the smell the rendering plant puts out. The start pay is twelve dollars an hour, but there is a lot of overtime. After a three-month probation period, we will start paying your medical and dental as well.

Sometimes we work fifty hours a week, and on occasion the weekends. Usually the guys work every other weekend. You would be working with a few of the older fellows at the plant. Most are older than I am but they are hard workers and have been with me for twenty some odd years. In fact, George, one of the old timers is going to be retiring soon. You might in time fill his position if you learn what he has to teach."

Nick paused waiting for a response from Shane.

"I'm willing to learn anything you can teach me. I'll work hard, be reliable and conscientious. That much I can offer."

"That's all I could ask. Do you have transportation?"

"That I don't have, Nick."

"I'm sure we could work something out. I can have Marvin drive you back and forth. He also lives here in town. How does that sound?"

"Sounds good to me."

"Good, we'll make your start date for Monday say 5:30 a.m. Make sure you bring along all your credentials, your social insurance number, that sort of thing. Plus I'll need your address to give to Marvin so he can pick you up, and if the number you called me from last night is the one where I can contact you, then I have it on file."

"Yep that's my cell number. I have an apartment at 333 Maple Crescent, apartment number three."

"You are renting from Abe Morhad. I've known him for years; he is quite the character."

"That is who he introduced himself as. He seems nice enough," Shane responded as he took the last swallow from his coffee, bored already from their conversation.

"Would you like another?" Nick asked.

"Nah, I think I'm going to head for home. But thanks anyway, Nick, and I'll see you Monday."

Shane rose from the table and approached the counter to pay his bill.

"Don't worry about it, Shane. I'll get it," Nick called out.

Shane looked over his shoulder and thanked him, then walked out into the warm mid-afternoon sun. He cared little about the job and even less about Nick. All that mattered to him was to be able to feed the monster inside without worry about where he could dispose of the bodies. In the week since his release, all he had been able to do was entice the monster, tease it. The more he did that the more he wanted to kill. However, even a monkey would figure out what was going on if he had shown up in New Kootenay and all of a sudden an array of deaths took place. He wasn't stupid. Timing and the opportunity to strike would be essential. For now, he was content in being as ordinary as the rest of the inhabitants of society.

Making his way back to his apartment on Maple Crescent, he double-checked the house number from which he saw Rachel leave, and for the first time noticed the sign hanging from the front porch. He squinted to make out the name, 'Dupree'. Smiling, he quickened his pace. He could assume that the Duprees knew the woman or they were family. Either way, he knew one more thing about her than she knew about him. Only time would tell what might come of that.

Entering his apartment, Shane wrote down both the name and address on a skimpy piece of paper. His one bedroom apartment was void of any furniture, other than a make-shift table, old lawn chair, a few pots and pans that he had picked up at a second hand store and a foamy that served as his bed. Eventually he would furnish the place, but for now, he liked the open space and the ease with which he could keep it clean.

Rachel, realizing that she had been gone longer than the hour she told her mother, now dialed her mom's phone number on her cell phone. "Mom, it is me, Rachel. I'm a little behind but should be home shortly."

"I was getting worried that you might be having car trouble again."

"Nope. The car is fine. I'm heading over to the drugstore. Are you sure there is nothing I can get for you?"

"Not off the top of my head. It is early though and if there is something I need, we can go together later on."

"I suppose."

"Would you like me to put on a fresh pot of coffee?"

"Pretty much coffee'd out, Mom."

"Alright. I'll see you in a bit."

"Yep."

Rachel turned her phone off and tossed the few bags she was carrying onto the front seat of her car. She walked the short distance to the strip mall drugstore. After making a few purchases, she made her way back to her car and finally back to her mother's place. With her shopping bags in hand, she entered the house and set them down on a foyer hutch until she could remove her shoes and spring jacket. It seemed quiet in the house and she called out to her mother, but there was no response.

Finally looking out the sliding glass door that led to the back garden, she was relieved to see that her mother was tending to some early spring gardening. Rachel stepped out onto the back deck and announced that she had returned, and then headed to her bedroom upstairs with her shopping bags. She had bought a few pairs of jeans, some dress pants, bra, panties, and a couple of cute spring shirts which she now put into a load of wash along with her bedding.

Slipping into a pair of clam digger pants and long sleeved shirt, she met her mother outside at the garden and helped her with what she could. They spent the entire afternoon outside, talking and joking. It was the closest Rachel felt towards her mother in a long time. She had always been a daddy's girl and often blamed her mother for his early demise. The truth was he died from coronary heart failure four years earlier. The car she drove, a midnight blue 1967 BMW 2000CS Coupe was once her father's, and when he passed away, her mother signed it over to her. The car was her baby and she had many memories of it from her childhood. Her dad restored it to perfection, and although he rarely let her help, she always recalled those rare occasions when he did to be the best of times.

Rachel was the only child of Anne and Frank Dupree. Growing up there was nothing that they could not offer her. She attended private schools and summer camps, went on month-long holidays to the Caribbean, Hawaii and Europe. Her father was one of the most sought-after architects. The Dupree Architect Development & Design Co. started out as a proprietorship but grew in leaps and bounds.

The Dupree name was stamped on hundreds, if not thousands of building structures, city parks, and million-dollar homes throughout both North and South America. Frank kept everything simple though and hired only three people. He sub-contracted the rest of the architecture business out to numerous construction companies that abided with his strict work and design ethics. Those companies then could take care of their own books, employees and the like. A year after he passed away, his three business partners bought out the Dupree name at a hefty price and took over the entire operation, although to a lesser extent. The only regret Frank Dupree ever had was the fact that Rachel hadn't assumed his role.

Rachel sometimes had that regret too, but not today. She was content working with her mother in the garden, talking about everything, and sometimes nothing at all. She couldn't know then that only one block away, Shane Brentwood was planning her execution. He was in no rush. He would stalk her first and when the time came, he would act.

Chapter 6

Tyler O'Brien rolled out of bed early that Saturday. He wanted an early start to the day. He hoped that Mr. Todd would be in better shape to continue with the few brief questions that he needed to clarify with him so that he could proceed with his investigation. The little bit of information he was able to get earlier wasn't quite enough for him. Clarification and a few more questions were indeed needed.

Blain was feeling better than he felt in the past few days, and when O'Brien finally made his way back to his room, he was sitting up in bed, reading that morning's newspaper. He looked up from it when his door opened and in stepped O'Brien.

"Good morning. Wasn't sure you were coming back."

"I won't take up much more of your time. I only want to clarify a few things. You're looking better; glad to see that."

"Yeah, I guess I'm pretty lucky. That woman who was also shot, did she survive per-chance?" Blain wanted to know.

He thought he knew the answer, but maybe there was a chance that she did survive.

"No, she was pronounced dead at the scene. It is speculated that the shooter also thought you were dead. You're lucky in that sense, I suppose; otherwise, it is likely he would have shot you twice."

Blain lowered his head and shook it.

"Damn, that is a shame about that woman. The two of them were fighting in the hotel hallway. I only wanted to stop them. I feel as though her death is due to that interference from me." He sighed, "Jesus, I hate having to carry that with me. I should've stayed out of it. She'd be alive at least."

"That is unlikely, Mr. Todd. If the man who shot you is the same man who shot my client's wife, she would be dead by now regardless of your interaction, and she would have likely been raped and humiliated beforehand. Trust me on this," O'Brien replied, as he took out his recorder and notepad again. "Can you clarify the description of the man again? You said he had a black tattoo on the top of his hand, and possibly brown dress shoes or sneakers. The shoes really aren't as important as the rest of his description, especially the tattoo. You also mentioned that he had salt and pepper hair? Is that how you remember it?"

"It is most definitely. The tattoo I'm certain was that of a raven or blackbird of some sort, with a church steeple, or cross in the background."

Blain thought for a minute.

"Yeah, it was a raven and church," he nodded his assurance. "And yes, he was wearing brown pants and brown shoes. He had a dark complexion too. I'm not sure about the color of his eyes, as I said last time he was wearing dark glasses. He was clean-shaven and not much taller than you are, 5'8" to 5'9", maybe even 6 ft. He wasn't that big a fellow, but he was quick. That is about all I can honestly remember."

O'Brien rose from his chair, turned off his recorder, and tucked his note pad into his shirt pocket.

"It all coincides with what you said yesterday, and also coincides with the description of the man I am looking for. Thank you very much, Mr. Todd. This will certainly help with my case. I appreciate you taking the time to talk to me under these circumstances, and I hope for you a speedy recovery."

O'Brien pulled out a business card and handed it to Blain.

"If anything else comes up, or you need a private investigator for anything, I hope you'll give me a call."

Blain took the card and looked at it.

"I will, thanks," he nodded his appreciation for the card.

"My pleasure, Mr. Todd. Good day," O'Brien said as he left Blain's bedside.

"Same to you, and good luck with your case. I hope you find this guy."

He turned and looked back at Blain.

"I'll find him, Mr. Todd."

O'Brien nodded as he opened the door and stepped out into the hallway.

Sure hope so, because if I find him first, there will be no judge or jury only an executioner, Blain thought as he switched to a more comfortable position in his hospital bed. He set the business card down on his bed-stand and closed his eyes. By now he knew the K.A.T. Agency was wondering where he was and that they likely had begun the process of removing his name from the database. He'd have five days from the date he was supposed to have checked in before they destroyed everything. It was a simple protocol. He knew it was important for him to make contact with the agency over the next few days. For now though, he needed rest.

Around 12:00 p.m., he opened his eyes. The doctor was standing next to him, his chart in his hand.

"I see you are awake, Mr. Todd. How are you feeling today?"

"I've felt better. I'm not used to getting lead in my stomach every day."

"No, I'm sure no one wants to be faced with that. You are recovering well though. There is no infection and the muscle is healing impressively. I think you are going to be alright. There may be some tenderness to your abdominal and mid back region for a few weeks, but it will dissipate."

"What about the nausea? That, I think bothers

me the most."

"Yes, well, that too is to be expected. As you heal, that will all go away. You are going to be fine, Mr. Todd, I assure you."

"Yeah, I imagine so," Blain replied as he looked toward the window. "When do you think I can be on my way?"

"You sound anxious to go."

The doctor half-chuckled.

"I was on my way to a cabin up in the Yukon to do some fishing, I guess you could say I'm quite anxious to get on with it."

"The police will be coming by later today to talk with you, I've been told. Once they interview you, I'll check on you again, and we'll decide from there. How does that sound?"

"Doesn't sound too promising," Blain replied.

"No worries, Mr. Todd. I'm pretty sure you'll be released today. You are doing well and I really see no reason to keep you from your holiday. I'll have a prescription for antibiotics and some pain killers for you. Are you allergic to anything?"

"Not as far as I know."

"Alright then."

The doctor put Blain's chart back.

"I'll come by again in a couple of hours. You could try to do some walking. It may be tough at first, but it'll benefit you in the long run."

"I'm not going to blow out the stitching, am I?"

"No. It may feel like that as you tighten your stomach muscles to walk. Just be careful, Mr. Todd. Everything will be alright."

The doctor smiled his assurance then turned and exited Blain's room.

Wow, didn't even get that doctor's name. Strange how he didn't introduce himself, he thought as he slowly pulled himself up to a sitting position and dangled his legs over the side of his bed. Standing now, he took his first few steps. The pain wasn't as bad as he thought it would be. Making his way over to his chart, he looked at it and the doctor's name.

"Dr. Umay, hmmm. Alright," he said quietly to himself as he turned and walked to the window.

Looking out, his mind wandered. He was thinking of Rachel and the more he thought the more he thought how much he did love her. It was hard not to think that he may have lost her. *Well, I guess it is, whatever, it is. For now, I have to get out of here and up to Yellow Lake,* Blain thought as he made his way around the room, walking as Dr. Umay suggested.

Finally, making himself comfortable, he began reading an outdoor magazine that was on the table beside the chair. He glanced through it from cover to cover a couple of times before the door opened and in walked another official looking man.

"Mr. Todd, I assume?" the man asked as he reached out his hand to shake Blain's.

"Correct," Blain began as he slowly rose, "and you are?" he asked with his hand outstretched.

"Special Constable, Harlow."

The two shook hands.

"I guess you know why I'm here?"

"I imagine you wish to ask me a few questions about the shooting."

"Yup. So, are you comfortable standing or would you prefer to sit?"

"The doctor tells me I should be walking some, so I'll pace."

"Very well."

Constable Harlow gestured toward the chair.

"Do you mind if I sit?"

"Not at all. Knock yourself out."

Blain stepped out of the way and began walking around the room.

"Can you give me a description of the man?"

"Yes, I can," he responded as he told Harlow everything he had told O'Brien earlier.

Harlow listened and wrote everything down.

"So the man was about 6'ft tall, dark complexion, salt and pepper hair, and was wearing dark glasses. Oh yeah, and had a tattoo on the top of his right hand, that of a raven and church steeple? Correct Mr. Todd?" Constable Harlow wanted to confirm.

"That would be him, yes indeed."

"Okay. Is there anything else you can remember, something that stands out, other than the tattoo?"

"Not really, no. You have to remember it happened fast. It didn't take him long to pull the trigger. I know when I approached him he was unarmed, so he was a quick draw. That stands out in my mind."

"I see. Alright, Mr. Todd. We have your information and description of the assailant. I don't think there is any reason to take up any more of your time."

The Constable rose from the chair.

"If we need you for anything else, we'll be in contact. Thank you again, Mr. Todd."

"You're welcome," Blain responded as the officer made his way to the door and exited.

Glad that is over with. I hope Dr. Umay gets here soon, he thought as he opened the closet where his clothes were and began to dress. Surprised that he had the cell phone provided to him by the Agency, he checked to see if there were any calls he had missed, but of course the battery was low and with no adapter to give it a boost, he'd have to wait to check and to make contact with K.A.T. Agency.

It wasn't long before the doctor came back with

his prescription. A few words and well-wishes were exchanged. Then, after signing the release form, he was on his way.

"You take it easy for a while, Mr. Todd," the doctor said as Blain began to leave the hospital. "And good luck with your fishing trip."

"I will, Doc. Thanks for fixing me up, and the good wishes."

Finally stepping outside for the first time in a few days, Blain inhaled deeply. He found that walking was somewhat aggravating, but he carried on. The more he walked the less pain he felt, and so he walked another block before waving down a taxi.

"Where you off to?" the driver asked as Blain opened the back door and sat down.

"The Heritage Hotel."

"You okay, mister? You look a little bit rough."

"Yeah, I just got out of the hospital. I'm fine though," he said as he made himself comfortable.

"Hospital eh, did you have some kind of surgery?"

The driver signaled, turned out into the street and made his way toward the Heritage.

"Pretty easy to tell, huh?"

"I drive this route often and every now and again, I pick up a fare who has left the hospital. I guess you could say I have an eye for folks who have had some kind of surgery."

"I had a surgery alright. Sure glad to be out of there now. I don't like hospitals all that much."

"I don't think many folks do."

The two grew silent as the driver switched lanes and turned down the street where the Heritage was located.

"Here we are," he said as he pulled up to the curb.

"I guess I was closer than I thought."

"Yeah, about three blocks. You'd still be walking though if you hadn't flagged me down," the driver chuckled.

"I suppose you are right, how much is the fare?" Blain asked as he opened the door to step out.

"Ten bucks will cover it," the driver responded as he looked at the meter.

Blain pulled out his wallet and handed the driver a $10 bill.

"Thanks for the ride; have a good day," he said as he stepped out onto the curb and closed the door.

"You too, mister, and get well."

The driver watched to make sure his fare made it to the front doors before he signaled and turned again into the street. The hotel manager met Blain at the front door and opened it for him.

"Hello, Mr. Todd. We have kept your room waiting for you. It was quite a courageous thing you did."

"I don't know if it was courageous or plain stupid. There could have been two dead people in your hallway. That doesn't sound courageous to me. It sounds stupid."

"It was the thought, I suppose. Not many folks would have tried to help as you did."

"There was no thought process in it at all. If I thought, maybe I wouldn't have been put in the hospital and that lady wouldn't be in the morgue."

"Mr. Todd, regardless of the outcome, you were more than heroic."

"Whatever, I only want to get to my room and rest for a bit."

"Yes, of course. Sorry to have kept you," the man said as he stepped aside and Blain walked passed him and up the stairs to his waiting room.

Inside it was as he had left it, other than the fresh linen on his bed and clean towels in the bathroom. He removed his shoes and lay on the bed. After resting for a few minutes, he rose and plugged the adapter into his cell phone to charge it. It would take maybe an hour, and so he lay back down and closed his eyes. It didn't take long before he dozed off.

He woke up at 4:00 p.m. Outside it was raining, and he briefly looked out the window and watched as the rain made puddles. He felt better, but he knew he wasn't quite 100% yet. Unplugging his cell phone from the adapter, he checked to make sure it was fully charged, then dialed the K.A.T. Agency. It rang a couple of times and finally Canbra answered.

"Entity?" the voice asked with caution.

"Yes. It is me. I'm back from the dead."

"What happened?"

"I tried to stop something that I should have left alone, and in my attempt I took a bullet in my gut. I'm recovering now and back at the hotel."

"The Heritage you mean?"

"Yep. I guess I'll need to reschedule my flight."

"Do you think you are well enough to carry out the objective?" Canbra asked with concern.

"As long as I breathe, I'll always be able to carry out my objective. Now, about that flight ticket, can you arrange it?"

"Of course I can. I'm looking right now. The next one leaves Canupe on Monday. I guess that gives you a day to rest. I dialed your cell number on Friday. A strange man answered. Are you aware of this?"

Blain was shocked to hear that.

"What?"

"I said I called you on Friday, and someone answered your phone. Do you know who that might have been?"

"I have no idea."

Blain thought for a moment.

"You said it was a man that answered?"

"Yes."

"Hmmm, strange that is. I have no idea who may have answered it. There was a private investigator named Tyler O'Brien who was hanging out in my room on that day. He's the only one I saw. It could be that he picked up. Don't know why he'd do that though. You didn't reveal anything to him did you?"

"No. As soon as I knew it wasn't you, I disconnected. I take it he was there to question you regarding that incident at the hotel that you mentioned earlier?"

"That is correct. Of course, I was using the alias Mr. Todd, and that is all he ever called me. He isn't any wiser on who I really am."

"That is a relief."

"Yeah, it is. Alright, so what time is the next flight to Yellow Lake on Monday?"

"Leaves Canupe at 10:00 a.m. The ticket has been secured. You can pick it up at the customer service counter when you get there. The documents and other things that you will need have been rerouted to that destination. It is amazing what a click of a button can do these days."

Blain half chuckled.

"Yeah, it is. Okay, Canbra, I shall contact you again once I make my destination and receive the documents and whatnot."

"Very good, Entity. I hope you get rested up and feel better on Monday."

"Me too. Regardless, I'll make the flight. I have no plans to step into anything again that doesn't concern me."

"We will talk soon. Bye for now, Entity."

"Yes. Bye for now."

They hung up their phones simultaneously. *Today, is a waste, and tomorrow isn't going to be any better,* Blain thought as he made his way to the chair and sat down.

Back at the agency, Canbra was waiting to confirm with Dwayne that 'Entity' was back on track and that he had simply been in a mishap that detained him from making the first flight. For now though, she wouldn't upload his data until he made contact with her again once he made his destination. Finishing up with what it was she was doing, she dialed Dwayne's number and filled him in. Dwayne smiled when he heard the news.

"I knew he would come through. He always does."

"Yes he does. Sometimes though, he does get himself into things that delay his progress. This is one of those times, I suppose."

"At least he is well, and nothing drastic has happened to him. I'm quite relieved."

"I think the majority of us are. The agency would certainly suffer if he wasn't with us."

"True enough. Alright Canbra. Thanks for filling me in. Shall I send his data back to you now, or are you going to wait for his second contact with you?"

"I'm going to wait for him to contact me again, yes."

"Good enough. We'll talk soon," Dwayne said as he hung up the phone.

Opening the agency's safe, he grabbed the thumb-drive that held all of Blain's ID's and aliases. It was better, he thought, to have quick access to it.

Meanwhile, back at the Heritage Hotel, Blain was contemplating whether he wanted to order food from the hotel restaurant or from the fast food joint across the street. He wasn't even sure that he could hold anything down. He was rather nauseated and in some pain. Perhaps food would have to wait. Instead, he stretched out on the bed and turned on the TV, which lulled him to sleep.

Waking a few hours later, he slid off the bed and paced his room. Keep walking the doctor had told him, and so he walked. He hadn't filled the prescription the doctor had given him, and now he wished that he had, if not for the antibiotics then for the painkillers. Finally sitting down again, he looked at his watch. It was 7:00 p.m. The day was done, and so was he. He'd have to wait to fill the prescription, and so he made himself as comfortable as he could and flipped through the channels. Bored with that, he turned it off, and sat in self- contemplation.

Chapter 7

At 9:00 p.m. that Saturday he slid beneath the sheets of his bed and closed his eyes. The pain he was feeling from the wound made it somewhat difficult for him to fall asleep, but eventually he felt his eyes get heavy, and he dozed off. It was the knock on the door the next morning at around 7:00 a.m. that woke him. Groggy-eyed he slipped out of bed thinking in his state that it was the chamber-maid coming to clean his room, he unlocked and opened it. Standing there with a pistol in his waistband and wearing dark glasses was the man who had shot him days earlier, or at least who he thought to be the man. There was no time to close the door as the man pushed his way in.

"Back up," the man said as he pointed his pistol and directed Blain to move back.

"I've never left any witnesses alive, and I'm not about to start now."

Blain standing there in his jogging pants slowly stepped back.

"You should have finished the job off, I suppose."

"That is exactly why I'm here now," the man said as he removed the salt and pepper wig on his head to reveal that he was completely bald.

He was wearing black leather gloves this time and the dark glasses on his face once again hid the color of his eyes.

"I've been watching you for a few days now. Was sure glad, to see you make your way back here. It makes it easier for me to kill you once and for all."

"What are you waiting for?" Blain asked without showing fear.

If he was going to die this way, it might as well be quick. He felt the barrel of the pistol slam across the bridge of his nose breaking it with a loud crack.

"I don't have any intention on making this quick," the man said as Blain fell back onto the bed clutching his now bloody nose.

"First off, I want to know who the hell you are."

"My name is none of your business. You might as well pull the trigger because you aren't going to get any answers from me."

"Is that right?"

The man reached over to the bed stand and grabbed the wallet sitting there. He opened it and looked at the ID.

"It says here your name is Ben Todd."

"Yeah, and I thought you had salt and pepper hair. Obviously, I was wrong. So maybe you are too."

"A smart guy, eh? Well, Ben, if that isn't your name, it matters little to me. It is the name I'll put down in my little book."

From his inside pocket, the man pulled out a silencer and keeping the .8mm Glock pointed at Blain, screwed it into place. He tied a towel around Blain's mouth and then cocking the weapon, he pointed it at his leg, threatening to shoot.

"You see Ben, I don't like to kill anyone without watching them squirm for a bit. I have few hours before I have to worry about some ditsy chambermaid. I'm betting I can punch six holes into you without killing you in that amount of time."

He looked Blain in the eye.

"So far you already have a broken nose. I can tell that by how swollen and black your eyes are getting. I know for fact it hurts like hell, too. Probably not as bad as the bullet I punched into your guts, but it hurts nonetheless."

All Blain needed was one opportunity to get the upper hand and the man standing before him would pay dearly for trying to intimidate him. Although his right eye was beginning to swell shut, he continued staring back at the man. The amount of blood he was losing, from where the man cracked him across the bridge of his nose, was minimal. The man though obviously enjoyed causing pain. Even without a gun, he'd likely be quite the opponent. Armed as he was, he certainly held an ace. Blain inhaled deeply as the man once more pointed the silenced pistol at him, and standing over him, drove his fist deep into Blain's stomach with as much heat as that from a baseball. Again, Blain winced in pain, sweat formed on his brow and tears stung his eyes.

"That's two," the man said as he stepped back and smiled. "Feeling some pain now, Ben? I bet you are. Even with that slug removed from your gut, it hurts, doesn't it?"

Blain couldn't answer with the towel wrapped around his face, but he did make gestures, showing he would waste no time in killing the man that stood before him.

"I'm sorry, Ben. I don't understand. What are you trying to say?" the man responded with disdain followed by a chuckle. "Where should I send my first bullet, Ben? Perhaps your kneecap? At this range, it will shatter like fine bone china. You'd probably pass out from the pain then, eh Ben?"

Blain shook his head in anger. Adrenalin coursed through his veins and his heart began to beat faster and faster; then, with all the power vested in him, he threw himself forward, knocking the man to the ground. The man's head hit the floor with a solid thud, and the glasses he was wearing slid across the floor. In as much pain as he was feeling, Blain managed to knock the pistol from the man's hand. Dropping one knee onto the man's throat, he pulled the towel from his face, and as quickly, stuffed it into his assailant's mouth.

The expression on the man's face was both that of surprise and fear, as Blain drove his own fist into the man's face, shattering his nose. It felt as though he had punched a baked potato that squished from the force of the blow. Grabbing him by the front of his shirt, he threw him onto the bed and in one fluid motion picked up the pistol.

"Guess what. The tables are now turned."

He pointed the gun between the man's eyes.

"I don't torture, but I do kill. You've picked on the wrong son of a bitch this time. Hand me your wallet, I'd like to know your name," Blain harassed.

He cared less who the man was.

The man sat up and pulled the towel out of his mouth.

"Fuck you. You want it, come and get it."

"Nope. Don't see a need in that. I really don't care who the fuck you are. Looks to me like you also have a broken nose. I'd say it is broke a helluva lot worse than mine. A big. improvement, I think."

"Are you afraid to shoot?"

"Afraid? Not at all."

Blain held the pistol to the man's temple and with as much force as the man used to punch him in the gut, he returned the favor, knocking him onto the bed.

"Hurts a bit, doesn't it?"

Grabbing him by the shirt collar, he pulled him up to a sitting position. Shoving the pistol up to his lips, Blain shook his head.

"Not a peep."

Tying the towel around the man's face, he pushed him back onto the bed.

"It's me now who has a few hours before worrying about the chamber maid."

The man was sitting up now, his eyes swollen shut, a constant trickle of blood ran down his face from his badly broken nose.

"You know what," Blain began, "I have a better plan for a fellow like you. Have you ever been to Yellow Lake, up in the Yukon? That is where I'm heading."

The man sat there in dizzying pain.

"I take that as a "no". It is real nice up there this time of year. I think I'm going to take you along. You'll really enjoy yourself," Blain finished as he sat down at the chair, picked up his cell phone, and dialed the K.A.T. Agency.

He kept the pistol pointed at the man. If he so much as moved or twitched, he'd send lead in his direction and take out his shoulder. His plan was simple: *'human testing'* on the piece of shit that sat before him on the bed. Human testing had, never been done with the K-15 virus. Now was the opportunity, and he wasn't about to pass that up. The phone rang a couple of times and finally Canbra picked it up.

"Hello, Entity. How are you today?"

"For a Sunday, as good as can be expected."

"You sound a bit nasally. Is anything wrong?"

"Wrong? Not at all, other than I have some pain, new pain even. Listen, I've decided to drive to Winnfield. Is that going to pose a problem?"

"Of course it is. We need you to start work on this A.S.A.P."

"I guess I should come clean with you."

"What is that supposed to mean?"

"The doctor told me when I left the hospital that I couldn't fly for a couple of weeks, three to four be exact. He said it could burst open my stitches and likely cause some kind of hemorrhage. I didn't want to believe him, but the way I am feeling I think I agree with him," Blain lied.

"Jesus Christ, Entity, why didn't you tell me that

in the first place?"

"I already told you why. I didn't want to believe him."

"You are okay to drive though?"

"Yep."

"How long do you suppose the drive will take you."

"If I leave this afternoon, I think I can make it to Winnfield in the next couple of days and Yellow Lake by Thursday at the latest, I would hope."

"You can't drive to Yellow Lake you know. You'll have to take a flight from there."

"Nope. There is another alternative. Rent me a boat from the Winnfield Marina. I'll boat in."

"What kind of boat do you want, Entity?" Canbra asked in defeat.

"A boat," Blain replied.

Any kind would do. He didn't care.

"It doesn't have to be anything fancy, as long as it can get me to Yellow Lake and up the tributary to Mud Creek."

"Well," Canbra replied as she rolled her eyes, "I guess there is no other option. Alright, I'll arrange for it and have the stuff you'll need delivered. Make sure you call in a few hours before you get there. We aren't going to be able to waste much more time on this. You'll have to leave directly for Yellow Lake when you get to Winnfield."

"Naturally. I'll let you know a few hours ahead of time before I get there. No worries."

"Good enough, Entity. Your boat and gear will be waiting for you."

"We'll talk soon," Blain said as the two of them hung up.

"Looks like we are going on a road trip, Mr. whatever your name is. I bet you are excited about that, eh? I'm going to take care of my nose first. Yours, on the other hand, I care little about."

Standing up from the chair, he walked over to the man sitting on the bed, and in one swoop, slammed the nearby desk phone into his head, knocking the man out cold.

"There, rest for a bit."

Gathering a small first aid kit that he carried with him, he made his way into the bathroom and cleaned up. Using a dampened cloth, he patted the blood off his face and from around his nose. Then, with nerves of steel, he placed his thumb and finger on his nose and snapped it into place, setting the broken bone. It cracked as he did that, and blood trickled over his top lip and into his mouth. He squinted in pain as his eyes slightly watered.

"Damn, that hurt," he said to himself as he waited for the pain to subside.

His eyes were swollen but not nearly as swollen as his assailant's. *At least I can see,* he thought as he finished cleaning up. Stuffing cotton balls up his nose to stop the bleeding and to help keep the broken bone from floating too much and to help it fuse together, he stepped out of the bathroom. The man was still out cold so he tossed a glass of water onto his face and slapped him.

"Wake up you piece of shit. I'm not about to carry you out the door."

The man shook his head as he came to.

"You're fucking dead, if I ever get the chance," he muttered, but his words were muffled by the towel around his face.

"Sorry, I don't understand that monkey English of yours."

Blain pulled the man up to a sitting position. With the pistol planted against the man's forehead, he gestured for him to stand up.

"I told you earlier that you and I are about to go

on a road trip. No use wasting any more time."

He made the man walk over to the chair and he pushed him into it.

"Now you sit there like a good dog, while I gather up my stuff."

Keeping the pistol pointed at the man, he gathered his overnight bag. Ripping the bloodstained sheets from the bed, he tossed them into the courtesy laundry bag next to his bed and zipped it closed. On their way out he would toss it down the laundry chute. Satisfied that he had covered up any signs of a struggle, he pulled on some clothes and gestured the man to stand up. Then, he untied the towel from around his captive's face and tossed it into the laundry bag.

"Come on, let's get going. Grab this laundry bag," Blain said as the man stood and followed his instructions. "We'll be passing a laundry chute down the hall. Don't try anything stupid, because I will not hesitate to pull this trigger. Go on, get going," Blain said as he grabbed the man's wig and forced him out the door.

He knew there wouldn't be many people out yet, and with luck, they would go unnoticed. Luck was with them, and they were able to exit through a side door. Two minutes later they were seated in Blain's car. It was 8:00 a.m.

"Where the fuck are you taking me? Do you honestly think you'll get away with this?" the man asked in anger and humiliation.

"I've already got away with it. I already told you where we are going. Now sit back and shut up."

Blain pointed the pistol at the man as they turned out of the underground parking lot and onto the street. He drove a short distance to the outskirts of Canupe, then, turned off the road. Forcing the man from the front seat to the back, he used plastic ties to secure the man's hands behind his back, and forcefully crossing the man's legs, he tied his ankles the same way. The man fought but Blain was always in control. With the man secured now, he taped his mouth shut with medical tape and frisked him for his wallet and extra shells for the 8mm Glock. Closing the car door, he returned to the driver's seat.

The stitches to his stomach due to the bit of fighting it took to get the man secured seeped, and blood soaked through his shirt. He pulled the shirt from the waistband of his Levi jeans and looked closely at the wound. *Ah, not so bad, I guess, could be a hell of a lot worse,* he thought as he signaled and turned out on to the highway. It was painful for him to drive but he would grin and bear it. Opening the man's wallet, he tossed it onto the front seat and thumbed through it as he continued to drive.

"So, you do have a name. Hector Hernandez, well, nice to meet you, Hector. Not so tough now are you?" he commented as he looked through his rear view mirror at the man sitting in the back seat.

Hector shook his head in anger. His eyes were swollen so badly that he couldn't see. His nose caked in blood was as black as his eyes were turning.

"I know if you could only speak, or should I say if I could only hear you. Too bad, Hector. I really don't want to listen to you. You thought you were pretty tough, didn't you?" Blain asked with little care. "The thing is you're nothing more than street scum. You get your kicks from beating up women and forcing yourself onto them. Those are the makings of a real tough man," Blain said with sarcasm.

He could tell from the protruding blood vessels pulsating on Hector's neck that the more he talked the madder Hector was getting.

"Maybe you should calm down some old boy.

We have a long drive ahead of us and I need you alive."

Around this same time back in New Kootenay, Rachel decided that she was going to head back home to Calimay. She decided to leave early the next day, Monday. The thought of a divorce from Blain was locked away for now in her mind. There had to be a better way and she was determined to discover it. She had no idea that Blain wasn't home. Her hope was that he'd meet her with open arms when she finally returned, early the next evening.

Behind a bush and looking in through the kitchen window stood Shane Brentwood. He was trying to read Rachel and her mother's lips as they sat at the kitchen table and spoke. He made out the word 'Calimay' and 'the drive back', but that was all. He knew what it likely meant to them, but, to him it meant he needed to move fast, something he hadn't expected. One thing was certain, if he didn't get a chance to take the younger woman captive, he'd certainly kill the older one, and that would bring the younger one back again. He would then at least have a second chance. Turning now, Shane made his way back to his apartment. The plan on how to take the younger lady captive was formulating in his head with every step he took.

His apartment was cool as he unlocked the door and stepped inside. Tossing the key on a cardboard box near the entrance, he made his way to the fridge and slugged back a drink of orange juice, wiping his mouth with his hand as he finished. *Got to get Miss Smokin' tonight,* he thought as he put the carton of juice back in the fridge. For now, he would sit and wait for complete darkness. He'd make his move in the wee hours of twilight when most were tucked away in their beds.

He had noticed while he watched Rachel and her mother that a side window was open, and that the simple window screen would be no match for a razor blade. It was there he would enter the house, providing the window remained opened. Plan 'B' would be simple mechanical or electrical vandalism to her car, anything to keep her from leaving. The more he thought about it the more he wished it was already done. His mouth got dry as he sat there. He was in a hypnotic trance. Nothing moved or sounded and the air was deathly still. Then, from around the corner in the next room the ringing of his cell phone erupted. Shane startled shook his head and slowly rose to meet the ringing sound. "Hello," he said as he put the phone to his ear.

"Hey Shane, this is Nick, Nick Burgress. How are you tonight?"

"Hello Nick. Might I ask the same question of you?"

"I'm fine. Are you going to be ready for work tomorrow?"

"Really haven't thought too much about it. I have been trying to get my place together and that, ah, but, yeah I guess I am. What time was it you said we start?"

"Between 5:30 and 6:00 a.m. I'll have Marvin drop by your place a little after 5:00 a.m. How does that sound?"

There was a pause as Shane contemplated. He knew, if nothing else, it would prove to be a good alibi for what he was planning that evening.

"Yeah, that'll be fine. What does Marvin drive? I'd like to be on the lookout for it."

"An old brown Jeep Wagoneer. You'll hear it pull up," Nick chuckled.

"Alright, I'll keep my eyes open. Thanks, Nick. See you tomorrow."

"You bet. See you then."

Shane listened until he heard the click on the other end, and then hung up. The clock on the wall seemed to echo as the seconds counted down to darkness. Shane lay down on his foam bed and drifted in and out of sleep. His dreams were laden with blood and mayhem. Then he heard it, the sound of a car horn. Startled and disoriented, he slowly rose from his bed on the floor. He had slept through the night. He had missed his chance.

Making his way to the window, he pulled the curtain open, and sure enough a brown Jeep Wagoneer sat idling in his drive with an older man sitting behind the wheel. Obviously, it was Marvin. Shane was neither elated nor enthused. Taking his time, he splashed water on his face and rinsed his mouth. After throwing on a pair of pants, he exited his apartment and introduced himself to the driver.

"Morning, I'm Shane."

"Hey, Shane, it's nice to meet you. Jump in, we have coffees to get."

Nodding, Shane made his way around to the passenger side and slid in next to Marvin.

"Excited about your first day?" Marvin asked as they pulled out onto the street.

"Excited? About what, killing pigs?" Shane responded with little interest.

"Ha ha. Got a sense of humour too, eh? That's good. You're going to need a sense of humour once those pigs start squealing. It's a shrilling sound, but one gets used to it soon enough."

"I bet."

Shane cared little about the conversation. He wasn't thinking about pigs, work, or even coffee. The only thing on his mind was the lady with the 'SMOKIN' license plate, and the fact that she may well be on her way back to Calimay. And so his day started.

The best part of the day as far as Shane cared, was when it finally ended. Back at his apartment, he doubted he would ever return to work. Something special had happened that day. He hadn't a clue about what it was, except that for now, the monster inside had been fed. The pigs he saw dying that day changed his mind about killing. It was an odd and overwhelming feeling. Had good won over the evil that for so many years he waited to release? Would he never have that desire to kill again? Had the monster been killed like the pigs?

Shane picked up the phone and dialed Nick's number. On the third ring, Nick picked it up.

"New Kootenay Rendering, Nick here. How can I help you?" he asked as he picked up the phone.

"Hi, Nick, this is Shane."

"Hello Shane. What can I help you with?"

"I appreciate the opportunity you gave me for work. I don't think I'm going to continue, though. I quit."

"Aw, shit. Well, I guess slaughtering pigs isn't for everybody. I thank you for calling and letting me know. You have a day's wage coming to you. I can send the check in with Sapphire tomorrow. You can pick it up at the Koffee House. How does that sound?"

"Sure. That will do. Thanks, Nick."

"No problem, Shane. Good luck to you," Nick replied as he hung up the phone somewhat disappointed.

He had seen many young folks just like Shane come and go. It was all part of the business.

Shane made his way into the small bathroom and turned on the shower to wash the stench from the pigs off his skin.

Chapter 8

Blain and Hector were getting to know one another, if one could call it that. They spent Sunday night sleeping on the side of the road, but not before Blain made sure that Hector couldn't get away. He tossed him into the trunk, securely tied and with fresh tape across his mouth. Hector fought him the entire time. Even after he was locked inside, he continued to fight by kicking and thrashing. Blain stretched out on the front seat and made himself as comfortable as he could, grinning as Hector fought himself in desperation. It took him close to an hour before Hector finally gave up and fell silent.

Early that Monday morning, near the same time that Shane was heading to his first and last day on the job at the New Kootenay Pork Product plant and before traffic got busy, Blain unlocked the trunk, yanked Hector out, and tossed him again into the back seat.

"Hope you slept well Hector. I did," he said as he closed the door.

Sliding into the driver seat, he fired up the car up and pulled onto the highway. Through the rear view mirror, he smiled at the man looking at him from the back seat.

"Maybe tonight I'll make the trunk a little more comfortable," he commented sarcastically.

They drove for another hour before he decided to pull off the road and rip the tape away from Hector's mouth.

"There, maybe you have a few words you'd like to share. I'm getting tired of doing all the talking."

"Did I tell you that you are a fucking dead man if I get my hands on you... you fucking little weasel," Hector burst out-loud with his first breath. "You're lucky you have these damn ties on as tight as they are, or

I'd wrap my hands around your neck and squeeze until your eyeballs pop out."

"Come on quit being such a baby. As tough as you are, you really don't have to talk like that. Here I am being nice to you, and you have to go and say something like that. Shame, shame, Hector, shame, shame," Blain said as he turned back to the steering wheel, signaled his move into traffic and continued driving.

They stopped a couple of times, first at a self-serve gas station where he filled the gas tank. Blain paid at the pump so he wouldn't have to leave the side of the car. Their next stop was a drive-through where he bought food and drink for both of them, warning Hector that if he tried anything foolish or even spoke, he'd shoot him. It was that simple. With the purchases made, they were again on their way.

"How am I supposed to eat this shit with my hands tied?"

"I don't know. If you are hungry, you'll figure it out. They are damn good burgers, I'll tell you that much. Smell good too, don't they?" Blain paused as he took another bite of his own burger. "Sorry about that Hector, I keep forgetting it is probably pretty tough for you to smell, with that broken nose and all. I guess you'll have to take my word for it."

"You are an asshole, a fucking asshole," Hector yelled as he bent over to the burger and fries that were sitting on the seat beside him and began to eat as though he was in a pie-eating contest.

Blain chuckled as he slurped from the drink in his hand.

"That a boy, Hector. I knew you'd figure it out."

Hector sat up with mustard and ketchup all over his face, some lettuce sticking to his nose.

"Fuck. I'm going to take pleasure in putting lead in you," he muttered as he once more leaned over and took a bite from the burger.

His pop spilled onto the seat and all he could do is slurp at it as it trickled toward the opposite door. Blain watched in the rear view mirror and took great pleasure in doing so.

"Awe, did your pop spill? That is too bad. What a terrible thing to have happened," he said with little care and a lot of glee. "You are doing a good job in lapping it up, just like the dog you are."

Hector rose again and looked at him through the mirror.

"If this dog ever gets off his leash, he's going to rip into you like he has rabies."

"I'm not worried about that. Dogs with rabies are shot. I would have no quibble in doing it either. So, behave yourself," Blain smiled, as he continued to eat and look around as he drove.

"Keep your smiles to yourself. I'm in no mood for your humour."

"I wasn't being humorous. Rest assured I'd have no problem shooting you. But I'd rather you be alive for what I have in store for you."

"Your only option when this is over will be to shoot me before I shoot you."

"I know. That is why what I have in store for you will result in exactly that, me shooting you."

"Give it your best and good luck with that."

"No luck is needed, Hector. All I need is a syringe and a bullet," Blain replied as he averted his eyes to the road sign ahead.

It read Winnfield 320 Km.

"That sign means we are getting close to your destiny. Should never have come back to try and kill me,

Hector. You should have waited for the law to round your sorry ass up."

The two grew silent as they continued on. At 7:00 p.m. that Monday, around the same time that Shane was showering, Blain pulled into a rest stop that was off the highway. It was there that they would rest before finishing their journey.

"Can I trust you enough to leave you in the back seat or should I toss you into the trunk again while we rest?"

"Do whatever you fucking want. I don't care," Hector replied.

"Really?"

"Yes, fucking really. I care little about what you do to me, because I know that eventually I'll do the same to you."

"That is very doubtful, Hector. When we get to where we are going and I do what I'm going to do to you, you'll already be dead, and introduced to a Hell you have never seen."

"Hell? I'm already there, Mr. Ben."

"Nope. Not the Hell I have in store for you. I guarantee that."

"Exactly, what kind of Hell do you think you can put me through? Huh, what kind? I think you are full of shit."

Hector tried to get comfortable in the back seat, but the ties to his ankles were making that difficult.

"You look a little bit uncomfortable there, Hector. Are the ties too tight?"

"As if you care."

"You are right, I don't care. Anyway," Blain stated as he reached for the medical tape, "I don't think I'm going to toss you in the trunk after all. But," he held up the tape, "I am going to tape your mouth shut. Then I'm going to rest my eyes for a few minutes. Remember this too," he said as he began taping Hectors mouth. "Your Glock," he showed it to Hector as a reminder, that he was in control, "is fully loaded. You try anything at all and I'll unload the entire thing. Then you'll never have that chance to get away and shoot me."

Blain smiled as he turned back around and stretched his legs out across the front seat of the car. He knew there was no way Hector could do anything without it alerting him, in which case he would not hesitate to kill him then and there. In fact, he half wanted it to turn out that way. The more time he spent with Hector the more he hated him. A part of him did want Hector to attempt an escape. That was Blain's illogical side.

One thing was for certain. If he didn't kill Hector before making the distance to his cabin on Mud Creek, the outcome was going to be the same. There were many times, he recalled, while his brother Trent was alive and the K.A.T Agency was only in the early stages, that they all discussed human testing. It was a barbaric thought back then, and even now, it seemed far-fetched. Nonetheless, it was probably one of the best and logical answers to solving the K-15 virus outbreak. Hector Hernandez, could give back to the people he had hurt, violated, raped and killed, by giving his own life in ambitious, almost scientific, research. Blain knew he was no scientist. He did know enough, however, to at least attempt such a feat. That was what his logical side wanted. Which one was going to win really depended on Hector.

How he would ever explain his findings using a live subject was beyond him. In fact, he doubted he would mention exactly how he discovered anything, if by some miracle he did find a cure or came up with a formula that could in one form or another at least control the K-15 virus. His idea was simple. Canbra had mentioned the first day she called him up to send him off to Yellow Lake to do the research that a live K-15 cell as well as a blood sample from a family named Brentwood, who were possibly the first generation of K-15 carriers, would be among his gear. There were other things she was sending as well, but with those two items only, he was certain he would be able to conduct a few simple tests.

His brother, Trent, made valid scientific points that a first generation carrier of this new type of Kuru likely developed in their own bodies a prophylactic serum that prevented the urges and needs from those suffering it the hunger for human flesh. Trent was never able to come up with the formula because there were no live subjects available or willing. Today they had their subject, a man named Hector Hernandez.

It was early evening as Rachel pulled into the driveway back home in Calimay. She was a bit surprised to see that Blain's car was gone. *Typical,* she thought to herself as she opened the door and stepped out of her car. There was a week's worth of newspapers stacked on their porch. She knew then that he had obviously been gone for at least that long.

"Should have followed through with that Goddamn divorce," she muttered to herself as she unlocked the front door.

Making her way inside she found the note on the table that Blain had left her. It didn't explain where he had gone, only that he was called out on business. *You couldn't even have phoned me you son of a bitch,* she thought as she tossed it into the garbage can. It was then she noticed that he had left behind, either purposely or accidently, the only communication device she had to contact him. Now, unless he called her, she had no way of contacting him. It wasn't the first time that he left his cell phone behind. It did however outrage her.

"Fucking asshole," she said beneath her breath as she gathered her bags from her car and unpacked. *Every fucking time, no matter what the problems that we have at home are, that son of a bitch always has an excuse either to leave or to avoid discussing it. I'm so sick of that shit. Goddamn it Blain, if you were here right now I'd smack you one,* she thought as she began hanging up her clothes.

Meanwhile Blain was finally waking up from the short nap he decided to take. Looking over to Hector, he smiled.

"Did you have a bit of a sleep?" he asked not really caring.

Of course, Hector, couldn't answer with the tape around his mouth. Blain sat up and opened his car door window. The early evening air felt good on his face and he inhaled deeply.

"The last road sign said we have about three hundred and twenty clicks to go before we get to Winnfield. I think we'll head up the road a few more miles. There is a campground ahead where we'll spend the night. Might even let you out to piss, but don't count on it," he commented as he looked at Hector.

Reaching across to the back-seat he pulled the tape from his face.

"There, does that feel better. No need to answer, because I don't really care."

"I have nothing to say about nothing, you prick. Do want you want; slap tape across my mouth, toss me in the trunk, beat me with a stick, if you desire. Eventually, you'll fuck up and then I'll do all those things to you."

"Should have had a nap, Hector, you are awful grumpy," he said as he turned around and started the car.

Pulling onto the highway, he signaled and continued heading north. The back roads they were taking certainly made it less likely there would be suspicions on why there was a man tied up in the back seat of his car. They had passed only twenty vehicles since they started their road trip. Most folks traveled along the main routes. Blain, though, always used the back roads, the ones less travelled. It always seemed quicker and less tedious, not to mention that the scenery was always better. It was during those trips that he would reflect on his personal life. This trip though was different; there was no time for reflection. This trip had to be as inconspicuous as possible. They drove for another forty-five minutes, barely sharing two words. Finally the sign for the campground came into view and he slowed down.

"There it is, the Shady Tree Campground. Not many folks use this place. We might be the only ones there, Hector old buddy."

"That doesn't mean shit though, does it? So I don't give a fuck."

"You are right about that it doesn't mean shit for you. For me on the other hand, it means I get to get out and stretch, maybe take a piss."

Blain slowed down more as he drove over the speed bumps that lead into the campground. As he expected he and Hector were the only ones there.

"Excellent. Look at that. Not another soul here."

Finding a place to park that was obscured somewhat by any possible passersby that evening or early next morning, he backed the car in. Anyone happening by would see only two people sleeping, unless of course they walked up to the car and looked in. Blain would meet them outside before that would happen. Besides, it was unlikely anyone would walk up to the car.

Shutting off the ignition, he opened his door and stepped out. Stretching and yawning, he made his way to a clump of bushes. *Ah, that feels better,* he thought as he did up his fly. Returning to the car, he opened the back door and pulled Hector out.

"I'm not going to cut those ankle ties, but I will cut the ones off that are on your hands if you need to piss."

He flicked open his lock-blade waiting for a response.

"I need to do more than piss. I haven't shit since the day we left."

"You don't need your feet free to shit. You can hobble over to that shit-house."

Blain pointed at it.

"But know that I will be right outside. Don't even try doing anything stupid. Kapeesh?"

"Whatever. Just cut these fucking wrist ties would you so I can get on with it."

Blain pulled out the Glock that was tucked into his waistband and pointed it directly at Hector as he cut the wrist ties.

"There, now get the fuck going."

He followed behind Hector as he hobbled to the outhouse.

"Don't be long," he said as Hector opened the door and stepped inside.

Ten minutes later Hector was again tossed into the back seat, his wrists again tied behind his back and a second set of ankle ties around his ankles. It was a precaution. Blain couldn't know for sure whether or not Hector had altered the ankle ties while he was in the outhouse so he simply added a couple more.

"How many of those fuckers do you need around my ankles, you son of a bitch?" Hector complained.

"As many as I think I need to keep you tied, and trust me, I have a whole box. Quit your complaining."

"Fuck you."

Hector spat as he tried to make himself comfortable.

"As tight as they are around my ankles, I'll probably never be able to walk again."

"That would be terrible, wouldn't it? Now shut the fuck up."

Blain stepped away from the door and walked over to the picnic table where he sat down. *This time tomorrow evening, we'll be getting close to Yellow Lake. I wonder how that son of a bitch is going to be in a boat,* he contemplated as he looked up to the sky and the stars that were beginning to flicker. It was a nice evening. There was a warm breeze blowing and loons on a nearby lake were calling. In fact, as far as he was concerned, it was the perfect evening, had it not been for the piece of garbage sitting in his car. He could hardly wait to get him to Mud Creek and the cabin. Only then would he have the peace he wished he had now as he sat there thinking. The evening grew darker and he made his way back inside his car and stretched out on the front seat. He looked back at Hector.

"I really find it revolting that I'm sitting here with you. Do you know that?"

"I feel revolted too. I'd just as well be lying in the trunk."

"Really?"

"Fucking right," Hector replied with hate and venom.

"Good, because that is exactly where I'm going to put you," Blain said as he sat up and opened his door.

Flinging open the back door, he grabbed Hector by his shirt and dragged him out. Slamming him against the car, he wrapped tape around his mouth, unlocked the trunk and threw him in.

"There, I feel better already. Get used to being in there too, because I don't think I'm going to let you out before we make it to Winnfield."

He watched as Hector's eyes got big and he started thrashing around.

"Kick and thrash all you want. You are going to be in there for ten hours tonight, and a good two hours tomorrow."

Slamming the trunk closed he returned to the front seat. Now in the silence and no bad breath spewing in from the back seat and the garbage tucked away in his trunk, he smiled, stretched out, and put his hands behind his head. As he lay there, Hector continued to thrash around inside the trunk much the way he had the night before.

Eventually he stopped and Blain closed his eyes for some real sleep. He was feeling the effects of both the drive and lack of food for the last couple of days. Hunger though really wasn't a problem. He'd eat in the morning and if he felt inclined, he'd feed Hector too. He wouldn't even have to remove him from the trunk. All he'd have to do was unlock the back-seat and tip it forward. The son of a bitch, as far as he was concerned, would remain in the trunk until he secured the boat in Winnfield. He was tired of listening to him and even more tired of looking at him. The sick bastard was going to get everything that was coming to him once they finally made their destination. There was no doubt about that in his mind.

Back in Calimay, Rachel was sitting on the couch in front of the TV watching reruns. A cup of coffee sat on the table next to her and on the couch was a shoebox, one she had only recently discovered. It was Blain's and she knew snooping through it wasn't the proper thing to do, but she was tired of the secrets. She hadn't let on to him that she knew a few things that she wasn't supposed to know, such as the fact that he owned the King Royal Hotel, or the fact that he worked for some kind of agency, although which one she wasn't sure. Her love for him had always outweighed any confrontations they would need to have if he discovered what she knew about these things. Instead, she let him believe that she knew only what he claimed, that he was a Software Developer whose work entailed a lot of travel.

She removed the box lid and started thumbing through the papers, but was unable to find anything in there that she didn't already know. There were no hidden secrets, no clues whatsoever on what agency he worked for, or for that matter what role he played. The only document that did catch her eye was one with only the letter "K" and the number "15". "K-15" is how it read. There was more on the document, but as a safety precaution it was invisible under ordinary light. It could be read via a black light, but Rachel couldn't have known that.

The document contained Trent Sweet's classification of the virus known as K-15, its symptoms and the prognosis of anyone who contracted it. Further down the page was classified information regarding the K.A.T. Agency and its operatives. In essence, it was all the information she was looking for, information that if leaked could destroy the entire K-15 operation, the K.A.T. Agency, and its efforts to control the deadly Kuru-15 outbreak. *What is K-15?* She wondered as she tried to remember if she ever heard Blain mention it. For the life of her, she could not remember any time when he may have said that.

There had to be a reason though, for him to write such a thing down, and keep it tucked away in the box. That much she knew. He wasn't the type to write something down like that without reason, and even if he did, he wouldn't likely keep it hidden in a box. The more she thought about it, the stranger it seemed. Maybe it was a ticket number of some sort, or a locker number. Whatever it was, her instincts told her that K15 held some kind of significance. She just didn't know what. She put the sheet back in the box, and replaced that at the top of Blain's closet where it sat along with all his other boxes of memorabilia.

Gathering fresh linen for their bed, she removed the week-old sheets and dressed the bed with the fresh ones. Then she made her way back to the living-room and finished what was left of her cold coffee. It was 10:00 p.m., and she yawned as she walked into the kitchen and set her empty coffee mug in the sink. After locking the doors and punching in the security code, she retreated to their bedroom and curled up with a book in her hand. The house was so silent, a silence she was growing used to, yet it bothered her to an extent. She was tired of being alone. She wanted something that could keep her mind occupied in times like these. She decided that she would go against Blain's will and get herself a dog.

At least, with a dog, she would have company when sitting outside on the deck when Blain was gone. She smiled at the thought of a puppy racing around their big empty house and playing in their larger-than-life backyard. Undoubtedly, a dog would keep her occupied with all the walks they would do together, and all the time and caring she would have to commit to it. *Yeah, that's what I'm going to do, I'm going to get myself a dog,* she thought as she pulled the blankets up around her neck and opened the book she planned to read. The only sounds, as time slipped by, were the sounds of her flipping pages as she read. Finally, with heavy eyes, she set the book down on the nightstand, closed her eyes, and fell asleep.

Chapter 9

Blain rolled out of the car early Tuesday morning, May 29th. He had slept well, better than he expected for sleeping on the front seat of his car. He even felt good; the wound to his gut wasn't as tight and aggravating. Things were looking up. A stretch and pee however were in order before he would check on Hector. *Yep, it is going to be a good day today. In a few hours, we'll be in Winnfield and once I get Hector loaded up in a boat and we get closer to Yellow Lake, it will even be better,* he thought as he finished his morning business and did up his fly.

To the east a spectacular sunrise painted the sky as the huge yellow sun slowly came in sight. The campground was as silent as the early morning dew that shimmered on the overgrown grasses that were scattered here and there. Birds chirped and fluttered by, complementing the serenity. Even a few butterflies were dancing in the breeze adding to the collage of colors in the sky. The only thing missing for such a beautiful morning, he realized, was Rachel. *If only she could see this,* he thought as he continued to gaze. The only thing making his reasons for being there intolerable was the garbage in the trunk of his car. At the present though, he cared little about Hector.

He wanted to take as much of the beauty in as he could before he opened the trunk. The likes of Hector, he knew, would certainly degrade the scenery. For a few minutes, he simply sat on the picnic table and reminisced. It was odd for him to feel as he did. It had been at least a year since he paid as much attention to the true beauty that surrounded him, everywhere and every-day. There were many contributors to this and only he knew what they were. Even the birds that day sounded different. It was almost as though an epiphany of peace enveloped him. It was so surreal that he had to shake his head to snap out of it. He had a job to do and a cure to find if he ever wanted to have that kind of peace.

Rising from the table, he made his way over to the back of his car and popped opened the trunk. Hector was his usual self as he glanced up to Blain and shook his head in hate and anger, trying to break loose from the ties that bound him. Reaching down Blain pulled the tape from his mouth.

"You'll never get out of those ties Hector. No use even trying."

"You fucking cocksucker, you've been standing outside for thirty fucking minutes and I need to piss. Get me the fuck out of here!" Hector bellowed with demand.

"Not so fast, old boy. I already told you I have no intentions on letting you out until we get to Winnfield."

"What am I supposed to do, piss my pants?"

Blain began to chuckle as he removed his lock-blade and cut the ties that he used the night before to hogtie Hector's feet and hands together.

"Nah, your piss would probably smell like the infection you are."

He grabbed him by his shirt and pulled him out of the trunk.

"What about my hands, are you going to cut them loose so I can piss?"

"You know the procedure, Hector. Your hands, yes, your feet, no."

He cut Hector's hands loose and they fell to his side, like they were arms of a rubber man.

"Now go on, go take your piss. I'll let you enjoy the fresh air for a few minutes before I stuff you back in the trunk."

"You son of a bitch. Are you really going to toss me back inside that fucking trunk?"

"Damn right I am. You best enjoy some fresh air because it isn't going to last long."

He watched as Hector hobbled over to a bush and took care of business.

"Feeling better?" he asked as though he cared.

"I'll be feeling better when I get my hands around your neck," Hector commented as he glared at him. "And if I ever get loose, you can bet that is exactly what I'm going to do."

"Alright, that is enough," Blain said as he walked over to him and pointed the Glock at his head. "Come on get a move on. You're going right back into the trunk. I'm already sick of your mouth."

Five minutes later Hector was once more back in the trunk, hogtied with his mouth taped shut.

"There, now I don't have to listen to you or for that matter look at your ugly face, you bald-headed piece of shit," Blain said as he slammed the trunk down.

As he made his way to the front of the car, he could hear the muffled sounds of Hector as he tried to yell with his mouth taped shut, spewing more venom and undoubtedly cursing him. Blain chuckled as he opened the driver side door and slid in. He waited a few minutes until Hector finally stopped thrashing; then, he fired up his car and they were on their way. An hour later, he pulled off the road unto the shoulder and dialed the K.A.T. Agency, using the cell phone provided to him by the Agency.

"Entity here," he began as Canbra answered. "I'm about an hour outside of Winnfield. Any news on my boat and accessories?"

"Yes, everything is in order. You are making better time than you first thought."

"I am. I've been driving steadily since leaving Canupe."

"No sleep for the wicked, I guess," Canbra responded. "How are you feeling?"

"Pretty good, other than being tired. I am certainly not in as much pain as I was a couple days ago. This boat, what kind is it?"

"I don't know too much about boats, but it is a twenty-one foot Stingray Cuddy Cabin. I hope it will get you to Yellow Lake."

"Nice boat. Do you know if it has sleeping quarters?"

"From what I understand, it does."

"Good, because it is going to take at least two more days to get to Yellow Lake and at least half a day to make the distance to Mud Creek. Who do I see at the Winnfield Marina? That is where the boat is, isn't it?"

"Yes. Ask for Gord. He has all the information. Just ask for him and tell him who you are. Your gear was delivered to a storage site not far from the marina called Nana's Storage. I'm not sure of the address, but Gord can tell you. Everything is stowed in the number three container. It was delivered only yesterday. Damn, I'm good eh?" Canbra chuckled.

"With today's technology it is hard not to be. Alright then, I guess that is it. I'll call in again when I get to Yellow Lake. After that, unless you have sent me a satellite and SAT phone with the gear, you won't be hearing from me again until I'm once more back at Yellow Lake. There is no cell phone service at Mud Creek."

"Of course there is a small satellite and SAT phone as well as a laptop. How else would you be able to relay any findings?"

"Yeah, I guess I should have known that."

"Duh," Canbra replied with a chuckle.

"Whatever. I guess I'll be off then. Talk to you in a day or two."

He waited for her reply.

"Okay Entity. Don't wreck the boat."

"Nah, would never do that," he responded as he shut off his phone.

Walking to the back of his car, he leaned with his back against the trunk, looking in the direction from which they had come.

"Hey, Hector, how are you feeling in there?"

The only response was a muffled sound and Hector kicking inside the trunk.

"Still alive at least. Not much further; another hour give or take a few minutes. I bet that makes you feel better," Blain smiled. "We'll be stopping soon to pick up some food, I'm god awful hungry. How about you?"

Only muffled sounds came from the trunk and no discerning words.

"Yeah, yeah, I hear you old boy. I'll make sure to pick you up something too."

Fifteen minutes later he pulled into a convenience food-store, filled up with gas and bought some snacks to go, jerky, pepperoni, and a couple of pop. It wasn't anything substantial, but it would have to suffice until they arrived in Winnfield, another forty-five minutes away.

"Hey, Hector," he called out as he pulled back onto the road. "I picked you up a pop and jerky. I'll pull off the road again in a bit and toss you some," Blain said with his mouthful of the most succulent pepperoni he ever ate. "I tell you Hector, the damn pepperoni I'm eating right now is the best ever."

He took a swig of the pop. "And the pop sure quenches the thirst. I bet you are thirsty eh, riding around it the trunk. I know I would be."

He chuckled as he pulled out another piece.

Hector unable to talk due to his mouth being taped, could only listen as his mouth salivated at the thought of finally being able to eat something. *Fucking guy, up there in the front eating and drinking while I'm being tossed around like a fucking rag doll. If I ever get my hands on him there will be hell to pay, and that son of a bitch will pay,* Hector thought as the car finally slowed down and pulled into a rest area. He heard the door open and expected the trunk to pop open, but instead he heard the back door open and a bit of noise. Then the back seat fell forward and there was Blain, all smiles.

"Guess I'll take that tape off your mouth so you can have a piece of this pepperoni. Don't know how you are going to drink, but, most dogs like yourself lap up liquids."

He yanked the tape from Hector's mouth.

"Ouch, I bet that hurt. I got a little bit of facial hair that time. God damn it, do you ever stink. Whew, I'm going to have to disinfect the trunk when I pull you out."

"Fuck you. It is fucking hot and stuffy back here."

"Always swearing up a storm, every time you open your mouth, eh Hector. How about you just keep quiet. Here," he started as he stuck a piece of pepperoni into Hector's mouth. "Chew on that and shut up. Use your wit to eat these others."

Blain tossed a couple more pieces to him.

"I'll even be a nice guy and open your pop. Look, I even brought you a straw."

He stuck it in the pop can and set that next to Hector's face as well.

"If you are careful you should be able to keep that pop from spilling. If not, I really don't care."

"How about some more of that pepperoni. I am hungry more than I am thirsty."

"Wow, I can't believe you said all that without swearing. Sure, here are a few more sticks," Blain replied as he tossed them to him. "Damn good stuff isn't it? Told you it was the best pepperoni I've ever eaten."

He watched as Hector wolfed them down right off the floor of the trunk. Dirt and dust covered his lips, but Hector didn't care. He was hungry. Next, he slid closer to the pop and sucked on the straw being careful not to spill it knowing full well, his captor wouldn't give a shit, or offer to help if he did.

"Feeling better now old chap?" Blain asked, with little care.

"I already told you when I'd feel better."

"That is right. You said you won't feel better until you get your hands around my throat. If you weren't such an asshole all the time, I might have offered you some beef jerky too, but I think I'll keep that to myself."

Closing the back door, he again slipped into the front seat.

"I'll let you have a bit of air for a while, but if you so much as make a peep, I'll tape that mouth of yours shut again and slam that seat back in place."

He waited for Hector to make some kind of retort, but he didn't. Instead he continued sucking on the straw in his pop. Blain tapped the floor pedal and watched through the rear view mirror as the pop Hector was sipping on bounced and sprayed all over his face, with trunk dust and dirt clinging to the sticky mess. Hector too bounced around like an old spare tire. Blain chuckled as he watched.

"How are you feeling now?" he questioned as he turned back onto the highway.

"You are a fucking asshole. That is all I got to say."

"I'm only getting started. There are worst things coming your way, Hector Hernadez, a lot worse."

"Nothing will ever compare to what I'll do to you, if I get my chance."

"I am afraid you'll never get a chance. On to a more civilized conversation. Do you know much about boats?"

"Yeah, they float on water."

"Indeed they do. Can you swim?"

"Why don't you drive and be quiet. I really don't like talking to you," Hector said with hate.

"I don't very much like talking to you either." Blain slammed on the brakes and skidded to a stop. Flinging open his door, he stepped out and opened the back door. "In fact, I think it is time to put tape across your fucking mouth."

Reaching for it, he ripped off a piece and slapped it across Hector's mouth.

"There that's better, I won't have to listen to your shit anymore."

Next, he slammed the backseat partition in place.

"I thought I was being nice by letting you have some air and light, but I don't feel like being nice any more. Enjoy yourself."

Muffled sounds from the trunk told him that Hector was pissed off, but he didn't care. As far as he was concerned Hector could stay locked up in the trunk until he took care of securing the boat and gathering his gear. Maybe even then he'd find some place to simply shoot the son of a bitch and toss his carcass in a ditch or over a bank. That though, he knew, wouldn't be as productive as testing him with the K-15 virus. He might discover something or he might not. The end result for Hector would be the same.

Finally, they were on the outskirts of Winnfield and he made a direct beeline to the marina. Parking his car, he walked down the wooded boardwalk to the front door and stepped inside. "Hello, I am Ben Todd," he said as he put out his hand to shake the man's hand behind the counter.

"Hello Mr. Todd. Is there something I can help you with?"

"Yeah, I'm looking for Gord. Is he around?"

"Sure is, just a minute. Hey, Gord," the man yelled into a back office. "There is somebody here to see you."

He turned back and looked at Blain.

"He'll be along shortly. Are you here to do some fishing?"

"A little bit, yep. I am heading up to Yellow Lake and then onwards to my cabin."

"Nice. Where is your cabin?" the man asked to be friendly.

"West of Yellow Lake near Fish Creek," he lied.

"Nice place Fish Creek. I was up there last weekend. Good fishing out of the northern inlet. A fellow caught a few twelve pound lake trout when I was there. I wasn't as lucky, but I did catch a five pounder. That was my biggest catch. Maybe you'll have better luck," the man smiled, "Oh, here comes Gord now."

"You hollered?" Gord asked.

"Yes I did. This gentleman," he pointed to Blain, "asked for you."

"Hello, I'm Gord. How can I help you?"

"I'm Ben Todd," Blain said as he reached for his wallet and produced ID.

"Right, I wasn't expecting you yet. You are here for the 21 foot Stingray."

"That is correct."

"Follow me. I'll take you to her."

Gord grabbed a set of keys that were hanging with a list of others from the back wall.

"It is a 1998, damn good shape too with very few hours."

Blain walked behind Gord as they exited the office.

"It has everything you'll need, a head, a kitchen, satellite TV, a stereo system, and of course sleeping quarters. One question Ben, what the hell, happened to your eyes? I haven't seen a shiner like that in a long time," Gord questioned out of curiosity.

"Ah, yeah, happened during a company softball game. I took one right between the eyes," Blain chuckled. "As for the boat, it is exactly what I was hoping for. I'm heading up to Yellow Lake and over to Fish Creek," Blain responded trying to avoid further questions regarding his blackened eyes.

"This baby will get you there and safely too. It'll get you across Lake Winnfield and up the river to Yellow Lake without even breaking a sweat."

They continued on to a boathouse. Finally making the distance, Gord unlocked the door and the two of them stepped inside.

"There it is. Nice one eh?"

Blain was shocked at how nice it was.

"Yes indeed, very nice."

"Go ahead, take a look inside. I'll open the big door so you can get out. Here are the keys, by the way."

Gord tossed them to Blain.

"Thank you."

He climbed onto the boat deck and stepped up to the captain's helm. It was everything he hoped and then some. It was midnight blue, with splashes of white and purple. The indoor-outdoor carpet on the floor was a light blue and the leather seats were white as fresh snow. The countertops in the pocket-sized kitchen were black marble. The bathroom/head was equipped with a sit down shower, toilet, and bathroom vanity with hot and cold taps.

"She sure is a nice one."

"Told you so," Gord smiled. "If there is nothing else, I guess I'll get back to the office. The fuel and water tanks are full. There is a booklet that explains all the controls and gauges at the Captain's helm. I am assuming you know how to captain a beast like this."

"I do indeed. I do have one other question. My gear is stored at Nana's Storage. I'm told it is near here?"

"It sure is. Head over to 2nd Street and go west. You'll see the sign. I'll leave the boathouse door unlocked for you. The boat was rented by your office for three weeks. Sounds like a nice long trip and holiday to me."

"It will be once I start pulling out the fish. Thank you very much, Gord," Blain said as he stepped onto the boathouse walkway.

"No problem. Enjoy yourself and be safe."

"I will be. Are there any papers for me to sign before I head off to Nana's?"

"Nope. It has all been taking care of. Go have some fun, Mr. Todd. You can park your vehicle at the Marina's reserved parking lot compound. Your spot is #7," Gord smiled as he entered the Marina's office.

Blain waved to him as he walked back to his car. It didn't take long to find Nana's Storage and within a few minutes he gathered all his gear and placed it in both the trunk and backseat, not caring if some of it was piled on top of Hector. Hector, of course, revolted by kicking and thrashing as though he were a stuck pig. Blain chuckled as he closed the trunk. Next, he headed for a local food store where he bought groceries for his trip. In the pet aisle, he took notice of an electric training/bark collar for a St. Bernard or 200 lb+ dog. *I doubt Hector is two-hundred lbs,* he smirked, *maybe I could use one.* In fact, he bought two of them. It was near 11:00 a.m. when he finally made his way back to the Marina.

He decided to take his time in loading the boat. The first thing he did was dock it nearest to where he had parked his car. It was somewhat obscured, but not completely hidden, and so he knew he needed to be cautious. The last thing he wanted was for someone to see him with Hector. He needed to load him without bringing too much attention to himself. He cleaned out one of the larger duffle bags that held some of his equipment and headed back to his car. Looking around he made sure that no one was near or could see him.

"Guess what, Hector. You get to slip inside this bag willingly or I'll simply force you in. Either way you need to get inside here."

Hector began rocking the car and thrashing about trying to make as much noise as he possibly could to bring attention to the situation. Blain simply ploughed his fist into the side of his head and knocked him out cold.

"I figured it was going to be like that," he said, as he stuffed Hector into the bag and tied the top closed.

He struggled for a few minutes getting him out of the trunk and slung over his shoulder, but eventually it all came together. With Hector tossed over his shoulder like a big sack of potatoes, he walked to the water's edge and tossed him on the floor of the boat with the rest of his gear. He returned once more to his car and parked it in the Marina's reserved parking compound. Making his way back to the boat, he pushed it off and headed out across Lake Winnfield toward Yellow Lake. Five minutes in, Hector began moving around. Slowing the boat, he let it drift on the water while he pulled the bag off.

"I told you that you could have made it easier on yourself by simply sliding inside this bag on your own. Now look at you. You have a big old bump on your head. Tragic," Blain said with a chuckle.

Hector tried kicking him as he thrashed and twisted on the floor of the boat. There wasn't much he could say with his mouth taped shut. He was certainly expressing himself though. Blain smiled and shook his head, then turned and went back to the helm and continued onward.

"You don't know when to quit do you Hector? Kicking and thrashing all the time isn't going to improve our relationship one damn bit. Where the hell do you expect to go way out here in the middle of this lake? Unless you are a good swimmer, there is absolutely nowhere for you to go. It would be best for you to simply smarten up, take what is coming to you, and live for the moment. I mean really, look at this beautiful scenery," Blain said, knowing full well that Hector had no view whatsoever lying there on the floor.

Looking back, he could tell that Hector was seeing black. His swollen eyes were glaring at him with the worst kind of hate one could possibly imagine.

"Ah, maybe once we get a little further out, I'll tie your ass up on the bow so I can keep my eye on you. I'm getting pretty tired of having to look back all the time. Then again, I'm not so sure I want to look at you in front of me either. You kind of make me sick."

Turning the throttle down he waited for the boat to drift.

"I will however, remove that tape so you can insult me and threaten me with all your crap. Out here, no one is going to see you or even hear your drivel except me. And I kind of want a few laughs."

He bent down and yanked the tape from Hector's mouth and face.

"There how is that?"

"You are a fucking..." Hector started, but Blain cut him off there.

"I know, I know, a fucking dead man."

"Exactly," Hector retorted with venom and hate.

Blain grabbed him by the scuff of his shirt and tossed him into a seat on the bow.

"How is that, a little more comfortable?" he asked as though hc cared. He raised his hand, "Ah, don't even reply. Sit there like a good Hector."

"Fuck you."

"Your mother should have washed your mouth out with soap a little more often, I think. Do you honestly believe that you are as mean and nasty as you want people to think? You are nothing but a rapist, murderer, and menace to society. You'll never hurt another person, I can promise you that. What can you promise me?"

"I can promise you that if I get out of these damn ties that bind me, I'll make quick work of you."

Hector turned his head away and looked out across the lake.

Blain floored the boat and turned it so sharply that Hector fell overboard, thrashing and kicking in the water to keep afloat as the boat circled around and stopped a few feet away.

"I could simply leave you there kicking like a mule and treading water. I don't suppose you could keep that up for too long before you drown. Would you like that Hector?"

"Maybe you should leave me in here, you keep telling me you are going to kill me anyway," Hector replied, calling his bluff.

"Alright then," Blain said as he turned back to the controls and started to leave.

He drove a few yards then stopped and looked back at Hector, who was now calling out in desperation.

"Are you fucking serious? You're going to leave me here to drown?" he called out as his head went under water.

Blain watched for a few seconds. Finally, Hector broke the surface and came up gasping for air.

"Are you going to behave?" Blain called back.

He wasn't going to let him drown. There would be no fun in that. Toying with him, however, was certainly entertaining. He began to laugh.

"I'll..." Hector began as he once more sunk beneath the whitecaps of the lake that suddenly began rocking the boat.

Blain waited to see if he would come back to the surface, and like a sunrise, there he was bobbing up and down.

"Have you had enough?" he called out as he turned the boat and headed back toward him.

"Fuck! You fucking win, come and get me you son of a bitch! I'm not going to be able to hold on much longer. Jesus Christ you are a prick! Hurry the fuck up."

The boat by now was only a few feet away.

"Before I pull you into the boat, are you going to promise to behave?"

"What the fuck do you..."

Hector again sank into the depths of the lake, but Blain was quick enough to grab him by his shirt collar and pulled him to the surface.

"I'll behave..." Hector retorted as he gasped at the air to fill his lungs. "I'll fucking behave."

"I knew you would see it my way." Blain pulled him inside. "That means no more threats, no more bullshit remarks. No speaking unless I speak to you. Got it!"

"Yeah, fuck whatever. Jesus, let me catch my breath."

Blain picked him up off the floor and made him sit down again in the bow.

"We've wasted too much time with this mockery. No more crap. Sit and be quiet."

Making his way back to the helm, he pushed the throttle forward and turned back in the direction of Yellow Lake. *Sometimes having a little fun gets away on us,* he thought as a smile crossed his face.

Back in New Kootenay, Shane Brentwood was spending the last of the paycheck that he got from Nick. He had picked it up from Sapphire, Nick's daughter, earlier that day at the Koffee House, where she worked. Sapphire met him at a table where he sat.

"You're Shane, right?" she asked.

"I am, yep. We actually met last week. Your dad interviewed me here for a job."

"Yeah, that's right. You are here to pick up your pay, then?"

"Am so. That and a coffee would be nice."

"Regular coffee, right? You don't like those other ones, if I remember correctly," Sapphire smiled.

"Correct again, thank you."

"I'll get it for you and I'll bring your check along as well."

Shane watched as she pranced away. For one reason or another, he didn't have the same desires he had the first time they met. She was very attractive to him, but he had no desire to hurt her. He could only associate this with the same feelings he had after putting in a day's work at the rendering plant. Something transpired that day, he had no idea what, except that the monster he thought he needed to feed no longer growled with hunger. It was as silent as a loft balloon catching a gentle breeze. Balloons though, he knew, sometimes popped. The oddness of the situation made him feel a bit uneasy. Was he finally free from thoughts of blood and gore, or was there something else brewing inside? He had never felt that way before, at least not while he was at the Calimay Mental Hospital, and he had only been released from that place for a little more than a week. *What was going on,* he thought as he waited for his coffee. It seemed like forever until finally Sapphire returned with both his coffee and his paycheck from her dad.

"Sorry for the wait," she said. "There was a bit of an accident in the kitchen. Our new guy is a bit of a dork."

She smiled and set his coffee down.

"Oh yeah, here is the check from my dad. Don't spend it all in one place," she joked.

Shane chuckled at her attempts to be humorous.

"Thank you," he said as he nodded at her.

"You are very welcome."

She was about to walk away and instead turned to him.

"You know what?" she began, "I don't know if you would be interested, but the Koffee House is looking for night staff. Maybe you have a resume to drop off?"

"Really? I might do that. Thanks for letting me know."

It was something he would certainly contemplate. What it all entailed he didn't know.

"If you decide, I'll even put in a good word for you," Sapphire winked at him and smiled.

"You would do that for me?"

"I sure would. Anyone who can work even one day for my dad shouldn't have any problem working here."

Shane chuckled as he nodded his head in agreement.

"Yeah, it was a pretty grueling day. The squealing and god-awful smell is what turned me off fast. And all that blood. I don't know how anyone could deal with that on a daily basis. Yuk."

"There are no horrible smells here and the only squealing you'll hear is the coffee grinder."

"True. Okay, you won me over. Who do I apply to? I'll drop a resume off tomorrow."

"Awesome. You can drop it off with me," Sapphire smiled.

"Alright then. Thank you again for letting me know."

"No problem, Shane. I'll see you later."

"Yeah, you certainly will."

Shane turned to his cup of coffee and took a swallow, as Sapphire strutted off. He was thinking about their conversation now as he walked the isles of the grocery store pushing a squeaking and off-balance grocery cart. Every now and again, his mind would fluctuate between Sapphire's beauty and the lady with the 'SMOKIN' license plate. He had made so many plans for both of them, yet now as he thought about those plans, they were rather revolting to him. It didn't by any means, mean that they were safe. He didn't know what would transpire over the next few weeks. All he knew for now was, those desires were subdued. *How could I have even have thought those things,* he wondered as he made his way to the cashier.

"Good afternoon," the old lady operating the cash registered said as he approached.

“Good afternoon back,” Shane replied, as he began loading the groceries on the counter.

The lady meticulously began punching in the costs of each item as it rolled by on the conveyer, and Shane watched as the numbers ran up.

“Is that everything for you?” she asked as she punched in the total.

“That is it for today, yep,” he replied as he fished into his pocket and pulled out some money.

“That will be one hundred and fifty eight dollars.”

Shane handed her $160. A few more strokes on the cash register and she handed back his change.

“Here is your change, sir.”

He took it and thanked her.

“Don’t forget to come back.”

She smiled at him and Shane nodded. With groceries in hand, he made his way back to his apartment and put them away. An hour later, bored as he was, he sat down at the makeshift table and scribbled out a resume. Most of it, in fact all of it were lies. The only job he ever had was the job he got from Nick.

He read it over a few times, then crumpled it up and tossed it on the floor. He decided he wasn’t going to lie with a trumped up resume. Instead, he’d talk directly to Sapphire. He’d tell her that he was completely new to the work force and that he was fresh out of college, or some crap like that. What else could he do? He needed a job. If he couldn’t dazzle them with brilliance he’d baffle them with bullshit. The ticking of the wall clock as loud as it was, like a swarm of crickets or frogs at night, made him look up to it. He noted the time to almost be 8:00 p.m. What was he going to do for the rest of the evening? He was bored out of his skull.

Rachel on the other hand wasn’t nearly as bored. The Bouviers des Flandres puppy she picked up that day for a mere $650 which she thought to be a great investment, was causing havoc and already destroyed a pair of her shoes. She hadn't named him yet, but the more she thought about a name the more 'Havoc' suited it. It was a beautiful dog there was no doubt about that, sired by a champion named 'Goliath'. The puppy, she knew, in time would likely become her best companion. With Blain constantly on business trips to here or there, in her opinion the puppy would be well worth all the training and carnage it could cause as it grew. She was chasing after it again as it ripped through the house darting this way and that terrorizing every room of their house with each bound and jump it made.

There were times she laughed at his antics and others where she tried to scold him, but the puppy wasn't having anything to do with that.

"Come on. Please quit being such a devil. Come here, come on puppy. Come sit beside me," Rachel said as she sat down on the spare bed in the spare room where she was finally able to catch up with him. "You are such a little bugger. Come here," she coaxed, "come on."

She patted the bed beside her. Finally, the puppy came close enough and she was able to scoop it up. Setting it down on the bed next to her, it began running in a circle urinating everywhere in its excitement.

"Oh my God, look what you are doing. Shame on you puppy."

Rachel stood up from the bed and ripped the covers and blankets off.

"I think I am going to call you Havoc, how does that sound, you silly thing?"

The puppy darted out the door and before Rachel could stop him, he knocked over a large vase in the hallway and it rolled toward the stairs. With a crash, it fell off the landing and smashed on the floor beneath.

Rachel tossed the blankets on the floor in exasperation and made her way downstairs. 'Havoc' as she named him was now lying on the couch, his big brown puppy dog eyes looking at her as though he had nothing to do with knocking over the vase.

"You, my friend, have already cost me a pair of expensive shoes and now this expensive vase Blain bought for me in Quebec. I thought you were going to be a nice puppy."

Havoc jumped off the couch and slowly approached her as though to say he was terribly sorry.

"Awe, that's alright. You'll eventually settle down, I understand your excitement of being in a new place. Come on, come over here, and give me a kiss."

Rachel bent down and sure enough, Havoc licked her face. He sat stock-still beside her while she cleaned up the broken vase.

"There," she said as she picked up the last few shards and put them in the wastebasket. "No more breaking things okay," Rachel smiled as she patted him, "you are such a big lush, aren't you?"

Havoc's cropped tailed thumped on the floor as he rolled over and she patted his belly.

"Yep, I think you and I are going to get along fine, providing you don't wreck anymore stuff. Come on, I'll give you treat," Rachel said as she made her way into the kitchen and the bag of puppy treats she bought.

Havoc followed close behind, and sat nicely as soon as she opened the bag.

"Good boy, Havoc, good boy," she cooed as she handed him a treat. "You go ahead and eat that, while I make myself a cup of tea. Then we'll sit on the couch and watch some television, how does that sound?" she asked as though he would answer.

Havoc didn't leave her side as she made her tea. He followed her back to the couch, hopped up on it and rested his head on her lap as she grabbed the TV remote and began switching through the channels.

"That's a good boy," she said as she scratched him behind the ears. "See this is called quiet time, we'll do it every night, you and me, alright Havoc?"

Taking a sip of her tea, she finally found something to watch.

They sat in each other's company as the evening slipped away, Havoc staying by her side. He even followed her upstairs to her bed and curled up on it.

"You're not going to pee on my bed are you?" she asked as she turned on the reading light.

Havoc looked at her and whimpered an apology for doing that to the other bed.

"Alright then as long as you don't pee on my bed you can stay."

Rachel smiled as she picked up the book on her nightstand and began reading. With Havoc lying beside her, she felt less lonely to some degree. There was no doubt in her mind that he would indeed be her protector as time went by. She read a chapter of her book, turned off the reading lamp and was soon fast asleep.

Blain and Hector made the distance across Lake Winnfield by now and were settling in for the evening as well. He anchored the boat at the Yellow Lake tributary of the Yellow River that fed Lake Winnfield. From there it was easily a four-hour trip up the river. There was no way he wanted to traverse the river in the receding daylight and so he anchored it where they sat now. For almost two hours as the boat drifted and swayed this way and that, neither one said much to the other. Blain looked through some of the gear he had been provided while Hector remained tied and seated in the bow.

"Fuck sakes man, you dropped anchor two or three hours ago. I'm fucking hungry, thirsty, and I need to take a shit."

Blain looked over to Hector.

"Really? You need all that?"

"What do you expect? I haven't eaten a damn thing since those pepperoni's you tossed to me earlier today in the fucking trunk of your car. Haven't had a damn drink either, except when I was almost drowning."

"Yeah, that was pretty entertaining," Blain said referring to Hector's dunk in the lake. "I suppose that act does deserve something. Let see..." he began, as he looked through the food he bought. "I'll open you a can of sardines."

"Are you serious? All you are going to offer are sardines?"

"What's wrong with sardines?" he asked as he continued looking at the food.

There were no sardines. He hated those almost as much as he hated Hector. He was simply toying with him.

"Nothing is wrong with sardines, but one little can isn't going feed me."

"You are lucky that I even offer you that. I could let you go hungry."

"Alright, I'll take the sardines."

"Nope, sorry but there aren't any," Blain said as he looked at him and began to laugh. "I hate sardines." He waved his hand in the air. "No worries Hector. I'll throw something to you. As for that shit, I'm not so sure I want you using the head. It is a pretty small toilet and I'm sure anyone who is as full of crap as you are, might break or at the least clog the damn thing up."

"I'll shit right here then," Hector threatened.

"Not sure I would be able to find you in the water if you did that because I'll throw you overboard. How about this, you shut up for a few minutes, squeeze you ass cheeks together a while longer, and after I toss some food to you and you still feel like you need to take a shit, I might reconsider."

Hector shook his head and looked out across the lake defeated once again.

"You know something, Mr. Todd," he started. "I've meant a lot of assholes in my life but you are probably the biggest."

"I'd rather be an asshole than a dick that can't get any unless it is by rape. Now shut up. Not another peep or I'll tape that mouth of yours shut until we get to where we are going. You'll get nothing to eat or drink then, not a fucking thing."

To curb both Hector's thirst and hunger, Blain settled on making him a can of soup. He set the bowl of soup on the bow's table and stuck a straw in the bowl. Hector didn't say two words.

Meanwhile Blain sat back and ate a nice thick salmon steak served with steamed vegees that he had picked up at the grocery store. It was quite comical to sit there and watch Hector sucking up the soup with a straw. Every time a wave hit the boat he would have to fight keep the bowl from sliding off the table and onto his lap.

"Enjoying your soup? This salmon steak is the bomb," Blain teased as Hector glared at him and was about to say something.

Blain shook his fork in his direction warning him, "Unuh, not a word. I have plenty of tape."

It was 10:00 p.m. when he finally allowed Hector to use the vessel's head. He cut the nylon-ties from Hector's wrists but left the ankle ties intact.

"There, now you can wipe your ass. I'm going to be right outside the door and if you try any funny stuff, and I mean anything, Hector, including fucking around with this vessel's plumbing, trying to get out of those ankle ties or anything like that, I will shoot you. Understood?"

Blain wanted confirmation that Hector understood and so he rammed the barrel of the Glock he held in his hand into Hector's temple.

"Understand?" he repeated.

"Fucking right I understand, okay," Hector responded with his hands in the air.

"Alright, get on with your business." Hector hobbled over to the head door, Blain close behind. "Don't take too long. In fact, I'm giving you exactly five minutes, starting now. Any longer and I'll simply open the door and shoot you where you sit. Go now, get on with it."

He pushed Hector forward.

"Hurry up."

With his finger on the trigger, he waited patiently. Finally he heard the toilet flush and Hector hobbled out.

"Don't come any closer. Turn around and put your hands on the wall." Blain gestured with the Glock. "That's it. Good Hector," he said as he frisked him and tied his wrists again.

Chapter 10

Blain woke early that Wednesday on May 30th, and despite Hector's snoring, he had managed to sleep well. The sun wasn't even cresting the mountains when he turned on the coffee pot. The only sounds were Hector's constant snoring and the odd shrill sound of seagulls that were piercing the early dawn. A calm wind gently blew across the lake and the waves it created caressed the hull of the boat and lapped up against the distant shore. While the coffee perked and Hector snored, he went to work in removing from the stern a few two-inch eyebolts that were used to tow a small life raft or dingy. Having neither he decided they were also the perfect size to tie up Hector and to keep him completely out of view.

All he needed to do was pick a good solid wall on the bottom deck and screw them in. The wall he decided to use was next to a storage closet. It was made of solid oak, and fastened to the boats frame with aluminum studs. Undoubtedly, it was both strong and solid. He was careful not to cause any cosmetic damage to the interior wall as he screwed the eyebolts in. With the task done, he yanked and pulled on them making sure they would handle the task. Satisfied, he returned to the top deck.

He had been sitting for a few minutes and was enjoying his morning coffee and the serenity, when he tilted his head. In the distance he thought he could hear the sound of an approaching boat, but it was too dark to see. He waited to be sure. It was the head-lamp of the approaching vessel that confirmed it. Jumping to his feet, he didn't even bother to wake Hector. He simply grabbed him and tossed him to the floor. Hector woke up in a fit cussing and cursing until he saw the Glock in Blain's hand pointing at him.

"Shut the fuck up, right now," Blain said as he gestured for him to stay down.

He could tell the approaching boat was not big enough to see the floor of his boat. Still, he needed to be cautious.

"Ahoy there," a man called out as his boat grew closer.

"Ahoy," Blain sounded back.

The small boat approached the portside of his vessel.

"Good morning," the man said.

"Good morning to you, too."

"Getting an early start to some fishing?" the man asked out of curiosity.

"Actually, I am waiting for some daylight. I'm heading up to Yellow Lake. Yourself?"

"Yep, just getting an early start. The mouth of the Yellow River is hopping with fish at this time of day."

"Yeah, that is what I've heard," Blain lied.

"Be careful when you head up-river to Yellow Lake. The river is fast this time of year."

The man patted the side of Blain's boat.

"I reckon though, this boat will do alright."

"I sure hope so. Thanks for the warning."

"No problem. Well, the fish aren't going to wait. I best get on with it. Have a good day," the man said as he continued on his way.

"You too," Blain called out. "Good luck with fishing."

"Thank you," the man replied as he waved.

Blain waved back as he watched the man and boat fade into the early dawn. Looking down at Hector who was sprawled out on the floor at his feet, he smiled.

"The old fellow was only being friendly. He's gone now, but I think you best stay where you are until we get up river some."

"What! You're going to leave me here on the fucking floor?"

"Pretty much, yep. You haven't a complaint about that do you?"

"What do you think? First, it is the trunk of your car, and now the floor of this fucking boat. Fucking right I have a complaint."

"That's what I figured," Blain said as he put his knee into Hector's chest and taped his mouth shut. "There, now I won't have to listen to your complaints."

He picked him up and shuffled him down to the bottom deck.

"Down here I won't have to look at you. You wreck the scenery and upset the balance of my day, you know that?"

He threw him to the floor and tied him to the eyebolts that he had secured into the wall for that exact reason, Hector fighting him the entire time. Finally, making his way to the top deck, he sat down in contemplation, enjoying his early morning coffee. It seemed as though time stood still and he took in every sight, smell, and glorious sound.

As the first rays of sunlight painted the morning, he pulled up anchor and headed for the river, waving at the few fishers who were casting their lines at the mouth of it. The river fought him most of the way and the boat was constantly being tossed to and fro, but he pressed on and the boat withstood the punishment the river threw at it. At 10:00 a.m. that morning, Yellow Lake came into view. He jetted out towards the middle of the lake, leaving the sandy shores and the river in his wake.

Slowing the vessel down, he came to a drifting stop. He wasn't planning on staying long, only long enough to have a rest and enjoy the view he now had of Yellow Lake. *Mud Creek isn't much further,* he thought as he looked out across the lake and the few boats that dotted it. *Sure hope this boat can make it up that tributary,* he contemplated. *If not, I guess I'll have to come up with a plan B.*

He knew that the Mud Creek tributary was both wide and deep, and he had seen boats as big as the one he was using on it. There were a few places he knew of that might cause issues, but there was nothing he could do about that. At least he needed to try. If the boat could only go so far, then so be it, he'd simply pack his gear in from that point; or better yet have Hector pack it. Either way, he was determined to make it to his cabin that day.

Looking at his fuel gauge, he realized he needed fuel. The Yellow Lake fuel station was a short distance away and he'd stop off there. They knew him and they would offer him any information on Mud Creek that he felt he needed. It was also near the Mud Creek entrance. Firstly, he wanted to rest. The trip up the Yellow River had taken its toll on him, and his nerves weren't quite ready to continue. With the boat drifting, Blain made his way to the bottom deck and checked on Hector.

"We're at Yellow Lake. Not much further."

He yanked the tape from Hector's mouth.

"How are you feeling?"

"Like I've been mixed up in a fucking blender. How do you think I feel?"

"Like you've been mixed up in a fucking blender," Blain smiled. "Anyway, I'm not here to converse, was only making sure you were still alive and tied. Going to be making a stop at a fuel station, then you'll likely get tossed around a bit more."

"Whatever. I really don't give a shit."

"Yeah, that is what I assumed alright."

Blain ripped off another piece of tape and once more taped Hector's mouth shut.

"You know, you are a lot more digestible when I don't have to listen to you."

He stood and kicked Hector in the leg as he made his way back to the helm. Sitting in the bow, he retrieved the cell phone and dialed the K.A.T Agency's number. It rang a couple of times and finally Canbra answered.

"Entity, how was the trip to Yellow Lake?"

"Brutal. But yes, I'm here now."

"Have you had a chance to look at the gear we provided?"

"Not yet, why?"

"I wanted to go over something with you."

"What would that be?"

"Inside one of the locked crates is a manila envelope. And..."

"Hold on a second," Blain interrupted, "if it is locked how am I suppose to open it? I haven't found any keys. Should I look for the crate now?" he asked as he began removing the canvass tarp that covered it all.

"Yeah, of course, that would help. Are you suffering some kind of dementia?" Canbra snickered.

"If I was, I wouldn't know it. Anyway, I'm looking through this stuff now and I haven't found a locked crate."

"Did I say crate?"

"Now who has dementia?" Blain replied. "Yes, you said crate."

"Wow, it isn't a crate, actually," Canbra began.

"No kidding, would it happen to be a Kevlar briefcase?" he asked as he found one. "If so, I haven't got a key to open it. What good is the envelope if I can't open the case?"

"Yes, it is a Kevlar case, and it isn't locked with a key lock. Put your thumb over the brand name logo."

He followed her instructions, a bit confused, but sure enough the case opened. "Okay, that is peachy. What of this envelope?" he asked as he looked through the contents of the briefcase.

"There should be a secured glass slide. Are you looking?"

"Yeah, yeah. Okay, so I have a glass slide. What about it?"

"Does it have any writing on it?"

"Nope. I imagine there should be though. Who could have forgotten such a detail as that? Let me guess, it was you, wasn't it?"

"Yes it was."

"And the last time we spoke you were bragging about being good," Blain teased as he shook his head.

"I guess that proves it then."

"Proves what?"

"That even when you are good, you can still screw up," Canbra chuckled.

"I suppose. I've never screwed up."

"Whatever, Entity. Geez, you are always so forward. Anyway, that slide you are looking at should be marked with a BDNA-XG."

"It isn't though," he said as he reached for a pen and wrote the information code down.

"No kidding. We went through that already. How about using your imagination and figure out how you can write that on there," she razzed.

"You want me to do that?"

"Very funny, Entity, I am assuming from that comment that you have already done that."

"Of course, but to be safe let me read it back to you so there are no more mistakes. BDNA-XG, correct?"

"Yep, the reference numbers on all other slides will correspond with each column in the reference document, except that one. You'll need to change from the reference document the number that is left over and doesn't have a match, to that of BDNA-XG."

"Can't you simply tell me which reference number that might be?"

"No. Unless of course, you want me, to read off to you almost seven hundred reference numbers."

"Forget that. Once I get to the cabin, I will go through it all. If I can't make sense of it then, I'll shoot you an email after I get the satellite in place and I have all gadgetry installed."

"Okay, sounds good to me. Other than that, how are you feeling? How is that bullet wound to your stomach healing?"

"Almost healed, I think. In fact I'll likely take the stitches out soon."

"Eeew, can't you leave that to a surgeon?"

"Won't be near a surgeon for a while and I don't want live with the god damn itching."

"I wonder about you sometimes, Entity. I think you are both mad and crazy."

"I have to be. Have you forgotten what I do for a living?"

"Good point. There is something else I wanted to tell you that might make your day even better."

"What's that?"

"Apparently the guy who shot you was also wanted for a few murders and rapes. They caught him yesterday, according to the newscast this morning."

"What?" Blain asked firmly. "You said they arrested the guy who shot me?"

"Yeah. I thought you would be happy about that."

There was a long silence as Blain digested what she said.

"Entity, are you there?" Canbra asked as she waited for his response.

"I'm here, I'm here. What else can you tell me about that and how do you know it is the guy who shot me?"

"The newscast mentioned he was involved with a shooting at the Heritage Hotel in Canupe on the same day you went off the map. It is a simple deduction of events that tells me it is likely the same guy. He's been charged with three counts of murder, five for rape, and one count of attempted murder. Apparently he might be charged with a few more crimes too, extortion being another and something else."

"I'm glad they caught him. We don't need scum like that walking the streets with all the other things going on in this world," Blain responded somewhat confused.

"I thought you would be glad to hear that."

"I certainly am. I hope he rots in prison. The authorities aren't going to have an easy time tracking down Mr. Ben Todd if they need him to testify," Blain pointed out with some concern.

He really wasn't interested in having to testify if it came down to that. It would put a damper on his current commitment.

"On the bright side it is only an alias, and a well-protected one at that. We can erase Ben Todd from the earth in one swoop," Canbra chuckled.

"I suppose. I'm just glad he survived. I wouldn't be here if he hadn't."

"Good one! Alright, Entity, I guess it is back to the grind. Don't worry too much about the authorities trying to track you or should I say track Ben Todd down to testify. Chances are it is going to take some time before your assailant sees a courtroom. Remember, this is Canada. I will talk to you once you get all the electronics in place at Mud Creek."

"Yes you will. Talk to you then, Canbra."

Blain turned off the cell phone. There were a few issues he needed to deal with. One was Hector; the other was his alias Ben Todd. He told both the O'Brien fellow and the local cops that he was headed to Yellow Lake on a fishing trip. Even the boat was listed under that name. The only thing that might slow the authorities down if they needed him to testify or identify his assailant in a line up, would be the fib that he told the marina, that he was heading to Fish Creek. *Ah, if they come, they come. There is nothing I'll be able to do to change that,* he thought as he put the manila envelope back inside the briefcase and locked it. Pulling the tarp back over it all, he made his way to the bow again and sat down.

If my friend Hector isn't who I thought him to be, I wonder then who the hell he is. He couldn't make any sense out of it. *Life just keeps getting more and more interesting every day,* he contemplated as he looked out across the lake. *Could be that the authorities have the wrong person in custody or I do.* Whatever the case, it certainly changed things.

Chapter 11

The truth was, Hector Hernandez' name was Rob Hartley *aka* 'On Point'. He was a onetime K.A.T. Operative. He went rogue shortly after Trent died, and it was said that he was responsible for killing over seventeen people in cold blood some months later. When the Agency discovered this, they sent another operative in to clean up the mess and to eradicate him, preventing the discovery of the Agency in the whole. It was reported back to the K.A.T. Agency, that the operation was a success and that Rob Hartley was no longer alive. The operative who was sent to clean up Rob's mess was respected and high ranking, so no one, not even Blain, doubted the report. Two years later the operative died of natural causes and the truth about Rob Hartley went with him to his grave. Now, Rob Hartley had appeared again.

Rob had spent the past decade trying to discover a cure for the K-15 virus as well. His vision though wasn't to share the cure with the world; rather he wanted the money he knew he could get. The seventeen people he murdered in the mid-1990's were used for non-documented, unscientific human testing, the first ever of its kind. It was a simple operation. He conducted the testing and his counterpart, K.A.T. Operative Chase Benton *aka* 'Shadow Chaser', the same operative who had been sent to kill him, supplied him with human subjects. His findings though were questionable and the experiments he conducted always showed false positives in his subjects. To prevent lengthy imprisonment for the ghastly experiments and brutality he inflicted on his subjects, his only recourse was to kill them all.

When the K.A.T. Agency discovered this and the weak link that Rob had become, conveniently it was Chase who was sent to clean up the mess. It was the perfect set-up. After Chase died, Rob continued on as a one-man research team. Only recently did he get wind that the K.A.T. Agency was close to finding the cure, and he set pace to discover it himself. He used every technique he could think of, right down to the tattoo on his hand and the salt and pepper wig, to convince Blain that he was the man who had shot him. The more he could learn what the K.A.T. Agency discovered, the closer he was to his own selfish goal. The millions of dollars he could get would be worth every humiliation Blain could throw at him or put him through. He didn't care if Blain thought he was a rapist or murderer. He didn't care if Blain hated the person he was pretending to be. All that mattered to him was being the first to go public with the cure for the ravenous K-15 virus, and the unlimited possibilities that would bring. The one thing he was counting on was Blain slipping up and his getting the upper hand on the situation. When that took place, and he was sure it would, he'd simply take over Blain's research and bury him somewhere.

He'd take all documentation, all the gear, the boat, everything, and disappear. It was pretty cut and dried as far as he was concerned. After all these years he remembered the tricks and magic that the K.A.T. Agency used. He even knew a few of their security codes to access certain selective information. In fact, he couldn't believe that the same passwords were still being used. But they were and he tapped into their databases. It was how he managed to get the information regarding the possible discovery of a cure and which operative was doing the research. That led him to Blain.

That, in itself, was a shock. He couldn't believe that the almighty Blain Sweet was still an Agency operative. Once he confirmed all that, he simply put his own plan in motion. So far it was working. It had been many years since he was a legitimate operative and he would never have recognized Blain had he not known who he was. It was obviously the same reason why Blain didn't recognize him; that, and the fact that he was now bald. Whatever the case, Rob had no intention to let Blain know who he really was.

Sitting in contemplation at the bow, Blain's thoughts were on what Canbra said about the man who shot him being apprehended. It made no sense to him whatsoever. Could the authorities have really screwed up that badly? Or was it he who had screwed up? Maybe the fellow who was tied up in the bottom deck, really wasn't who he though him to be. *The tattoo, the face, even his damn skin tone is exactly how I remember that guy. If he isn't the shooter, who the Hell is he and why did he even show up at my room?* he thought as he looked to the starboard of his vessel and the fuel station he could faintly make out. *Humph, well, I'm getting nothing done sitting here; best make waves.* He stood up and traipsed over to the helm, took the Captain's seat and proceeded in the direction of the Yellow Lake fuel station.

Old Neil Chadwyk was running the pumps that day. The Chadwyks were the only people on the lake who operated a fuel station, and when folks left Yellow Lake, Neil was the caretaker for the many privately owned cabins and cottages that scattered the shoreline. He was also the fellow who kept an eye on Blain's cabin. He'd go up that way once or twice a month using an old hiking and ATV trail. In the winter he sledded the distance or on occasion snow-shoed.

"Hello Mr. Chadwyk, how have you been?" Blain asked as he drifted towards the fuel dock.

"You got to be kidding me, Mr. Todd! How in hell have you been?" Neil Chadwyk responded as he recognized Blain.

"Pretty good, Neil, pretty good."

"Nice rig you have there. How much did that set you back?"

"I couldn't afford something like this. It's a rental, Neil. Fill her up."

"Here to do some fishing I suppose, eh?"

"Depends, I have a few different things I have to do up at the cabin. You don't suppose this rig can make it up to there, do you?"

"Hell yeah. The creek this year is higher and wider than ever before. It grows bigger every year it seems. Others have made it to Mud Creek and back with the same sized rigs. I don't see why it would be any different for you. Might have a problem at the quarter-mile mark near that sandbar, but once you pass that spot it'll be clear sailing. Just be careful and keep your eye on the hull. If you don't end up grounded, you'll be okay," Neil chuckled. "And if you do end up grounded, there is always someone boating up and down there. You'd get help."

The sound of the gas pump stopping alerted Neil.

"Whoa, alright your tank is full."

"What is the damage Neil?"

"Sixty-two dollars and fifty four cents. Big fuel tank this old girl has. Cash or credit Mr. Todd?"

Blain reached into his pocket and pulled out a credit card.

"Put it on this, Neil."

He handed Neil the card.

"You bet Ben, thank you."

Neil stepped into the small fuel station office and returned a few moments later.

"Good to go, Ben," he said as he handed the card back. "How long you planning on staying up at your cabin?"

"It depends I guess. I've booked three weeks off, so I might stay that long. I imagine the old cabin might be in disarray. It's been a year or two since I was there last. I'll putter around for a couple of days and fix a few things. Sure hope the generator is working. The last time it was giving me a bit of a problem."

"I was up that way last week. The cabin was fine when I last checked; everything is boarded up. That generator is an old Millwire Generator, isn't it?"

"Yep."

"Ah, it'll be fine. If it gives you any issues, feel free to come back here. I can send Joe or Roger up to get it working."

"How are those twins of yours?"

"Same as always; drinking too much and driving the rest of us sane folk crazy. Joe's doing alright, I suppose. Roger on the other hand wasn't taken out to the wood shed often enough," Neil chuckled. "Ah, they're both in their early 30's now. I only wish they'd both act it."

"They say time and age changes people. Maybe they'll change."

"I doubt that. Spoiled rotten both of them. That is where the Mrs. and I went wrong, raising those two knuckleheads and giving them everything they wanted, but didn't need. Oh well, they have their own kids to deal with now. By the way, it looks like you were in fight yourself. Those are nasty black eyes."

Neil shook his head and smirked.

Blain scratched the side of his face.

"Happened during a company softball game. I took one right on the nose," he chuckled, "anyway, Neil, I best make waves. If I have any problems with the generator, I'll let you know. How does that sound?"

"Suits me fine. Alright, Ben. Take your time up near that sandbar. It is best to stay left I've heard."

"Left it is. Thanks again, Neil. We'll talk soon."

Neil waved as Blain turned the boat and headed towards the Mud Creek tributary. It didn't take long after that to make the distance to his Mud Creek cabin. The sandbar didn't cause him any problems other than the fact that he had to slow down to almost a rowing pace, but he managed. Finally, he could see his cabin's boat dock. Slowing the boat to drifting speed, he pulled up alongside the old rickety thing. He could see the cabin's tin roof from there. It reflected like a mirror in sunlight. Mooring the boat, he stepped onto the dock and tied it securely. The trail to the cabin was overgrown and it took him a few moments to make the distance, but there it was, there was his home for the next three weeks. He smiled as he stood outside and looked at it. As Neil told him, all the windows were still boarded up telling him that no one had been there since his last visit. He sighed in relief to finally, be there, it was such a beautiful place.

The cabin itself was nestled beneath and surrounded by birch and cedar. A few weeds and ferns took over the small yard. The old rail fence that skirted the cabin was broken in a few places, but it was nothing he wouldn't be able to fix. All in all everything was as he had left it the last time he was there.

"Home sweet home," he said as he unlocked the door and stepped inside.

Other than the musky stale air inside, all was good. The first thing he did was remove the boards that covered the windows, opened the shutters, and slid the windows open to let the cabin breathe.

He looked into a back room that he and Trent converted into their lab. They designed it specifically for that reason. Other than the way it was set up, it looked like an ordinary room only it was a lot cleaner than any room in the cabin. Two of the walls were lined with bench tables and drawers, and in one corner sat a desk where they did their writing and computing work. Before he could use it, he would have to go through the process of cleaning, and disinfected it as best as he could, he didn't want to contaminate any of the research slides. He looked in the direction of the desk, and managed a smile. Although Trent had been gone for years, it was at that desk where he made some of his best discoveries and wrote some of his best scientific medical essays regarding K-15. *Maybe I will make the next discovery,* he thought. *I miss you, brother.*

Next, he walked outside to the back of the cabin and entered the generator shack. He checked the three 45 gallon drums of diesel fuel that were on hand, making sure at least one drum was full. Satisfied, he filled the generator's tank, checked the oil and wiring. A visual of the belts told him they were fine. He sprayed some "get up and go" into the carburetor and held his breath as he pushed the big button that started it. It sputtered and coughed a few times spewing smoke. Finally, the silence of the mid-morning was broken as it whined to a start, then slowed to an almost silent constant note as it kicked down.

"Excellent," he said as he flicked the switch that powered up his cabin.

The gravity fed water cistern was full as well and he turned on the electric water pump that pumped water into the cabin. Everything was perfect.

He sat down on the porch and looked around. He certainly missed being there. As far as he was concerned, it was heaven, the best place on earth. Away from all the hustle and bustle of civilization, his only wish was that he was there under different circumstances. But he wasn't; he was there for one reason only and that was research. God, he hated research; he'd rather eat a handful of grubs. The K.A.T. Agency however needed him to conduct the research and so he would. This time though, things were going to be different. This time there was a live subject involved.

Now as he thought about that, he wasn't sure that would be feasible. If Hector wasn't who he thought he was, there'd be no way he'd be able to proceed with that type of testing. So, what would he do with Hector?

The fact remained that Hector had muscled his way into his hotel room, busted his nose, and threatened to kill him. Whether he was the man wanted by the authorities for murder and rape, he was in Blain's opinion a dirt bag. One thing was for certain, he couldn't simply let him go. He wanted answers; he wanted to know who exactly this man named Hector was, and what the hell he wanted.

He tried to think back if there was ever a time where their paths crossed, but nothing jumped out at him. Was Hector a family member of one of the many K-15 carriers that he killed? Was he simply out for revenge? These were questions that he couldn't answer. In time though, it would all become clear. *I best get him unloaded along with all the gear, knickknacks, and pollywogs,* he thought as he returned to the boat. Climbing onboard, he made his way to the bottom deck.

"Ready to see your new home?" he asked as he ripped the tape from Hector's mouth.

"Wondered why the boat stopped and you weren't around. So, we're here then?"

"Sure are," Blain responded as he untied him and helped him to his feet. "Today is your lucky day."

"Why is that?"

"It is quite the walk up to the cabin, and I have no intention to carry you, so I'll be untying your feet this time, but not your hands."

"Not afraid I'll try to run?"

"Go ahead, I have the Glock. Not a soul would hear. And there is no place for you to go. You'd never get far."

"Don't ever count on that."

"Oh but I do, Hector."

Blain pulled out his lock blade and cut the ankle ties.

"There, now get a move on."

"Whatever," Hector said with disdain as Blain pushed him towards the two steps that lead to the upper deck.

"Fucking slow down would you. Christ sakes I haven't walked in a couple days let the blood get to my feet."

"No time for your belly aching; just keep moving."

He pushed Hector up the stairs with the Glock pushed into the small of his back.

"There, now you can step off onto the dock. I'm right behind you."

"Fuck you!" Hector retorted.

At that point Blain simply pushed him overboard and he landed with a solid thud onto the dock.

"You fucking asshole! I could've broken something."

"I don't care. Stand up and get going."

He waved the Glock at him as Hector finally stood up and began walking.

"That a boy, keep going that way. We'll be there soon."

Blain followed behind as they made the distance to the cabin.

"There it is old boy. Nice eh?"

"Looks like shit to me."

"Yeah well, get used to it. You won't be leaving here."

"We'll see about that."

Blain shook his head.

"Yes we will. Now get inside."

He tied him up again and continued to gather the rest of his gear. An hour later, he sat down at the table and sighed.

"Whew, going to be a hot one today," he commented as he wiped the sweat from his brow. "I should've had you packing this gear instead."

"I wouldn't have done it. I'm not your fucking slave."

"You would have done it if I told you too. Mind you, you probably would have ruined my day."

"What the fuck do you plan on doing with me anyway? I'm kind of getting sick of the charade."

"I'm not sure what I'm going to do with you, Hector. A few things have come up since we left Canupe. I can tell you this much, I have three weeks to decide."

Blain rose from the table and began putting his food supplies away.

"You know what? I am not sure I picked up enough food to feed you too. What a shame that is," he said as he put the last of it away. "You might get real hungry around here."

Of course, he had bought plenty of food for both of them, but he got a real kick out of razzing Hector.

"Again, I'm not amused. I don't care if you got enough food or not. I don't plan on sticking around for three weeks."

"That is funny. I don't think you have much of a choice."

"You'd be surprised."

"I doubt that."

Blain set his laptop and microscopes on the table.

"You see all this stuff here, Hector? What do you think it is for?"

"I really don't give a shit. Maybe you are some kind of faggoty author or something," he replied, knowing full well what all the equipment was for.

"Faggoty? I don't think that is even an English word."

"You are the author. I guess you would know."

"No Hector, I'm not an author. I work for an agency that does research on genetics and DNA of certain people who are infected with a disease much like Kuru. Do you know what that is Hector? I'll give you the exact definition. It is a progressive disease of the central nervous system marked by increasing lack of coordination. Eventually it leads to paralysis and death, usually within a year. Does it sound interesting so far Hector?" Blain asked as he looked at him.

"I've seen Old Yeller too. Sounds like simple rabies to me."

"Really?"

"Fuck, you know what. I don't even care what it is that you do."

"Maybe if I continue you'll understand. Kuru is thought to been transmitted by cannibalistic consumption of diseased brain tissue. They say that because the disease disappeared when cannibalism was abandoned. Research has proven that it originated in Africa. Can you believe that? All the way from Africa. The difference is, since it has somehow found its way to the western world, things have changed. Those infected today crave human flesh. I bet you find that hard to believe eh?"

"Everything you say I find hard to believe. You are a fucking no-mind in my books. I shouldn't have wasted my time back at that hotel. I should have killed you then."

"You got that right. Because now I'm in the driver's seat and I'm not nearly as dimwitted as you."

"What? Are you going to kill me?"

"That depends. I'll either kill you, or mess you up so badly that you'll beg for me to kill you. I'm not sure which. As I said, I have three weeks to decide."

"Don't take your time in deciding."

"That is the fun part, taking my time."

The cabin grew silent as Blain sorted out the gear that Canbra sent. Finding the 12-inch satellite, he set it and all the coaxial wiring that came with it to the side. Next, he gathered the Kevlar briefcase and set that on the kitchen counter, the satellite phone was in its box, and he wasn't amused that he'd have to activate and set it up. *Canbra, Canbra, Canbra, why would you send me an un-activated satellite phone, and a Genesis brand at that. I hate when you do stuff like this,* he thought as he shook his head and set it down.

Next, he found a box of latex medical gloves and a pretty white lab coat. He chuckled at the coat, "yeah as if," he said to himself as he hung it over the back of a chair. In another plastic sealed box, he found a bunch of Verbatim 185 MB Pocket CD-R's approximately 21 minutes each. He counted forty of them. Each was numbered and each number was referenced by a code and folder.

"Yeah, this going to be real fun," Blain muttered, "I haven't even started yet and already I'm sick of it."

"What's that you're saying?" Hector asked as though Blain had been speaking directly to him.

"Nothing to concern yourself with. Besides, I wasn't talking to you anyway," he replied as he carried on.

In a bigger box, he found the folders and other documentation, as well as a brand new box of microscope slides, lights, and batteries. Tweezers and syringes along with a few test tubes were in another plastic sealed container. A few of the tubes had sediment in them with printed labels of what each contained. In the same box were two bernz-o-matic lab torches, and few other gadgets that would make his research and portable lab as efficient as possible. Canbra hadn't forgotten one thing. Everything he needed and some things he didn't were amongst his gear. There would be no turning back or excuses he could make for not being productive. The worst part he knew was all the damn cross-referencing and reading he'd have to do with what the Agency supplied him and the documentation Trent had on the K-15 virus. Those documents he would get to once everything else was in place. They were in a weather-proof briefcase, buried in the ground not far from where the cabin sat. With everything now sorted out, he looked at his watch. It was going on to 1:00 p.m.

"Still think I'm an author with all this lab looking stuff, Hector?"

He sat down again at the table, and waited for a response.

"Maybe you are a mad scientist. As I said earlier, I really couldn't care less."

"You will care eventually, Hector, because you might be part of an experiment. I mean really, who would miss you? You are a piece of shit; a rapist and murderer, aren't you?"

"I don't think it matters to you what I am. Sounds to me like you already have your mind made up."

"That I do, Hector, that I do. That is why I brought you here. No one will have a clue on what I might or might not do to you. You were quite willing to kill me. Only thing was you didn't know what you were stepping into, or for that matter what I'm capable of.

You bit off more than you'll ever be able to chew, Hector."

The cabin fell silent again as Blain stood, picked up the satellite and cable and went outside. With Blain away now, Hector tried to get loose, but the more he struggled the tighter the nylon-lock ties got. He finally gave up a short while later, cussing, and cursing beneath his breath.

Back in New Kootenay, Shane was returning to his apartment. He had spent the majority of his day touring the side of town where he lived and where he would soon be working. He spoke with Sapphire earlier that day and the interview went well. He was excited in a sense. The pay wasn't good but on top of gratuities it would certainly suffice until something better came along. What he looked forward to most of all was the possibility of getting to know Sapphire on an intimate level. He thought back to the first time he saw her and how he wanted nothing more than to rip her clothes off and have his way with her.

Fortunately, for her and all other residents of New Kootenay, that isn't how he felt now. That evil was lost somewhere between killing pigs, and when he quit that job. There was nothing that could guarantee however that the evil wouldn't return. Only time had the answer to that.

His first shift at the Koffee House was scheduled for that Friday. He was expected to be on the clock from 4:00 p.m. until midnight. What he was going to do with himself until then he didn't know, but boredom was probably going to play a role.

In Calimay, back at Blain and Rachel's house, things were topsy-turvy. Havoc, Rachel's newly acquired friend, was tearing up their Kentucky bluegrass yard. He had dug four holes already and every time Rachel fixed one and scolded him, he'd dig another. She finally gave up trying to stay ahead of him. She was sitting on the back deck watching him as he continued the assault on their lawn. In her hand, she held a chilled glass of Vodka and orange juice.

"You know what Havoc? You are pain in the ass, but I love you anyway you silly thing. Go ahead and tear that lawn up I could care less, it is Blain's baby," she chuckled as she took a long drink. "Whatever you do, don't touch the flower beds, those are mine," she threatened as she took another drink.

By now, Blain was on the roof of his cabin, setting up the satellite. It didn't take long and soon he found himself trying to set up the satellite phone. Everything else was a go, the internet was up and his email account was active, but the phone was giving him problems. *God I hate trying to activate these phones,* he thought as he struggled with the set up. Thirty minutes later he was no closer to activating it. Then, he returned the damn thing to the box.

"That's enough of that," he said to himself as he tossed the box and phone on the counter.

For the next three hours, he did his best in cleaning up the research room; then spent another two hours setting it up, so that everything was in its place and all files were in chronological order. He double-checked the ten-inch monitor that was hooked up to a small camera in the corner of the cabin's open concept kitchen and living-room. He could see Hector but not very well. The monitor would have to be focused in a bit more. Other than that he was set. All systems were "go".

He sent a brief email to Canbra stating that he was finally at his cabin, and that he was unable to set up the phone. That was the extent off his first evening. After tossing Hector a few pieces of beef jerky and an old blanket, he made up his own bed. He cared little on how Hector was going to eat the jerky with his hands still tied, but at least he was fed. By 10:00 p.m., he stretched out with his hands behind his head and drifted, his mind racing with what tomorrow would bring.

Chapter 12

Thursday morning as he rolled out of bed and made his way into the kitchen, he kicked Hector awake.

"Good morning Hector, how'd you sleep? I slept well," he razzed as he walked into the kitchen and began to make morning coffee.

"Of course you slept well. You weren't tied up and sitting on a fucking floor."

"Aw, so you didn't sleep well. That is too bad. Maybe some coffee will make you feel better?"

"How am I supposed to drink coffee with my fucking hands behind my back?"

"I might untie those hands and maybe even let you sit at the table with me. We can be like old friends."

"I'm not any friend of yours."

"Yeah, that is a good point. Alright then, I guess I'll sit here by myself and enjoy a coffee. You can sit there and watch."

"Of course, after all you are quite amusing to watch," Hector retorted with a snort.

"Not nearly as amusing as you. Boy, this coffee tastes good," Blain teased as he brought the cup to his lips. "Are you sure you don't want to join me?"

"What do you think?"

"I would think that by now, you are hungry and likely a bit parched. I imagine it was tough trying to eat that jerky I tossed you last night."

"You are so fucking humorous."

"I know. I kill myself laughing every now and again, especially at your expense. So, I'll ask you again, care to join me?"

"I'll sit at the table with you, but don't expect any friendly conversation."

"Good," Blain said as he stood up and made his way over to Hector.

Yanking him to his feet, he pushed him toward the table and sat him in a chair, then cut the ties from his wrists.

"While we're sitting here, don't try anything stupid. Remember," he, began as he flashed Hector the Glock, "you try anything and this day will be your last on earth. Understood?" he questioned with authority as he poured Hector a coffee and set it down in front of him. "You can help yourself to the sugar and cream."

Blain motioned to the bowls on the table as he sat back down.

"I drink mine black, but thanks for the hospitality," Hector responded with hate as he brought the cup to his mouth and took a long drink. It seemed like forever since he last drank anything and the hot liquid, although almost burning his tongue, felt good as it found its way down his throat and into an empty stomach. As he held his cup to his lips and drank, Blain for the first time paid attention to the tattoo on the top of Hector's hand. The ten-second close-up view only made him want to look more closely.

"What exactly is that tattoo on your hand supposed to be?"

"What does it look like to you?" Hector responded.

"I don't know, I haven't really looked," he said as he quickly grabbed Hector's hand and looked more closely.

It was then he noticed a difference between the tattoo on Hector's hand and the one that he could remember being on his assailant's. His mind raced. So sure had he been that Hector was the man who shot him in the hallway of the hotel that he hadn't paid any attention to the tattoo at all. Now he wished in hindsight that he had.

There was a difference indeed. The one on Hector's hand clearly depicted a Crow, and in the background a church steeple. By the looks of it, it was a recent tattoo. He knew then that there was more to Hector than he initially thought. His mind would never forget the tattoo on his assailant's hand. It was burnt into his mind like the look on the face of the woman who the man killed. His tattoo was not nearly as professional and looked more like a homemade job of a Crow and some other crap in the background. It lacked the clarity and professionalism of Hector's. There was no way the two men were the same. This piqued his interest even more on who Hector was.

"Now that I've had a good look at it, I'd say it is a Crow and a church. Nice tattoo by the way," he said as he let go of Hector's hand.

"You'd be right. That is exactly what it is," Hector responded with suspicion as he once more brought his coffee to his lips.

He was no longer playing Blain. In fact, it was Blain who was now playing him. He knew now that Hector wasn't the man he thought he was. Nonetheless, it wasn't going to change the way he looked upon him, or for that matter the way he treated him. Back in the recesses of his mind, things were beginning to click. The more he thought about it, the more there seemed to be some kind of familiarity about Hector. For now though, it eluded him, but something was certainly there, and in time, he'd know exactly what.

"You can help yourself to more coffee, if you like. It'll be the last you get until later."

"What about some food? I haven't eaten anything except jerky and pepperoni."

"I don't eat breakfast, Hector. I will be eating lunch though. I figure you can wait until then."

“That is four or five hours away. Fuck! Can’t you give me some toast or something?”

“I could, but I won’t. You’ll wait until I eat. If you don’t want more coffee, then I guess this little table sit is over. Come on, Hector, back to the floor.”

Blain stood up with the Glock in his hand. Tying Hector securely once more on the floor, he made his way into the research room. Turning on his laptop, he received two emails. One was spam and the other was from Canbra. He read the email which detailed how he could set up the satellite phone and gave the number the phone was assigned. It was part of the puzzle he was missing. Canbra wrote that it was important for the Agency to have contact with him both through email and via voice.

Although it really made no sense to him why, he followed through with her instructions on setting up the phone. It was surprisingly easy, and he shook his head. The only thing he had missed in trying it himself was using the # key after he entered the activation code. The number it was assigned automatically came up on the screen, and again he needed to press the # key to finish with the set up. Voila, it was activated, simple. He dialed the Agency’s office to make sure it worked and Canbra answered.

“Hello Entity. It didn’t take you long to set that phone up did it?”

“I was missing one vital step, pressing the number key. I’m here now and all systems are up and running.”

“Good to know. Regarding your health, how are you faring?”

“The gut wound is fine and I’m feeling good. I have no complaints.”

“There were a few attacks that took place over the last couple of days. The K-15 carriers are back at it.”

"Really? Where did these attacks take place?"

"Forge and Elkhill."

"Those two places are close together, not much distance between them both. Could it be the same carrier?"

"Operatives, Echo and Oakwood are looking into that. It is possible."

"Has anything been proven as to why the attacks stopped? It's been a couple of weeks since the last, hasn't it?"

"Over three weeks to be exact. Not sure why. No one is."

"I don't think I recall a dry spell that long ever. It is something that really needs to be looked at."

"Agreed, and we are doing just that. So far though, we've come up with no concrete evidence. It almost seems as though our assault campaigns are actually working."

"I think from what we know about K-15, is that it is never going to end until all carriers are dead or we come up with a cure."

"That goes without saying, but something is going on for the attacks to have slowed down as much as they have."

"Or seemed? Maybe that is what we are overlooking. The fact that it never slowed down at all, maybe the carriers are getting smarter and are only wounding their victims to replenish their masses."

"That might explain it. You would think though, that anyone who was attacked would at least report such a thing to the authorities," Canbra stated with reluctance.

"True. I would agree, but something is going on. I don't know, Canbra. My opinion is that of Trent's. He always said the best way to fight this was with human testing conducted in a controlled setting."

"That, Entity, is impossible. We can't do that. You of all people should know better. That is totally out of the question."

"I know. I honestly don't see how doing any kind of testing on anything *'but'* is going to give us any answers. What about doing a human blood test?"

"We've done that. The results are always inconclusive."

"Ah, that is right. Maybe the tests that were performed were done incorrectly? I never could figure out how blood testing was not conclusive? It honestly doesn't make sense. Blood is blood isn't it?"

"It is, but it doesn't work. I would suggest a monkey, but there are no monkeys around here."

"Have you ever been to a pet store, Canbra?"

"Of course I have, but those monkeys are meant to be pets," Canbra said with hesitance.

"Whether they are meant to be pets or not, I think a monkey would be a good candidate. I'm sure the Agency has some pull and could secure a lab monkey from somewhere. Maybe an operative could steal one from a zoo," Blain responded with indifference. Using a monkey, as far as he was concerned, was a very good idea.

"You're not seriously suggesting that are you?"

"You said we need to do some live testing. Why wouldn't you think about that?"

"It seems inhumane, but it also sounds plausible. Maybe I will see if I can't get a lab subject from one of the universities or something."

"Yeah. Simple."

"Not really. There is a lot of red tape and as you know the K.A.T. Agency doesn't even exist, so we'd have to come up with some kind elaborate fib."

"That is easy enough. You know all the avenues to take. It shouldn't take more than a couple of days with all your knowledge and expertise," Blain pointed out. "I think that is something we should have done a long time ago. We'd probably have already found a cure or something."

There was a short pause as Canbra contemplated.

"When the Agency started we had no idea what we were looking at, or if we were simply dealing with a rabies type virus. It has taken all these years to narrow it down to the Kuru virus. Now though, since we are that much further ahead, maybe we should start looking at live testing. I guess a monkey is the closest thing we'll ever get to a human."

"I concur. There you have it, Canbra; you have my ideas and blessings," Blain chuckled.

"The idea has to be approved by others. You and I can't make that decision."

"Really? Says who?" Blain stepped out of the cabin into the cool morning and looked around.

There was mist rising from Mud Creek and the sun was breaking through the fog that hung around the mountains like a halo.

"Why can't you simply go about doing what it is you need to do to get us a monkey?"

"It is protocol, Entity."

"I think it was Trent and I that came up with that protocol. It only makes sense that I'm the one who can change it and I just did," Blain made clear.

"You don't think it is unfair to the others involved?"

"Hell, no. I think it is unfair that there are people infected and we are getting close to new discoveries, but we have to constantly wait for this, that, or the other thing. That is unfair to those infected. I say do what you can to get a monkey. Tell Gonsite and the others I said so. End of discussion as far as I'm concerned."

"Alright, Entity. I will see what I can come up with over the next few days. Do we even want to mention it to the rest of the crew?"

"I don't care either way. I know what you are doing, and you know I have said go. What else is there to say? The only issue I see is getting Gonsite to do the testing. If he isn't willing, then he'll have to answer to me. Do what you can Canbra. I'll carry on with what it is you have me doing here. If anything comes up with these newest attacks in Forge and Elkhill, make sure you contact me. The same goes for the monkey."

"Will do, Entity," Canbra said as she waited for his response.

"Good. Then get at it."

"Goodbye, Entity."

"We'll talk soon," Blain responded as he shut the phone off, and strapped it to his waistband.

He continued his gaze toward the eastern mountains and watched as the sun broke through the halo of fog. The first rays of sun reflected off the shimmering dewdrops that held on tightly to the blades of grass that scattered the cabin's yard. Looking at his watch he noted the time to be 8:00 a.m. *Getting a nice early start, that is for sure,* he thought as he walked around the cabin taking notes of certain things he needed to fix. His mind drifted as he picked up a few pieces of old garbage that had blown off the creek from passers-by. He tossed them in the burning barrel as he passed it.

Making his way down to the dock where his rental boat was moored, he climbed the small ladder and stepped in. Untwisting the eyebolts that he secured in the bottom deck wall, he put them in his pocket, knowing he'd have a use for them eventually. Satisfied that the boat was afloat and that the creek hadn't receded, he turned and walked back towards the cabin. Using a stick he picked up off the trail, he began swatting down the overgrown weeds that had taken over the trail. It wasn't something he meant to spend too much time on, just something to do for fun. He cared little if the trail was overgrown or not. This task only gave him those extra few minutes to be outside before he'd have to get on with his research. He didn't even know what it was he was supposed to be doing yet. It would all be explained in the pocket CD-R's and documents in the Kevlar briefcase; that much he did know.

Standing on the porch outside the cabin, he looked around at the pleasantries that surrounded him. He could hear the creek as it rushed by. The wildflowers and weeds that filled up the canvas of his view were solemn and peaceful. A mild summer breeze gently blew carrying with it the scents of cedar and pine. A few geese coasted by on the creek, tooting and squabbling as they made their way downstream. *If only I was here, to only...be here without strings,* he thought, as he turned and stepped inside.

"I guess it is time for me to get at it. You're not going to miss me are you?" Blain joked as he removed his boots and slipped on a pair of anti-static Nike running shoes. "There, that feels better," he said as he stood up and walked around a bit. "I hate breaking in shoes. How about you, Hector?" Blain asked to make meagre conversation.

"Only pansies wear sneakers."

Blain stopped for a moment. What Hector said was another clue as to who he wasn't, and he certainly wasn't the man who shot him. That man who shot him was wearing shoes.

"What do you mean? Haven't you ever put on a pair of new shoes that pinch your toes?" Blain was simply doing his best to get more information out of him, regarding shoes.

"I haven't worn shoes for years," Hector pointed out with sincerity and conviction.

He had no clue that the information he was supplying was actually helping Blain out.

"What? You wear only boots?"

"Is that a problem?"

"No, not at all. It only seems kind of weird to me. I wear boots too, but I sure like slipping into a good pair of shoes once in a while."

"Shoes, as I said, are for pansies."

Blain waved his hand through the air.

"To each his own, I suppose. Anyway, I'm going to be inside that room," he began as he pointed to the big heavy door. "The door will be closed, but if you look over to this corner here, you will see I can always watch you."

He pointed across the room to a camera that was set up in the top corner of the wall. It was there so that he and Trent could converse via video when one or the other was breaking from their research, back in the day when Trent was alive. It helped to keep the door to their lab closed and was used by them to be more of an intercom type thing. The video was an added bonus.

"Let me guess," Hector stated, "you'll be able to see me?"

"Very good Hector, that is exactly right. I will indeed be watching you."

"I don't fucking care, watch all you want. It is obvious that I'm not going anywhere."

"It is obvious to me. I'm not so sure it is obvious to you. I think you're going to jump at the first chance to either screw up my day or attempt some kind of stupid escape."

"No one can call you stupid for thinking that," Hector offered with a scoff.

"No, but I can certainly call you stupid if you try. The Glock will not be far from my side. Keep that in mind," Blain pointed out with authority.

"I get the point," Hector replied.

"Good. Then I guess I'll get on with it."

Blain picked up the briefcase and stepped inside his makeshift lab. The first thing he did was turn on the outer room camera and the small 10 inch monitor. He played with the focus until he could see Hector.

"There you are. Smile," he said to himself.

Sitting down at the desk, he pressed his thumb against the briefcase logo and it popped opened. Gathering the relevant documents to get him started, he began looking through them, highlighting text and taking notes as he read. It was all gibberish to him but he pressed on. Finally, a few hours into it, he closed the last folder he was looking at, and rose from the desk. *Not a thing pops out at me on what it is I'm supposed to be looking for or even doing. Man, I hate research,* he thought as he stepped out of the room.

It wasn't so much the research he was doing, rather all the other things that were on his mind: his wife Rachel, his marriage, and who the hell Hector was. All these things were playing on his mind making it hard for him to concentrate. Professionally, he knew he should simply move forward and forget his personal troubles. His job was always best done that way. He was always an 'operative' first and an 'operative researcher' second. There was no denying he hated research, to him it was boring and unfulfilling. Out in the field though, hunting and tracking down K-15 carriers was his specialty, and he was damn good too. He sucked at researching, reading text, writing formulas, reading more text. It was all so boring. Sighing, he looked toward Hector.

"Are you ready to eat something?"

"I've been ready to eat for three or four days. Told you that this morning."

"Yeah, yeah, and I told you, that you would eat, when I ate. I'm about to eat, would you like to eat too? That is the question. A simple yes or no suffices."

"Excuse me from not being cordial. Yeah, of course I'd like to eat. Is that better?" Hector responded with venom.

Blain chuckled.

"That is better, I might teach you some manners after all. Not that you'll ever have a chance to use them."

"Not that I ever would sounds better to me. You might think you are getting away with something here, but really you're not."

"Really? What exactly do you mean Hector? Do you think scat like you would be missed? Do you think someone is going to find you? As far as I'm concerned, I've already got away with whatever it is I have in store for you. No one is looking for you, and there is no way you will escape."

"Probably not. I think you are harmless though. I think you had a whim and I think your whim has been quashed. I think you are too fucking scared."

"I'll be honest with you I have second-hand reports that you aren't who I initially thought you were. You played me; you did a damn good job too. What I know now, is that you somehow managed to get information about my condition when I was released from the hospital after I was shot in the gut. You even managed to get information on what my true assailant looked like, and I'm betting you got that information on the day it happened or the day after.

You probably got that information from a witness. The one thing that stuck out in your mind was the fact that the man had a tattoo, probably described by said witness as a Crow and church or something along that line. The smart man that you are, you found the nearest tattoo shop. You see Hector, I'm no tattoo connoisseur, but I do know the difference between a newer tattoo and one that might be years old. Any idiot can figure that out. Yours, my friend, can't be any older than a couple of weeks give or take a few days. That is why you were wearing gloves when you busted into my hotel room. Does that about sum it up Hector?" Blain asked as he stood and made his way to where Hector sat and yanked him to his feet. "My mistake was I should have clued into that. Weakness and pain though sometimes blots out logical thinking, which is what happened in my case. I got the upper-hand though, didn't I, Hector?"

He pushed him toward the table and made him sit.

"You think you are pretty smart I bet, figuring out all that crap. Think of how smart and brazen I must be to have done all that. I'm way fucking more superior than you, aren't I?" Hector questioned with hostility.

"Superiority hasn't got a thing to do with it. It was all about luck. I'll grant you this, though; it does take a bit of ingenuity. In that area you did well." Blain sat across from him and smiled. "Now that I know who you aren't, do you mind telling me who you are and why you played me? Or, would you rather not? Trust me, it matters little to me. You are the guy that muscled his way into my hotel room and busted my nose with the barrel of this Glock."

Blain waved it in front of him reaffirming the fact that it was now in his hands.

"I'm not going to say a fucking word more on the subject. I'll leave that up to you to figure out. You seem to have done pretty well so far, if you believe in magical mystery worlds," Hector snorted as though daring Blain.

"There is no magic or mystery, Hector. Everything I've said is as close to or exactly the way you pulled it off. You don't have to tell me anything more, nor would it benefit you, so I don't care. One thing is for certain. When all is said and done, the outcome, regardless, is still going to be the same. We'll leave it at that."

Rising from the table, he made his way into the kitchen where he proceeded to make each of them a few tuna salad sandwiches. He was onto Hector now, there was no doubt about it, if he didn't want to talk that was fine. He would get the answers he was looking for either by way of an admission or forcefully. Either way was fine by him. Although, in his mind, forcefully was more appealing for a dirt bag such as Hector.

"Hope you don't mind tuna. Actually, I really don't care if you do or don't. It is what I'm having and I don't take requests," Blain said as he sat back down and handed Hector a plate with a couple of sandwiches on it. "Go ahead, eat up old chap."

"Really? My hands are still tied, you moron."

Blain chuckled. "And by calling me a moron is going to help you how?"

"Again, excuse my fucking mouth. Will you or will you not untie my fucking hands?"

"I suppose I might, depends though on the whether."

"What the fuck does the weather have to do with it?" Hector questioned with anger as he salivated at the thought of finally eating something.

"Whether I do or whether I don't," Blain laughed as he rose and pushed Hector forward so that he could untie his hands, giving him the freedom to eat.

As soon as his hands were free, he began shoving one of the sandwiches into his mouth. He dug in like a mad man.

"Slow down Hector. I wouldn't want you choking and dying on me."

Truthfully, Blain wouldn't have cared.

"I told you I was fucking hungry. POWs even get fed, you cocksucker," Hector responded as he picked up a second piece and shoveled it into his mouth.

"POWs are prisoners of war. You on the other hand are a simple prisoner, nothing more. You are an insult to POWs, Hector," Blain retorted as he too ate another sandwich.

They finished the rest of their lunch with their eyes locked, neither one speaking to the other. It was during that ten minutes that Hector's body odor got the best of Blain. Luckily he was finished or he would have gagged at the smell.

"Jesus Christ, you stink. Whew. I think you need shower."

"You don't smell like a bed of roses either. At least I have an excuse."

"What would that be?" Blain coughed at the smell.

"Being stuffed in a fucking trunk of car might have something to do with it," Hector commented.

"Yeah, I suppose that might have an adverse effect. Either way, you stink like shit."

Blain grabbed him by the scruff of his shirt. Dragging him into the bathroom, he turned on the shower and tossed him in, clothes and all.

"Rinse some of that odor off."

He retrieved a bottle of dish soap and squirted it over Hector's head.

"Make some lather and don't forget to rinse. Come on hurry up. I don't want to stand here all day."

"You are a fucking maniac, you son of a bitch!" Hector retorted, as Blain used an old toilet brush that was tucked- away in the corner to scrub him down.

When the last of the suds and soapy water escaped down the drain, he pulled him out, and forced him back to the floor.

He sniffed at the air.

"There that's better, you still stink but not nearly as badly," Blain said as he made his way back to the table and sat down. "I'll take my shower the conventional way."

He smirked as he looked at Hector who was sitting on the floor, sopping wet. He could tell Hector was both humiliated and angry.

"A prisoner, Hector. That is all that you are."

"Kiss my fucking ass."

"Don't be so anal," Blain commented. "Be grateful that I used that old toilet brush to scrub the fleas off."

"It is you that should be grateful that I didn't shove it up your ass. Now, leave me the fuck alone."

"I'd say you're a bit hostile."

"No shit, Sherlock. Don't you have something better to do than to sit there and heckle me," Hector spewed with anger.

"I most certainly do and I plan on getting to it, but right now I'm kind of enjoying your humiliation. It isn't every day that I get to watch such a comedy unfold. If only you saw the look on your face when I started scrubbing you with that toilet brush you would be laughing too," Blain chuckled.

"The only time I'll be laughing is when I stomp on your throat."

"I know, I know," Blain waved his hand through the air. "Only in your dreams will you ever be able to do that. You might be good, but you aren't that good."

Blain rose from the table and made his way outside. The afternoon sun was a blessing and he absorbed its rays. Inhaling deeply, he contemplated the rest of his day. By rights, he knew he should be nose deep in research, but it was only Thursday. He decided to put researching off and instead went about repairing the fence that skirted his cabin. It didn't take long and the fresh air helped clear his head.

It was while he was finishing with repairs to the fence that he heard the sound of an approaching watercraft. He walked back to the cabin and waited. He knew he would have plenty of time to react if it approached closer. He had no reason to fear who might be approaching. The cabin was his and so was the land it sat on. What he didn't need was someone discovering that he wasn't alone. That would put a new twist to the current situation. If the boat came closer, he'd have no other choice than to hide Hector. Standing still and listening he was able to discern that the sound was growing fainter, which likely meant the boat had turned back. He was relieved, but remained cautious as he continued to work outside. For the rest of the day as he puttered around fixing this and fixing that, no other sounds echoed, except the sound of his handsaw and hammer or that of the birds that chirped or the occasional sound of chattering squirrels.

Chapter 13

At 4:00 p.m., he put his tools away in the shed and entered his cabin. Hector was almost dry from his forced shower earlier that day, but his mood hadn't changed. He wasn't happy at how easily Blain manhandled him, or for that matter left him sitting on the floor with wet clothes on and his ankles and wrists tied, while he went outside and enjoyed some sunshine.

"It was a beautiful day Hector. The sun was warm and bright, birds were chirping and I sure enjoyed being away from your stench. Mind you, you don't stink to terribly now. You even got a free clothes wash from the deal."

Blain chuckled as he waited for Hector to retort, but he didn't. He sat there on the floor with a look of hate and misery on his face. He had nothing to say about anything. He was indeed beginning to feel defeat.

"What's the matter? I was half hoping you'd have something to say. But I kind of like the silence too."

Reaching over to the kitchen counter to a bowl of oranges sitting there, he grabbed two and tossed one at Hector. It bounced off his forehead and landed in his lap.

"That's three points for me," Blain said as he peeled his orange. "Go ahead Hector, enjoy."

"Yeah, I'll do just that," Hector said as he shook his head and looked down at the succulent piece of fruit on his lap.

He did want it, but he wasn't going to entertain Blain anymore by trying to eat with his hands tied.

"You know what I'm getting real tired of being your babysitter. I have another idea. Not sure you'll like it, but it might give you jolt."

"Really?" Hector finally responded.

"Yes, really. I picked up a couple of shock collars."

"Shock collars?"

"Yeah, shock collars designed for a two-hundred pound St. Bernard."

Blain retrieved the first collar. Making his way over to Hector, he yanked him up to a standing position, pushed him against the wall and forced the collar around his neck. Stepping back, he pushed the button on the collar's receiver to activate it and then pushed the button on the transmitter. Hector jumped as an electric charge jolted him.

"See told you, you'd get a jolt out of it." Blain laughed, as he pushed the button again. "I think I've found another way to entertain myself. This could be fun," he said as he made his way to the table and sat down.

Pressing the button in quick successions, Hector's head involuntarily jerked from side to side and then he slid down the wall.

"I can't fucking believe you are doing this to me."

He pressed the button again. Hector's eyes doubled in size and his head banged against the wall with a solid thud.

"Ouch, that one looked like it hurt. Might be the fact that you're still sitting in water, or did you piss yourself?"

"Fuck you," Hector retorted as his ears continued to ring, and his muscles relaxed.

"One more," Blain said as he pushed the button again for a sixth time. Hector's entire body stiffened and his mouth snapped shut.

"Not bad for fifteen volts eh? Did any fillings weld together?" Blain razzed. "The good thing is,

Hector, it is fully rechargeable. I think there is even a way to boost the voltage for really bad dogs."

"You are a fucking asshole."

"Be nice, you don't want me to press that button again, do you?"

"I don't think it makes much of a difference what I want. Press away, if you feel so inclined."

Hector at that point really could have cared less.

"Nah, I've had my fun." Blain set the collar transmitter down on the table. "But don't doubt I won't use it again."

"I wouldn't put it past you," Hector responded.

Blain chuckled as he read from the package on how to increase the voltage.

"Yep, it says here I can boost the voltage another 5 volts, but I won't have to, will I, Hector?"

"Boost it, don't boost it. I don't fucking care."

"That isn't the answer I was looking for. I was thinking if you said no, that I might untie your feet and tie your hands in front, rather than behind your back. Since you aren't willing to behave, obviously I'll have to increase the voltage. And as far as I'm concerned you can remained tied as you are."

Reaching for the transmitter, he began fiddling with the voltage control.

"Wait," Hector started. "I'll behave."

"Really? What changed you mind?"

"The fact, that you were going to untie my feet, so I could at least fucking walk around with a little bit of freedom. Being tied up like this is getting stale."

"I didn't say I would untie them. I said I might."

"Oh fuck, here we go again. Always the fucking wise guy eh?"

"I'll tell you what," Blain contemplated for a minute. "I'll untie your feet so you can walk around for a while, and if you behave I'll think about tying your hands up front. You piss me off once though, and I'll strip you naked and pour pancake syrup all over you, then I'll hang you upside down above a red ant nest that I know of, and leave you there for the pesky little critters to eat your brains out."

"Fine. I'll abide. What about this fucking dog collar?"

He wanted that removed as well.

"Nope, that stays right where it is. The deal is I'll untie your feet. That's it," Blain made clear.

"Fine."

Rising from the table, he cut the ties from around Hector's ankles.

"I'm not going to help you stand up. You can figure that out yourself." He turned and walked back to the table. "Also, don't forget about Mr. Glock. Now go ahead, get up if you can and stretch your legs."

Hector struggled to his feet and began walking around stretching his aching legs. His feet felt like pincushions with every step he took. Blain kept a close eye on him as he watched. Both the Glock and the collar transmitter were within his reach. If Hector tried anything, he'd either shoot him or shock him or both. It wouldn't matter to him as long as he stayed in control.

"Tell me, how does it feel to walk?" Blain questioned as though he cared.

"A lot better than sitting with my fucking legs tied and crossed. Not sure my feet are working though. Can't even fucking feel them."

"All part of the benefits of being tied up for four days. Keep walking; the feeling will come back."

For thirty minutes straight Hector walked in circles around the cabin. Blain watched his every move. Finally, he pulled up to the table and sat down.

"I take it your feet have feeling now?" Blain asked.

"Like as if you'd care."

"You are right, I wouldn't care less. Now that you are walking though, I think I can get some use out of you tomorrow."

"Oh? What kind of use?" Hector asked with little enthusiasm.

"I have some grunt work to do outside. I think you'd make the perfect grunt."

"How am I going to be able to do anything with my fucking hands tied behind my back?"

"That'll change. I'll tie them up front so that you can use them," Blain smiled.

He really didn't have any work for him, but that didn't mean he couldn't invent some, and invent some, he would.

"What about now? What about tying them up front now?" Hector questioned.

"Maybe when we eat I'll untie one and tie the other to the leg of your chair. For now, though, I really don't see any point. Besides, I'm not sure I can trust you."

"Whatever. So, when are we going to eat?"

"That depends on the weather, I suppose."

"Let me guess whether we eat or whether we don't."

"Nope. It depends on the weather. I plan on BBQing a couple of big, thick steaks."

Hector shook his head at Blain's wit. He hated it as much as he hated him.

"What about me, are you going to tie me up again or what?"

"Probably, but not inside, I'll tie you to the porch somewhere. Can't leave you all alone in here with your feet not being tied. Mind you I could tie them again."

"I'd rather be tied to the porch. I haven't had any fresh air since we got here."

“True enough, but I’m not so sure you deserve any fresh air,” Blain smirked. “We’ve only been here since yesterday. You had all kinds of fresh air when we boated up, not to mention while we drove.”

“While we drove, I was in the trunk or have you forgotten that?” Hector retaliated. “I need some air, man.”

“Tomorrow you’ll get all kinds of fresh air. So don’t bother trying to plead with me. If I decide to let you out, you’ll be tied to the porch. Enough said about that.”

Hector sighed in defeat.

“Well, fuck it. Do whatever you want. I’m tired of this shit.”

“Sounds like you’re ready to start answering some questions.”

“You haven’t beaten me down that much. I have no answers for you. Figure this shit out yourself. I’m fucking done,” Hector replied as he turned his head and looked around.

Blain smiled as he reached for the collar transmitter and gave Hector another jolt. It knocked him right out of the chair he was sitting in.

“Jesus fucking Christ! You son of a bitch; stop with that crap would you.”

“Nah, it is too much fun. You’re like a marionette that I can make jump with the push of a button. Seems like this thing works best when you’re close too.”

He laughed as Hector rose from the floor, his face red with anger.

“Cheer up, be glad I’m not putting bullets in you. Now go on, go sit back down on the floor like a good boy. I’m tired of your bantering. You’ve walked a bit and stretched. Now it’s time to sit back down in your spot." Blain gestured toward the floor. "Go on, get over there, and sit down."

Hector shook his head as he meandered over and sat down on the floor.

"Good boy," Blain remarked as he rose from the table. "I'm going to get our steaks ready and until they are, I don't want to hear a word from you, and I certainly don't want to see you get up."

Hector glared at him with so much gut-filled hate that he had to bite his lip to keep himself from speaking.

Back in Calimay, Rachel was nursing her hangover. She drank so much the day before that even now she felt a little drunk. Havoc lay at her feet waiting to go outside, but Rachel wasn't in the mood for fresh air. All she wanted was more coffee and some food. Her mind was racing with thoughts of Blain and why he hadn't called her yet. It perturbed her that he left behind the only means she had to contact him, his cell phone. He rarely left that behind, but for one reason or another, this time he had.

"You know what, Havoc? I am so mad at Blain right now I could strangle him. Who the hell does he think he is that he doesn't have to phone home? At least I showed him some courteousness and phoned. Fuck!" She shook her head. "I don't know, maybe we should go back to my mother's."

She sat in silence as she weighed her options and poured herself another coffee.

"Fuck it. We'll stay here. He has to come home eventually and when he does, he's going to get it from both sides. If he phones he'll get it then too." She took a long swig of her coffee and slammed the cup down. "I think tomorrow we're going to pay his office a visit. I have a feeling there is something I am missing. If I find out he's been rolling around in the hay with someone else or has been filling my head with lies for all these years, I'll hit him with the biggest divorce suit I can. I'll take this fucking house, his fucking car, everything that son-of-a-bitch owns and then some."

She was mad there was no doubt about it. As mad as she was, however, she was also quite saddened that he wasn't sitting beside her. She missed him terribly. Reaching for her package of cigarettes, she pulled one out and fired it up. Inhaling deeply she sighed, then broke down and began to cry. Her heart was breaking with every thought she had of him. There was no denying how much she truly loved him and the more she thought of that the harder she sobbed.

"Please, Blain, please phone me. I need to know you are okay."

She cried until her eyes hurt and her tears ran dry.

Blain too was missing Rachel as he rubbed down the two steaks with spices and rolled a couple of potatoes in foil. He contemplated phoning her at her mother's where he assumed her to be. He wasn't sure however, if she was ready to talk, or for that matter even wanted to. He had left his cell phone back home intentionally and now as he prepared his and Hector's dinner he wished he hadn't, but every time he was out in the field he always used the phone provided by the Agency and authorized in the name of the alias he was using. Instead, he decided he'd wait a day or two longer. If the urge to call her didn't change he'd do exactly that. For now, he'd continue on as he had been.

Although his heart wanted to hear her voice, he wasn't sure he wanted to hear the ultimatum which he felt for sure was going to be a divorce. He wasn't prepared for that; it was the last thing he wanted. He never loved anyone as much as he loved her; she was everything to him, his heart his soul, everything. He could freely admit in his own mind now, that for the past year their marriage had been on the rocks, and now as it came down to the final blow, he wanted nothing more than to turn back time. Yet, he prepared himself for the loneliness and misery that might be his future. He looked over to Hector.

"The steak and spuds are ready to be tossed on the BBQ. Can I trust you not to move a smidge or do I need to tie your legs again?"

"I'll let you decide."

"Alright," Blain said as he walked over to him, turned him over onto his stomach, and tied his legs. "There, you can lie like that for now. Keep your face planted. If I come back in here and see that you have moved, you won't like what I'll do."

"I thought you said you were going to tie me to the porch?"

"You keep getting the word 'might' mixed up with 'will'. You do know the difference, don't you?" Blain shook his head. "I still might. I just want to get the BBQ and this grub started. If you stay as you are and don't move, I'll take you out."

Gathering up the plate of steaks, he stuck them back into the fridge. The potatoes needed to go on first and cook for a while before the steaks would see the flames. Grabbing the foil wrapped potatoes, he exited the cabin and set them on the porch railing as he went and fished out his BBQ. Pulling it out of storage and closer to the cabin, he looked over all the fittings, removing any dirt or debris he found. Then he checked the burner and propane tank. Satisfied that the BBQ and propane tank were safe, he hooked it up and pushed the electric igniter. In a sudden rush of gas and spark, the BBQ with a loud *whoosh,* came to life. He watched the flames stabilize to a nice blue hue and burn at a constant level. *Now that is indeed a beautiful sight,* he thought as he closed the lid and waited for the temperature to rise a bit, before he tossed on the potatoes.

Back inside he was somewhat amused in a humorous way that Hector had indeed not moved.

"Glad you listened. I thought for sure you would have at least rolled onto your back. I guess you are starting to see the light being so damn obedient and all, what's up with that Hector?"

"I'm tired of all the fucking games is all."

"Ah, you are beginning to see the light then?"

"Fuck that. You said you'd take me outside if I didn't move. So, what of it? Are you going to take me outside or what the fuck?"

"Did I say I'd take you outside?" Blain razzed.

"Fucking right you did."

"Alright, but your feet and hands stay tied." Pulling him to his feet, Blain pushed him out the door. "You can sit right here," he said as he kicked Hector's feet out from under him and let him fall to the porch deck. "You can squirm your way up against the wall."

"Obviously," Hector retorted as he looked up to Blain. "Thanks for all your fucking help."

"Don't mention it."

Blain made his way over to the BBQ and checked on the potatoes.

"Yep a little while longer, Hector, and these outdoors are going to be filled with the smell of grilling steak. The only thing missing is good company."

An hour later Hector sat at the table, his legs still tied and his right hand tied to the leg of the chair, waiting patiently for his plate of food.

"Here you go. And 'no' you don't get a knife and 'no' I'm not cutting the steak for you."

Blain set a plate down in front of him.

"Dig in. You won't be eating again until tomorrow at noon."

Hector didn't speak. He was too busy enjoying the steak and potatoes, the first real food he had eaten in days. He didn't care if the steak was cut or not. He simply stabbed the fork into it and brought it up to his lips. It melted in his mouth like butter on a warm summer day and he was going to savor every bite. Blain waited until he finished with his steak before he spoke.

"You know what, Hector?"

"What?" Hector responded as he put a mouthful of potatoes in his mouth.

"Now that I'm done with my steak, I think I'm going to have a shower, without the toilet brush." Blain smiled as he pushed his empty plate to the side and leaned back in his chair.

"Your humour only intensifies my hate for you. Do you know that?"

"I do. You know what else that means, don't you?"

"Yeah, while you're showering, you're going to tie me up again."

"Exactly. So hurry up and finish."

Standing now, he set his plate on the kitchen counter. Making his way into the spare bedroom he turned up the mattress against the wall and took the bed frame apart.

"I've decided, Hector, that this will be your very own room," he said loud enough for him to hear.

"How pleasant," Hector responded as he finished with his own dinner.

"Yeah. You'll get a mattress, but not a bed frame. I'm removing it, and anything else I think that might tempt you to try something stupid."

"You don't think I'd try anything do you?" Hector responded with sarcasm.

"I don't think. I know you would."

Blain screwed the eyebolts into the wall. Testing them to make sure that they were secure and that they couldn't simply be pulled out, he yanked on them.

"I almost have it all ready for you."

A few minutes later, satisfied that the room was clear of anything that could harm him or tempt Hector, he made his way back to the table.

"Yep, all done. I see that you are too. Good."

He put the muzzle of the Glock to Hector's head and untied him.

"Come on, stand up. Let's go see your new room."

Hector rose from the table cussing and cursing but not struggling.

"That's it, nice and slow."

Blain pushed him into the room and threw him onto the mattress.

"Feels better than that hard floor, eh?" he said as he tied him to the eyebolts. "There, nice and comfy."

"I'm not going to complain, but what are the chances that you can untie my fucking boots? My feet hurt like hell and I haven't had the boots off in almost a week."

"Are you asking me what I think you are?"

"Just untie the fucker's; I'll kick them off."

"You know, Hector. You are beginning to be a real pain in the ass."

Blain pulled the laces and untied them.

"There. I'll wait here while you kick them off."

After a few attempts, Hector managed to get them off. Instantly the room filled with an odor so bad that Blain gagged.

"Holy Christ. Your feet stink worse than your BO."

"What do you expect? I haven't taken them off in a week."

"There isn't a hygienic bone in your body, either way. You can lie in your own stench. I'm going for a shower."

Blain exited and closed the door. Looking into the mirror, he noted that his blackened eyes weren't as black as they had been. Now the bruises were a sickly yellow where the black once was. Even his nose was nearly normal, although he did notice it was a bit out of alignment. The entrance and exit wounds, to his abdominal and lower back appeared to be healing. All the same, it was quite evident what caused the wounds. He would have to do some quick talking once Rachel discovered them. *It could be worse I suppose,* he thought as he turned on the shower and removed his clothes.

"Yuk, I stink almost as much as Hector," he said as he stepped into the shower stall and lathered up.

Ten minutes later, slipping into a set of clean clothes, he shaved.

"That's better," he said as he cleaned the razor and washed his whiskers down the drain.

Hanging up his towel, he exited the bathroom and turned on the coffee pot. At 9:00 p.m., he checked one last time on his guest. Satisfied he was tied, he tossed him the same blanket from the night before.

"Sleep tight," he said as he closed the door.

Sitting down with a fresh cup of coffee, he sighed. Day one had ended. At 11:00 p.m., he retreated to his own room.

Chapter 14

He rolled out of bed the next morning at 6:00 a.m. It was Friday, June 1st, 2007. Splashing water on his face, he looked into the mirror. *What am I going to accomplish today?* he thought as he dried his hands and face. He decided to leave the researching until Monday, and spend the entire week doing exactly that. At least, that was his plan, but plans didn't always come together. Sometimes it was better to see what would happen rather than make any firm decisions.

"Rise and shine. Daylight in the swamp," he hollered as he opened Hector's door. "Come on old chap, wake up, it's Friday and we got shit to do."

Turning, he walked into the kitchen and turned the coffee pot on.

"When the coffee is done, I'll untie you so that we can get on with it," he said loud enough for Hector to hear.

"What exactly is it that we have to get on with?" Hector responded with a tired voice.

"I don't know. I'll think of something," Blain replied as he sat down. "I told you yesterday I have some grunt work for you."

"Yeah, well you still haven't told me what it is. I'm not sure I'm up to doing any work."

"It doesn't matter if you are up to it or not. I need some things done, and you, my friend, are the person who is going to do it. Simple."

"Whatever," Hector responded from the other room as he yawned and closed his eyes again. Blain picked up the collar transmitter and pressed the button.

"Fuck you!" Hector yelled from the other room as the shock jolted him to wakefulness.

Blain laughed.

"The coffee is almost done. Do you want some or not?"

"You're already getting on my nerves, do you know that?"

He couldn't help himself and he pressed the button again.

"I don't care. Now answer the question. Do you want some or not?"

"Fuck! Is it necessary to keep fucking around with that collar thing? I'm fucking awake, alright. Jesus, give me a break."

"You didn't answer the question. Should I push the button again?"

"Alright, yeah, I want some coffee, and I need to piss too."

"I didn't ask if you needed to piss."

"Well I do. I have a pooh cramp too."

Blain started to laugh. "A pooh cramp? Jesus that is the funniest thing you have said."

"How about untying me and letting me get on with it? Come on," Hector pleaded with concern.

"No, the coffee isn't done yet. I said when the coffee was done, I'd untie you."

"How much longer?" Hector wanted to know.

It felt as though he was going to mess himself if it wasn't soon.

"I don't know, a few more minutes."

"I can't wait a few more minutes. Jesus, I'm going to crap myself. God damn it, can't you untie me? I need to use the crapper real bad."

Blain sat at the table wiping away the tears that were streaming down his cheeks because he was laughing so hard. Finally, he stood up and untied Hector.

"Go on, go take care of your business, I'll give you the usual five minutes."

He pushed Hector toward the bathroom door.

"Don't forget about the Glock in my hand. Keep the door open too. I don't want you thinking you can get away with something. When you're done I'll be checking that collar."

Blain made his way back to the table and sat down. He poured two cups of coffee and waited five minutes.

"Alright Hector, time is up," he said from the table. "Get your ass out here."

"Yeah, yeah, I'm on my way," Hector replied as he flushed the toilet and stepped out.

Blain remained sitting at the table with the Glock pointed at Hector as he made his way over.

"Turn around and spread out against that wall, so I can frisk you. I'm not taking any chances with you."

He waited while Hector followed his command.

"What am I going to do, beat you to death with a paper roll?" Hector asked as he spread out against the wall.

Rising from the table, Blain frisked him.

"Are you happy? I haven't got a fucking thing on me."

Blain slapped him across the back of the head.

"What the fuck was that for?"

"I wanted to slap you. That is a good enough reason for me. Now go sit down."

Blain followed and the two of them sat down at the table and drank their coffee.

"I have to tell you Hector, I'm getting real sick and tired of always tying you and untying you."

"I'm sick of that shit too."

"If only I could trust you. I don't see that happening though, do you?"

"What do you think? I took a shit in your shitty shitter, and I'm sitting here drinking your shitty coffee. Have I tried anything?" Hector pointed out.

"I'll take that into consideration as I contemplate whether or not to simply shoot you, especially now since I know you aren't who I thought you were, and that really pisses me off."

"Shoot me, don't shoot me. I don't care. Your ploy to get me to talk isn't going work. You won't get two words out of me, except these two, 'fuck you'."

As soon as Hector said those words, Blain pressed his finger down on the transmitter button and held it there as he pointed the muzzle of the Glock against Hector's forehead. Hector's eyes grew wide, and his neck muscles stiffened from the constant voltage as he began twitching. His eyes rolled back in his head and he fell over, falling to the floor with a foamy broth of saliva around his lips. Even as he lay there on the floor his legs kicking and arms flailing like a slaughtered pig, Blain kept his finger on the button, releasing it only when the charge was completely dispensed.

The look on Blain's face would have darkened any room. He was sick and tired of Hector, his bad mouth, his persona, everything about him, Blain hated. Who the hell was he? That question bothered him the most ever since he learned that the man who put a slug through his gut was sitting in a jailhouse somewhere. What really made his mind tick was when he looked closer at Hector's tattoo to discover that there was a noticeable difference between the two. That was when it really hit home for him. It was then he knew without a doubt that there was more to Hector then a simple attack in a hotel hallway, and although he was certain of this he was no closer to discovering his true identity.

It was while he stood there looking down at Hector's limp body that an idea came to mind, one that he wished now he thought of earlier. Using an old rubber stamp pad that miraculously held ink, he took fingerprints from Hector's right hand, and copied them to a piece of clean paper. *I must be getting slow, why I didn't think of this earlier is beyond me,* Blain thought as he shook his head and looked at the copy. *Yeah, these will work,* he set the piece of paper down on the table and wiped Hector's hand clean so that when he finally came back to the living he wouldn't have a clue. Blain wasn't about to tell him, either.

The next thing he needed to do was find someone or someway to have the prints analyzed. He would have been able to ask Canbra if only he had a scanner, but since he didn't that was out of the question. His SAT phone did have a camera however, and he could take a picture and shoot her a Jpeg through email. The more he thought of that, the more unrealistic it became. Jpegs wouldn't be as concrete as having the original hardcopy analyzed. Not only that, but things could happen to Jpegs especially if shot through a cyberspace connection and not directly uploaded to a secure data centre of some kind. For now, it would seem he simply had a copy of Hector's prints. For now, that would have to do. Kicking Hector to make sure he was still out cold, Blain took the piece of paper and inkpad and stored them out of view. He was on his second cup of coffee when Hector finally came to.

"What, what happened?" Hector stuttered as he tried to sit up.

"My anger got the best of me and I put you to sleep. How do you feel?"

"Not as good as I did earlier. You turned my lights off with this fucking collar, didn't you?"

"I did. It worked like a hot damn too."

"Jesus Christ, my head hurts and my heart feels like it exploded. I can't believe you did that."

Hector struggled to his feet and sat back down.

"Believe it. I'll do it again too if you so much as speak another word. Sit there and be quiet while I decide on what I'm going to do with you."

He was on edge and Hector's presence wasn't improving his mood. Finally, after a few minutes of silence, he rose from the table, muscled Hector back into his room and once more tied him up.

"The work I had for you can wait, and since I don't want to look at you or for that matter listen to you, you'll remain tied up until I decide otherwise, or you decide to tell me who you really are. Good day, Hector."

Blain spat as he exited and closed the door.

Now that his morning was ruined, he finished his coffee and went outside. Much like the early evenings around Mud Creek, early dawn was a world of its own. The calm he felt as he looked around was like no other calm, other than the calm he felt when embraced in Rachel's arms. God he missed being near her and especially now during the crisis they were having. Their marriage wasn't what it used to be, that was for sure, and he knew what the causes were.

It all started a year earlier in 2006. He could almost pinpoint the day. It was the day he killed an entire family of five, all due to a stupid virus that no one except the K.A.T. Agency wanted to admit existed, or for that matter even offer some kind of assistance. It was a day that would always be branded in the recesses of his mind like that of a steer branded with an iron. The scents, the screams, the smells, he remembered it all, right down to when he drew their blood into five vials, soaked their dead bodies in kerosene and without a thought of remorse tossed a match. From that day on his heart and mind weighed heavily on him. Never before had he been responsible for killing so many at one time and an entire family at that. He quit looking at things for their beauty, and instead hid in a shallow shell of self.

He began to grow more distant every day and within months, he thought he had found the perfect self he could be, an uncaring and unemotional being.

Blain shook his head as he reminisced. He had been wrong to adopt that role as his real self. Now the things in life that meant something, like his marriage, peace, beauty, and any humanity that he acknowledged, hung on an unbalanced beam that crossed through his life. He was tired of chasing an evil he knew could never be eradicated. He was tired of all the killing in the name of finding a cure or discovery that for over a decade he and all the other operatives were no closer to finding. He even doubted the research he was there to do would be of any help.

Nothing has helped so far. Why would this new research be any different? Blain questioned himself as he walked to the creek. *I guess I'll never know until I get at it.* He focused his eyes on the rising sun and the colorful sunrise its rays painted across the horizon. It was during that time that it hit him like a ton of bricks. Hector's familiarity was due to that fact that he was actually Rob Hartley *aka* 'On Point'. Blain shook his head in both confusion and uncertainty. Rob was supposed to be dead. *Dead he isn't, I'm betting,* Blain thought as he turned back to the cabin. It made sense to him now as he conjured up the face of Rob in his mind and compared it to that of Hector's aged face. The only difference was that Hector was bald and had a foul mouth, something he recalled Rob never had. It was obviously all part of the persona he was portraying.

Why didn't I see that sooner? God damn it. He was both elated and angry. No matter how he looked at it, Rob was a murderer and a weak link. Hell, he was no better or worse than the Hector character he was portraying as far as Blain was concerned. With the question on who Hector was now answered, Blain had a list of new questions that needed answers. Why was Rob alive? What was his motive? Did he know something that no one else knew? Was it simple revenge?

The most pressing question in his mind was how Chase Benton, the man sent to kill Rob and to clean up his mess years earlier, was involved. Chase was one of the K.A.T. Agency's best operatives ranked only below himself. A leak such as that could tumble the entire organization. The populace of K-15 virus carriers would grow as those infected, procreated, or wounded their victim's only, in attempts to quench their thirst and populate their masses. It would be a dark world, and he wasn't going to let that happen.

He couldn't simply blurt out what he knew. Rob would then close up like a clam, and not he or the Agency would have any answers on why he was alive, what Chase's part was, or if Rob knew something that no one else did. The more Blain thought about it, the more challenging the situation seemed. Caution, wit, luck, and intelligence in the form of research and investigation were going to have to come into play if the answers he was seeking were to be found.

He felt as though there wasn't anybody he could trust, not even Canbra. If there had been a leak, who was to say at what level. There was no way he could simply snap a picture of Hector and send it to Canbra to confirm that he was indeed Rob Hartley. Any information the K.A.T may have held, including photos, were always destroyed when an operative died or was discharged from the agency. There would be no pictures to compare. His best hope were the prints he took that morning, but there were no feasible answers on how to have them analyzed. For now, he'd play his cards slowly and make sure that he had a royal flush and not a simple pair, before he went that route.

With a shovel in hand, he walked around to the other side of the cabin where the big rock was. It was from there that he would excavate Trent's research documents. He had gone through them before. He found nothing then and was convinced that he would find nothing now. The main reason however, that he wanted the documents at that time was to search for any references to Rob Hartley. From what he could remember, Trent, did have vital information on certain K.A.T. Operatives. Blain though, couldn't remember if there was anything on Rob. It took only a few minutes to find the lid to the wooden-box. Clearing the dirt away, he opened it, reached inside, and pulled out the weather-proof briefcase. *Still intact, good,* he thought as he set it to the side and covered up the lid with the sod and dirt he removed. Leaning the shovel against his cabin, he entered and made his way directly to the research room.

Opening the briefcase, he gathered all the documents and formulas and began going through them, looking only for references regarding Chase and Rob. Disappointment followed next. There were no references to either name. *Hmmm, well that was pointless.* Returning the documents to the case, he did a quick tidy up of the contents on his desk and checked his email. There was nothing in his inbox, and so he shut the laptop off and exited. *Everything is going to have to wait until Monday, I'll spend more time with all that crap then,* he thought as he poured a coffee.

He went over in his mind the events of the morning, his epiphany on who Hector truly was, and the fact that there was a real possibility that there had been a security breach or information leak. How else would Hector have known that he was in Canupe at the Heritage Hotel? Everything else Hector could have easily have found out, but not that fact that he was even in Canupe. That was secure information, and if Hector knew that, then he either hacked the information, which in itself was a major security issue, or someone working in the Agency was also working with him.

Either way, he knew that it would be up to him to initiate a probe into the possibilities. The only people who could ever know that Hector was even there were he and Hector. Everyone else would have to remain in the dark until he knew more. If it was an inside breach then whoever was involved knew by now that he was alive and that Hector failed at whatever it was he was trying to do. If a simple security hacking job, then it would mean that the entire Agency could fall prey to hackers. For Blain, that possibility was a real issue. He knew little about computers other than when he punched keys, text appeared on a word document and with the stroke of a few more keys, he could send the document anywhere in the world. That was about the extent of his knowledge. He knew how to logon and log off, how to send and receive. That was it.

It seemed ironic as he sat there. For years he had been playing the part of a computer software developer in his real life, yet he knew nothing about computer code. He left that to the computer techs and gurus. Finishing his coffee, he rose from the table and checked in on Hector, who was now sleeping. Closing the door, he made it a point to recharge the collar transmitter and adjusted the voltage output to the highest setting. Hector would get a real jolt the next time he used it. Blain smiled as he plugged it in.

Looking at his watch, he noted the time to be 10:00 a.m., in four hours the transmitter would be fully charged and ready for the next battle. With no desire to spend the rest of the day indoors, or for that matter hash over in his mind what he now knew about Hector, he grabbed his fishing rod and headed to his favorite fishing hole along Mud Creek. Today, he would fish.

Back in Calimay, Rachel and Havoc were making their way to Blain's office. Maybe she could dig something up that she didn't know. Maybe she would find answers to why he had grown so distant. Maybe she would find nothing at all and her suspicions were just that, simple suspicions. As of late, she was having many. She was certain she would find the answers there. But even after going through the office and all of Blain's crap lying around, she found nothing that proved he wasn't who he claimed to be.

"I feel dirty going through his stuff without him being here, you know that, Havoc. I must be crazy to have thought he has been lying to me. I don't know, I just feel as though there is something, I am missing. Whatever it is, it isn't here," Rachel said as she began putting the things she snooped through away. "Come on, let's head for home, Havoc. You've been a good boy and deserve some play time."

Rachel smiled as she took him by his leash and headed to her car. There were no lies or indications of extramarital affairs that she found. She was satisfied that Blain and she were simply going through a bit of a spell, and that there was a glint of hope for their marriage after all.

Shane Brentwood looked up at the clock on the wall. He had five hours to go before he would be pulling his first shift at the Koffee House in New Kootenay. He was nervous and excited all at the same time, even the palms of his hands were sweating. He knew though that it was all due to the anticipation of a new job and maybe even a new life. He was excited, perhaps even titillated, that he would be working so closely with Sapphire. She had been in every one of his dreams since he got the job. They weren't dreams of violence and rape, such as he was so used to having. They were dreams of genuine happiness, serenity, and peace. They were dreams he thought he was incapable of having. He took it as a sign of change and he wanted those dreams to be as real as the air he breathed. Fantasy and reality though could often be confused, but Shane was convinced that it would be his reality. He hoped that he and Sapphire would become more than friends. Setting his alarm clock to go off at 3:00 p.m., and with these thoughts, he closed his eyes and waited to meet Sapphire in his dreams.

Blain stood on the shore of Mud Creek, a fishing rod in his hand. Already he caught a couple of nice trout and was hoping to catch a couple more.

"This is the life," he said to himself as he cast into the water.

He watched as the bobber floated down stream and into an eddy. It twirled and floated closer to the shore and then suddenly disappeared. Blain yanked on the rod and began reeling his line in. There was no doubt that a fish had taken his bait. From the way it battled, he could tell that it was at least a couple of pounds. It broke the surface and jumped, thrashing in the air. It dived again into the water like a missile.

"Hell yeah! That is a brute," Blain blurted out as he reeled faster and brought the fish in closer.

He could see that it was a brown trout and by no means was it small. In a sudden burst of energy, it broke the surface once again only a few feet from where he stood. Then, as suddenly, it dived once more and snapped the line taking with it, the bobber and all.

No fucking way! Shit! That really pisses me off. The line is too old I guess. It shouldn't have broken that easily, Blain thought as he reeled in the now empty line.

"You aren't going to get away from me. I'll be back."

He raised his fist in the air.

"I'll get you. Damn fish anyway," he muttered as he gathered up the two he landed.

With no extra hooks, he made his way back to the cabin and cleaned his catch.

"Lunch," he said to himself as he removed their guts.

It had been a long time since he had eaten fresh trout and the two he caught were a bit too big for any frying pan he had. He fired up the BBQ deciding that was how they deserved to be cooked. As the flames warmed up the grill, he went inside and wrapped them in foil with butter and onions. He took the time then to check in on Hector. Opening his door, he made his way in and kicked him.

"Hey, Hector, wake up! Lunch soon. Hope you like fresh trout."

Hector opened his eyes and looked at him.

"Trout?" he asked. "I fucking hate fresh water fish," he said as a matter-of-fact.

"That's too bad. I caught a couple nice ones, and they'll be ready in a few minutes. All the more for me, I guess."

Blain shrugged his shoulders. Making his way outside he slapped them on the BBQ. It took a couple of minutes before he could hear the sizzling as the butter melted and the combination of cooking fish and onions permeated the air making him lick his lips in anticipation. If Hector didn't want any, it didn't matter to him, as far as he was concerned he could then stay tied up. That would make his day better. He wouldn't have to listen to or even look at him.

It was while he was eating that the rain moved in. The thunder was sudden and rumbled in the distance like a bowling ball rolling down a lane. It was followed by a crack of lightning that streaked across the now darkening sky. *Damn it, where the Hell did that spring from?* He watched from the cover of the porch, as the clouds grew darker. In only minutes the rain came. It was so hard and fast that the sound of it as it hit the metal roof of the cabin drowned out all other ambient sounds. Torrents of water boiled over the cabin's roof and eaves as though someone was standing on top with a garden hose. *Wow, I haven't seen rain like this in a long time,* he thought as he sat down on one of the chairs.

Lightning danced across the sky giving him a show that would rival any laser exhibit made by man. Clouds of dust rose from the ground as though a hundred horses were galloping by as the rain pummeled the dry, dusty earth. With one final roll of thunder and show of lightning, the rain slowed to a moderate and constant pitter-patter. The clouds in the sky told him that this was only the beginning of a long, needed rainstorm. It may have thrown a wrench into his lazy day, but by no means did it ruin it. The cleansing scent was refreshing and he inhaled deeply the sweet smell of wet earth and grass.

When the wind picked up and the tall evergreens swayed this way and that, dancing with the north wind that now blew, he rose from the chair and entered the cabin. The torrential downpour continued until evening as did the thunder and lightning, blocked out only on occasion as gusts of wind howled by and took over with haunting resonance. Hector remained tied the entire time as Blain continued with his day. Unable to fish and with no desire to work on his research, he spent the majority of the time tidying up. An idea came to his mind as he did this. He decided the best way to keep from having to constantly tie and untie Hector, would be to make some changes to the room he kept him in, making it as escape proof as possible.

All the tools and supplies he would need for the remodeling were out in the storage shed. There were boards, a few lengths of rebar leftover from when the concrete foundation for the water cistern was poured, boxes of nails and spikes, boxes of screws and bolts. He smiled as he thought about it and was glad they had left the remaining supplies on the property after they updated the cabin and outbuildings. Trent always said that '*one day it might all come in handy, might as well leave it here*'. Blain nodded his head as he remembered, it was so clear that he could almost hear Trent saying it. *Well, you were right, Trent, it will come in handy,* he thought to himself as he reminisced. It was too late to start now, but in the morning that was exactly what he would do.

It would be simple. He would use the rebar to bar up the one window in the room. He would reinforce the door and reverse the lock so it could be locked from the outside. Hell, he'd even add a couple of bar locks to the outside of the door with whatever rebar was left after he barred the window. The only time he'd have to look at Hector after that was when he needed to use the bathroom. He wouldn't even have to sit with him when he ate as he could make a slot in the door and feed him that way. He chuckled at how mad Hector was going to get, when he broke the news to him. One thing was for certain, he wouldn't have to listen to his constant bantering about being tied up. It would make his research a lot less distracting. He opened Hector's door and looked in on him.

"Still alive or what?" he asked.

"I'll live a lot longer than you."

"So you are alive? Damn," Blain responded back with the same amount of hatred in his voice as Hector had used.

"My fucking hands are swelling from these ties, my fucking feet feel like a voodoo doll being stabbed with pins, and I'm fucking hungry."

"That was your choice to be hungry, but remember you don't like fish and I don't take requests."

"That was already hours ago."

"True, and I had fish for supper too."

"Of course, you fucking did," Hector snorted. "I guess I wait until tomorrow."

"Maybe. There is a lot of fish left. I might have that for lunch tomorrow too," Blain chuckled. "Maybe I'll throw you something, maybe I won't," he said as he closed the door.

"Arc you just going to leave me here tied up like this, or are you at least going to let me have another walk about?" Fuck!" Hector hollered from behind the now closed door.

Blain simply chose to ignore him, and made his way over to the kitchen where he slapped some peanut butter and jam onto a couple pieces of bread, and returned to Hector's room.

"Here, have this," he said as he tossed it to him making sure it landed on his lap, so that he had at least a fighting chance to get it into his mouth and eat it.

"How am I supposed to eat it with my hands tied?" Hector bellowed.

"Same way you ate the jerky the other night. Figure it out, Hector."

He closed the door and walked away as Hector spewed out a list of obscenities and empty threats. Blain wasted no time in grabbing the now fully charged collar transmitter and pressed the button.

"Holy fucking Christ! God damn it!" Hector cried as the jolt hit him like a hammer, causing him to drop the sandwich that he struggled to get in his mouth. "You fucking son of a bitch!" he hollered, "I just managed to get that sandwich in my fucking mouth. Fuck!"

"Shut up in there and I won't have to shut you up from out here."

"You...!" Hector relented knowing what the outcome would be.

"That's better," Blain responded. "Keep it quiet in there and eat your PB and J sandwich."

At 10:00 p.m., when the rain returned and continued its assault, he made his way to bed and closed his eyes as it pelted the tin roof and lulled him to sleep.

Chapter 15

The rain continued through the night and as he looked out the window to the creek, he noticed how much it had actually risen. It was brown with mud and rolled by with destructive force. He could hear the sound of the boat as it rubbed and clunked against the wooded dock. Luckily, it remained moored. The last thing he needed was for it to break loose or the dock to wash away. The sky was clear, however, and the sun was shining. As long as no more rain came for a few days it wouldn't take long for the swelling creek to return to normal.

Turning on the coffee pot, he ventured into the bathroom and took care of his bladder, brushed his teeth and splashed water on his face. His plan for the day was the same as the plan he had made the night before. Pouring two coffees, he set them on the table and opened Hector's door.

"Hey. Wake up," he said as he walked over to him with the Glock in his hand.

Hector looked at him groggy eyed. Blain untied his hands from the eyebolts in the wall.

"Come on, get up. You have five minutes to shit or piss or both. Hurry up," he said as he gestured with the Glock for Hector to get up and get moving.

It took Hector a couple of minutes, but finally he was up and at it.

"Go ahead, take yourself in the direction of the shitter, and take your piss. I'll be waiting with Glock in hand."

He watched as Hector stumbled into the bathroom. Five minutes later Hector came out and Blain went through the same ritual as every day, frisking him to make sure he had nothing on him or, for that matter, tampered with the shock collar around his neck. Satisfied, the two sat down to their morning coffee.

"Guess what I have on my agenda today, Hector?" Blain offered as he took a drink from his coffee.

"Do you think that I really care what you have on your agenda?" Hector snorted as he looked into Blain's eyes. "Because, if you do. Trust me I don't."

"I think you might be interested," Blain smiled.

"No. I'm not, but I'm sure you're going to tell me anyway."

"Indeed I am. I'm going to turn your room into a prison cell. What do you think of that?"

"It'll only make it easier for me to get my hands on you. Are you sure you want to do that?" Hector retorted as he took a drink.

"On the contrary, Hector, it is going to make it a lot less likely that you'll ever get the chance. I won't have to constantly babysit you. I'll feed you through a slot in the door and let you out once a day to shit and piss. That'll be the extent of our contact, until I find some other use for you or shoot you."

"You've been talking that crap since the first day. Yet, here I am."

"Yeah, well keep counting the days, Hector, you don't have many left."

Twenty minutes later, Blain tied him up again so that he could keep an eye on him as he went about reconstructing the room. It took him the better part of the day, but finally, he was finished. The slot in the door through which Hector would receive his food when he felt like feeding him, was the perfect size for a cup and plate and was easily closed so that Hector couldn't look outside his room.

The rebar on the outside of the window was the most problematic thing he had to contend with, but he managed with some ingenuity and even reduced the window opening, making it a lot less appealing to try and slither through. Satisfied, he stood back and looked it over. *Yep, that will keep him in. He'll never get through that without me knowing.* Blain gathered up the tools he used and put them back in the shed. Next, he muscled Hector into the room and, keeping the Glock pressed against his temple, he untied him. Since there was no more need for the shock collar, he unbuckled that as well and removed it, then pushed him onto the bed.

"Don't move from that spot until you hear the door being locked."

Slowly he backed out the door and locked it. Looking through the slot in the door, he told Hector to enjoy his new home and then closed it preventing Hector from seeing outside the room.

Blain added a few more touches to the door. Using two lengths of rebar, he secured them in an 'X' across the door and frame, using the eyebolts that he used to tie Hector to the wall. It so happened that they were the perfect size and the rebar slid through them, as though that was what they were for. He checked everything when he was done. He was satisfied that there was no way Hector would be able to escape through the heavy door without alerting him. Even if he somehow managed to break the simple door lock, the rebar would prevent the door from opening unless the rebar was removed from the outside first.

Wasting no time, Hector flung open the curtains and looked at the bars that now covered the window on the outside. He shook his head. Blain had certainly gone the distance in making his escape or an attempt to escape next to impossible. Not only were there bars, but Blain had also reduced the window opening, making it impossible for him to even squeeze through if he did manage to bend a few of the bars. He had to try something though. Sliding the window open he wrapped his hands around a couple of the bars to see if he could loosen or bend them, but it was futile.

Fucking, son of a bitch. Who the fuck keeps metal bars out in the fucking woods, he thought as he looked around the room for any hope of escape. Defeated yet again, he slumped onto the mattress as anger and hate bubbled through his veins. He couldn't even attempt an escape through the walls. They were solid log, with a few pieces of drywall or paneling here or there to liven up the decor, but ultimately solid log. For now it was obvious that Blain had him right where he wanted him.

That didn't mean he wouldn't try to escape and he looked toward the door, big and heavy as it was. It was, he noted, his only means out. Rising from the mattress, he tested the lock and jiggled the handle as he pushed up against door to see if it had any give. He could tell that it was rigged. *That fucking guy has thought of everything,* Hector sat back down on the mattress shaking his head. His only hope of escape as far as he could tell now, was if Blain slipped up. By all accounts, he knew that was as unlikely as snow in July. Blain had outwitted him; there was no denying that. It pissed him off a great deal too, as he sat there looking around in hopelessness and defeat. His hope for escape or discovering the cure for K-15 on his own and all the money it would be worth was nothing more than a pitiful dream.

Was it time to admit defeat? Was it time to tell Blain exactly who he really was? Was it time to offer up what he knew about K-15 and fill Blain in on the human testing he already conducted, and the results, which, although meager, offered a few answers. With more testing and formulas that he was missing, which he knew the Agency had, he was certain he'd be able to complete the research and undoubtedly discover a cure. What would Blain's reaction be though when and if he admitted that he was, in all actuality, Rob Hartley.

These things and others raced through his mind. Hector lay on the mattress and looked up to the ceiling, his mind drifting with possibilities. He knew that the Agency was holding some very interesting evidence regarding a cure. It was right there within his reach, but as things were, he'd never get a chance to see it as long as he was Hector Hernandez, or for that matter even if he did admit who he really was. He was a rogue operative, a murderer in the eyes of the Agency and its operatives. Even though all the things his accusers accused him of, in reality, brought him closer to finding a cure, in the eyes of those who knew nothing about the research he conducted, he was a simple murderer, a weak link. The only one who understood what it was that he was doing had been Chase and Chase was dead. For now, Hector decided he would ride the waves. His lips would remain sealed. He would wait to see if things changed, and maybe, just maybe, he would get the one chance he needed to escape. If and when he did, he would take with him all the classified information the Agency held and plant Blain in the ground.

Blain sat at the table a fresh cup of coffee in his hands. He was pleased with the work he did in reconstructing Hector's room. There was no possible way he could escape. He was unsure what it was he was going to do with him. Simply killing him was out of the question; nor could he use him as a human guinea pig, although that was a very enticing idea. It didn't mean he couldn't continue to threaten him with that. The reality was that when the three weeks were up, he'd turn him over to the Agency and let the others decide his fate. Blain was by no means a coldblooded murderer. Killing

Hector wasn't something he wanted on his hands, but if it came down to his life or Hector's, he wouldn't think twice.

The weekend passed without incident and when Blain rolled out of bed on Monday, the only thing on his mind was the dreaded research he would now begin. The fun and games were over and it was time to buckle down and get on with the one reason he was there. Hector was secured in his room, and as of late hadn't really caused many problems. He let him out every morning to use the facilities, fed him at noon and dinnertime, and the two were never in contact with each other for more than ten minutes a day. The words they exchanged never amounted to more than a few brief sentences, sometimes it was friendly, sometimes not.

With a coffee in hand he made his way into his research room and turned on his laptop. The first thing he did was check his email. No one except Canbra had his email address, no one, that is, except a bunch of bloody spammers and theirs were the only messages he received that morning. He deleted them all, then plugged in the first Pocket CD-R and opened the first folder burnt on to it. There was a list of documents, each about four pages long, so he read them all, jotting down notes that he thought were relevant. He went through the first ten CD-R's using the same technique of scribbling out notes on things that he found worthy. It seemed to him that a lot of the information was either irrelevant or complete nonsense, and some of it he didn't even pay attention to, due to his drifting mind. By 3:00 p.m., he was tired of it all, his eyes burned from the amount of reading he had done, and he was a bag of nerves. Whatever, it was that he was supposed to be looking for, after comparing notes with the documents that Trent wrote still made no sense to him.

By mid-week, after shuffling through most of documents and thirty-six of the forty Pocket CD-R's and no closer to finding anything that made sense he knew then, as he had from the beginning, that he was not the man for the job. He sat at the table that Wednesday, June 6th, so defeated by the research that he was miserable. Nothing made any sense. Nothing proved one thing or the other. It had been a waste of his time and the Agency's. He might as well have been there only to fish.

The only thing that he had discovered was the fact that Rob Hartley was alive, and the only one who knew that was Blain. The possibility that a security leak had unfolded right beneath the Agency's eyes was the one thing he really wanted to investigate. The research was beyond his capabilities. Discovering that Rob was alive, and how he managed to breach the Agency's security was more appealing. Although not nearly as important as discovering a cure or antidote for the K-15 virus, it was nonetheless important. Perhaps during that investigation something more concrete would come about.

Yawning, he rested his elbows on the table and put his head in his hands as he contemplated. For three days from sunup until sundown, he had done nothing except read, write, and research, and what came from it was a big fat zero. He sighed as he went over it all in his mind one final time. Files, folders, formulas and sentences, they twirled around in his mind like a carrousel, making him almost feel sick. Nothing though, even came from that. There was no use for him to carry on with the bloody research, and from that day on, he would make it perfectly clear that he wanted nothing to with it ever. The Agency had people for exactly that, and as far as he was concerned, they were the ones that should be doing it. He was a field operative, not a field researcher. It was time for him to pull rank. Picking up his SAT phone he dialed the Agency. Canbra answered after few short rings.

"Entity, how is the research going?" was the first thing that came out of her mouth.

"Are you sitting down?"

"Yes," Canbra answered, hoping that he had news for her.

"Good, because what I have to say, isn't going to impress you one bit."

"Why?" she asked hesitantly.

"Because, I have not discovered a damn thing, I am putting the research off."

"You can't do that."

"Yes I can, Canbra, and I am. I've decided to return to Calimay in the next couple of days. I'll bring all of Trent's research with me. Someone else, perhaps Gonsite, can take over. I'm fed up with it all. I know nothing about the shit I've been reading. It makes no sense for me to continue with it. It is a blatant waste of time."

"How can you say that? I've supplied you with everything. You can't give up like that."

"You know, Canbra, that I would never give up if I was making some kind of progress. Since I'm not, the longer I'm on this, the longer it is going to take. Gonsite or even someone else more qualified in the research department is more likely to make heads or tails out of it all. As I said, I will gather all of Trent's work and hand it over to whoever is next in line. But, I am done with it."

"Well, since you have put it that way, I guess I can't argue."

"Nope. Not you or anyone else for that matter. I do have a few questions."

"What are they?"

"Firstly, how has the monkey possibility been going? Any luck in being able to secure a test subject?"

"I do have a couple of leads, but nothing can be done with it for a couple more weeks. I am waiting for a Professor Schuler who may or may not offer his assistance."

"See, you have made more progress than I. Next, what about the recent attacks in Forge and Elkhill. Any news from that operation?"

"Nothing concrete except the ME has declared the attacks as an animal attack, likely a cougar. Basically, it was a dead end. Not even the operatives sent to investigate came back with anything worth mentioning."

"Is it plausible to think that the killings by the carriers of K-15 have slowed?"

"They have definitely slowed down to a snail's pace. It is almost as though they have gone into some kind of remission or hibernation. It may very well be that they are no longer killing, just simply replenishing their masses as you said before."

"That does sound frightening. It is hard to believe however that if the carriers are only wounding their victims to replenish their masses, why haven't any of the victims come forward?"

"That I don't know. Perhaps the carriers aren't wounding their victims the same way as before. Maybe the victims aren't even aware that they have been attacked."

"That is a scary thought. Is it possible that they are now using simple bodily fluids such as saliva, or from intercourse?"

"Yes. It is possible that the K-15 virus may have morphed into a communicable infection transmitted by sexual intercourse, and even saliva is a possibility.

We've been looking into that for a while. See, you are a researcher, Entity."

"I'm afraid not. I'm only suggesting other possibilities. Something is going on, Canbra. I think we are all aware of that. If corpses haven't been showing up, then it is obvious that something else is transpiring or there are no more carriers alive. That, I think, is very unlikely."

"I would not disagree. But, until we discover otherwise, the world as we know it is no safer then it was six months ago. I was hoping that your research was going to come up with a few answers."

"Forget that. I'm done with researching."

"I know. You've already pointed that out."

"Yes I have and I mean to stick by it too. I will never do research again. My job has always been field operative. I kill K-15 carriers. That is what I do. I am not a biogenetic researcher, nor am I a geneticist. I am an assassin first and foremost."

"Yes you are, and I do understand where you are coming from. It is like asking a mechanic to wire a house. Their specialty is DC not AC. I get it, Entity."

"Good. Alright then, now that you know where I stand on this research thing, let's move on. I'll head back to Calimay in a couple of days. I do have something that needs to be looked into, but I'm not about to say anything on the plastic."

"Why? It is a secure line?"

"Secure or not makes no difference to me. Once I get back to Calimay I'll be setting up a conference in person with all available field operatives, researchers, and legal moguls, including you too. Until then though, I trust you will not mention it."

"You can count on it, Entity. Should I let the others know that you are returning?"

"You can certainly do that. Go through every researcher's personal records as well. I want the Agency's best on Trent's stuff. Likely, that will be Gonsite. If you find someone else with more credentials, keep it to yourself until we meet. I'll decide from there."

"Understood, is there anything else?" Canbra questioned. It wasn't every day that Entity pulled rank, but that is exactly what he was doing now.

"Nope, other than I will stay in contact with you until I return to Calimay."

"Good enough. Alright, Entity. We'll see you when you make your way back. Bye for now."

"Indeed. Goodbye, Canbra." Blain turned his SAT phone off. Standing now, he made his way to the coffee pot and poured a cup. *No more need to read shit I don't understand,* he sighed as he took a drink. What bothered him now no matter how farfetched it sounded, was the idea that the K-15 virus may have morphed into a sexually transmitted disease (STD). It was unnerving, but obviously, something was going on. That fact in itself was certainly worth concern. Sitting, he tried to imagine what the prognosis of those infected would be if the K-15 virus had morphed into a STD. Would those infected simply die from Kuru-like symptoms? Would it go deeper than that? If K-15 had morphed into an unidentified STD, the world was in a lot of trouble, more so than now when carriers were simply killing their victims. There was no point however in fretting over the possibility. There were no findings yet that proved it. *The world better keep its fingers crossed,* Blain thought as he took a drink of his coffee.

He spent a couple of hours packing up the equipment and research documents that Canbra supplied. Since he didn't need it anymore, there was no reason not to pack it up. He would never have to look at it again. He took special care with Trent's findings.

Those he knew were the key to answers the Agency needed. Although he and Trent agreed that the information would be for their eyes only, Blain knew there was no way he'd ever be able to understand it, and that the best thing would be for someone else to study it. He looked around the room as though Trent was with him as he reminisced. *It has to be this way, Trent. I can't make any sense of it. Hope you understand.* He set the last folder and Hector's prints into the briefcase and packed it with the rest of the stuff. The room now empty of all research equipment, Blain looked around. *Maybe one day this can be used for something else,* he thought as he closed the door. The equipment and gear were scattered across the main living area of the cabin, and he stacked it all into one pile and threw an old blanket over it to keep prying eyes from seeing exactly what it all was. The only equipment that he didn't pack were his SAT phone and the satellite dish which he would get to later. The SAT phone he'd keep close.

He felt good knowing that he did try his best to understand all the research and mumbo-jumbo. He felt even better knowing that the cabin would no longer be used for that reason, *'research'*. Perhaps he could surprise Rachel with a home away from home. He knew she would love it. It was rustic, modern, and secluded. The only way in was by boat or hiking trail. It was the perfect gift. She often asked him to buy a cabin or cottage and he always told her that one day he might. *Today is the day, that this cabin becomes a place of retreat for both of us,* Blain smiled as he thought about that. It had been a part of his life for a long time and he was enthralled that he would now be able to share it with her.

There were a few problems with that though. The man that stayed at the cabin and who was known by the locals of Yellow Lake, was Ben Todd, his alias. *A minor detail,* Blain thought as he scratched his chin. He could simply tell Rachel that was the name he had given them. Undoubtedly, she would then ask 'why' and he'd have to give her some kind of excuse. Then there was the problem of why he had owned it for so long without telling her. *Hmmm maybe not a minor detail after all,* Blain reminisced as he thought about it. He loved that cabin and he wanted to keep it. *Ah, I'll deal with it, somehow, someway,* he decided as he drank his coffee. Looking at his watch he noted the time to be 6:00 p.m. *Best get on with cooking some food. The animal in the pen is probably hungry by now,* he thought, referring to Hector. Making his way into the kitchen he tossed some food together. It was nothing special, but it was food and it would suffice. His mind really wasn't on making a gourmet dinner; besides he wasn't hungry. The food was for Hector. Opening the door slot, he peered in. Hector was standing looking out the window through the small opening.

"Hey, Hector, come and get it," he said as he waited for Hector to approach. Sliding the plate to him, he smiled.

"Hope you enjoy it."

"Thanks, although I don't know why I'm thanking you," Hector replied as he took the plate from Blain.

"By the way, we're going to be leaving here sooner than I thought."

"We?" Hector asked somewhat confused.

"That is what I said."

Hector looked at Blain through the door slot.

"No bullets for me, then?" he asked with a smirk. "I knew you were all talk."

"I'm not done with you yet. There are some other people you need to meet."

That is all Blain said as he closed the slot and made his way outside to take down the satellite. It didn't take him long. Putting it back in its box along with the coaxial cables, he stacked it with the rest of the stuff in the middle of the floor.

"There, already to move," he said quietly to himself as he wiped his hands on his pants.

He looked around the cabin knowing he would have to make changes to it before he left there. The first thing he did was turn the research room into a simple spare room. He took down the bench tables and piled them outside near the burning barrel. The desk he moved into a different corner. There was nothing wrong with having a desk in there.

Next, he tossed the 10-inch security monitor into an empty box, yanked out the wiring that connected it to the camera in the opposite room, and finally took the camera itself down. He tucked it all into the box and set it to the side. Hector's room would be next and he decided he'd make those changes on their last day, after Hector was tied up somewhere. It would take a bit of work, he knew, but the last thing he wanted was to leave the cabin as it was. The next time he came there, if things went as planned, he'd be there with Rachel.

With enough daylight remaining, he grabbed an axe from the shed and proceeded to knock apart the bench tables into manageable burning pieces. Adding a few of the smaller pieces to the burning barrel, he dosed the wood with diesel fuel and tossed in a match. Flames danced to life, and smoke billowed into the air as the wood and debris began to burn. His mind raced with memories and visions back to the times when he and Trent sat at the tables hashing over this, that, and the other thing, as they conversed on the importance of eradicating the K-15 virus. It seemed like only yesterday and he did feel heartsick. In life, he knew that sometimes things were best burned from memory or at least put to rest in the recesses of the human mind. He would never forget the times he and Trent spent there, nor could he ever speak of it. It would have to remain as an Arcanum.

Picking up another piece to add, he felt something bounce off his foot and he looked down. There at the toe of his boot was a flat green plastic case. He knew exactly what it was, a 3.5 inch floppy disk case. Setting down the piece of table that he was going to toss into the fire, he bent down and picked up case. Inside there were two floppy disks, labeled 'Floppy 1' and 'Floppy 2'. That was it.

"What in the hell are these?" he questioned himself as he stood up and looked them over closely. The handwriting he knew was Trent's. *Geez, would you look at that. Wow, I've never seen these before. What the hell,* he thought as he stepped back and sat down at the bench to continue studying them.

Obviously, they were of some importance otherwise Trent would not have kept them. *Huh, well they'll be coming with me,* Blain put them in his shirt pocket. Until he had a chance to look at them, he wasn't going to let anyone else. The problem was that they were 3.5 inch floppy disks and the laptop he had at the cabin didn't have a floppy reader. Everything nowadays was CD or DVD. His old computer back home though had those capabilities, and not until he got there would he even be able look at them. *Hope they are still good,* he thought as he looked under the piece of tabletop from which they had fallen, making sure it held no more secrets. He could see where the floppies had been taped, but there was nothing else. Satisfied, he tossed the piece into the barrel and watched as it took to flame.

Every piece he added after that he made sure that he wasn't throwing something into the fire that he should otherwise keep. Although by now it was pushing 10:00 p.m., he added a few more pieces of scrap wood. Sitting on the bench, he watched the evening grow darker. It was peaceful as he sat there, his mind racing with memories. The only sounds that echoed were the sounds of the flames, as they danced precariously in the warm evening breeze that gently blew and tousled his hair. Wednesday, at Mud Creek, had come to an exceptional end.

Chapter 16

Blain woke with a new outlook regarding his cabin. For the past fourteen-years, it had been used for nothing more than a vessel to do research. No more would that be the case. From that day forward it would simply be a cabin, a place of retreat and good times. It even seemed to Blain that the cabin itself felt a sigh of relief and took on a new glow. Feeling as good as he was, there were hurdles he needed to cross before he could bring Rachel there, but ultimately that was his goal. It would be their place, their piece of heaven. He looked into the bathroom mirror and smiled. *Yep, for Rachel and me,* he thought.

Setting his morning coffee on the table, he unlocked Hector's door and woke him.

"Hey get up. You know the routine, come on," Blain said with the Glock in his hand as he waited for Hector to roll out of bed.

"Yeah, yeah," Hector responded as he rose and made his way past Blain and into the bathroom.

"Any chance I can get a shower today?"

"I'll think about it. Why? Can't you stand your own smell?"

"I haven't gotten cleaned up since you scrubbed me down with that toilet brush. The whiskers on my face are making me scratch all night long."

"So you're asking for a conventional shower and a shave. Huh, maybe I'll allow that. You haven't given me much of a problem lately. Maybe that'll be your reward."

"Whatever," Hector said as he walked over to the table where Blain sat.

"I know. Up against the wall."

Hector rolled his eyes as he turned and went spread eagle up against the wall as Blain frisked him.

"I'd think by now this wouldn't be necessary."

"Think that all you want. As long as you are my prisoner," Blain chuckled, "this is the way it is going to be every time you are out of my sight. I'd think by now you'd be used to it."

Finding nothing on Hector, he pushed him toward the table.

"There is your coffee. Grab it and right back into that room you go."

"Yeah, I know the routine."

Hector picked his cup of coffee up and returned to the room with Blain behind him and the Glock he held in his hand shoved into the small of his back.

"What about that shower and shave?" he asked as Blain closed the door and locked it.

"You'll get your answer soon enough. Drink your coffee and relax a bit," Blain replied as he put the door security bars in place.

It probably was a good idea to allow Hector to clean up. He was starting to smell quite putrid as far as Blain was concerned. Making his way to the bathroom, he removed everything from inside, except a bar of soap, a bottle of shampoo, a disposable razor, and clean towel. When the time came, he'd stay alert, making sure Hector didn't try anything stupid.

As the morning edged on, he walked down to the dock and checked on the boat and the creek level. It had receded more than he expected in the past few days, but it was deep enough that the boat continued to float. Luckily, Mud Creek was a goliath of creeks. Wide and deep as it was now, not always could a boat as big make it to the cabin. Usually they used canoes or small aluminum boats. The creek, though, was changing and by the looks of it, it wasn't about to get any smaller. Climbing the few rungs of the ladder, he stepped up onto the deck, and checked the boat over for minor damage from the storm that hit a few days earlier.

Other than a few broken branches and pine needles that scattered the deck, which he cleaned up and tossed overboard, the boat looked as good as it did the day he picked it up from the Winnfield Marina. He sat down at the helm and turned the key. Letting it idle for a few minutes, he checked the gauges and whatnots. *Good to go, I'd say. You are a good old girl, you know that,* Blain thought as he patted the helm's dash and removed the key. *I think I'm going to find out if you are for sale. Can't have a cabin near a lake without a good boat. You'd be worth every penny, too,* he smiled as he stepped away from the captain's seat. Returning to the cabin, he unlocked Hector's door to let him shower.

"If you still want to clean up, now is your chance. Chop, chop."

He waited for Hector to get it together.

"Really, you're going to let me shower?" Hector asked with doubt and shock.

"Well, we have a creek to navigate, a lake and a river, and then a long drive back to Calimay. I'm not so sure I would be able to handle your stench for that long. Besides, as I said, it is your reward for being as cordial as you have been as of late," Blain razzed. "Now come on, get a move on. There is a towel, soap, and razor waiting."

"Fucking eh, it is going to feel good to wash up. As for being cordial, dream fucking on, buddy," Hector retorted as he made his way to the bathroom.

"Just get the fuck on with it. I'll be waiting," Blain responded as pushed Hector in. "The door by the way remains open."

Walking the few steps to the table, he sat down, keeping his eye on the bathroom as he waited for Hector to finish. It seemed like forever, but finally the shower shut off and the bathroom taps turned on. A few minutes later, Hector came out shaved and clean.

"You almost look like someone I once knew, except you're bald." Blain looked at him and smiled. It was subtle hint, but Hector didn't clue in.

"Trust me, I'm no one you have ever known."

"Yeah, I know. The guy that I knew is dead and had hair. Anyway, no use standing there, you know the routine, up against the wall," he said as he rose from table, Glock in hand and frisked him. "Alright, off to your cage. Come on, get a move on."

Blain gestured as Hector turned and walked back to his room.

"We'll be leaving here tomorrow sometime, so until then, good day," he said as he closed the door and locked it.

"What about lunch?" Hector asked from behind the door.

"You'll get it when you get it," Blain responded as he slid the last bar in place. "Might even throw some meat at you today. Would you like that, Hector?" he asked as though he cared.

"Fuck, a shower, a shave, and meat all in one day. You got to be kidding?" Hector retorted with uncouth mannerism.

Blain paid little attention as he made his way outside and sat on the porch. Putting his hands behind his head, he stretched out his legs and yawned. The silence of mid-morning and the warm sun felt good as he sat there and basked in all its splendor. Hector was cleaned up, the boat was fine, and all the gear that he brought with him on that visit was packed and ready to be loaded back onto the boat. There was nothing left to do but wait until the next morning and dawn's early light.

At 1:00 p.m. that day, he tossed a few cobs of corn on the barbeque and waited for them to cook before he slapped on a half a dozen thick pork chops. An hour later with Hector fed and his own stomach full, Blain too, took some time to shower and shave. Dressing in some clean clothes, he turned on the coffee pot and waited for a fresh cup before he once more ventured outside into the blissfulness of late afternoon. There was nothing grander in his opinion. The warm breeze and serenity was magical as he sat there and listened to the sounds of the creek as it drifted by. Everything was as it should be.

Shane Brentwood looked out his living-room window. He was doing well at his new job at the Koffee House. He worked six days already and made $200 plus in gratuities alone. After his first shift that past Friday, he wasn't sure it was anything he would stick with. So far, though, he was enjoying it. He worked with Sapphire three times out of the six days he had worked. This coming Friday, he'd be working with her again. He was on permanent nights and although it messed up his days, he was growing used to it. The idea of being that close to Sapphire on those occasions that they worked together, made the evening-shift in his opinion worth every wakeful hour. The old wants of murder and mayhem had not yet reared their ugly head, but he did feel the pangs of sexuality and desire to be with a woman for the first time whenever he was close to her. He had left the Calimay Mental Hospital weeks earlier with two desires: murder, and rape. Since then, that desire faded away like snow on a spring day.

He wasn't sure if he should be grateful things turned around for him, or if he should be concerned. For years while he was a mental patient, the fantasies of murder and rape bounced around in his head, leaving him with the impression and convincing him that was what he was supposed to do. Now it seemed that the desire was bleached from his mind. Even the voice that told him to kill when he was a child, grew silent since his release and it confused him. His desire however to wrap his lips around a woman's breast, and to engage in all-out carnal knowledge remained strong. The only thing that had changed in the temptation of that was his desire to make it forceful. Reminiscing, Shane closed the curtains, slipped on his shoes, and exited his apartment. His next shift at the Koffee House was one hour away and he always liked to get there early.

Back in Calimay, Rachel was lounging on the back deck. Her day had been pleasant and she was enjoying the serenity and peacefulness of late afternoon, much the way Blain was up at Mud Creek. The only difference was that she was in good company. Havoc was at her side. It amazed her how big he had grown in only a week. Even his soft puppy fur was turning to the wiry type his breed, Bouvier des Flandres or Bouvier for short, was known for. His size also portrayed the blood that ran through his veins. Rachel looked down at him by her feet, and smiled.

"I'm sure glad you aren't like that bitch mother of yours. She seemed a bit nasty to me. You though, are as sweet as honey from a hive."

Rachel used her foot to give him a belly rub as he lay there at her feet. She had seen both of his parents. The sire, Goliath, was magnificent in both size and demeanor. The bitch, Livina as she was called, seemed a little offish to Rachel. She was pleased Havoc wasn't showing any of those traits. He had his own personality, the star of her day.

"I can hardly wait to see what Blain is going to say about you. I hope he is okay, Havoc, I really do. I wish he'd give me a call." Rachel averted her eyes to a few birds on a telephone line as she thought about him. "I'm sure he has his reasons though."

She sighed, "I'm just being a mampy-pampy. It is partly my fault. If I hadn't gone to my mother's when I did, I would at least know where he was off to and when I could expect him back."

She looked down at Havoc again, who was now sitting and looking at her, his stubby tail scraping across the deck as he wagged it.

"I am sure glad I have you. I probably would have drunk myself into a stupor, and smashed all of his stuff by now if it wasn't for you," she reminisced as she thought about that. "Which reminds me, I probably should look around, for a lawn maintenance guy to fix all those holes you have dug in Blain's Kentucky bluegrass."

She smiled and half chuckled at the same time as she looked at the mess.

"If we leave it, he'll go completely bonkers. I would probably have to call the Calimay Mental Hospital to bring a straightjacket for him, and have him carted off," she said in fun as she stood from the chair she was sitting in. "Come on, Havoc, let's go inside and see what we can throw together for eats. I'm a little hungry and I think you want a treat."

Rachel opened the sliding glass door and they entered the house. True to his usual self, Havoc darted across the hardwood floor, slipping, and sliding. He jumped onto the couch and off the other side coming to a skidding halt at the kitchen table.

"You silly thing you," Rachel said as she made her way into the kitchen and handed him his treat. "I'm going to need a floor polisher too, if you keep that up."

With the treat in his mouth and paying no heed to Rachel, he darted out of the kitchen and jumped onto the couch again, this time lying down as he devoured the treat in a few gleeful chomps. Rachel crossed her arms and watched in delight, shaking her head at his slaphappy antics.

"You are crazy, Havoc, you really are, but I wouldn't want you any other way."

Turning she reached into the cupboard and took out a loaf of bread. Not in the mood to cook anything, she decided on the simplest thing, a ham and cheese sandwich and a glass of ice tea. Sitting at the kitchen table, she looked through a Home Makers magazine, and ate while Havoc slept on the couch. It had been a perfect afternoon.

It was near 7:00 p.m. when Blain finally found the energy to cook his and Hector's last supper they would have together up at Mud Creek. He went all out too, barbequing steaks, sausage, corn on the cob, potatoes, a tray of chicken wings and another six pork chops. He didn't do it to make the evening special. He simply cooked that much to get rid of some of the food he had bought. Anything that was cooked and left over, he would take with them as they headed back to Calimay. That way they wouldn't have to stop for food, only gas.

The rest of the food that he had brought to the cabin he would open up and dump in the bush for the bears, coyotes, or worms, whichever got to it first. The only things he would be leaving in the cabin were the furniture and kitchen utensils. Everything else needed to be disposed of, so that when he did finally return with Rachel whenever that would be, the cabin would seem brand new to both of them.

He wished now that he hadn't cut the slot in Hector's door, and wasn't sure how he would deal with that. It wasn't something he could easily hide unless, of course, he removed the door completely. *I wonder what she would say about that, seeing a food slot cut out of a door,* Blain thought with a smirk. *Ahh, I'll remove the damn thing completely and store it generator shack. We'll pick up a new door later. She'll never know.* He waved his hand through the air, *no problem.*

With all the food he cooked now slapped onto a couple of plates, Blain made his way back inside the cabin and set it all down.

"Hope you are hungry, Hector; got quite a feast going on out here," he said loud enough for Hector to hear. "I figured I best cook as much of it as I care to, since we aren't going to need it after tomorrow."

"I am. Bring it on. What the hell do you have?" Hector responded with vigor as he made his way to the door and waited.

"Sausage, chops, chicken wings, steak, corn, and potatoes. What do you want to start with?"

"Fuck, toss some of each onto my plate. I'll fucking eat it."

"I bet you will," Blain said as he filled Hector's plate.

Making his way over to the door he opened the slot and slid the plate through.

"Don't choke on it," he said as walked back to the table and filled up his own plate.

After a second helping of chicken wings, he was stuffed. Hector, on the other hand, asked for thirds.

"You got to be kidding," Blain said as he put another chop and a couple of wings onto Hector's plate. "Pace yourself, because that is all you'll be getting tonight."

"I haven't eaten like this since we made this fucking stupid trip. And if the return trip isn't going to be any different, I want to be full. You practically starved me the last time," Hector said as he took the plate from the other side of the door, like a ravished wolf.

"I should have starved you, because then I wouldn't need to listen to you or be in your presence. I could have simply buried you along the way."

"Yeah, well you had other plans, didn't you?" Hector responded with fake disposition as always, as he tried to make himself sound big and bad.

"Don't think that I don't have plans for you, Hector. Think of it this way. My plan has only changed. There is a bigger picture unfolding, trust me."

"Really, I think you are as full of shit as the day I busted into your hotel room," Hector said as he wiped his mouth free of the sauce from the chicken wing he was eating.

Blain walked away from the door shaking his head. He was done with him. Hector's bellowing as he continued to throw insults and empty threats went in one ear and out the other. Even as he wandered around outside, putting the BBQ and the shovel away, and generally tidying up so that he had fewer things to do in the morning, even then he could hear the muffled voice of Hector carrying on, wanting some kind of response. Most of the time Blain chuckled at his play on words, but he didn't give him the satisfaction of any kind of response and eventually Hector shut up, knowing that his goading was landing on deaf ears.

It was dark when he made his way back inside. Walking over to Hector's door, he slid opened the slot and peered in.

"Hey, how about handing me your plate, now that you have licked it clean."

"Why don't you come and get it?" Hector responded.

"Why all of a sudden are you being such an ass?"

"I'm testing you. I don't think you have the balls to come in here while I have it in my hand."

"It is true. You could break it into a few pieces before I got this door open. Being the stupid fuck that you are, you might try to lash out at me. I can't have that, Hector."

Blain pulled the Glock from his waistband and pointed it directly at Hector.

"So, I would suggest you bring me your plate."

"Or what?"

"You know what, Hector. I don't think you have any negotiating power here at all. You are a little man with a ceramic plate. I'm the guy with the 8mm Glock," Blain chuckled.

"I'll tell you this much. I'll get another chance or opportunity to knock you on your ass as we make our way back to Calimay. I long for that." Hector rose from his mattress and reluctantly handed his plate to Blain. "Don't think that I'm handing this to you because of fear."

"Whether it is fear or common sense makes no difference to me. I only want to do the dishes. Thank you for your plate by the way," Blain said with aggravation as he put the Glock back in his waistband.

Closing the door slot, he turned and walked away. *Boy he's stupid some times,* he thought as he began doing up the dishes, *correction, all the time. I'd rather be talking with Rob than the character of Hector. What a piece of work he is. Would never have thought anyone as educated could act so uneducated and vulgar as Hector. Oh well, I'll let him have his fun for now, tomorrow I'll let him know what I know about him.* Blain shrugged his shoulders as he finished up.

Chapter 17

It was hot outside already when he woke Friday. He didn't bother with letting Hector out, nor did he make any coffee. Instead, he went to work immediately packing the boat and disposing of the leftover foodstuff that he no longer needed since he was heading back a week early. When he was finished with those tasks, he muscled Hector out of the room, tossed him onto the floor, and tied his hands and ankles. Next he took down the door and stowed it away as he had planned. Without slowing down to take a breath, he removed the bars that he had installed in the window of Hector's one-time room. It was 9:00 a.m., when he was finally able to sit down. The whole morning, it seemed, was rushed, but he could sigh with relief that the work was done.

"We're not even going to have coffee today, Hector. I'm going to catch my breath and then we'll be off."

"I'm thrilled. What about letting me piss?"

"There are a couple of things I want to tell you before that. Firstly, your name isn't Hector Hernandez."

Hector looked at him with surprise.

"What do you mean by that? You saw my ID."

"Yeah, ID's are easy to fake, I'm sure you know all about that. Your real name, Hector is Rob Hartley. We worked together, remember?"

"What are you talking about?" Hector asked. "I'd never laid eyes on you until the day in the hotel."

"That my friend is complete bull. Tell me, what was it you were hoping to find on that day when you busted into my hotel room?"

"I, ummm, I... fuck you."

Hector was at a loss for words. Blain had figured out who he was. He wasn't sure, though, that he would admit it. His mind raced, how long had Blain known, and if he knew, how did he find out? He had done everything to conceal his real identity, even came up with a character and a name. He thought back to the time they did work together, when Trent was alive. It was true that they were friends back then, not to mention colleagues. Hector sat still as he looked into Blain's eyes and waited for him to say more.

"Look, I have a copy of your fingerprints. I recognize your face, even though it has aged, and you do look awful funny with no hair, but you are Rob Hartley. Now you can continue to be Hector, but when we make it back to Calimay, I will prove to you that you are Rob. The prints might help with that, or they might not. I know for certain, that when I drag your ass into the K.A.T. Agency, a panel of your peers will prove it. Then we'll all have to decide what it is we're going to do with you. I mean, after all, you killed seventeen people. We all know that. Or, you can come clean with me now and save us both the trouble. The only thing that has me disgruntled is why you are alive. You were supposed to have been taken out years ago. Either you and Chase Benton were in cahoots together while you killed those people or there is more to this story then the rest of us know. So, what's it going to be, Hector or Rob?"

It was at that moment Hector realized that there was no use in carrying on. He was sick of the character he was acting; he was sick of being part of the problem and not part of the solution. He was beaten at his own game, and in a sense, he was glad for that. To come clean with all that he knew and all that he did would lessen the weight of it all. For years, he had wanted to do exactly that, the only thing that stopped him were the consequences he would face for seventeen murders. He knew what happened to those proven guilty of such, but he was tired of the act and he began to come clean.

"Alright, you win. I am Rob."

Hector lowered his head as he thought about what he would say next.

"Those people that you all thought I killed in cold-blood were actually test subjects for the K-15 virus we've all been fighting. Chase and I were indeed working together. He found the subjects and I did the testing. It wasn't cold-blooded killing Blain, Ben, or Entity, whichever one it is that you want to be called."

Rob looked deep into Blain's eyes.

"We were so close to finding a cure, and when the hit on me was ordered and Chase was the man who was supposed to end it, we came up with a plan to make it seem as though the hit had been made. Right up until Chase died, we worked together on the sidelines. The subjects we used were of the criminal element, folks who committed atrocities like rape or murder. Although they were charged with their crimes, our awesome Justice system let them walk. It wasn't as though we picked people off the street. We were selective."

Rob went silent for a few minutes as he contemplated.

"Obviously then, there is, or was more to the story than we all thought. Why didn't you and Chase come forward? What was the point in keeping it from the Agency, or better yet why didn't you come to me then?" Blain was curious to know.

"Think about that, Blain. What were we supposed to say? That we were doing human testing? The Agency was against that. Not you or anyone else would have accepted that. Chase and I decided we were better off keeping it silent, but we were going to come forward if we found anything substantial. The only thing is, we never did. The test subjects usually ended up sick, but they showed no symptoms of what we knew about K-15."

"You said the two of you were getting close to finding a cure. How close exactly?" Blain asked.

"Close enough to know we were missing only a few key elements. I'm going to be honest with you, I broke into your hotel room to confront you and force you to hand over your research. I knew you didn't have any of that with you, and that you needed to get to a drop site. I was going to do to you what you did to me, take you captive, force you to the drop site and take everything that the Agency sent."

"What were you going to do with me after that?"

"The only thing I could have done," Rob averted his eyes, leaving Blain to decide what that was.

"You were going to kill me then?"

"Yes."

Blain shook his head.

"What were you going to do with your findings, if by chance you did find a cure? I'm assuming since you were going to take me out, your intent wasn't to benefit the world as a whole, more like you were going to hand it over to the highest bidder. Pharmaceutical companies could make a lot of money from a discovery like that. You would have been rich, Rob."

"Something like that, yes."

"Next, I'd like to know where you got the information on where I was, and what it was I was assigned to do. Can you tell me that, Rob? I hate to think there is someone working at the Agency who has been handing out classified information."

"No, it is nothing like that. I've been working solo since Chase passed. I managed to breach a few data files on the Agency's mainframe."

"Really? How easy was that?"

Blain needed to know so that he could contact Canbra and get the issue taken care of directly. If it was easy, then by chance it was possible it wouldn't be long before someone else breached the mainframe and Agency's security. That would not be good.

"Far from easy, unless you happen to know a few old passwords. I tapped in to the mainframe with two of the three passwords I could remember from when I was an operative. Without those passwords, trust me, the Agency's security is unsurpassable. Gonsite really knows his stuff. The only thing I can't understand is why those passwords are active after all this time. I remember the Agency was quite adamant about changing them every six months or so," Rob replied with sincerity.

"What are the passwords? You can help yourself out here by telling me."

"The passwords for the data files I accessed are: wrung7270-perso, all lowercase. That'll access personnel files. The second one is XX10-RES-NW7721, all uppercase. That will access current up to date research. What is going to happen to me, Blain?" Rob asked with concern.

"That depends. I can't let you walk away. You know too much. I can't simply kill you, because I'm no murderer. That is why I'm taking you back. You have already helped yourself out a bit by filling me in on how you managed to get classified information. That doesn't mean however that all things are peachy. You understand that, right?"

"Obviously."

"Alright. I'm going to make a call to Canbra and have those passwords changed. I won't mention that I got the information from an alive Rob Hartley, or that you are even here with me right now. We have a lot to talk about Rob, and I aim on getting all the answers as to what it is you know about K-15, what your research showed exclusively, and anything else that pops in my head. Your cooperation will be dutifully noted by me. For now, be quiet while I make the call."

Blain picked up his SAT phone and dialed the Agency's number. A couple of rings later, Canbra came on the line.

"Hello Entity."

"Canbra, listen closely. I hope you are near your computer."

"I am. What is going on, Entity?" she asked with excitement hoping it was good news.

"There is a real possibility that the Agency's mainframe or at least a couple of the data folders are accessible with an old password from years ago."

"What are you talking about?"

"Quit talking and I will tell you. I'm going to blab off a couple of passwords. I want you to tell me if they are familiar. Are you ready?"

"Yes, go ahead." Canbra responded as she got ready to punch the keys on her keyboard.

"Okay, the first one is all lowercase, wrung7270-perso." Blain waited for a response.

"That one is for personnel files," Canbra said with shock and concern. "Something has to be done about that a.s.a.p.! Next one."

"All uppercase, XX10-RES-NW7721."

"Oh my God! Where did you get this information? It looks as though we have been compromised, Entity. That one is for classified research."

"I know. Those passwords have been used forever. You know what that means? It means any one of the Agency operatives who has been discharged or retired can continue to access those files. Whoever is in charge of that hasn't changed them. I'm not sure if it was Gonsite who was supposed to be taking care of things like that or one of his lackeys. Whoever is responsible, have them correct the problem immediately. I'll have words with them when I get back."

"Where did that information come from, Entity?"

"For now it doesn't matter. Just have the problem looked into. I'll fill everyone in when I get back."

"So, then you are heading for home today?"

"Correct."

"Okay, Entity. I'll have these issues looked into. I feel partly to blame because I use the first password quite often, and probably should have had it changed, I just never thought. Anyway, I will see you when you make your way here. Bye."

"TTFN," Blain said as he hung up the phone. "There, that takes care of that problem." Blain looked over to Rob. "I need to know right now if I can trust you. I'm tired of Hector. He really pisses me off," Blain chuckled. "I'd much rather be sitting here with an old friend, so, what of it Rob? Are you ready to be my friend?"

"I feel pretty bad for what I was trying to do, Blain, and I am sorry. I don't see any reason to carry on with the charade, and I am starting to feel better than I have in years by coming clean to you. My research was never meant to discredit the Agency. When I had to kill those seventeen people, I knew that is exactly what would have happened. I've carried that around for a long time, but I do not feel remorse for those who were my test subjects. They all should have been in prison where they belonged. Not one of them was innocent. I want to make that clear. Yes, I am ready to be Rob again," Rob pointed out.

"To tell you the truth, Rob, if they're found not guilty in a court of law, then they are in the eyes of the law, not guilty, completely innocent. I know where you are coming from though, and I feel the same way as you do on the subject. That is why I brought Hector here. I honestly thought you were the man who shot me in the hallway, but it turned out that you weren't.

That is when my plan to use Hector as a human guinea pig changed. I still didn't know who exactly you were though, and I couldn't simply stick you with a syringe unless you were that man who shot me in the hallway. He too was a rapist and murderer and God knows what else. When you busted in on me, that is exactly who I thought you were. However, Hector was the man who broke my nose, but not the same man who sent me to hospital with a lead slug in my gut. We've always had a few things in common, Rob. That is one of them. If you mean what you say about being a friend again, we can work through this. You have to be honest with me and no fucking tricks."

"I am done with tricks, Blain, and I am ready to accept what is coming to me for disgracing the Agency and not following protocol."

The cabin became silent as each of them went over in their minds what the other had said. Finally, Blain stood up and untied Rob.

"I'm trusting you, Rob. I know that is what Trent would have done. I'm keeping the Glock, though. I hope you understand?"

Blain made his way back to the table and sat down, gesturing for Rob to do the same.

"Feel free, you are no longer a prisoner to me; you are a colleague and friend. There are a lot of things we need to clear up and now that you are not Hector, we can talk."

Rob stood up from the floor and sat across from Blain.

"I thought this day would never come. I have a few questions of my own."

"I imagine you do. Feel free to start asking," Blain said as he listened.

"It was you, Chase said, who authorized the hit on me. Is that true?"

"In a sense, but there were others who were in favour of it as well. You understand why we were left with no choice to do that, don't you?"

"I do. I could never put it out of my mind though, that it was you."

Again, the cabin grew silent as the two reminisced.

"I mean, I understand why, but I would have thought it would have been you that may have stood in my corner. I know that I bent every one of the Agency's protocols and did some unorthodox things, but I did it all to try and speed up the process of coming up with something concrete that we could have used to put an end to K-15. When Trent died, I honestly thought it was going to be the agency's downfall, and any research we were doing then was going to end. I approached Chase and we came up with another plan. If the Agency was going to go tits up, we wanted to be able to continue, even if we did it alone without the backing of the Agency. Finding a cure meant that much to us."

Rob sighed as he thought back to the meetings he and Chase had. Finally he continued.

"When word got out that I had gone rogue and was a vicious murderer and when Chase approached me and told me the Agency wanted me out of the picture literally, we faked the hit. From that day on, I worked on the sidelines and Chase helped whenever he could. When he died, we were both in so deep, there was no turning back, at least not for me. I kept up with the research, but gave up on live subjects for experimental testing, since it wasn't proving anything anyway. For years, I tried to make sense of K-15, but I was never getting any closer than when Chase and I were in on it together. Basically, I gave up.

Then, not even a month ago, I breached the security to personnel and research files in the Agency's database. I learned that there was a decline in K-15 carrier attacks, missing persons, etcetera. I also learned that the Agency was getting closer to a cure, and that you were being commissioned to head a research objective in that regard. I made up some fake ID, and became Hector."

"You've been busy. Let me guess. Once you figured all that out, you thought you'd be able to coerce me into giving you all the information, so that if there was a discovery to be found you'd be the man to find it."

"Pretty much, except there was a flaw. When I made my way to the hotel you were staying at in Canupe, you were already in the hospital. As you suggested the other day, I found a witness and got a description of the man who shot you, and was told he had a tattoo on his hand, so I did exactly what you said I did. I used the tattoo description that the witness gave me to have one made for my own hand. I knew when you got out of the hospital you would be in no shape to make sense out of who I was or if I was the man who shot you. The rest I adlibbed," Rob said as he took a few moments for Blain to respond.

"You did a fine job too. I was convinced you were exactly that man. I was even more convinced when you blatantly broke my nose. But, I got you back," Blain smiled. "It wasn't until I spoke with Canbra when we got to Yellow Lake and she mentioned my assailant had actually been picked up. That is when it all began to fall apart for you. At first, I thought maybe the authorities picked up the wrong person by mistake. Then, when I looked more closely at your tattoo, I could tell it was too professional to be the one that was on the hand of the man who shot me. At that point, I was convinced you weren't that guy. But I didn't know who you were yet, not until I thought about you. I don't even know why I did, but your face conjured up in my mind and all the pieces came together.

I decided then that I wouldn't say a thing though, until I brought you back to Calimay, that is, until I got so sick of Hector that I wanted him to be gone. That is when I decided I was going to tell you that I knew who you really were. I'm glad now that I did because I really hate Hector. He's an obnoxious piece of work," Blain smirked.

"I didn't like him either," Rob chuckled. "So, now that we know who, what, and why. What's next?"

"Well, no one knows you are alive except me. You have some research, the Agency has research, and Trent has research. You're a researcher, or at least someone who can make heads or tails from it. You are computer savvy. You are everything that I am not. The right thing to do, I think, is to join forces. No one has to know you are the late Rob Hartley. We could carry on with research back in Calimay, but do it for the benefit of finding a cure, not for money.

If we discover something that is beneficial, the K.A.T. Agency gets the credit and reaps any monetary gains from such. In other words, you go into deep cover and work for me," Blain suggested with sincerity. "I can't send you on your way. That would be detrimental to the Agency's cause. Besides, I'd rather have you working for us than against us. That is my conclusion." Blain leaned back in his chair. "However, I can't force you to do that. I can pick up this phone though, and have the Agency set it up so you take the fall for the deaths of seventeen people, I don't think there is a statute of limitations for mass murder. We have all the information to have that done, as you probably know. I hate to put it to you that way, Rob, but those are the only alternatives I can foresee. One or two. I'll let you decide."

"Obviously, I prefer alternative one. How are we going to pull it off, though? There are those still working for the Agency who may be able to recognize me."

"No worries. You won't be working at the Agency per se. Again, we have two options. You can work from whatever lab it is that you have already or we use my private office. I prefer the latter simply because it is easier for me."

"You would trust me enough to let me work from my lab even though you haven't a clue on where that may be?"

"Why not? Are you forgetting alternative two from the first two alternatives?" Blain asked with a smile.

Rob chuckled and shook his head. "I see where you are going with this now. Okay, so I'll work out of your office. What about all the lab equipment we need. From what I remember of your office, it doesn't have any."

"You would be right. That doesn't mean we can't get any. All the stuff I brought here could be used once it has been decommissioned from the Agency's use. All I need to do is have it signed off. I can have Canbra do that easily enough. You probably have better equipment in your lab," Blain pointed out. "Field research equipment that the Agency uses is always cheap, but it does do the job."

"My equipment is old and failing. I'd rather use the stuff you had. From what I saw of it, it is better than the equipment I have," Rob confirmed.

"There we have it then. I'll get it decommissioned. Consider it commandeered." Blain nodded. "The files, folders, and all the other stuff, like blood slides, virus slides, etcetera will have to be turned in to Gonsite. He keeps a close eye on that kind of stuff. It doesn't mean, though, that we can't make copies of the text documents that the Agency has provided before I turn it all back in. You'll basically be starting from scratch, other than the research you have already gathered on your own, and whatever it is you can decipher from Trent's research." Blain paused as he shook his head and caught a breath. "I know I couldn't figure anything out, but maybe you'll have better luck."

"Only time will tell, I suppose. I'll need to gather my research from my lab, and all other pertinent information from where I've been hiding all these years. Have you ever heard of a little place called Fruitmont?" Rob asked.

"I have. So, that is where you have been, eh?"

"Yep. I've been there for well over ten years. I have an acreage on Polarty Rd, five miles from my nearest neighbor."

"Hmmm," Blain stroked his chin. "Quite rural. Interesting. Maybe it would be better to continue with our research from there. My office isn't nearly as concealed as that. It is what, about a hundred clicks from Calimay? That could work."

"I would have no problem continuing it from there. I just wasn't sure how you would feel about it."

"I hold seventeen aces, Rob that spell out murder," Blain winked at him and smiled.

"That you do. You would trust me then?"

"I'll answer your question with a question. Do you want to go to prison or do you want to help the world recover from a virus that could ignite the beginning of the end?"

"I think you already know the answer. Whether or not you had that to hold over my head, my answer would be the same. I want to help."

Blain nodded his head in approval.

"Good. I knew you would. It is settled then. We'll replace all your old equipment with the stuff in the boat, and go from there. I don't know what you've been living on for the past decade, but I'll pay you fairly from my own pocket."

"No need to pay me, Blain. I have money put away, enough to spread out for another couple of years if needed. If after that nothing has changed, and we aren't any closer to eradicating K-15, I might then start looking to you for money," Rob smiled as he reached across the table and offered his hand in a show of sincerity.

Blain offered his as well and the two shook their hands sealing their allegiance to one another and to working together in an effort to eradicate the K-15 virus.

A new, yet old, friendship was rekindled that day at Mud Creek. The more they conversed, the more they became like the two friends and colleagues they once were. They joked about how they had broken each other's noses. They laughed about the arguments and empty threats they had made too, and generally reacquainted themselves until there was no animosity whatsoever between them. Then, with a final look around the place where their friendship was restored, Blain locked up the cabin, shut down the generator, and they headed back to Calimay.

"It is going to be nice to enjoy the return trip," Rob said as Blain fired up the boat.

"I concur. If things go well, we should be home in a few days, if we push for it."

"Push on, old friend, push on," Rob sounded off as he looked into the wind.

Chapter 18

Luck was with them and they made the distance to Winnfield by early Sunday afternoon. Blain pulled the boat up to the dock, and he and Rob stepped out. “Here is where the road trip begins. I’m just going to go inside and let the Marina know their boat is back. You’re welcome to tag along.”

“Nah, I’ll wait here. Besides, I never got to look around at how peaceful and pleasant it is the last time,” Rob smiled.

“I’ll be right back,” Blain said as he entered the Marina. “Hello,” he said as he opened the door.

There was a new guy behind the counter. Blain introduced himself as Ben Todd and that he was returning the vessel a week early.

“Was there a problem with your trip?” the man asked as he stood up and leaned on the counter.

“Not at all. It was a great trip. I don’t suppose Gord is around today?”

“Nope, only me. I’m Dave.”

“Nice to meet you, Dave. I wanted to ask Gord if you guys were interested in selling that 21 foot Stingray, Cuddy Cab that I used? I fell in love with it. It was indeed everything I expected it to be.”

“I’m not sure it is for sale. But, you could call Gord tomorrow. He’ll be here then. That is about all I can offer.”

“Alright. Anyway, the boat is back. I just have to unload it. Here are the keys.” Blain handed Dave the keys.

“I guess you have a refund coming, a week’s worth of rental to be exact. Go ahead and unload your gear and I’ll work out the refund.”

Dave turned his head and began working on Blain’s refund.

"As for the refund, can you reverse the charges onto the credit card my company used? Makes it easier for me."

"Not a problem. Will do."

"Perfect. Thanks, Dave. I'll unload and then you can have your walk through."

Dave nodded at him.

"Sounds good, Mr. Todd. Let me know when you are done."

"I will," Blain said as he exited.

He and Rob unloaded the gear from the boat onto the dock. It didn't take the two of them long. Dave walked through the boat and making sure there wasn't any new damage. Satisfied, he stepped onto the dock with Blain and Rob.

"Looks good to me. I guess that is it, then. Thanks for taking care of it. If you are interested in buying it, don't forget to call Gord. Bye for now, Mr. Todd," Dave said as he made his way back inside.

"I guess we best get this stuff loaded into the car," Blain said as he and Rob each grabbed something and walked up the ramp that led to the Marina's reserved parking. It didn't take long with both men carrying. By 1:30 p.m. they were heading out of Winnfield on their journey back to Calimay and Fruitmont.

They drove all day and through the night, switching drivers every three-hundred clicks or so, while the other slept or just sat back and relaxed. It was 2:30 a.m. on Tuesday, when they pulled over and rested. They had been driving hard for over thirty-six hours and were feeling the fatigue that came with it. For three solid hours they slept, and when they finally woke up it was early pre-dawn. Blain wanted to make the distance back to Calimay by late evening. He hoped to get there by at least 9:00-10:00 p.m. He felt good as he took over the driver's seat and Rob moved over.

"Going to drive solid until Calimay. You can stay with Rachel and me tonight and maybe we'll head to Fruitmont on Wednesday or maybe rest for a day and head out on Thursday. I'll call ahead, of course, to make sure Rachel, if she's around, knows that we'll be having a guest. I'll introduce you as one of my colleagues from work. She presumes I'm a software developer. She knows nothing about what I really do. I hope to keep it that way too."

"No problem, my lips are sealed. Shall I be Rob or Hector?" Rob smiled as he rolled down his window to let the early morning mountain air caress his face.

"For God's sake don't be Hector. I might be tempted to shoot him," Blain too smiled and shook his head as he rolled down his own window. "I'll introduce you as Rob Sharpley, if you prefer to conceal your real name. There really is no need though."

"Nah, you can use my last name. I trust you enough. If you are a software developer, what kind of software do you develop? It might be good for me to know, just in case I need to answer a question or three," Rob pointed out.

"Good point. I've always told her that I develop apps, etcetera." Blain scratched his whiskered face as he pulled out onto the highway. "I honestly don't know how I've gotten away with that little lie, since I know very little about computers."

"If it has been working for you, there is no point in changing it. Apps, it is," Rob said as he winked at him.

"True. Sometimes though I wish I could change it. I get sick of being someone I'm not. But, I also know if she knew what it was I really do, I would be single," Blain half chuckled.

"I understand that. Trust me, I understand that."

The cab of the car grew silent as they reflected on what being a K.A.T. Operative entailed: lies and deceit. The Agency and its operatives had to remain classified, and no one, not even loved ones, needed to know about its existence. For every operative, not just Blain or Rob, but everyone who had taken the Agency oath, lived double lives. It was all part of the protocol. Perhaps one day that would change. Blain was one of the luckier ones. He had a fall back plan. When he finally did step away from the Agency to pursue a new life, he would make his living from the hotel he owned in Calimay, the King Royal. He would have the freedom then to tell Rachel that he actually owned it. Until then, it would remain as another deception, like all the other deceptions in his life he had embraced since becoming a K.A.T. Operative.

They drove in silence for a distance rarely conversing as they reminisced. When they did talk, it was all trivial and nonsensical, but it kept their spirits high. They stopped at a rest area that was near a small lake at 1:00 p.m. It was their first full stop since early morning. The sun was hot and sweat formed on their brows and upper lips as they looked out across the lake at its glorified beauty. Whitecaps rolled in and gently caressed the grassy shore, as a mild breeze picked up.

"I stopped looking at all this beauty a year or so ago. Man, have I ever been missing a lot," Blain said as he sat down at one of the tables.

"Only a year? I haven't looked at it either for at least a decade. We've certainly have been missing out. What was your reason for turning all this off?" Rob asked out of curiosity, as he averted his eyes once more across the lake.

"Ah, it was all part of an assault campaign."

He tried not to answer more, but found it hard not to continue. Maybe it was due to the fact that he was finally able to talk about it, although it seemed odd that he was talking about it with Rob.

"I was sent into a hot spot. There hadn't been many attacks in this particular area, but we did have good information on a carrier's whereabouts."

Blain paused as he remembered in more detail.

"There was a problem though. One carrier turned out to be actually five carriers. I don't know to this day how that information was ever missed or if the way it was relayed to me was perceived wrong. It turned out the five carriers all belonged to one family. I wiped them out because that is what we do, but I tell you, I've never killed that many in one outing. I guess that is when I stopped looking around, you know, at the real things in life, the things that mean something, like this lake," Blain finished there as he looked on.

"Our experiences certainly differ. I quit looking around when the Agency thought of me as a murderer. I feel no remorse for those seventeen, but I have often thought about the carriers I have killed also. We have to remember though, if we hadn't killed any of the carriers, the world wouldn't be as it is now. Fourteen plus years of free running carriers would have sent the K-15 virus on a rampant spree no less deadly than the plague. Think about that. At least the Agency has been able to slow it down. There is no reason to feel bad about that, Blain," Rob was quick to point out.

"I suppose not, but in fourteen years we haven't even began to scrape the surface of what K-15 actually is, how to slow it down medically, or find a cure or antidote. I wonder if we ever will. Even now, I am certain it is as viral as it was at the beginning. Every time I turn around, I am faced with more questions; in fact, we all are. For instance, as you mentioned, when you were breaching the Agency's security you noted that the killings had slowed down. Although they have, we aren't sure why.

We don't know if it is because it has gone airborne, which is the worst case scenario, or, if it has turned into an STD. Could you imagine that? What would the symptoms be? You know, would they be different and would body parts simply start falling off or would one simply die from unknown causes. It is frustrating as Hell," Blain said as he looked to the horizon.

"Our research is meant to figure that out. There has to be an answer, Blain. Once we get looking at all the information we both have, I'm betting it will then only be a matter of time, maybe only months. There has to be something we can learn from all the research and information. No use in letting it eat at you. No pun intended," Rob teased. "I say we leave it at that and wait and see."

"Yeah, I concur. Anyway, we should head out again, no use wasting our time worrying here. We can worry while we drive," Blain chuckled, "Come on, let's go."

"You okay to drive or should we switch?" Rob asked as they made their way back to the car.

"Nah, I'm fine. We're only about four hours away," Blain responded as he opened the driver side door and slipped in. "I feel better now that we took in some fresh air and rested a while."

"It was definitely a well-deserved break," Rob agreed as Blain turned the car back onto the highway for the second time that day.

Friendly chatter ensued. As time went by, they grew silent and talked sporadically. It was a nice drive, and Rob was glad to be seeing it and not tied up in the trunk, being bounced around like the spare tire. Four hours later, they pulled in to a gas station in Canupe, filled up with gas, bought a few snacks, and switched drivers. They were going to make it to Calimay in four days as Blain hoped.

An hour outside of Calimay he put his call into Rachel. It had been a few weeks since they had spoken, and to hear her voice on the other end as she picked up the phone, made his heart skip a beat. He had thought for sure that she wouldn't be home yet.

"Rachel?" he asked as he heard her sit down.

"Oh my God! Blain! I have missed you. Please tell me you are on your way home."

"I am, hon. I'm bringing a colleague with me. I hope you don't mind. He needs to spend the night. He missed his flight, so I offered to let him crash at our place."

"I don't care who you bring with you, I'm just so glad you are on your way home. I have a surprise for you too."

"I hope it isn't divorce papers," Blain half chuckled.

"No, no, not at all. I changed my mind about that for now," she teased. "My surprise is better than that."

"What is it?"

"You'll have to wait until you get home. I'll set out fresh linen for your friend. Shall I make some coffee?"

"We won't be pulling into the driveway for at least another hour. So, maybe you just want to go to bed," he hinted. "I'll introduce you to Rob in the morning."

"I'll set the coffee pot up so all you'll have to do is turn it on, if you guys decide you want some. How does that sound?"

"That sounds great, Rachel. Thank you very much. I'll see you when I get there."

"You know where I'll be, Blain, so don't be too long. I love you," she said with sincerity and glee.

"I love you too. Bye for now, hon." Blain turned off his phone. "It is settled. No problem with you staying at our place, Rob. You won't get a chance to meet Rachel until tomorrow, unless she stays awake and waits for us."

"That suits me. I'd rather be cleaned up before I meet your wife, anyway. Which reminds me, I don't suppose there is a mall open at this time of night in Calimay? I wouldn't mind picking up some clothes." Rob replied.

"No worries, we'll wash those duds tonight and you are quite welcome to use the shower. You'll have clean clothes for tomorrow. We can head over to Walmart for something in the morning."

"Yeah, I guess so. I need only a few things. Okay, no problem. Question though, do you seriously shop at Walmart?"

"For sure I do. Nothing wrong with Walmart," Blain smiled.

"Fruitmont doesn't have one. I usually buy my stuff from a Hardware/Clothing store unless, of course, I'm in the city," Rob chuckled. "I guess Walmart isn't much different."

"Nope, pretty much has everything one could need."

They drove in silence, as the evening grew darker. At 10:30 p.m. they pulled into Blain's driveway. Rachel immediately looked out the bedroom window. Relieved that indeed it was Blain, she closed the curtain and dimmed the light as she waited to be in his arms.

"Nice house you have. Wow. Looks like a castle," Rob teased as they stepped out of the car.

Blain only took a few steps when he heard a dog barking.

"That is weird, we don't own a dog."

It was then it dawned on him that the dog was the surprise Rachel was obviously talking about. He could tell it was upstairs and he hoped it was locked in a room. It barked a few more times and then Blain heard Rachel's voice telling it to be quiet, which meant she was waiting for him. It excited him as he thought about it.

"Sounds like you do now," Rob said as Blain unlocked the door.

"Yep, I'd say so."

Flicking on the kitchen light the two removed their footwear and entered. Blain gestured for Rob to sit down.

"Want a coffee, Rob?"

"Thanks, Blain. I would drink a coffee," Rob said as he looked around. "Indeed, nice place you have here."

"Rachel and I designed it ourselves, or should I say, Rachel did," Blain commented as he turned the coffee pot on.

"She is an architect then?" Rob asked.

"Not by trade, more like by blood. Her father was one of the best. I guess she learned from him. It's like a natural instinct for her. I couldn't have drawn up the plans myself." Blain poured each of them a coffee. "Here, grab your cup and I'll show you around."

"Sure," Rob said with enthusiasm as he stood from the table and followed Blain.

Blain gave him the grand tour of the main floor, and showed him where his room for the night would be. He showed him the bathroom and laundry room offering him the use of each. Then they sat down in the living room and talked a bit longer while they finished their coffee.

"I hate to be a stickler, Blain, but I wouldn't mind getting on with a shower and washing up these clothes."

"Yeah, okay, Rob. Help yourself to whatever you need. I think I'll have a quick shower and shave myself in the upstairs bathroom. There are towels and things in the linen closet, so have at her. I'll talk to you in the morning, Rob."

"Looking forward to it, Blain. I'll see you then."

Rob made his way into the bathroom, and turned on the shower. Blain stood from his chair, took their cups back into the kitchen, and set them in the sink. Then he went upstairs to the shower himself, and to the waiting arms of Rachel. She noticed right away the fresh scar that marred his stomach. She hadn't noticed the one in his back yet, but she would.

"What happened there, Blain? My God, are you okay?" Rachel asked as she rose from the bed in shock.

"It is okay, Rachel. Settle down. It's nothing to worry about. I was in a bit of an accident a couple of days after you left to go to your mother's," Blain stated as he tried to come up with more on the subject, or better yet, a way to explain it. He really hadn't thought about it until then.

"I imagine it was an accident, but what happened?" Rachel repeated with concern.

It was the sound of her voice that made him contemplate telling her the truth. In fact, the only way he'd be able to explain the wound would be to tell her that he had been shot. There was no other way to explain it. He would of course have to fill in the lines with half-truths; that much he knew.

He simply started making up the story in his head as quickly as his mouth said the words.

"I tried to prevent a tiff a couple were having at the airport. I guess I said something I shouldn't have and the next thing I knew, the guy pulled out a gun and fired a shot. Then the two ran like Hell. I never saw them again and woke up a few days later in the hospital."

Rachel listened in complete and utter alarm.

"You were fucking shot! Oh my God, Blain why didn't you call. I, I, can't believe this; and you tell it like it means nothing. Are you crazy Blain?"

"Umm, I guess you don't want to see the exit wound?" he asked meekly as he turned his back to her.

If he was going to get it, he might as well get it all at once. Rachel's eyes grew big. She felt as though she was going to pass out. She braced herself against their bathroom door to keep from falling over. She couldn't believe what she was seeing or for that matter hearing. Blain had been shot and the bullet had ripped right through him. She couldn't fathom it and she turned and darted into the bathroom. Blain followed close behind and comforted her.

"It is okay, Rachel. Trust me, I didn't feel a thing," he cooed as he wrapped her up in his arms.

It was the wrong thing to say, obviously.

"Jesus, Blain," she began as she beat upon his chest. "What if I lost you? What if you died and I didn't know where the Hell you were? Good God, Blain, I would be a total mess, more than I am now."

She began to sob, as Blain comforted her.

"Come on Rachel, I'm here now and I am alive. I'll keep my nose out of other people's business from now on, I promise."

Rachel looked into his eyes, her face tear streaked.

"You promise?"

"I do. I promise, Rachel."

A few minutes later, they made their way back into bed and picked up where they left off. It was the most erogenous love making they had enjoyed in what seemed like forever. Sweating bullets and breathing hard they fell into sexual bliss as they cooed each other.

"That was magnificent. God I have missed you, Blain."

"I have missed you too, Rachel, more than you will ever know."

He squeezed her close and smiled.

"Now, I know I heard a dog. Where is he?" Blain asked as he smirked at her.

"Oh, yeah, Havoc. I almost forgot all about him. He seems to have taken a shining to the spare room. I'll go get him."

Rachel began to pull the covers off but Blain stopped her.

"Nah, I'll meet the dog tomorrow. Tell me, what kind of name is Havoc? And what kind of dog are we talking about here?"

"He's the sweetest thing, Blain. You are going to love him. He's a Bouvier."

"A Bouvier?" he questioned.

"Yep, a purebred too."

She smiled as she kissed him.

"He's going to be big, isn't he?"

"I sure hope so. That is why I bought him?"

"Bought?" Blain questioned as he raised an eyebrow and smiled.

"Yes. He will be well worth the six hundred and fifty dollars we spent."

Rachel looked deep into Blain's eyes.

"Since you don't want to meet him until tomorrow, the horse's nose is still wet and longing for you," she said as she reached down and slowly brought his manhood to life. "I've never made love to a man with bullet wounds before," she teased.

They made love for the second time that evening and finally they fell into each other's arms exhausted and spent. There was nothing in the world that could have separated their embrace, nothing that is, except the lonely howl of Havoc in the next room.

"I don't think Havoc wants to wait until tomorrow to meet you," Rachel commented as she ran her fingers up and down Blain's chest. "Should I get him?"

Blain looked at her and shook his head.

"No, I don't want to let you go. The dog can wait."

"Tell me, where have you been?" Rachel asked as she curled up closer to his warmth.

"I was sent to Montreal again. The trip was good, except of course when I was shot," he subtly joked as Rachel pinched his nipple at that comment.

"Ouch, geez. Anyway, we made some decent sales pitches and have brought a couple more computer gurus in on our latest software. But enough of that. How was your trip to your mother's? I hope she is well."

"You know mother; she is doing great. Has her garden, and that great big house all to herself. I think she should take in boarders. I mean really, she has five spare rooms. Either she should get boarders or a house nanny, someone to help her out and keep her from being lonely. I was going to mention that to her, but this last trip wasn't a good time for me to approach the issue. I was too busy fretting and wondering about us."

She looked into his eyes.

"I almost did file divorce papers, Blain. You do know that, right?"

"Yeah, I know and I'm sorry you ever felt that way. I don't want a divorce, Rachel, but I can't walk away from my work either." Blain sighed as he looked up to the ceiling.

"I know. I realized that when I was at mother's. We took vows, Blain, and those vows mean something to me. How about you, do they mean anything to you?"

"Of course they do. I wouldn't have said them when I slipped that ring on your finger if they meant nothing to me."

The two of them grew silent as they thought about their lives together.

"I admit that I haven't been as cordial to you as I should be. This past year has really been a downer for me and I don't know why," he lied as he averted his eyes to her.

"I do. You've been spending too much time on business trips. That will take its toll on anybody, I'm sure. When was the last time you had any time off. I bet you don't even know?"

"You're right, I don't know when it was that I had time off last. Keeping the software company satisfied isn't an easy task. It is quite demanding." Blain paused for a moment. "I'll see about taking some time off here in the next month or so. I can't right now because we are close to closing a million dollar plus deal. If I push and make the deal, and it doesn't go sour on us, the company will owe me time off then," Blain fibbed.

"There is hope then, that'll you get some time off?" Rachel asked with sincerity.

"I think so, yep."

"That's better, I guess, than no hope. Oh, geez, look at the time, Blain, we should go to sleep." Rachel yawned. "You must be tired." she said as she closed her eyes.

"I am, but talking with you has woken me up, in more ways than one. I'm glad you are here with me right now, Rachel."

Blain kissed her head as he twirled some of her hair through his fingers. It didn't take long before she was sleeping. Blain kept his arm around her as he reminisced. One day he would have to come clean with her. One day he would have to explain away all the lies he had told. One day their lives would be normal.

Chapter 19

Blain woke an hour before either Rachel or Rob. He let both of them sleep as he freshened up and got a pot of coffee going. The whining and whimpering of the puppy upstairs brought Blain to the door. He slowly opened it, not sure what it was he was going to find. There sitting on the floor looking up at him was Havoc, with a look on his face of 'who are you'.

The mattress from the spare bed was torn up, looking like a piece of paper that had gone through a shredder. Blain's mouth dropped open as he looked around at all the stuffing that scattered the room.

"You did all this?"

Blain stepped inside the room closing the door to keep the monster in as he glanced around aghast, at what he was seeing.

"Holy crap! Looks like you even tried, to dig your way through the wall. And, Rachel said I was going to like you. This, my friend, isn't a very good introduction."

He shook his head as Havoc sniffed at him. His scent was familiar because it was all through the house. Havoc, satisfied that Blain belonged there, jumped onto the torn mattress wagging his stubby tail, trying to prove how cute he really was. He playfully growled at him and buried his head in the mess of sheets and covers as he watched Blain.

"Hmmm, I see now why Rachel named you Havoc. Maybe she should have named you Fred or something."

He scratched his face in annoyance at the disastrous mess the room was in.

"So, Havoc, how do you expect to pay for all this?" Blain teased as he looked at the dog, sitting there all innocent, as though tearing up the room was his rebellious way for them not answering his call the night before.

Havoc's charm, was working for him. Blain was slowly coming around, especially when he looked at Havoc who was looking back at him, tilting his head from side to side as though in confusion. But if Blain could understand him, Havoc would have been saying, 'wait until you see your Kentucky Bluegrass.' Blain crossed his arms, as he looked on.

"Well, anyway, I'm Blain."

He stepped closer and patted Havoc.

"Rachel says you're going to be worth the six hundred and fifty bucks we spent for you. When I look around here, you've already cost me, with a new mattress, some drywall repairs, some new sheets, blankets, and pillows, in my humble estimation at least triple of what we paid for you. You're going to spend a long time paying off this debt, Havoc. For now, I'm betting you need to go outside. The only thing I don't see on the floor is the mess I would have rather seen. I guess that is one plus for you. Come on, I'll take you out."

Blain opened the door and Havoc darted past him, down the stairs and directly to the back glass door. Blain. close behind, opened it and let him out. Then, as he turned to walk to the kitchen, from the corner of his eye he caught a glimpse of something. Turning quickly, he looked out onto the backyard. All he saw at first were mounds of dirt. Then the pain of what he was seeing became clear as he opened the door and stepped out onto the back deck. His Kentucky bluegrass lawn was in disarray. A dozen holes took up his view; each one looked to be bigger than the other. Not one hole was in Rachel's flower garden.

Blain's mouth dropped opened for the second time that morning.

"You got to be kidding me," he muttered to himself as he walked over to the first hole. "Havoc, come here!" he demanded of the dog, which surprisingly came to him and sat down. "I am assuming you did this," Blain started as Havoc, now realizing the reason why Blain had called him, lay down and rolled over onto his back, looking at his caller upside down.

Looking around, Blain shook his head.

"You know what you have done here?" he asked as though Havoc would answer. "You've dug up my pristine lawn. I can't have that, Havoc, no sir. This lawn cost an arm and a leg, not to mention the hours and hours I've spent keeping it up. Man, you are into me for a lot now."

Blain rose and made his way back to the deck and sat down. His mind rattled out all the work ahead of him to correct the mess his lawn was in. *Rachel said I'd love this damn dog,* he thought as he reminisced. Havoc, now done with his morning routine, pranced up the stairs and sat next to Blain.

"You know what I think. I think you have some behavioral problems. You don't just rip up a man's lawn, and you most certainly don't try to break down or dig through a man's castle wall. Nor do you rip up mattresses, blankets, sheets, and pillows." He averted his eyes again out across his mangled lawn. "But what really gets me is that you chose my lawn as opposed to the damn shrubs and flower beds. That, my friend, isn't normal."

Havoc just looked on at him as though to say, 'I get it. Now, what about my morning treat? Rachel always gets me a morning treat. So, what of it bud?'

"Maybe you should go to reform school." Blain looked at him and smiled. "I have to admit you do kind of grow on a person."

He stood up and made his way back inside. He barely had the door open when Havoc once again darted past him and slid across the floor, then jumped onto the couch and off the other side, sliding across the floor and coming to a stop near the kitchen table. This was Havoc's normal entrance. Blain was shocked. It was humorous and costly all at the same time. Looking closer to the hardwood floor with daylight now shining through the big glass windows, he could plainly see that Havoc had been doing that for a while. There were a few big gouges and a few simple scratches, but all in all it would cost money to be fixed. Things were certainly going to have to change.

Finally, he made his way into the kitchen and poured a coffee. Havoc sat patiently as he waited for his morning treat; however, Blain had no idea that is what he was waiting for. It was Havoc's glaring stare and the fact that he hadn't moved, that Blain realized he was missing something.

"Umm, what is it? What, ah, what am I missing, Havoc?" Blain asked as he looked around, finally eyeing the bag of dog treats. "Hmm, is this what you are waiting for?" He reached over and grabbed the bag. "I bet it is eh? I'm not so sure you deserve one though." Blain teased as Havoc tilted his head and wagged his tail. Blain chuckled as he reached inside and pulled out a treat. "Alright here you go," he said as he tossed it to him. Havoc caught it in mid-flight and darted to the couch.

"What? You eat that on there?" Blain asked with shock. "I don't know about that, Havoc. Geez, some things certainly have to change."

He took a swig of his coffee and looked on as Havoc curled up and went to sleep. Blain only shook his head and smiled. *I kind of do like him,* he thought as he finished his first coffee of the day. He was halfway through his second cup when Rob made his way into the kitchen and sat with him.

"How did you sleep, Rob?'

"Better than I have in weeks," Rob smiled. "It was odd to sleep without having ties around my ankles and wrists."

"You'll never have to go through that again, at least not by my hand."

Blain poured him a coffee and handed it to him.

"Thanks, Blain. So, where is this wife of yours?" he asked with anticipation. "I can't wait to meet her. Anyone who can put up with you, must be a helluva woman." Rob teased as he chuckled and took a drink of his coffee.

"I imagine she'll be along soon. It is almost 9:00 a.m. Usually she gets up around this time. She's going to be in a huff when she sees how much the little bugger of a dog destroyed one bed and a bunch of linens. Nice dog and all, but I think he has abnormal tendencies."

"What kind of a dog is it?"

"A Bouvier. He's sleeping right now on the couch," Blain pointed. "He's been crashed out there for almost an hour, hasn't moved."

Rob looked toward the couch.

"Not very old is he?"

"I don't know. A couple of months, maybe three," Blain shrugged his shoulders as he took a sip of his coffee. "He made a mess of my lawn too. I couldn't believe it this morning when I looked outside. He's dug a dozen or so holes, each one bigger than the other." Blain chuckled. "Quite tragic, I'd say. It is going to take some time to fix up. Oh well, he's a puppy and I guess that is his natural instinct. Only wish he had taken his frustration out on the shrubs, and not my lawn. He even tried to dig his way through an upstairs bedroom, can you believe that?"

"Rambunctious little fellow. Bouvier's grow big. Enjoy his puppyhood, Blain. When he's full grown he's going to be a brute with attitude."

Rob brought his cup to his lips, when all of a sudden a shriek of anger came from upstairs. Both Rob and Blain looked at each other their eyes big.

"I think Rachel has discovered the mess in that room I was telling you about," Blain smiled. "She sounds madder than I was."

"HAVOC! Come here right now!" Rachel yelled.

Havoc sat at attention and looked upstairs, then into the kitchen. When he noticed another person sitting with Blain, he jumped off the couch and came running in, barking and growling until Rob let him sniff his hand. Knowing now that the new man sitting with Blain wasn't a threat, he crawled underneath the table and lay down. Again, Rachel called his name, but Havoc wasn't budging. Blain and Rob started to laugh.

"Havoc! I don't want to have to come down there and get you. March your four little paws up here right now," Rachel yelled a second time.

Blain kicked him from underneath the table.

"Go on, listen to Rachel I think she wants to have words with you."

It took some time, but finally Havoc marched off to answer Rachel's call. He lowered his head as he marched on, like a soldier going into war. He knew exactly what it was he had done and maybe if he put on his cute side, Rachel wouldn't have the heart to scold him too badly.

"What have you done here, Havoc?" Rachel scolded as he climbed the stairs to meet her. She was pointing at the bedroom and shaking her head. "You've destroyed my mattress, some sheets, and blankets, some fucking pillows even. What is the matter with you?" she asked as he approached the top stair.

His big droopy eyes and stubby tail were expressing an apology that only a puppy could ever offer and as he grew closer, Rachel let her scolding guard down and crouched to be closer to his level.

"You know you were bad, don't you, my lil' Havoc Shmavoc."

Rachel looked into his eyes and all anger dissipated due to his cuteness.

"You can't do things like that and not expect to get into trouble. No more bad stuff, okay."

She tickled his chin and then kissed him on top of his head.

"I'll forgive you this time, or should I say, I'll forgive you again." Rachel smiled as she stood up and made her way into the bathroom to shower and freshen up.

After a coffee and an introduction to their houseguest Rob, she would think about cleaning the mess up.

Havoc, knowing that he had come very close to receiving a scolding as never before, lay down on the upstairs foyer floor at the top of the stairs and patiently waited for Rachel. For thirty minutes he didn't move. He knew his place. He was Rachel's protector and she was his provider. He liked Blain too, but not as much as he liked Rachel. Finally, Rachel opened the door and stepped out.

"Good boy, Havoc, I am so glad you waited for me. Have you met Rob yet?" she asked as she bent down and petted him.

Havoc, wagged his tail and sat up.

"Alright, let's go, come on Havoc."

Rachel and Havoc made their way into the kitchen where Blain and Rob were seated.

"Good morning, you two."

She stepped toward Rob and reached out her hand.

"Hi, I am Rachel and you must be Rob?"

Havoc sat beside her feet and looked on.

Rob pushed his chair out and standing to show his respect shook her hand.

"Yes. I am Rob. Very nice to meet you Rachel."

Rob nodded his head. He was awestruck by her beauty. She had beautiful eyes and cherry lips, the kind that every man wanted to nibble. He stood still as he stared at her. Rachel, noting this, smiled and looked over to Blain who was smiling back.

"My pleasure too, Rob. Go on, go ahead and sit down. I'll join you boys with a coffee."

She turned and poured a cup as Rob sat down.

"How long have you known Blain, Rob?" she asked as she added her condiments with her back turned to both of them.

Rob looked over to Blain and Blain shrugged his shoulders gesturing for him to go ahead and adlib.

"Ah, I guess about five years."

He looked over to Blain for assurance and Blain nodded for him to carry on.

"We umm worked together on one of the Apps for weather when we first met. We run into each other every now and again at seminars and the like. I work out of the main office in Sherwild, Montana."

"You're from the States?" Rachel asked as she sat down.

"Yeah, well, I work there for a few months a year. I am actually a Canadian and live in Fruitmont."

"That is a pretty place, Fruitmont, not far from here. How come I'm only meeting Rob now, Blain?" she asked as she looked at him and brought her cup to her lips.

"I found out only on this last trip to Montreal that he lived near us. I always thought he was an American," Blain smiled.

"That is true," Rob stated, "in fact he always teased me about that. When I missed my flight back to Montana, we ran into each other at the Canupe International. The next flight to Montana was hours away, and since I was heading back home after that flight anyways, Blain offered to drive me back to Fruitmont," Rob responded as he took a drink of his own coffee.

"It was late though, and we decided to come here," Blain added.

"I hope you enjoy your stay with us, Rob. I don't imagine the two of you will be heading to Fruitmont today after driving all that way last night from Canupe."

"I don't know," Blain shrugged his shoulders. "Neither one of us is expected back in the office until Monday, unless, of course, something comes up. It is up to Rob."

"To be honest, I wouldn't mind getting home today. I have a ton of crap to do."

"No problem, Rob. I don't mind driving you back today, but you are welcome to stay."

"Thanks for that Blain, and I likely would if I didn't have so much to do."

"Well, if the two of you decide to go, make sure you let me know, Blain. I have a few things I need to do. Havoc really made a mess of that room, didn't he?" she chuckled, "I can't believe he did all that. He must have been leery of the two new people in his house."

"What about my lawn. Now, that is a travesty," Blain responded as he shook his head. "Not to mention, of course, the hardwood flooring in the living room. He's already cost us more than what you paid."

They all started to laugh as Havoc looked up at them and rolled over onto his back as if to say, 'I'm not all that bad'.

For the better part of the morning, the three sat and conversed as they swilled back a pot of coffee.

It was Rachel who took the first step in getting motivated.

"I have to tell you guys," she began as she rose from the table, "that it has been fun talking and listening to you both, but I have a big mess upstairs to clean, and then I have to go to town for a bit. So, until I see you fellows later, have a good day boys."

She set her cup in the sink and pranced off upstairs to the mess Havoc left for her. Of course, Havoc trotted alongside and lay outside the bedroom door as she put things back in order.

Blain and Rob now ventured outside and were sitting on the back deck as the late morning sun cast shadows from the trees and buildings that surrounded Blain and Rachel's home.

"Blain!" Rachel yelled from an upstairs window.

Blain looked up to her and acknowledged he had heard her.

"Do you think you and Rob can take this ruined mattress down to the garage?"

"Sure," Blain replied as he and Rob made their way upstairs.

A few minutes later after struggling with the damn thing they managed to stand it upright against a sidewall.

Rob's mouth dropped when he saw Rachel's car.

"Wow, that there is a beautiful ride. It's a 1967 BMW 2000CS Coupe. Love the color too, midnight blue. Is this yours?"

"No chance. That is Rachel's car. It is indeed nice. Her father rebuilt it while she grew up. Every part is an original stock part. Took him many years to rebuild, so I have been told. It does have a few engine quirks, but nothing worth concern. Would you like to go for a ride? I can see if she'll let us."

"I would never turn down a ride in one of these. That would be great, if she doesn't mind."

"Nah, she lets me drive it every now and again. I'll ask. Hang on."

Blain made his way back inside the house and upstairs to the room she was cleaning.

"Psst, hey, Rachel," Blain said from the door as he watched her cleaning.

God, she looked good. For a few minutes, he stared at her, and every one of her luscious curves.

"Hey, Rachel," he said a bit louder this time.

Rachel turned her head and looked at him in surprise.

"Jesus, Blain you startled me. Are you and Rob leaving?" she asked thinking that was the reason he was standing there.

"No, I wanted to see if you didn't mind me taking him for a ride in your car. He loves it. Seems to know a bit about BMW's as well. What do you say?" Blain pleaded, with that cocky smile of his.

"I don't know. You aren't going to go rat racing are you?"

"No, not at all. I'd never do that to your car."

"Yeah, right. I guess so. Go ahead, my dear," she jostled him. "But, don't come back if you scratch it."

"Thank you. I'll be careful."

As quickly as he said that, he was down the stairs like an excited kid. Grabbing her key from the key plaque next to the garage door, he opened it and stepped in.

"Let's go," he said as he held up the keys a big smile across his face.

"Excellent!" Rob said as they opened their doors and sat down.

Blain pressed the automatic garage door remote and waited a few seconds. Putting the key in the ignition, he fired up the sporty little car. He backed out with caution, but once on the street, all caution was lost in the wind as he squealed the tires in every gear as he raced away. Rachel heard every shift and squeal as she looked out the window and shook her head. She would indeed be having words with him.

"She sure has good pick up speed. Nice." Rob started bobbing his head grinning from ear to ear.

Blain too was smiling. They were like two kids with new pedal bikes as they raced around the back streets of Calimay. Rachel's car didn't wheeze once. It was as though it knew every curve and it clung to the pavement with every turn. Blain pulled into an empty parking lot and slowed to a crawl, then with a burst of speed began burning doughnuts, smoke bellowed into the air as the squealing tires echoed in the silence pre-noon. Blain and Rob, both laughing hard, soon lost their smiles when the police shut them down.

"Awe shit! The cops. Fuck," Blain said as he slowed down and shut the car off waiting for the officer to approach.

"Good morning, Blain," the officer started. "Blowing off a little steam this afternoon?" he asked as he looked at the rubber marks. "It looks as though you've been having some fun." He scratched the side of his face. "I can't believe Rachel allowed you to take her baby out."

"I ah, well, I yeah, I guess I wasn't thinking, John. The parking lot is empty though," Blain commented as he tried to make an excuse.

"I see that. The streets aren't though. We got a complaint about a car that fits the description of this beauty, racing around. That wouldn't have been you, would it?"

John already knew the answer.

"Never. I'd never do a thing like that, John. You know me better than that."

John started to chuckle.

"I honestly don't think there are many cars in Calimay that look like Rachel's. I'm pretty sure about that. It must have been you."

John started writing out a ticket.

"You have your license handy, Blain? You might as well hand it over to me, as well as the insurance and registration."

"Come on, John, give me a break?" Blain said as he reached into the glove box for Rachel's papers. "Here are these," he handed them to John as he fished out his license, "and here is my license."

"Thank you, Blain. I'll just be a minute," John said as he made his way back to his squad car.

"Rachel is going to lose it after this," Blain half chuckled. "Oh well, I was having a blast. That was fun wasn't it?"

"For sure. I'm only glad it is you being busted and not me."

Rob began to laugh.

"These BMW's raced the circuit back in the seventies. They were built for speed, and this one doesn't lack any of that. You could probably burn the tires right off. Oh, look, here comes your friend," Rob smiled as he averted his eyes.

"Here you go Blain."

John handed him the ticket.

"It is a stunting fine. You have thirty days to pay it or to go to court and dispute it."

"Shit, John, you must've filled it out wrong. The fine is for three hundred and eight bucks. That can't be right... can it?"

"It sure is. That is the going rate, Blain," John chuckled, "if I got you for speeding too, it would be at least twice that. Have a good day, Blain, and no more stunting, alright?" John said as he tapped the roof of the car.

"Yeah, no problem, John, thanks for ruining my day," Blain razzed as he smiled.

John stepped away and headed back to his squad car.

"I guess our fun is done. What do you say, Rob? Want to go for a coffee down by the beach?"

"Sure. I didn't know Calimay had a beach."

"It isn't much of a beach, but there is a good little coffee shop near it."

Blain turned the car on and headed out of the parking lot toward the Calimay public beach. The small lake was man-made but it served its purpose when the weather was at its hottest. The coffee shop was a franchise of the 'Koffee House' that was also in New Kootenay. It wasn't a big place, but the coffee was always fresh and hot. They served other things too, like smoothies, iced teas and coffees, pop, and doughnuts. Blain drove the speed limit not wanting to receive another ticket. It was a short drive but relaxing.

"There it is, the Calimay 'Koffee House'. Doesn't look like much does it?" Blain questioned as the found a parking spot.

"Looks okay to me. I can already smell the coffee. That's always a good sign when you can smell the food and stuff before you get inside," Rob responded as they walked the short distance.

When they were sitting down at a table facing the lake, Dawn, one of the waitresses who knew Blain approached. She was a sweet looking woman, not too tall, not too short, not too big, and not too small. Her shoulder length hair was flaxen, her eyes were smoky blue. She had a smile that was as beautiful as the face it was on. There was nothing about Dawn that was ugly.

"Good to see you, Blain. We haven't seen you in a while, and you have the little ladies car, too," Dawn smiled. "The usual Blain?"

"Yeah, thanks Dawn. What about you, Rob? You want a regular or one of those fancy types of coffee?"

Rob looked up to Dawn.

"I'll have a regular coffee, black, please."

"Sure. Okay. I'll be back shortly," she said as she pranced away.

"I'll give Calimay this much. There sure are a lot of nice women living here," Rob said as he looked toward Dawn.

"How old do you figure she is?"

"Dawn?" Blain asked. "I imagine she's at least in her early forties. Doesn't look it though, does she," Blain commented.

"Not at all. I was thinking late twenties, early thirties. She sure is nice, wow. Forty eh, isn't that something? She could eat crackers in my bed anytime," Rob said with a smile as she returned with their coffee.

"Here you go, guys." She set the cups down, and true to her persona, she struck up a conversation with them both.

"So, what's new, Blain? How is Rachel? We haven't seen you two in a while."

"I just got back from Montreal again, and Rachel was at her mother's for a week or so. Excuse me for being rude," Blain stated as he looked over to Rob. "This is Rob, by the way. He's, a colleague of mine. Rob, this is Dawn, she's a friend of Rachel's," he said as he took a sip of his coffee and watched where the introduction went from there.

“Nice to meet you, Rob,” Dawn said as she stuck out her hand to shake his.

“Nice to meet you too, Dawn.”

Rob shook her hand.

“So, you work with our Blainer, eh?” That was Blain’s nickname that some of his friends used. “That must get tiring sometimes,” she teased.

“Well, you know Blainer. It is better to work with him than to have him as a boss,” Rob answered with a smile.

“Is that what they say?” Dawn asked. “I always knew he was nasty.”

“Come on, I’m not nasty,” Blain responded as he looked at her. “You’re the one that is nasty,” he teased.

“You’ll never know, Mr. Blainer,” she flirted. “Anyway guys, I should be getting back at it. The day has only started. If you want anything else, holler. It was nice meeting you, Rob. Maybe I’ll see you again at one of Blain and Rachel’s lawn parties. You’ll never forget one of those,” she chuckled.

“Maybe,” Rob replied. “It was nice meeting you too, Dawn.” She waved at them as she strutted back to the floor and started taking orders.

“Lawn parties?” Rob asked as he took a drink from the cup in his hand.

“Yeah, Rachel puts together these little lawn parties every now and again. They are fun sometimes, and other times not so. I’m really not much of a partying type fellow. I do let loose once in a while though. That is when those parties are fun,” Blain smirked.

“If you ever have one and Dawn is coming, don’t forget about Rob,” Rob replied as the two of them chuckled, “or I might have to send our old friend Hector around.”

"No, never. I'd shoot him. That damn guy got under my nails. I hope and pray that I never run into somebody like that for real. I'm still trying to fathom how you were able to live in the shell of that thing," Blain chuckled and shook his head. "Yep, he was something else." He raised his coffee cup in the air offering a toast. "Rest in Peace, Hector," he said as he took a drink.

"I don't know how either," Rob said as he followed Blain's lead and repeated the toast. "I don't know how you managed to keep yourself from shooting him."

As the Calimay 'Koffee House' began to fill up with patrons, Blain and Rob left.

"What time do you have there, Blain?" Rob asked as they made their way back to Rachel's car and got inside.

Blain looked at his watch briefly.

"Almost 2:00 p.m., Rachel is probably wondering where her car is. We best head for home."

"Yeah, you want to head to Fruitmont today and set up?"

"We could. It probably would be best. The sooner we get going on it the sooner we can get on with it."

Blain rolled down his window and slowly backed out of the parking spot. They took a long route back that skirted the man-made lake and rolling hills of the Calimay Mental Hospital, then southerly past the King Royal Hotel and Blain's pretend office.

"The hotel looks the same. Is your office still in the basement?" Rob asked. He knew nothing about the fact that Blain also owned the hotel, but he could recall being in his office on a couple of different occasions while he was an operative.

"Yep. I continue to fake my existence and career out of the dungeon. I haven't been there in a couple of weeks though, and I certainly don't miss it."

It was 2:30 p.m., when they pulled back into Blain driveway.

"Here we are. I best hide this ticket. If Rachel finds out I'll be grounded from driving her car," Blain chuckled as he stuffed it into his pants pocket.

They had barely stepped out of the car when Rachel was standing there with her arms crossed.

"Speedy Gonzales or what, Blain? Was it necessary to speed away like that?"

"I was only having some fun, Rachel. No big deal."

Blain shrugged his shoulders.

"Look I brought it back without a scratch."

"Next time, if there ever is a next time, how about waiting until you are out of ear shot. I get freaked out when you take off in my car like that."

"Alright, I won't misbehave while driving your car ever again."

"Good. I have fresh lemonade made if you boys are thirsty. It is in the fridge. Havoc and I are going for our walk. I'll talk to you guys later."

"Wait a minute, I'm going to take Rob home. I might not be here when you get back." Blain leaned forward and kissed her. "But, I will be back later this evening. Okay?"

"You don't want to spend another night, Rob?" Rachel asked.

"I have a lot of work to catch up on. It was certainly nice meeting you though. I'll probably see you again sometime. Thanks for your hospitality, Rachel."

"You are welcome, Rob, and I hope I do see you again. Alright, Blain, I'll talk to you when you get back tonight. Come on, Havoc, let's go," she said as she strutted off and waved to them both.

"I guess we should grab a drink of lemonade; then we'll head off. No use wasting time."

Blain opened the door and they found their way into the kitchen. He poured a couple of tall glasses of Rachel's lemonade and they sat down at the table.

"What about the equipment? Are you going to have it decommissioned?"

"I almost forgot about that. No worries. I'll get on it first thing tomorrow. I'd rather call Canbra from my office. We have to make copies of the relevant documents too. Do you have a photo copier?" Blain asked.

"I have a three in one, a fax, photo copier, and printer."

Rob took a drink of his lemonade.

"Man, that sure makes a fellow pucker, doesn't it? Good though."

"I know. It is between too sweet and succulently sour. I don't know how she makes it, but it always quenches the thirst. Okay, so our plan is I'll photo copy the documents tomorrow and fax them to you."

"That is where we'll start, undoubtedly," Rob said as he wrote down and handed Blain his email address and fax number.

Blain took the piece of paper, looked at it, and stuffed it in his pocket.

"Thanks," he said as finished his lemonade.

At 3:00 p.m. they headed out. It took a little over an hour to make the distance to Rob's place. It was indeed secluded. It was set with the backdrop of the Evergreen Mountains. Even now in late June, snow still covered its peaks.

"Here we are," Rob said as he opened the door and stepped out of Blain's car. "I've sure missed being here."

"I'd miss this too. It's quite serene and peaceful."

Blain looked around.

"Have you spent much time up in those mountains?"

"That is where I get my food, Blain. I have hunted most of the area up there. I always find something to stuff in my freezer."

"I didn't know you hunted," Blain commented as he unlocked the trunk so they could get to the equipment.

"While I was an operative, I didn't. It has only been in the last ten or so years that I started. I got a sweet rifle collection that I'll show you."

Rob bent over into the trunk and grabbed one of the boxes.

"Come on, let's get this stuff set up or at least unpacked."

"Yeah, yeah. I was taken away by the area. Very nice." Blain nodded as he too grabbed a box. "Lead the way Rob."

He followed Rob into his house. It wasn't a big house. It had two bedrooms, a living-room and kitchen which spread out across the main floor. A loft looked down over it all and that was where Rob did his research. The second bedroom was Rob's gunroom, and the wall was loaded with vertical and horizontal gun racks. Rob showed it to Blain after they unloaded the car.

"Nice collection. You must have at least what, ah twenty or thirty rifles. Nice collection of hand guns too. I take it that blank spot there is for this Glock?"

Blain pulled it out from his waistband and handed it to Rob.

"I won't be needing this anymore. It is yours, so here you go."

"Yep, that is where it belongs."

Rob unlocked the door and put it back.

"There, now you can see the collection in its entirety."

"Very impressive collection, indeed. How long does it take to accumulate that many?"

"I spent about five years getting them all. The first rifle I ever owned was the .270 Remington. It takes down most of the game around here. The rest were bought in chronological order starting from that end of the cabinet. Some I have only fired once or twice. This one, .408 Cheyenne Tactical," Rob pointed at it, "I bought only a few months ago and haven't even shot it yet. I'll use it this Fall though. Have you ever hunted, Blain?"

"Other than K-15 carriers, I can honestly say no."

"Maybe you'd like to tag along some time. I head up into the mountains on the first day of hunting season. I have a chalet or cabin as well. I spend two weeks at a time there when I'm hunting. It is a straight hike, though, no roads or boats. Not even ATVs can get to it."

"Thanks for the invite, but I haven't even got a hunting license," Blain commented as he continued to look at all of Rob's rifles and handguns.

"That doesn't mean you can't get one. You'd have all summer. You should think about it. It is quite a good time. I promise I won't tie you up at my cabin," Rob razzed.

Blain smiled and looked at him.

"I wouldn't have tied you up either, hadn't you been Hector."

He shook his head at Rob's comment.

"I know. I was only teasing you. Would you like a coffee, Blain? It'll only take a few minutes to make."

Blain was looking with great interest at Rob's .408 CT. It was an awesome looking rifle. The camo design was black and purple and the scope attached looked like one from a sniper movie. He knew very little about rifles. Handguns had always been his preferred weapon. He looked over to Rob to answer his question.

"Sorry about that, Rob. I was caught up in the moment looking at this .408 of yours, but sure I'll have a coffee. You don't mind if I take a closer look at it, do you?"

"Not at all. You can take it out of the cabinet if you want. Have a look through that scope. It is deadly."

Rob turned and began to make coffee. Blain had the rifle in his hand by now and was looking out a window through the scope at a pile of debris near the bush line three to four-hundred yards away. The rifle felt good in his hands. It wasn't too heavy and it wasn't too light, but it did have some weight. The smell of gun oil and the rifle's newness wafted up his nose.

"Quite the scope, I'd say. I can see clear over to that pile of debris by the bush line. It's almost as though I'm standing there. Amazing."

Blain lowered it from his shoulder and put it back in the cabinet.

"Maybe I will contemplate hunting with you sometime, Rob."

He closed the cabinet door, walked over to the table and sat down.

"Sure, that would be great."

Rob poured each of them a coffee and offered Blain condiments.

"Here are sugar and whitener. Help yourself, Blain."

Sitting, he looked around. It had been a few weeks since he was last home and it sure felt good.

"There is nothing like Home Sweet Home is there?"

"No kidding, especially when you go through as much as we have in the past few weeks. The coffee smells good, Rob, thank you very much," Blain commented as he took a swallow. "Yep, that is good coffee."

"What do you suggest we start with in this research?" Rob now asked as he took a drink from his own cup.

"I'll copy all the documents tomorrow, and have Canbra decommission the equipment. I'll be heading to the main K.A.T Agency next week to drop off the rest. I say we start where you left off. You'll get all the recent discoveries and theories. Amongst the equipment, I also have a live K-15 virus sample. I haven't figured out how to keep that though, or if we can run some tests on it before next week. It is already Thursday. I think it important that we get a sample somehow, someway. I was also given a sample of DNA. Canbra says it is relevant. I'm not sure where the sample came from, but she says it leads to the Brentwood family, whoever they are," Blain shrugged. "I haven't done any research on that sample nor the live K-15 sample. I don't have a clue what it all means. She seems pretty adamant though that it is a significant find."

Rob sat in contemplation for a few minutes.

"You said Brentwood?" he asked with curiosity, as though it meant something to him.

"That is what she said. Why? Do you know that name?"

"I've heard the name before, but I can't think of where or why. It does sound familiar. Humph." Rob stroked his chin as he tried to remember.

"For the life of me, I can't remember. Strange, I know I have heard it before. Not sure how significant that is, though. There are probably a lot of Brentwoods."

"I said the same thing. Apparently the Agency tested a few family members that were willing to be tested. She said the ones they tested though, didn't have the same DNA structure as the Brentwood DNA that she was looking into. She said that the family with that DNA may very well be a first generation carriers. If that turns out to be the case, then maybe we'll be that much closer to discovering a cure."

Rob took another drink of his coffee.

"I know Trent was always adamant that tracking down a first generation carrier would make all the difference. So, that is how close the Agency actually is, eh?"

"In Canbra's mind, yes. I'm going to remain skeptical until we have some hard evidence. I hope we won't have to wait too long."

Blain finished his coffee and rose from the table.

"I should be shoving off, Rob. It is getting close to 5:00 p.m."

He scribbled out a cell phone number and handed it to Rob.

"You can contact me at that number. Oops, almost forgot, I should give you my email address as well."

He scribbled that out too.

"There now, you have my cell number and email address. Use either one when you need to make contact. I'm going to head back now, Rob, so good luck in your research. Make sure you keep me posted on any findings."

"You can count on that," Rob said as he walked Blain to the door. "I am looking forward to getting on with this, Blain. It is as important to me as it is to any and all operatives that we kick this thing in the ass. I'll do all I can to help out," Rob said with sincerity and satisfaction that he was reactivated and working closely with Blain once more.

"Remember the seventeen aces that I hold, Rob."

Blain smiled as he opened his car door and slipped inside. Waving, he headed back to Calimay. He trusted Rob and was as pleased as he was that they were going to be working together. Rob was a good friend back in the day. He was also a good researcher, perhaps not as good as Gonsite, but he was better than Blain and Blain knew it. *I hope he doesn't go rogue again, I have seventeen aces up my sleeve if he does, and if that isn't a solution, I'll be the one to kill him this time,* he thought as he drove.

At 6:30 p.m., he pulled into his driveway. The only thing he heard as he opened the door was Havoc barking. Again he was locked in the upstairs bedroom. Blain would get to him after he read the note on the table.

Shortly after he left there had been some tragic events. Rachel's mother had fallen ill and was in the hospital in New Kootenay. Rachel tried to call him, but he hadn't had his cell phone turned on and only now as he read the note left for him did he check his voice mail. Sure enough, at around 3:30 p.m., Rachel had called him and explained everything that he had just read in the note. She left Havoc at home, knowing that she would be spending time at her mother's side in the hospital and wouldn't be able to care for him. He shook his head as he set the note down.

Sitting himself, he ran his hand through his hair as he contemplated on whether or not he should head to

New Kootenay. Instead, he decided to wait for Rachel to call him later that evening as she promised. He would discuss it with her then. Making his way upstairs, he let Havoc out and they went outside for a bit.

"Looks like it is you and me for now, Havoc. I haven't been home for more than 24 hrs and already things have gone for a shit. I sure hope Anne, Rachel's mom, is going to be okay. Rachel will be devastated if anything happens to her."

Blain scratched his chin as Havoc scooted down the deck stairs and over to his favorite tree.

"That is why that grass is all yellow. Maybe you should switch trees or something. You've made such a mess of my lawn, Havoc, I'm not sure it'll ever be the same again. Damn mutt anyway."

At 7:30 p.m., Rachel called.

"Hello, Blain."

"Hi, how is your mom? Is she going to be okay?"

"I haven't talked to the doctors yet or have seen her. I'm heading that way now. I wanted to let you know I'm here. I'll talk to you later maybe or I'll phone you tomorrow. Stay by the phone or at least keep your cell phone on. I love you, Blain."

"I love you to pieces too. Yeah, phone me later or tomorrow. Should I maybe pack some things and head out that way?"

"There really is no point in that. As far as I know, she'll be home in a day or two. If it turns out to be serious and I'm going to be here longer, then you could come here. Make sure you take Havoc for his walks. He likes to be walked in the early morning or mid-afternoon. I don't think he cares which just as long as he gets walked."

"Don't worry about Havoc, Rachel. Your concern should be for your mom right now."

"You are right. Okay, I'll call you later, love you."

"Love you back. Talk to you later. Bye."

Blain waited for her to hang up before he did the same.

"That was Rachel, Havoc, she's safe. I'm glad she phoned. I feel better knowing. What is it that we're going to do for the next couple of days? She says I have to walk you every day. Don't count on that though, Havoc. The yard is big enough for you to run around. I don't think there is much more damage that you can do to it. I am glad you haven't dug any more holes. I guess one of the things we can do is fix those. We'll do that sometime before Rachel gets back."

Blain rose from the deck table and using a measuring tape, measured the circumference of each hole, so that he would get a close proximity of how much Kentucky blue grass sod he would need. With that done, he and Havoc retreated inside. The house was cool and silent. For the first time, he realized how silent and lonely it was without Rachel being there. *That poor girl. All those times I left for weeks on end must have really been lonely for her. I understand her choler now,* he thought, as he turned on the kitchen radio for noise. Tossing Havoc a treat, he poured himself some lemonade and wandered upstairs to have a better look at the drywall repair he also needed to do. It wasn't as bad as he first thought and some tape and drywall mud would fix it.

It would be better to let Havoc have run of the house and close the doors to the rooms we don't want him in. It would probably make him feel better than being caged up and probably save us some money too. Blain shook his head as he tried to decide which was best. After all, if Havoc was locked up in a room, how would he ever be expected to protect the house, which was obviously why Rachel picked him up in the first place? That, and of course, Havoc was to keep her from being lonely and to offer her companionship, something Blain knew he hadn't offered a great deal of lately, and chances were he wouldn't be able to for a while.

At 10:00 p.m., Rachel phoned. The news wasn't dire but it wasn't the best either. Her mom had suffered a stroke and there was a chance of permanent damage. The doctors, however, were skeptical that would be the case. She was a healthy and strong woman, they told Rachel. If things went as they expected, she might be released the following Monday. There were tests that the doctors wanted to do before they made a final decision.

"That is better news then what it could've been. At least she is going to be okay," Blain said hesitatingly, not sure if Rachel saw it as good news or not. After all, it was her mother.

"It is better than her having a heart attack. There is no doubt about that. I only hope she's going to be okay. I am not ready to lose her."

There was silence from both ends as they contemplated and hoped for the same, that she would be okay.

"While I'm here, I'm going to see about getting her a live-in caregiver. She will likely come out of this okay, but I don't know what will happen the next time, if there is a next time. I think she needs someone living with her to be safe."

"I wouldn't disagree. Should I come to New Kootenay?"

"I'd love to have you here, but I don't think it is necessary unless things change for the worst. It is Wednesday today. Will you and Havoc be okay until Monday or Tuesday next week?"

"We'll be fine. You only need to worry about and deal with what it is you need to deal with over there. Havoc and I are starting to see eye to eye," Blain teased.

"Be nice to him, Blain. He's only a puppy. Anyway, I'm tired from the drive and from going to the hospital. I think I'm going to head to bed. Keep your cell phone charged and on, and the home phone plugged in. I know how you like to unplug it," she chuckled. "I'll phone sometime tomorrow; evening is probably best, because I will likely be at the hospital all day."

"Okay. I'll keep the phone and my cell phone on. Phone me anytime if there is a change for better or for worse. I love you."

"I love you too," she said as they hung up.

"It is official, Havoc. Looks like you'll be coming with me to the office tomorrow. Rachel likely isn't going to be back until early next week. I haven't had company in my office all day ever. You'll be the first. As for the stuff we need to do around here, we have six maybe seven days to get things in order."

Chapter 20

Thursday, June 14th, 2007, Blain woke at his usual time and dressed. He had let Havoc have complete reign of the house the night before and was impressed that there was no damage to anything that he noticed. Havoc hadn't even crapped on the floor. He waited to be let out as Blain's morning coffee perked. Pouring a cup, Blain grabbed the cordless phone and phone book, opened the sliding glass door to the backyard and let Havoc out to take care of business. He sat down at the deck table with his coffee and listened to the birds as he drank his first cup.

At 8:00 a.m., he began looking through the phone book, and finding what he was looking for, he dialed the number.

"Good morning, Calimay Yard Maintenance and Sod Farm, how can we help you?"

"Good morning. This is Blain Sweet. I was wondering if I might be able to get someone to come by and do some yard work?"

"What do you need done?"

"My wife bought a dog, and I have a Kentucky bluegrass lawn. The damn thing dug some holes. I'm hoping you fellows have a slab of sod."

"Yep, we have Kentucky Bluegrass. How much was it you said you needed?"

"One roll, however wide a roll is, and about five to six feet long, if that is possible?"

"We can do that. You want us to patch the holes?"

"Yes, and maybe give the lawn a quick manicure," he chuckled with hope.

Usually it was something that he would do, but with all he had going on, he knew he was pressed for time.

"Sure, what is the address?"

"Three-sixty Magenta Flats. Any chance someone can get to it before the weekend?"

"I can probably have someone there tomorrow morning. Will you be around?"

"It depends on what time that is. I head to the office at around 9:00 a.m."

"I couldn't get anyone there by that time, 10:00 a.m. works though."

"I'll leave the back gate open in that case. You can go ahead and do it. I'll swing by after work and get the invoice."

"You could do that if you like, but we'll also leave one on site."

"Sounds good, thank you very much," Blain said as he hung up the phone.

"Hey, Havoc, come on, we have to get going. I have a bunch of stuff I need to photo copy," he called out as Havoc came running to his call. "You get to go for a car ride and spend the whole day with me. It is going to be as boring as hell."

With Havoc at his side, he locked the house down and the two of them were off. He arrived at his office at 8:45 a.m. Pulling up to the door before he parked, he unloaded the box of documents he needed to photocopy and send to Rob. He left Havoc inside his office as he parked.

Making his way back to his office, he was glad to see that Havoc was simply lying on the floor next to his desk.

"Good boy, Havoc."

He reached down and rewarded him with a pat.

"This is where I work. This is the dungeon. Welcome," Blain commented as he looked around. "We'll be spending a lot of time here over the next little while."

He sat down at his desk and dialed Canbra's number to check in, to make arrangements to deliver Trent's documents, and to have a sit down with some of the K.A.T. Operatives. They needed to tighten up the slack on a few security issues, and he wanted to hand select those to whom he was going turn over Trent's work. In his mind it was obviously going to be Gonsite, but things sometimes change, and he wouldn't know for sure until the meeting took place.

"Hello, Canbra," he said as she answered.

"Hey, Entity, you are back I'm assuming."

"Your assumption would be correct. How are things? Any news on any attacks or possible attacks?"

"Not a one that we are aware of. Things have really been slow. It is a good thing, but also a scary thing too."

"I hear you. We've been at it for over fourteen years. Maybe we've wiped the carriers out?" Blain said with doubt. They could always hope.

"It would be nice if that were true. Then again, who is to say that isn't the case. I went back a month to the last attack. It took place in Rosedale. Operative 'Ten Seventy' tracked down the carrier. Since that tracking and assassination, it has been dead quiet. Excuse the pun," she chuckled.

"Rosedale, eh? Hmmm, maybe we should concentrate our efforts in that area."

"Ten Seventy has been stationed there since, and he hasn't found anything substantial."

"Maybe we should send in another operative to that same location. Two sets of eyes are better than one," Blain commented.

"We could. We have a few who are sitting idle. Who do you want to send?"

"That depends on who is available, I guess. How long is the list?"

"There are five idle operatives," Canbra answered.

"Okay, well, do me a favor. Have those five meet with me. I don't think I'll be able to make it there before Wednesday or Thursday next week. Have their personnel files and credentials available for me then."

"Then, when?" she asked.

"Thursday, next week. If I can't make it, I'll see them here in Calimay. You can courier me their files. I'll know one way or the other by Wednesday the 20th."

"Is that when you will also return the documents and equipment we sent?"

"Oh yeah, about that. I need the equipment written off the books. But yes, that is when I'll return the documents and drop off Trent's findings."

"Why do you need the equipment decommissioned?" Canbra asked with curiosity.

"I had a mishap in the boat and lost some in Lake Winnfield. I was able to save the documents, laptop, test-tubes, and microscope slides though. Everything else is swimming."

"I don't know about that, Entity. It sounds kind of fishy to me," she teased as she went about looking up the items that were sent and with a click of the button, decommissioned them.

"I imagine that is how the equipment feels too," Blain chuckled. "Anyway, decommission them."

There was nothing more he wanted to or needed to say, and Canbra suspected that.

"Okay, it is done. Anything else, Entity?"

"Nope, I'll talk to you next week unless, of course, something else comes up. Don't forget to keep me in the loop on any attacks or other happenings. I'm by my phone 24/7."

"I know. If anything comes about between now and when we speak next, you'll be the first to know, after me."

"Good; we'll talk next week for sure. Bye for now, Canbra."

Blain hung up the phone. He looked down to Havoc who continued to lie by his desk.

"That takes care of that. Now, we get to make some noise."

He stood up and made his way over to his photocopier, and began copying the box of documents. There was no way he was going to fax that many pieces to Rob and instead decided to send the copies via courier. He called him up to let him know. They decided then, that since he wasn't going to fax any of it, and was going to send it by courier, it probably wouldn't hurt to make copies of the documents that were burned to the 40 pocket CD-R's as well.

Rob gave him easy to follow instructions on how to accomplish that, by simply sending the documents from the pocket CD-R's to a few folders that he could create on his desktop computer and then burn those folders onto a set of new DVD-R's preferably the bigger ones, like the 4.7 GB 120 Minute type.

It all sounded simple as Rob explained it. Blain gave it a try. It was in his opinion easier said than done, especially with his minimal experience. He finally gave up trying and decided to look on the internet for step-by-step easy to follow instructions and printed them off. Now with it written in black and white, he followed the instructions a few times and was soon comfortable enough to proceed. It took eight, DVD-Rs to completely copy and burn the 40 smaller CD-Rs, but he succeeded.

"Would you look at that, Havoc. I learned how to burn DVD disks. Don't have to use only my thumb-drive now."

He felt good about that, and leaned back in his chair pleased with his accomplishment.

Putting the DVD's into another small shipping box, he stowed it in the bigger box that held the documents. Then picked up his office phone and dialed the Calimay Courier Service. By 3:00 p.m. that afternoon, the documents were on their way. The driver assured him that the package would arrive at its destination in Fruitmont by 6:00 p.m. that evening. With the tasks of photocopying, burning the DVD's, and getting the equipment decommissioned, he decided he was finished for the day and closed up shop.

He and Havoc arrived home at 4:00 p.m. Immediately he went to work in fixing a few things. With a bucket of premixed drywall mud and drywall tape in his hand, he taped over the hole in the wall where Havoc tried to dig through. He slapped a liberal amount of mud on the tape and feathered it out so it looked smooth. It would need at least one more coat to finish, but that would be another day. Looking at the box spring on the bed and reading its size he ordered a new mattress from Sears. Things were moving along nicely and he accomplished the few meagre tasks that were not so pressing but rather cosmetic.

The hardwood floor was next on his list, and he tried to scrub the scuffs and scratches out, but it was futile. His elbow-grease wasn't enough to change the look. For now he would leave it, there was no point in laying down new flooring. Havoc would probably ruin that as well.

At 6:00 p.m. the phone rang and he answered it after the third ring. It was Rachel. Her mother was improving and the doctors determined that the damage to her arteries was indeed reversible. They were going to put her on blood-thinning medication, and she would have to follow a strict diet, but all in all, things were looking up. She was not by any means out of the dark, but if she followed the doctor's advice and stuck to a healthy regimen and diet, in a few months she would be her usual self, and could look forward to a long life.

The news, in Blain's opinion, was good, and Rachel did tend to agree. She would, however, while she was there, continue to look for a live-in person to help her mother with day-to-day living. It was true her mother was getting old and the help would make things easier for her. Convincing her mother that a live-in was a good idea would certainly be another story and take a lot of convincing. Her mother was independent and she loved her life and her privacy as it was. She was never one for change.

There were a few different options. One was to move her mother to Calimay so that she could live with them. Blain, though, wasn't sure about that. He did love Rachel's mother as his own, but she was often meddling in their business, and at times could be nasty. It was an option though, and he would never turn Rachel's mother away. If it came down to that, he'd live with it. Another option and one Blain was more inclined to agree on was to buy her a small house in Calimay, so that Rachel could keep an eye on her. The biggest problem with that though, was that she probably would never want to leave New Kootenay or, for that matter, sell her house. Another option was to sell their house in Calimay and buy one in New Kootenay, and move Blain's office there. Blain hummed and hawed at that idea, but nonetheless he didn't say "no".

The best thing would be to find a live in, so that they wouldn't have to fight over the other options. Their marriage was in enough of an uproar and although they were slowly working on their problems, things hadn't completely turned around for them yet. Blain knew though that the closer the K.A.T. Agency came to solving the K-15 riddle and abolishing the virus' spread, the closer he and Rachel were to mending their marriage. He also knew that it may never happen, and their marriage would simply fall off the bluffs of their union and shatter on the rocky shore below. They were hanging on to what was left of their marriage by a thin thread, and the thread could break anytime over anything. Having to sell their house and move could very well be the scissors that cut that thread.

It would be hard for both of them to do, but it was an option that could very well keep Rachel's mother alive and well for another decade or more. The idea wasn't completely out of the question. It was, however, one that neither Blain nor Rachel wanted to accept yet. For now, Rachel would look for other alternatives. She and Blain could both be wrong and her mother might very well agree to a live-in, or for that matter agree to sell the big lonely house she was living in and move to Calimay. Rachel would know more as the days progressed and she slowly brought the topic up. For now, they would wait and see.

Their conversation lasted well over forty-five minutes and with a final assurance that everything was hunky-dory at Blain's end and that Havoc was fine and behaving, they said their "I love you's", bid each other good night and hung up their phones. Rachel would call again on Saturday, as she had made plans with a girlfriend to spend a few hours at the local spa and do some late night shopping on Friday. Blain was okay with that. It gave him some time to reflect. Besides, he needed to go through a few things that he could do only at home. His desktop computer at the office didn't have a 3.5 floppy disk drive, but the one in their basement's recreation room did, and he had two floppy disks that needed to be looked at. Without having to worry about Rachel calling him on Friday, he could look through them without disturbance. He wasn't going to attempt that now, though. He had already spent enough time playing with computers that day.

The clock on the wall read 7:00 p.m., and so he dialed Rob's cell phone to confirm that the package he sent had arrived. The phone rang a couple of times before Rob answered.

"Hey, Rob. How is it going?" Blain asked as he poured a coffee.

"Blain, glad you called. I received the package. There is certainly a lot of stuff to go through. Glad you managed to burn me those DVDs. I'll be getting to those soon. Did you know that Trent mentions the name Brentwood in one of the documents he wrote?"

"I had no idea. It must've been in one of the ones I didn't look at. What else does it say about that?" Blain wanted to know.

Obviously if the Agency was looking at the Brentwood family name and Trent had made reference to the same name, there was reason for it. He was both elated and curious as he waited for Rob to respond.

"It is a reference to a guy name Anvil Brentwood. It reads that Anvil was suffering from a type of Kuru. I don't know where he got that information, or if this Anvil fellow even exists, but that is what he has written down and makes reference to. The writing has faded over the years, but the little bit I told you just now is easy enough to read. I don't know how you could have missed it, Blain. It is in one of the first folders that I opened. There was no rhyme or reason on why I picked that folder either."

Rob was as curious as Blain was now that Trent also made reference to the Brentwood name.

"Anvil Brentwood, eh? That is interesting. I think that is a good starting point. With Trent referencing him it makes it even more intriguing. As you go through it all, Rob, make sure you keep your eye open for any other information regarding that name. Trent often encrypted things. That could be why I was never really able to understand some of the stuff he wrote. I can honestly say, though, that I have never read the folder you are talking about. Not even when I made the photocopies did I see anything like that."

Blain took a swallow of coffee as he made his way over to the kitchen table and sat down.

"I've been thumbing through this folder and I can say I do recognize some encryption going on. It might be hard to decipher it. I will, however, certainly do my best, Blain. As for everything else, that is also going to take time. Is there any chance that you can do some foot work and see what physical evidence you can come up with on where this Anvil fellow might be? He might even be dead by now, if he ever existed at all," Rob continued thumbing back and forth through the pages of the folder.

"For sure, I can do that and I will. It is the best information I have heard, and that type of investigating is right down my aisle. I can't believe you found it so quickly, or for that matter how I missed it."

It did seemed strange, but, strange things often happened in life. He was certainly glad that Rob was working on it with him. He wasn't sure now if he wanted to hand over Trent's documents to the Agency or not. There would be a lot of bureaucracy and rules of engagement that the Agency would have to follow in order to do such an investigation on who Anvil Brentwood was. On his own, he could bypass all the crap and get right to it, and run all the risks himself.

"I haven't got the folders here at home, but I do have them at my office. Can you tell me which folder holds that information. That way I can remove it from what I have committed to handing over to the Agency. If they have never seen it, they certainly won't miss it. It might be best, in fact, to remove any other references to Anvil Brentwood you come across in Trent's work," Blain added as he reached for a pen and piece of paper to write down the folder information.

He was getting more excited now at what he might find on the floppy disk.

"Yeah, I can give you the document reference number that I'm looking at. It is marked as miscellaneous A-5 1993. It is easy enough to miss being that it is faded so badly. That is probably why you didn't see it."

Blain wrote down the number as he listened to Rob.

"That is possible, I suppose. So the document number is A-5 1993 correct?" he asked, waiting for confirmation.

"That is it, yep. It is one of the documents that he wrote out by hand. It looks as though you have photocopied a few of those."

There was a pause as Rob flipped through some of it.

"The more I read the more I think I'm going to be awake all night," Rob chuckled as he looked at a few more documents.

He found nothing more on the name.

"Looks to me that the one piece of information on the Brentwood name is all there is. Of course, the encryptions, if I can decode them, may reveal more."

"Hmmm, okay. Do what you can, Rob and feel free to call my cell anytime as you go through the folders and whatnots. I'll see what kind of information I can dig up on this Anvil fellow."

Blain paused as he tried to think of anything else to relay to Rob, but nothing popped up.

"I guess that will be all. We have a good start I think," he added as he doodled on the piece of paper in front of him.

"I guess, yeah okay... hold on a second, Blain. I just came across something else."

"What is that?" Blain wanted to know.

"I found an abbreviation that I have often used for a floppy disk, but I don't see any floppy disks in the package you sent."

"Floppy disks?" Blain questioned as though he were surprised.

"That is right. You don't know if Trent kept anything like that do you?"

"You have everything of Trent's as far as I know. I don't recall any floppy disks amongst anything I have seen," he lied. "What does the abbreviation read?"

"Simply 'flpy-3doc'. That, to me sounds like a floppy disk. I could be wrong though."

Blain quickly scribbled it out and circled it. If it was a floppy disk and the number 3 represented a third floppy, he was missing one.

"You think that means a floppy disk?"

"It is definitely an abbreviation for one, I think. Seems strange I know, but I think Trent may have information on floppy disks somewhere too. I'm going to have to see what I can find out about that. Perhaps there is a reference somewhere. Any chance he could have stored something like a floppy disk in a security box at a bank or something?"

Rob knew it was an impossible question to answer. Trent though was certainly referring to a floppy disk as far as he was concerned.

"That is a good question. I guess it is possible, but I wouldn't know where to start looking."

"Maybe as I go through all of his stuff something will pop up. I guess I'll get at it and will let you know if anything comes of it. There are a lot of documents and stuff to go through," Rob admitted.

"Well, do what you can, and yeah my line is always open. Thanks for what you have already given me and good luck in deciphering it all."

"Alright. We'll talk again soon, Blain. Bye for now," Rob said as he hung up the phone.

Blain rose from the table and poured another coffee. He wanted to see, now more than ever, what was on the two floppy disks he had found at the cabin. Curiosity convinced him to go downstairs and turn on his computer. As it booted up he sat down and inserted the first floppy. All it contained were a few pictures of him and Trent standing by their cabin, their arms over each other's shoulders. The pictures were a bit opaque due to the fact that the camera they were using wasn't at all that good, and the timed picture setting rarely worked. He chuckled as he remembered that camera, and the trouble they had with it. The two of them did everything together right up until Trent's untimely death. They started the K.A.T. Agency, bought the cabin, and split the cost 70-30 on the King Royal Hotel, all of which Blain owned now. Had it not been for Trent's 30% though, the King Royal wouldn't be his today.

He owed Trent a lot. That was probably one of the biggest driving forces behind his willingness to continue as a K.A.T. Operative. It was because of Trent that the world would not suffer from a virus so unpredictable that the symptoms included cannibalism. It was his wish to put an end to the spread of the K-15 virus, and when the scientific, medical, and governmental communities shunned his findings, he did what he always did. He continued on with his own research despite futile efforts to gain support. Ultimately, his work led to the formation of the K.A.T.

Agency. For fourteen years the Agency had been able to thwart any noticeable increase and spreading of the K-15 virus due to Trent's findings. Granted, Blain knew that it wasn't under control, but it was safe to say that the Agency certainly slowed down public exposure.

The cabin back then looked like hell and as he gazed at the pictures, his mind raced with memories. He missed Trent, and the pictures he was looking at only made him miss him more. There was one curious picture that caught his eye. He remembered the day it was taken as though it were only yesterday. It was the first day that they laid their eyes on the cabin after buying it a few days earlier. What caught his attention as he looked at the picture was the fact that it was taken by one of the property stakes and Trent was pointing at the stake while his arm was draped over Blain's shoulder.

It seemed odd that Trent was doing that. There was no reason. It was as if he was telling him something. He looked at the other pictures too, but always went back to that one particular picture. It seemed uncanny. Maybe it was because it was the first picture taken on the cabin's property, or maybe there was a greater reason. Whatever the reason, he sat transfixed as he stared into Trent's eyes and chuckled at his quirky smile. *Those were the good old days. How I wish you were alive. You were my best friend,* Blain, reminisced as he wiped a tear away from his cheek. *You are trying to tell me something, aren't you,* he thought to himself as he continued to stare at the picture.

He brought his hand to his face and stroked his whiskered chin as he sat in contemplation and wonderment. He finished his entire cup of coffee sitting there and staring at the picture, as memories of Trent palpitated his mind. Not often did he think about the tragedy that befell Trent. It was however always in the back of his mind.

As he sat there that evening, he thought about that tragedy now. Trent had been out on a typical K-15 carrier assassination operation, but something went terribly wrong. No one knew exactly what, except that he didn't return. As the weeks passed and turned into months, the discovery of a body that was in the general location of where the assassination was to have taken place turned up. Hampering the identification was the fact that the body was burnt beyond recognition, and body parts were missing.

There were good reasons for those concerned to objectively believe that indeed the corpse was that of Trent. If it were the K-15 carrier he set out to kill that day, the corpse itself would have retained all its limbs. There would have been no reason for them to go missing. Of course, it was always possible that animals could scatter body parts, but nine times out of ten, body parts scattered by animals could be located in the area. Trent's never were. Blain decided then that since he was the only living relative, there would be no autopsy, and instead he made funeral arrangements and laid his brother to rest. He often wondered over the years as he did now, if he had made the right decision. With no confirmation from a ME that indeed the body was that of Trent's, all he ever had to go on was the premise that it was. There was no other explanation for his disappearance except that he did meet his demise that day.

It was hard for Blain to fathom that thirteen years had passed since his death. *It has been a long time, Trent, since I have thought about that day. The Agency has grown and we are making progress, however only time will tell if we have succeeded in eradicating the K-15 virus.* He continued to stare at his brother's picture as the words read out in his mind. Finally, with a sigh and a click of the mouse button, he closed off the picture. *I'll always have memories,* he thought as he picked up his empty cup and headed back upstairs. He wasn't in the mood to look through the other floppy. His mind was filled with too many memories and he wanted to hold on to them for a while longer before taking on that task. He sat with Havoc at his feet at the kitchen table and reminisced. At 11:00 p.m., he went to bed.

Chapter 21

Blain made his way with coffee in hand to the outside deck, Havoc trailing close behind. Again, Havoc hadn't made a mess overnight, and again, Blain rewarded him for behaving. Sitting down at the table, he took his time drinking his coffee and listened to the sounds of early morning. He watched as Havoc ran around chasing a few robins that were looking for worms. The morning air was exhilarating and he felt good to be alive. A gentle breeze tousled his hair as he drank his coffee. Squinting, he looked in the direction of the rising sun. It was going to be another blistering hot June day, and he was glad he'd be at his office as the dungeon was always cool.

His watch read 7:00 a.m. and in a few hours the yard maintenance crew would be around to fix his lawn and give it a quick mow. When he got home that evening his lawn would look as good as he wished it looked now. He would make an effort after that to keep it up as he always had, as long as Havoc refrained from digging in it and tearing it up. Hearing the paperboy, he walked around to the front of the house and picked up that day's newspaper. With a fresh coffee, he thumbed through it. There was not much going on in the town of Calimay. The funnies though, brought a chuckle.

At 8:00 a.m. he and Havoc headed to the dungeon. He didn't know what he was going to do when he got there. That was the thing about his job. Not every day was the same, and sometimes the days seemed brutally long as he waited to be called out by the Agency. Lately there had been no calls. Lately things were as dull as a butter knife. He wasn't sure it was a good or a bad thing, but something had to give. Something was bound to come up soon. He could not remember a time when things were so slow between attacks, deaths, or assassinations, and he was desperate for some kind of action. The K-15 carriers were still out there, somewhere. K.A.T. only needed to find them. The eyes and ears the Agency scattered all across British Columbia were certainly not hearing or seeing anything significant.

It was a time of uneasiness amongst all the K.A.T. Agency operatives. Maybe, it was the calm before the storm, and it would only be a matter of time before the carriers continued with their vicious and barbaric killing sprees. Maybe the K-15 virus had burned itself out, but more than likely it morphed to a different set of characteristics. That was the thing about K-15. If it wanted to change its viral strains, it simply changed them. It had morphed from Kuru-like symptoms to symptoms that included gruesome murderous impulses and even cannibalism in the years that the Agency battled it. No one could say it hadn't changed again. That was probably the biggest fear those fighting it shared, and not until it was discovered as a new strain, if it did morph, would anyone be the wiser.

It was close to 9:00 a.m. when Blain unlocked his office door and he and Havoc entered. They had made a stop on their way and bought coffee and doughnuts. It was probably a mistake on his part. By the time they made it to the office, Havoc had helped himself to a couple of doughnuts and destroyed the box that held them. He now carried in his hands the surviving few and Havoc was eyeing those as well.

"Forget it, you've already eaten enough."

Setting the four doughnuts down on his desk, he turned on his computer and clicked on Google maps. From the conversation with Canbra earlier that week, he learned that the last K-15 carrier to be detected, over a month ago, was discovered in Rosedale. He knew the area, but there were two things that concerned him. One was the fact that not many K-15 attacks ever took place in the eastern corridor of British Columbia. It was possible that was about to change. The second was the fact that New Kootenay was also in that same region. Looking at the map on his screen, he felt some relief noting that New Kootenay was hundreds of kilometers away from Rosedale. However, it was imperative in his mind that the Agency conduct a deep sweep of the entire eastern corridor. If there was one carrier, there could certainly be two.

The Agency had very little presence in that region due to the lack of attacks. Maybe it was time to change that. Maybe the K-15 virus was about to be unleashed in eastern British Columbia, and if it crossed the Rocky Mountains, Canada and the world in whole would be in desperate shape. The K.A.T. Agency had managed to keep it isolated all these years. However, they were not equipped to reach across Canada. The eastern part of the province could very well be in a lot of trouble. If the Agency didn't move quickly, a possible uncontrolled epidemic could be on the rise.

He didn't bother phoning Canbra and instead sent her an email, telling her to send the five idle operatives directly to the eastern corridor along the Rocky Mountains. He didn't care to which towns or cities they were sent as long as they were sent. Five operatives were better than none. He also suggested sending others that weren't on any particular assignment. The more operatives they could send that way, the quicker they would be able to decide if indeed the K-15 virus was making its way East. The fact alone that attacks in that region were so sporadic and then to have the only attack in a month happen there, seemed very odd.

Taking some time now, he plugged through Trent's documents looking for Document A-5 1993.

Finding it, he noticed that as Rob had mentioned, it was quite faded. He could however, make out exactly what Rob read to him. Whatever was written, below that was next to impossible to see, let alone read. The faded scribbling looked exactly like that, 'scribbling'. *I don't see how anyone can read beyond what Trent has written about Anvil Brentwood. That is too bad. It could be something quite relevant,* he thought as he removed the document from the folder and set it to the side. Trent would not have written down anything like that without reason and he was determined to discover that reason.

He was about to head out the door to a local sandwich shop a block away and take Havoc on a walk with him when he received a reply email from Canbra. The five operatives that he had requested to be sent to the eastern corridor were now in motion, and were on their way to various towns and cities that dotted the main highways from British Columbia to Alberta. Their trained eyes would certainly help curtail any possibilities of the K-15 virus crossing over the Rocky Mountains into eastern Canada. Blain felt more at ease knowing that. It was obvious to him that since there had been very few new developments on any K-15 carriers in the western part of the province, and the fact that last carrier was discovered in the eastern corridor, it was quite likely others were heading east as well.

He replied to the email requesting a list of operatives that were already in the area and the names of the operatives that were now on their way. Canbra always left things like that out. With the email now sent, he rose from his desk and shut down his computer.

"Come on Havoc, lunch is calling. What do you figure, a short walk or should we be lazy and drive?"

Havoc rolled over on his back as though telling Blain that he was quite content as he was.

"A lazy fellow today are you? Alright, we'll drive. It is quicker at least." He gently nudged Havoc. "Come on, let's go."

Finally, Havoc stood up and followed Blain out the door and to the car.

It took only a few moments to get to the deli drive through. After making his order and paying at the window, he decided to take a detour to the Calimay local library to see if he could come up with something in regard to the name of Anvil Brentwood. Firstly, he drove the short distance home and put Havoc in charge of the house. It was getting hot and there was no point in having the dog tag along if he could simply drop him off at home first. Adjusting the controlled air conditioning, he put food in Havoc's dish and gave him fresh water.

"I'll be back in an hour or so, and if I'm feeling up to it we'll head back to the dungeon. Be good while I'm gone Havoc," Blain said as he exited and locked the door.

It took him a few minutes to drive to the library. He drove slowly so he could finish his sandwich and soft drink. He was relieved to see that the library parking lot wasn't packed. He pulled in and parked, then made his way inside.

"Afternoon Blain, what brings you here this time of day?' the librarian asked as he walked up to the counter.

"I need to look at some old archives in regard to some software," he lied. "Any chance I can get in there today?" he asked, referring to the archived section of the library which was behind locked doors.

Only one person was allowed to be in the library's archive room at any one time. It was always best to call ahead. Sometimes it wasn't worth the effort to simply show up. Today though, Blain simply showed up.

"I think it is actually unlocked, Blain, so go ahead. How are you enjoying this beautiful spring we're having?"

"I think it has the makings of a hot summer. Hopefully, I'll be away in a cooler climate when that happens," Blain chuckled as he made his way to the archives room. "I shouldn't be long."

"No worries. No one has been in there for at least a week."

"Thanks, Leanne," Blain replied as he opened the door and stepped inside the cramped, one desk room.

He went directly to the microfiche and began browsing old newspaper clippings and death certificates dating back to the early 90's and up. It seemed ironic that there he was once more doing research. He shook his head and chuckled, since he had declared to Canbra he never would. This kind of research though was relatively understandable and so it bothered him little.

He was quite surprised to come across the name of Tyler O'Brien, but there it was in black and white. *Imagine that, what the hell is this all about,* he thought as he read on. It was a press release in regard to the shooting of a felon named, Norm Bradley who was wanted for assault and murder. It read that it was O'Brien who pulled the trigger. The event took place in Fruitmont, six years earlier in 2001.

The clipping continued to read that shortly afterwards, Tyler O'Brien, was ranked up to lieutenancy for one of Henderson & Co's PI Agency's and sent off to Ridgeville. That was the gist of the article. Blain decided then to keep his eyes open for any other articles that were of interest regarding the infamous Tyler O'Brien, the same PI who interviewed him weeks earlier at the Canupe General Hospital after the incident at the Heritage Hotel.

An hour of being cooped up was beginning to take its toll on him and since he had found nothing on anyone named Anvil Brentwood, he decided to come back another day. It was, if nothing else, interesting to read what he found about Tyler O'Brien.

"The archive room is free now, Leanne. Thanks for letting me in there today," Blain said as he made his way up to the counter.

"Did you find what you were looking for?" she questioned as she finished stamping out a book for a member.

"I did find a few articles, yep," he said as he nodded to her and exited the glass doors.

He opened the windows of his car as soon as he sat down. It was extremely hot inside, from being directly under the mid-day sun. He waited a few moments to let some air in before slowly pulling on to the street and heading for home.

It was only a 1:10 p.m. when he pulled into the driveway. He noticed the long curtains in their living-room were pulled down and the thick curtain rod that held them in place was dangling diagonally across the big bay window. *Aw, shit,* he muttered as he turned off his car and looked on. There was Havoc, panting at the window as though, he was having a great time. Blain, shook his head as he opened his car door. Stepping out, he caught from the corner of his eye, the curtain rod dropping from view as Havoc turned to meet him. In his haste, he managed to get tangled up pulling the rod from the wall. He was correct in his assumption as he opened the front door. There stood an excited Havoc with the curtain and curtain rod behind him on the kitchen floor, torn and shredded.

"Holy crap, do you know what kind of trouble we're going to be in when Rachel sees that. I have no idea where to get one of those long frilly curtains. Havoc, Havoc, Havoc, what have you done?"

Blain slipped off his shoes and made his way to the shredded mess of brass and material. He was relieved to see there was no other damage to the house. Shaking his head, he picked up the parts and pieces. It was his fault for leaving Havoc alone and so he refrained from scolding him.

With the mess cleaned up and the rod back in place, Blain sat down at the table and poured a cup of coffee. It was from the morning and so it wasn't as good as he hoped; still he swallowed it down. At 2:00 p.m., he decided to head back to his office to make sure everything was locked up and to pick up his cell-phone that he used to keep in contact with the Agency. At the same time, he would get any email or voice mail that might be waiting. He was hoping to hear from Rob. Chances were he stayed up all night reading and examining the documents he had sent to him the day before. With Havoc loaded up, he started his car and turned out of the driveway making his way to the dungeon.

It was locked up and everything was turned off. There were no voice mails, and he wasn't sure he wanted to turn on his computer to check for emails. However it was cool in the office and he decided to beat the heat. Turning the computer on, he waited for it to boot up and run through its scans etceteras. It usually took a couple of minutes and he used that time to skim through a few more of the documents that were scattered across his desk, putting each away as he did so. Finally, the computer was ready and he checked his email.

A return email from Canbra was in his inbox. He clicked it opened and read the names of the Operatives who were already in the New Kootenay area. They were 'Scarecrow' and 'Cinder'.

The names of the five that were en-route were Operatives 'Echo', 'Oakwood', 'Ten Seventy', 'Tangiera' and 'Crosshair'. The five of them as well as the two that were already in the immediate area were undoubtedly quite the force, in his mind. He replied to Canbra telling her that her selection was good. All seven operatives had been with the K.A.T. Agency for a long time, and were responsible for 210 plus assassinations of K-15 carriers among them. With an average of thirty kills each, give or take a couple, they knew what they were doing, and that is what made them the force they were.

With operatives like that moving into the eastern corridor, it was safe to say that any carrier in that area would be disposed of quickly. The Agency wouldn't know either way, if any K-15 carriers by chance had moved that way until the operatives were settled and began their search. Blain was hopeful that within the week the Agency would get its answer. *A lot can happen in a week and with people like Rob working on research, it would even be better to discover a cure, or a preventable antidote,* Blain sighed as he thought about that. There was always hope.

Back in New Kootenay, Shane Brentwood happened to look out his front window when the car drove past. He was surprised to see the license plate. It was without a doubt the same car and driver who weeks earlier he had seen parked in the driveway of the Dupree home, only a few blocks away. This was the woman who he first saw along the lonely highway as he made his way to New Kootenay. He didn't know how he should react. The desire to kill was no longer a desire or a need. Still, he stared out the window as the car turned toward the downtown core. A small desire to see the woman that was driving that car again filled his gut with excitement.

He didn't want to hurt her only look at her again. That is what his mind told him, but unbeknownst to him, the sight of the car and the possibility of touching the woman woke up the monster, and for a brief moment in time his mind flashed back to the plan he made for her weeks earlier; then, as suddenly, it faded. He shook his head. *No, I can't let it take me over,* he thought as he stepped away from the window. Things were going well. He was getting to know Sapphire in a different way. They were becoming fast and trusted friends, and he didn't want the monster to wake and change things. He didn't want that to happen. He had to keep it suppressed.

Making his way into the bathroom, he splashed cold water on his face to snap himself out of the sick fantasies that were once more beginning to take shape in his mind. He looked at himself in the mirror and deep into his own eyes. *I will not change. I will not let it change me,* he thought as he continued to stare at the face staring back at him. It was as though he was looking at someone else. Averting his eyes now, he looked out the bathroom door to the clock on the wall. He had one hour before his next shift at the Koffee House started, and with that, he stepped away from the mirror and exited the bathroom.

Things went from bad to worst with each thought he had of the woman driving the car with the 'SMOKIN' license plate, and even more so when later that Friday evening, three hours into his shift, the woman and a friend showed up at the Koffee House. Shane tried to stay hidden from her view and continued to work in the back, sneaking peeks every chance he had.

Indeed, it was the same woman. To see her in full view and not sitting in a car only aroused him more. She was as beautiful as he imagined and looked exactly the way he remembered her. A twitch in his stomach reversed time and once more a great desire to have his way with her woke the silent killer that for a time bedded down in the pit of his gut. Awakened now by thoughts of perversion, it simmered and waited.

Shane turned his attention to what he was doing in the kitchen, trying desperately to avoid his desires. The harder he tried, the faster and more vivid the fantasies he once conjured about murder, mayhem, and wrongful conduct battled in his skull. With agonizing brilliancy it seemed to blind him. Biting the inside of his cheek, the metallic taste of blood trickled down his throat, as he battled on, his good against his evil. Then, like a flash, the fantasies vanished into the recesses of his mind and visions of slaughtered pigs and their squealing radiated for a moment. Like a flick from a switch, those too vanished into darkness. Shane shook his head as, he snapped out of his reverie.

Rachel had no reason to look in his direction, but she did and for a brief moment their eyes locked. She offered a meek smile and turned back to her friend sitting opposite her.

"I saw that guy a few weeks ago when I came here."

She spoke softly to not be overheard.

"It was kind of creepy, actually. My damn car broke down and I was pulled off the road. Anyway, to make a long story short, he walked by and asked if he could help. Of course I said no, and then he walked away, but stopped where I could see him, and just stood there hitchhiking. It was creepy."

She took a sip of her coffee as she waited for her friend Kali to respond.

"He looks kind of cute, I would say. Look at him, he's almost dreamy," Kali chuckled, "Did you give him a ride?"

"No, I drove right by when the car finally started," Rachel smirked with embarrassment.

"What a meanie, I would have given him a ride. He can't be that old. What made you creep out?"

"I don't know, probably my own imagination. I wasn't having a very good day. Let's just say that."

"Fair enough. Anyway, I still think he's kind of cute. I'm going to ask Sapphire what his name is the next time I see her. Maybe I can convince him to buy me a drink sometime."

Kali winked at her. She was always such a flirt, but, she was single and as far as Rachel was concerned, her business was her business.

She shook her head, "Oh, come on Kali, he's probably half your age."

"I know. That is what makes him cute; that, and the fact that he is new to town."

"Get your mind out of the gutter, Kali, geez," Rachel smiled. "You sound like you are desperate or something."

Kali shrugged her shoulders.

"Maybe I am," she chuckled as she finished the last of her coffee. "Anyway, it is getting on to 7:30 p.m. We should probably hit the shops if we want to get in some shopping. A new boutique has opened. I'll take you there."

"Yeah, I think if we stay here much longer you'll get even more hot and bothered. Come on, I'll buy the coffees and you buy the first drink later. How does that sound?" Rachel joked.

"Sounds good to me. I'll meet you out at the car," Kali said as the two rose from their table.

Rachel made her way to the counter and Shane approached. He didn't want to at first, but it was his job after all and so far he had kept himself under control.

"Hello," he said in a friendly voice.

"Hello."

Rachel handed him their bill, hoping he hadn't noticed her.

"That'll be three dollars even," Shane said as he punched in the keys. "How is the car running?" he asked letting her know he did recognize her.

"Excuse me?" Rachel questioned as though she was oblivious to his question.

"Your car, how is it running? I saw you along the highway a few weeks ago."

Shane remained friendly as he pried.

"Oh, that was you. Oh my god, I didn't recognize you. How are you?" Rachel questioned as she handed him a $5 bill. "You can keep the change for the young lady who served us."

"Yeah, that was me. I'll make sure Beth gets a two dollar tip," Shane said his heart speeding up as he looked at her. "I'm doing okay I guess to answer your other question."

"Good to know. I'm sorry I didn't pick you up, but a woman alone in a car along a desolate highway has to be careful."

Rachel offered an apologetic smile.

"Yeah, no problem. I got a ride only a few minutes later. No hard feelings," Shane smiled back.

"Good, alright. Have a good night."

Rachel turned and made her way out to her car. Kali was already seated.

"What took so long? You were flirting with him, weren't you?" she joked as she looked at Rachel.

"No. I was only apologizing for not picking him up. And you know what? Under those lights, he is kind of cute," she chuckled as she pulled out of the parking lot and headed to the city.

"I told you so. Did you get his name?" Kali teased.

"No, I'm married," Rachel chuckled, "besides we're probably both old enough to be his mother."

"Nothing wrong with a little flirting, Rach, geez you are married not buried."

"Kali! Shame on you. I haven't flirted with anyone in years, I've probably forgotten how."

"No. A woman never forgets how to flirt. Anyway, enough of that talk," Kali said as she wound down her window. It was a warm evening as they pulled up to the new boutique in downtown New Kootenay.

"Well here it is, the 'Clothesline Ladies Store'. They have a really nice selection of cute apparel," Kali mentioned as they parked.

"It looks nice from out here," Rachel said as she turned her car off and they stepped out.

"You are going to love it, Rachel. I was here last week and bought a treasure trove of lingerie at a very decent price too. Come on, let's get to it."

Kali lead the way inside. The boutique was all that Kali said it was. They spent a few minutes browsing and Rachel picked out a few different pieces of lingerie. It was different from any of the stuff she bought before. Usually her garments were satin or silk. The ones she was going to buy today were leather, black and shiny. She might be a little embarrassed when she purchased them she knew, but she did have to admit they looked damn good on her when she tried them on. Kali also admitted the same.

"Oh, Rachel, Blain is going to love you in that get up. You look stunning," Kali commented as she gave her opinion on how good Rachel looked.

"I hope he doesn't get scared away. I have never bought leather before."

Rachel shrugged her shoulders smugly and offered her quirky smile as she returned to the dressing room.

"He'll be everything except scared, Rachel. Trust me. You've even got me worked up."

Rachel began to laugh as she dressed back into her shopping clothes.

"Are you flirting with me, Kali?"

"I'll never tell," Kali responded as she looked on another rack of good time bedtime attire.

"Well, if you were, just so you know, I'm married," Rachel chuckled as she made her way over to her. "God, there is even some nice stuff on this rack. I love this lacy unmentionable," she said as she touched it to see how it felt between her fingers. "I should grab this too," she said as she removed it from the rack and draped it over her arm with the others she was going to buy.

Kali also bought a few camisoles to add to the slew of bedtime wear she already owned. She was quite the lingerie connoisseur, but she too looked stunning in all that she bought. Kali's long, dirty blonde hair hung down to her lower back, her big doe-full brown eyes were always cheerful, and her voluptuous red lips and beautiful smile were enough to please anyone. She melted many men's hearts and even a few women too. Her body was very athletic and her breasts were firm and taut. She was single and for as long as Rachel and she were friends, she always had been. She was a one nightstand type of woman and rarely stayed with any man for more than a few months. Her sexual prowess was a normal heterosexual one, but she did have experiences with women on occasion. Rachel, though didn't know that.

"We should maybe pick up a bottle of wine and go back to your mother's and try these on again. What say you Rachel?"

"Sure, we could do that. What about the movie we were going to see?"

"We can see it some other time or we could go. It is up to you, I suppose," Kali said as the two approached the cashier counter.

"Well, wine and a quiet night sounds good to me. Sure, let's do that. Then I can at least be by the phone in case Blain or mother's doctor calls."

She laid her items on the counter and waited for Kali to finish with her purchases.

"Great. We can have a girls' night out, but at home. Sounds fun to me."

Kali reached into her purse and pulled out her credit card, to pay for the items.

"What kind of wine should we get?" she asked as the cashier took the card.

"I don't know. I like a medium kind of sweet red wine a Blush or something," Rachel suggested as Kali removed her shopping bag, and Rachel moved up to pay for her own purchases.

"Okay, sweet and dry it is. I'll meet you at the car," Kali said as she exited and waited.

"If I may make a suggestion on the wine," the young lady running the cash registered began.

"Sure, what would you suggest?" Rachel asked, as the lady continued ringing up her purchases.

"A Riesling wine is very good. It is a white wine, but very good. The best red in my opinion is a Merlot."

She looked at the cash register as she punched in the total cost of Rachel's purchases.

"That will be two hundred and fifty six dollars. Will you be paying cash, credit card or debit?"

She looked back at Rachel.

"I'll use debit," Rachel said as she reached into her purse and found her debit card.

She slid it through the handheld debit card slot and punched in her numbers.

"So, you would suggest a Merlot?" she questioned as she waited for her receipt.

"Oh, for sure I would. A Blush is good too, though," the cashier said as she handed Rachel her shopping bag. "There you go. You girls have fun tonight."

The cashier smiled as Rachel turned and made her way out to meet Kali.

"Guess our next stop is the Liquor Store," Rachel said as she seated herself behind the wheel and started her car.

"Yeah, the best one is on Main and Parkway. It isn't far. Besides it'll give us a few minutes to whistle at the hunks walking around," Kali chuckled. "So you like a sweet medium wine. I always thought you liked white wine."

Kali ran her fingers through her hair trying to straighten it up from having the window rolled down.

"Actually, I like both. I just feel like red wine tonight."

"We'll get both, a red and a white."

"Gee, are you out to get drunk?" Rachel asked with a smirk as she slowed down for a streetlight.

"Why not? We haven't tied one on together for ages. I think it would be fun."

Kali looked out her window and smiled.

"I suppose. It can't hurt. Okay, so we'll get two bottles. I'm not sure how we'll feel in the morning, but it'll be Saturday so who cares," Rachel replied as the light changed to green and they continued on their way.

It was close to 9:00 p.m. when they finally pulled into Rachel's mother's driveway.

"Here we are," she said as she turned her car off.

"Yep, here we are. It has been a while since I've been here. Looks like your mom has kept everything pretty much the way it has always been. I hope she gets well, Rachel. She is doing okay isn't she?" Kali asked as they made their way to the front door and Rachel unlocked it.

"Yeah, she is doing well. Might even be home by early next week. The doctors wanted to keep her in the hospital for a few more days. All her tests were good though. They're just being cautious, which, as far as I'm concerned, is appreciated. I don't want her getting any worse. She's too young and full of spunk, you know."

Rachel opened the door and the two stepped inside. Setting their purchases on the kitchen table Rachel looked at Kali.

"Red or white to start with?" she asked as she found two wine glasses.

"I'll have whatever you are having."

"Red it is," Rachel said as she poured them each a glass.

Turning back to the table where Kali sat, she handed her a glass.

"Do you want to go sit in the living-room? I think I have some old Neil Diamond records kicking around here."

"I haven't heard Neil in ages. Yeah, for sure."

Kali rose from the table and followed Rachel.

"God, I can't even remember the last time I heard any Neil Diamond, come to think of it," she commented as she sat down on the couch.

"Me neither, but I love his dreamy voice."

Rachel set her glass of wine down on the fireplace mantel and began looking through all the old vinyl records that her mother kept. Kali sat back and watched sipping her wine. She and Rachel had been friends for over twenty years and she always found her to be quite attractive. It stirred her a bit as she looked on staring at Rachel's backside. She even gave herself a quick little tweak between her legs. *Perhaps after a few more glasses of wine, and showing off the lingerie we each bought, things could progress to a sexual level,* she thought. It would be an unforgettable experience, and likely the first woman to woman experience that she ever had, Kali reminisced as she looked on.

"Ah, I found one," Rachel said as she turned to show Kali just as Kali removed her hand from between her own legs.

Rachel caught it from the corner of her eye and she smiled as though she had seen nothing.

"Look at this Kali, Neil Diamond's greatest hits."

She began to chuckle as she turned back toward the record player and set the record to play.

"I love this song, Rachel. Come on let's dance."

Kali stood up and began dancing by herself, totally in tune with beat. Rachel stared back at her and almost blushing stood up and began to dance too. By the third song on the first side of the album, they were dancing together, wine glasses in their hands, innocently flirting with each other, whimsically of course, or so Rachel thought. The more they danced, the steamer things seemed to get, and by the time the red wine was gone and the white wine was cracked opened, it was obvious to both where it was all leading.

It started with the lingerie show each put on for the other under candlelight. By 1:00 a.m. they were lying beside each other on the living room floor with pillows propped up under their heads as they continued to sip wine and talk, every now and again running their fingers over each other in a sensual pleasing manner.

It was around this time that Shane was on his way home, and only because of curiosity and wonderment did he walk pass the Dupree home. He could see the flickering candlelight as he stood on the street looking in and he could hear the sound of light music playing softly. It was faint, but he could hear it. Curiosity and bad intent made him approach closer to the house and peer through another window. From there he could see the two women lying on the floor, wine glasses in their hands, both dressed scantily in lingerie. He felt his heart speed up and a lustful urge as he stepped away, both embarrassed that he looked and titillated at what he saw. Quickly he made his way back onto the street and out of the Dupree yard.

After walking only to the end of the street, he had a great desire to see more and he doubled back entering the backyard of the home. He had scouted the house out before and knew that the big glass door in the backyard looked directly into the living room where the two women lay. He was more than quiet as he made his way near it and peered in. The two women were now both standing, their arms wrapped around each other as they swayed this way and that, dancing to the softly playing music.

The lingerie that each wore made the scene that much more exciting. He felt tingly and aroused, as he watched on. He had never seen women in that state of half-dress. His eyes glued to them as they continued to engage in the sensual acts they employed on one another. It was a night he never would forget. As the candles inside were blown out one by one, and Rachel and Kali walked hand in hand to the bedroom, Shane turned and walked home, his mind unraveling with intrigue and sexuality. Oddly, not once as stared did he feel the monster's presence. What he did feel was simple curiosity and a desire to finally lie with a woman and experience the sexual bliss that came with it. It was as he sat alone in his apartment that he felt a sudden urge and desire to conjure up the monster. He wanted it to push him back to the house and into the room into which the two women retreated.

He wanted to smell their skin and hair, suckle their breasts and fondle them, but the monster lay dormant. Shane shook his head as he realized what he was thinking and he turned the switch in his mind off. He wanted his good to be with him when he experienced a woman for the first time, not his bad. Yet his good didn't know how to play the game forward, but his evil did. Confusion and right from wrong battled in his mind like a screaming opera as he sat there alone and discontented. Finally, his eyes grew weary and he retreated to his bedroom. Sleep took him quickly and as he dozed, visions of the scantily dressed women premiered in his dreams, dancing and swaying this way and that as they caressed each other.

Chapter 22

It was early Saturday morning when the knock to his front door woke Blain. It was Rob.

"Hey, Rob. Wow, what is going on? It's early. Just 6:00 a.m. You must have some news that couldn't wait. Come on in, I'll get coffee going," Blain said as he invited him in.

"Yeah, coffee sounds good. I've discovered two things, but you best be sitting down when I tell you."

Rob made his way to the kitchen table and sat down.

"What have you come up with Rob? You must've been busy to have come up with something so soon. Sure hope it is good news."

Blain sat across from him as they waited for the coffee to be ready.

"I have a little of both, good and not so good. Firstly, I don't know how, he found me, but... are you ready for this, Blain? Your brother Trent has contacted me. He isn't dead. He's been in Uganda, Africa."

Blain pushed his chair out and stood up quickly. "What?" he asked in shock as though Rob was completely out of his mind.

"He is coming back to Calimay with a possible antidote for K-15. Apparently, he's been down in Africa and has for the past 13 years been working at the Uganda Disease Control. I know this sounds like bullshit, but believe me, Blain, it was Trent. No one else could have known what he knew when he called me."

Rob paused for a moment as he noted Blain's discontent.

"He mentioned the cabin at Mud Creek and said that there is some more documentation in a wooden box buried near one of the property stakes. He said that he put it there when you guys first saw the cabin. He said the document explains the discovery of a possible antidote that needed to be researched. Blain, are you listening?"

Blain shook his head.

"Yeah, yeah, carry on."

"The Uganda Government has kept him hidden and protected for all these years. They were very close to discovering an antidote for what they call 'Laughing Disease' a new form of Kuru that hit Uganda hard in the early 90's. They discovered Trent's research and read all the scientific documentation that he wrote. It was their belief that he was as close to discovering an antidote as they were, and they offered him a deal he couldn't turn down.

I'm not sure why he faked his death other than to protect the K.A.T. Agency. Maybe he thought it was best for the Agency to carry on while he headed to Africa. The research he said that he was doing down there has taken twelve years to complete, and only this year in March was it completed. He said they used human guinea pigs, and have now confirmed that the antidote or cure has been successful in curing the human subjects that they used."

Rob took a breath as he looked into Blain's eyes and waited for a response.

Blain ran his fingers through his hair trying to grasp all that he said.

"Holy shit! I don't know what to think. This is unbelievable. Are you certain it wasn't someone else?"

"It couldn't have been. Who else could have known as much as he did about me, Chase, and your cabin at Mud Creek? I know how hard it is to believe, but he said he'll be back here in the next few days. He called from a hotel pay phone in Uganda, so I don't even have a number for him. I honestly don't know what to think either, but I'm most certain it was Trent," Rob said in all seriousness and sincerity.

"I don't understand why he didn't contact me. That makes no sense."

Blain grew silent for a moment as he contemplated.

"Come here, I need to show you something."

He gestured for Rob to follow him downstairs to his computer.

"When we were up at Mud Creek, I did find a couple of 3.5 floppy disks, two to be exact. I didn't say anything when you asked if I knew if it was possible that Trent had something like that because I wanted to look at them for myself first. I've looked at one that was full of pictures he and I took."

Blain turned on his computer as he and Rob pulled up chairs.

"I don't see how pictures are going to help us here, Blain," Rob commented as they waited for the computer to boot up.

"There is one picture that might. Hang on, I'll show you."

He reached into his desk drawer and pulled out the two floppies.

"These are the two I found," he said as he slipped the first one into the floppy disk drive of his computer.

Scrolling, he found the picture he was looking for.

"Look closely at that, Rob. Trent seems to be pointing at a property stake. I'm betting that is where the missing floppy and other documents are, if what the caller, be it Trent or someone else, was referring to when they contacted you," Blain said hesitantly not so sure that the caller was indeed Trent.

Until he saw him for himself, he would remain skeptical.

Rob looked closely at the picture and was convinced that was what Trent or 'the caller' was referring too.

"I'd say that is a pretty telling picture. Of course, he's pointing directly at that stake. That only convinces me more that it was Trent I was speaking with. I can't imagine anyone else knowing all that he did."

"Well, that is the question; was it Trent, or was it someone else?"

Blain shrugged his shoulders, he wanted nothing more than for the caller to be Trent, but he had his doubts.

"Anyway, moving on from that, it looks as though another trip to Mud Creek is needed. Did the caller say anything else, such as when he was going to be in Calimay or who he would contact then? Anything like that?"

"No. Only that he would be arriving in a few days. I never thought to clarify when he would be here. In hindsight, I guess I should have."

"What we know is this. Someone claiming to be Trent, or on a long shot was Trent, has said that there is more information regarding K-15 buried near a property stake at the cabin in Mud Creek. We also know or have been told that this person has an antidote secured that was developed in Uganda, Africa, that it has been in development for thirteen years and is now formulated. We also know this person claimed to be Trent. Until that can be confirmed, however, I have reservations, to be honest with you. It only adds to the mystery, though. You and I know that his body was never identified by a coroner. It was only speculation that it was his body we buried. It is definitely a mystery now, Rob. We're going to have to move fast and see what comes of it all.

You said you also had something else to share. What is it?" Blain asked as he ejected the floppy and put it back in its case.

"The not so good news is that my research over these last few days has shown that K-15 is about to or already has morphed to an STD. It seems to change every five to seven years from one thing to another. That is the bad news. It is about to change again from the cannibalistic symptoms we are now familiar with to one that can and will be spread via sexual contact. If we can't come up with something soon, the human race is going to be doomed."

"Christ sakes, Canbra and I discussed this. The Agency was doing research on that possibility too. There was nothing concrete though; they were only looking into it. How were you able to come up with this concept?"

"With the stuff Chase and I were able to discover way back when and with what Trent found out and the stuff that the Agency was working on in the research they gave you to do. I discovered that there are likely five stages of K-15. We're already in the fourth stage, where it is now an STD. The first stage is Kuru. The second is K-15. The symptoms then, as you are aware, were murderous rampages committed by those infected, almost like a human form of rabies. The third stage is what we have been battling since, you know, cannibalism. I don't have a clue what the fifth stage is, but I am positive the fourth stage of K-15 will be spread through sexual contact. The fifth stage is anyone's guess, but I'd bet it will include birth deformities or neurological disorders. In other words, we may see a rise in birth defects of all types from mental to physical.

It isn't farfetched to say that those men who are infected who impregnate women, or women carriers who become pregnant, will be giving birth to children who are born killers. Alternately, they will be born so incapacitated by physical deformities that they will not survive. It won't be pretty either way."

Rob sighed as he thought about a world like that.

"That is a gloomy outlook. I'm not sure how exactly I want to play these cards. Should we or should we not inform the Agency? Or, are we better off waiting to see what comes our way in the next few days, after we retrieve whatever it is Trent has buried up at Mud Creek?" Blain questioned.

"My opinion is this. I say we wait and see if Trent shows up and we or you get whatever it is that is up at Mud Creek."

There was a short pause.

"You said you haven't looked at this floppy."

Rob picked up the second floppy.

"I think we should have a look right now. It might even have more information."

He handed it to Blain.

"I agree."

Blain took it from him and plugged it into the disk drive. There was only one folder on it, and he opened it. The folder contained another picture with a simple caption that read 'black light'. The picture was that of a piece of paper that read 'K-15'. There was nothing else visible. It did, however, look familiar and was in Blain's own handwriting.

"What the hell could that mean, 'black light'? That is in Trent's writing. The 'K-15' though, was done by my hand, but I've probably written that on thousands of pieces of paper over the years. What could it mean? I, I don't get it."

Then it came back to him.

"Wait a second! I remember writing that down for Trent once on a piece of paper. He was busy on the phone or something and asked me to write it down, so I did and he took it from me."

Blain grew silent as he reminisced and tried to remember what happened after that.

"The next day that same piece of paper that I wrote K-15 on was on my desk again, but there was no writing whatsoever on it, which is how and why I can remember, because it seemed odd. I think I tossed it into a box. I can't remember if I ever threw the box out or not. Of course, it was so long ago I likely have since then. I still don't understand what 'black light' means."

"That is weird. Humph, what the heck," Rob stroked his whiskered chin in deep thought.

"I know there was a time when I was in research for the Agency and not a field assassin, we sometimes goofed around with a type of novelty ink that could only be viewed under black light. That is probably what he is alluding to. You don't think there is any chance you still have that box?"

"It's been years and I haven't seen that scrap piece of paper since. I imagine it has been tossed out by now. To be certain I'd have to look through all the crap I have stored at the office. It is easily enough done."

Blain looked again at his computer screen and the Jpeg of the piece of paper.

"I can't believe that these two floppy's contain only Jpegs. If there is a third, I'm betting it is up at Mud Creek. I wonder, though, if it will contain only Jpegs too?"

"We'll never know until we find out what Trent has buried near that stake. I say we come up with an idea soon, Blain. I don't know. Maybe I can head to Mud Creek and you can stick around here and wait to see if Trent contacts you. Umm, I, ah well, I'm not sure what you want to do."

"I agree we have to find out what exactly is going on. I think, however, that I should head to Mud Creek. Whoever this person is, Trent or not, is more likely to contact you, since they made contact with you first," Blain responded as he sighed. "Explaining another trip to Rachel isn't going to be easy."

The two made their way back upstairs and to the kitchen. Blain poured each of them a coffee and they sat at the table, talking amicably.

"By the way," Blain started, "you said you have been living in Fruitmont for ten years or so. Did you ever hear the name Tyler O'Brien?" he asked as he took a drink of his coffee.

"Hmm, O'Brien? No, I don't think I have. Remember, I live in the boonies, I don't spend much time in town. Why do you ask?"

"Was curious. I went to the library yesterday to see if I could find anything on the name Brentwood. I didn't, but I did come across a small article about a private investigator named Tyler O'Brien who shot and killed a fellow. I thought it was kind of strange since Tyler O'Brien was the investigator who questioned me after I was shot in Canupe."

Rob was thinking back trying to remember if maybe he did know a Tyler O'Brien, but nothing jumped out at him.

"And he is from Fruitmont?"

"I guess he was, but he was sent to Ridgeville or something like that. I really didn't pay much attention to the gist of the story. Was just interesting is all. Thought maybe you might have heard of him."

"Nope. That name doesn't ring a bell at all. There is a Henderson & Co Private Investigating Firm in Fruitmont. It is probably the only one. Likely your friend worked from there."

Rob stood up and gestured to Blain if he wanted another coffee and if it was okay for him to help himself to a refill.

"Yeah, I'll take another."

Blain handed Rob his cup.

"I do remember that the office he worked from was Henderson & Co. In fact, that is what his business card says too. So, you don't recall a story where a PI killed some guy in Fruitmont or near Fruitmont?"

Rob handed Blain his coffee as he sat down.

"Humph, honestly I don't recall. You seem pretty interested in this O'Brien fellow. Why is that?" Rob asked out of curiosity.

"Not really. I only thought that maybe you knew him."

They sat in silence for a few moments and enjoyed their coffee. Havoc lay on the floor next to Blain's feet. He began to chuckle as he recalled the damage Havoc did to Rachel's living-room curtains and he told the story to Rob.

"Damn dog. Yesterday when I went to the library I left the little pipsqueak alone. By the time I got home he had ripped the living-room curtains and curtain rod completely off the wall. They were scattered across the floor, ripped and torn."

Blain half chuckled and shook his head.

"Don't know what I'm going to do with him if Rachel doesn't come back soon. She had to go to New Kootenay again. Her mother fell ill. Not sure when she's coming back, but I assume I'll be gone by then. There doesn't seem to be enough hours in a day"

Blain sighed.

"Shit, I have to get back to Mud Creek, and at the same time somehow get over to Clarkston and meet up with some of the operatives at the Agency's office. I hate that drive, so flat and straight. Oh well, so be it. Such is life."

"I hear you. I never liked that drive much either. When are you supposed to show up there?"

"Thursday of next week or so I said to Canbra. Not sure I'll make it now."

Blain brought his cup to his lips and took a drink.

Swallowing, he added, "Not sure I want to go all the way back to Mud Creek either. I'd hate to miss out on what is going to happen presumably in the next couple of days with that caller of yours. I think, I'll hold off until we know what is what. You seem to have got quite far with the research without whatever it is that is up at Mud Creek."

"True enough. Whatever it is, it isn't something that is needed yet. The best thing probably is to stick around, and see if Trent shows up. Then there will be no need for another trip up there, unless, of course, it is something that is relevant."

Blain nodded his head.

"Yeah, I don't see any need right now. Besides, if I can find that box where I tossed that piece of paper that needs to be viewed under a black light, there might be something to that. Plus, I'm still trying to track down that name 'Anvil Brentwood'. Another trip to Mud Creek would slow that investigation down. I'll probably head over to the dungeon sometime today and see if I can't come up with the box or a lead on the name. What about you, what do you have planned?"

"I'll probably head back home in a bit and stick by the phone in case the caller calls back. There is some stuff I could still be doing back there. I can't say for sure that we have come up with any conclusions today, other than there is definitely something buried up at your cabin, and that we now know what 'black light' means."

Rob half chuckled.

"That is about all we have resolved. I had to come here though to let you know about that caller and what my opinion is regarding the research I've done these past few days. I guess it wasn't a total loss."

"That it wasn't, Rob. If you hadn't filled me in about the caller and the black light deal, I wouldn't have had a clue. I appreciate your perseverance too in the research you have done."

"A lot of it was already compiled. With everything you gave me, it has been that much easier. There are undoubtedly some things that obviously can't be overlooked and there are some things that can be. Once you figure that out, the research will always point you in the right direction. It does take patience and a bit of an imagination though, and some understanding of formulas and encryption," Rob replied as he stood up. "Anyway, the day isn't going to get any longer. I think I'm going to head out, Blain. I have an hour's drive ahead of me and a folder of documents four inches thick. I'd best get to it."

Blain now rose from the table too, and put their cups in the sink before walking Rob to the door.

"Yeah. I'll be near my phone and I'll take a look around my office for that piece of paper. Hope I find it. It would be interesting to see what it reads. You have to let me know as soon as you hear from the caller again. I'll keep my phone on 24/7 until I hear from you. And don't be a stranger, Rob. Feel free to pop by anytime night or day. If I'm not here, I'm usually at my office."

"Okay, Blain. I'll be sure to contact you with anything else that comes about. Maybe I should email you the findings of my research regarding the morphing of K-15. It is easier to understand in black and white. Might be an idea to shoot it to Canbra. I don't know, it is up to you."

Rob shrugged his shoulders as he bent down to put on his boots.

"You can certainly send it to me, but I won't be sending it to the Agency yet. I want to find out if this caller is indeed Trent. If he is, well, I'll fill in the Agency with everything we know then. But I'll do it when I head to Clarkston next week. If it is Trent, he can come with me. We'll get your name cleared up too, Rob. I think the K.A.T. Agency will have a place for you in the end. You do good work, and I appreciate your commitment to the project."

"I don't know, Blain. I kind of like being a free agent. I wouldn't be too upset, though, if you did clear my name. Then maybe I can start living openly again and not in obscurity. But who knows? Maybe I will come back to the Agency. For now, I think we should continue to carry on as we are until we have more answers than we do questions; for example, who the hell is that caller and what the hell is up at Mud Creek?" Rob said as he opened the door and stepped out into the cool morning.

"Indeed we will, Rob. Alright then. I guess I'll see you next time."

"You bet, Blain. We'll see you."

Rob made his way to his truck and pulled out of the driveway waving as he headed in the direction of home. Blain returned the gesture and watched as Rob turned down the street and out of site.

Interesting stuff he had for me. Sure glad he filled me in on that black light secret. Now if only I could find that damn piece of paper, Blain thought as he entered the house. There were other things on his mind too. *Who was the caller? Could it have been Trent?* After contemplating everything, running it all through his mind and processing all possibilities, his conclusion was that indeed it was possible. He would certainly give him an earful if it turned out to be so. *Why would he leave for Africa and not tell me?* Blain couldn't understand that, but he knew Trent and if Trent had a reason for disappearing as he had, then he would not hesitate to explain it to him when they met again.

Still, it bothered him to a degree that his own brother would do that. He must have had his reasons. Blain poured himself another coffee and sat once more at the table, reveling in the possibility of being reunited with Trent, and he smiled. *Going to keep my fingers crossed for the time being, though. It could be someone else,* he thought as he took a drink. He looked over to the wall clock. It was a little after 9:00 a.m. Since it was Saturday, he decided to hang at home and enjoy his manicured lawn and the sunshine. Maybe he'd finally get his chance to stretch out on his hammock and sip a cool drink. With coffee in hand, he made his way out to the deck, Havoc close behind. "Don't be digging any holes, you crazy dog. We just had that all fixed up," Blain said as Havoc darted out onto the lawn and began rolling in the flush, cool grass.

Birds chirped and crows cawed, and Havoc, well, he was being Havoc. Even before Blain could make it to the bottom step to scold him, he had dug another hole.

"No, Havoc, no! Bad dog, go on, go lie down. Jesus Christ, enough of that," Blain scolded as Havoc ran onto the deck and lay down with a sulking look on his face.

Kicking dirt back into the hole, Blain stomped on it to pack it in. So began his Saturday at home.

Rachel and Kali were slowly rolling out of bed, both a little embarrassed at the fact that they had spent the night together.

"I slept well. How about you, Rachel?" Kali asked as she rose from the bed.

"I have a bit of a headache, but I would say I slept well too. I can't believe we did what we did."

Rachel meekly smiled as she too now rose from the bed. It wasn't as bad as she thought it would have been. In fact, the night had been pleasant. It only seemed odd to her since she had never been with another woman. She felt some guilt, but it faded as they took turns showering and cleaning up. One day she would tell Blain, but for now it would remain a secret between herself and Kali. It was 10:00 a.m., when they finally sat down at the kitchen table and had their morning coffee.

"What are your plans for today, Kali?" Rachel asked as she sipped her coffee.

"I'm not sure, but I think I'll head for home soon and lounge. What about you?" she asked. "Maybe later today you can swing by my place and have a dip in the pool."

"I wish I could, but I have to go see mother sometime, plus I told Blain I would call him today. Other than that, I think I'll take it easy today. Maybe I'll spend the afternoon sun tanning on the deck. I'll probably have to do some minor gardening too. I really hate that type of work when I have to do it."

Rachel wrinkled up her nose as she smiled.

"You're not going to tell anyone about last night are you?"

She was embarrassed that she even asked, but she didn't want it getting around that the two of them had actually pleasured each other.

"No, don't worry about it, Rachel. My lips are sealed."

Kali took a drink of her coffee.

"It wasn't all that bad was it?"

"No actually, it was a very nice experience. I have a feeling though that you have done it before with a woman."

“I have a few times, but I don’t practice it. I like men too.”

“Obviously, the way you were checking out the guy at the Koffee House yesterday.”

Kali began to chuckle.

“Yeah, I like them younger than I. The old fellows don’t do for me what the younger ones do. I guess I’m a bit of a pervert.”

She winked at Rachel.

“I really enjoyed last night with you though. You are a beautiful woman, Rachel, very sexy too.”

“Thanks Kali. You too are very sexy. I never thought I’d ever roll around with a woman, but since I have, and it was my first time too, I’m glad it was with you. You really knew how to make me feel.”

Rachel was blushing as she said that.

“I just go with the motion. I know what I like, so I guess it is easy to figure out what another woman might also like. I’m glad that we did it.”

“I am too in a way. I’ve always admired you. You are a good friend, and now you are even a better friend. I feel kind of shy talking about it, but I am glad things unfolded as they did. Blain is going to be so intrigued when I finally tell him, if I ever do. I might keep it a secret.”

She began to smirk.

“He has often teased me about fooling around with a woman, and now that I have, I would probably do it again.”

“I’ll do it with you anytime, Rachel.”

Kali smiled as she rose from the table.

“I guess I’ll toddle off. It is getting on to 11:00 a.m. and I have a house to clean and laundry to do. Maybe you can call me later after you see your mother. Make sure you tell her I said ‘hi’. I might even swing by her room myself later. But to be honest, I really find hospitals to be a drag."

Kali slipped on her shoes.

"Anyway Rach, if you get bored later you can always call me. Being that it is Saturday though, I might be out on the prowl."

Kali began to laugh, "Maybe I'll swing by the Koffee House later and see if that dreamy looking guy is there."

"You are crazy, Kali, you know that."

"I know, but if I wasn't crazy I think I'd be pretty dull. Craziness is the spice of life and I love my life. I'm independent, I have my own money, and I have fun. What more could a single gal want, eh?"

"Yeah, sometimes I wonder how my life would have turned out if Blain and I hadn't married. Would I still be single, or would I be married to an asshole? Now I wonder if maybe I would have been a lesbian," Rachel chuckled as she kissed Kali on the cheek.

"I think you would be much the way that I am, independent and obviously rich," Kali said as she looked around the house.

"I often wondered why your family never kept your dad's business. He sure knew how to build houses. You probably would have been an awesome architect. Your and Blain's house in Calimay proves that."

"I don't know. Dad was always away working. The only time we ever spent time together was when we went on our holidays, and even then we went away. I don't have the same desire as he had to be constantly on the move. He was indeed a great architect though. There is no doubt about that. Me, well, I can design houses, but I could have never filled his shoes. I'm glad for the way my life has turned out. I'm married to a great man, although sometimes a little unruly. Still, he's mine and I'm his. That is what makes me happy."

"I have to admit, the two of you are a great pair. Anyway, I guess I should get."

Kali turned and exited, Rachel close behind.

"Maybe I will call you later, Kali. Maybe we could have dinner or something. Either way, I want to hang out with you again before I head back to Calimay," Rachel said as she stood on the porch.

"When do you think you'll be heading back?"

"Not until I get mother home and settled. By the way, you wouldn't happen to know any homemakers who live in, do you?"

"Like a nanny, you mean?"

"Well, someone who can help my mom out. It would be great if they were a nurse or something. I just don't want to have to hire one from the hospital. I'd rather hire someone who my mom would like. So far she doesn't like many of the nurses there."

"I don't blame her. I'll keep my ears open. If I hear of anyone like that, I'll let you know. It sounds to me that you want someone who can keep her company and to help her out around the house."

"Exactly, just someone she gets along with and who can help her with the day to day chores and shopping, that kind of thing."

"Okay, I'll ask around a bit. I do know of one girl, well, she's more of a woman than a girl, but she is younger than we are. She has done that type of work. She actually lived with my aunt until she passed away. She would probably want something long term, if she isn't already working. I'll check."

"Thanks, Kali," Rachel said as Kali opened her car door and slipped inside, waving as she pulled out of the driveway.

Rachel waved back, smiled, and blew her a kiss. *Last night, my God! I can't believe I did that with her,* Rachel thought as she entered her mother's house and closed the door behind her. *It was sure fun though. Her tongue knew where every one of my tickle spots are.* Rachel shuddered with exhilaration as she thought about it and how good it actually felt.

Kali happened to be driving by as Shane was walking to the store and she spotted him. Slowing her convertible down, she honked her horn and waved.

"Do you need a ride?" she asked as she slowed down to a stop.

Shane looked over and recognized her. He walked over to her car and smiled.

"I'm only going a couple of blocks to the grocery store, but I'll certainly take a ride if it isn't out of your way," he said as he leaned on the car door.

"Sure, no problem. Hop in," Kali commented as she waited for him to be seated. "You work at the Koffee House, right?"

"I do, yes."

"Yeah, I saw you last night. My friend Rachel and I stopped there for early evening coffee."

"Rachel; she's the lady with blue car, right?" Shane asked.

"Yep, that is her. By the way, my name is Kali."

"Nice to meet you, Kali. I'm Shane."

"Nice to meet you too, Shane. That is a nice name, by the way."

"I guess, but so is Kali," Shane chuckled as he looked her over.

She was nice looking. She had a beautiful smile, big breasts, blondish hair, and a tight body that begged to be ravished. He could tell by the way she moved the night before as he spied on them both, that she was very sexual as well. He felt tinges in his stomach as he thought about what he had witnessed.

"So, Shane, I haven't seen you around before. Are you new to New Kootenay?"

"Yeah, I've been here almost a month."

"Really? How long have you been working at the Koffee House?"

"Three weeks."

"You must know Sapphire? She's my niece."

"No way! Really?" Shane asked with excitement. He indeed knew her, and was quite fond of her in more ways than one. "Yeah, I know her. She is the one who hired me. Very nice girl."

"She sure is. I don't get along so well with her mother, my sister, but I certainly adore her."

"So then you are related to Nick?"

"I am. He's my brother-in-law. How do you know him? You must have met him at the Koffee House."

"I did, but I also worked one day with him when I first came here."

"Eew, at the processing plant?"

"Yeah, I was able to hold on for one day. I quit after that."

"I don't blame you. I get sick to my stomach from the smell whenever I visit my sister. Their house sits way back from the plant, but still you can smell that horrible odor. Yuck."

Kali slowed down as she pulled into the grocery store parking lot.

"Well, here we are. I'm going to pick up a few things too, so I can give you a ride back also if you like," Kali said as she closed the convertible's roof and the two of them stepped out.

"That would be great, thanks," Shane said as they walked the short distance to the sliding glass doors. He waited for Kali to go in first and he followed looking briefly at her from behind. The perfume she was wearing made his heart skip a beat. She smelled good and he silently inhaled her scent. Kali wasn't fooled. She could feel his eyes on her, and in a way it made her feel sexy and she felt a tinge of her own.

"I have to pick up a few things from the fruit and vegee produce department, and then I'll meet you back at the car. How does that sound?" she asked as she turned and looked at him.

"Sure," Shane said as he felt himself grow flush. "I'll meet you back at your car," he said as he turned and walked in the opposite direction.

Kali smiled as she now watched him. *Yum yum,* she thought to herself as she made her way to the produce section. *Could I ever have fun with that young hunk. He seems so shy, it makes me wonder if he's ever been with a girl. Oh well, I'll never know I guess, unless of course, I pick him up and bring him home,* she smiled to herself as she thought about that.

Shane too was having similar thoughts, although they were a lot more devious then hers. *I'd love to see that woman nude again and close up this time, I'd fondle her in ways she has never been fondled. I bet she would be a great sex toy,* he thought as he made his own purchases. The two met back at Kali's car and she drove him back to his place.

"Oh geez, you live here? I live down four houses from here on the other side of the street. We're closer than we knew. How do you like renting from Morhad?"

"It is okay. He doesn't bother me. The rent is decent I guess, and the apartment isn't old and dilapidated. It's pretty modern and I like that. I'd invite you in, but I have to get some sleep before work tonight," Shane said to be friendly.

"You work tonight?"

"Yes, from 4:00 until closing at 12:00 midnight. I seem to have been stuck with the night shift," he said as he half chuckled and grabbed his bags from her back seat.

"Well, maybe after you work you could stop by my place, or I could pick you up and we could have a few drinks. What do you think of that?" Kali asked as she smiled that smile of hers. "I have a pool table. Do you like pool, Shane?"

"Honestly, I stayed away from the arcades when I grew up, so I can't say. I have never played so I don't know."

"I think you would like it, so what do you say? I could teach you. Unless, of course, you think I'm being totally absurd. After all, we only just met."

"I don't think you are being absurd at all. I haven't met many people since I moved her, other than Sapphire and few other people from work. Sapphire and I are good friends, and since you are her aunt, I feel like I already know you. I think you are being quite kind actually, so sure I'd love to learn how to play pool."

"Good, so I'll pick you up at around midnight. We can go to my place and have a few drinks and play some pool. What do you like to drink?"

"Pop," Shane said meekly.

"Straight pop?" Kali chuckled.

"I haven't drunk much either. I kind of stayed away from all that stuff."

"Pop it is. No problem."

She knew then that Shane was certainly sheltered and she was feeling herself grow antsy, and her mind fluctuated between reality and fantasy as she conjured up the two of them playing pool in her basement.

"Alright, Shane, I'll see you tonight," Kali said as she waved and slowly pulled out onto the street and headed for home.

Shane waved as she pulled away, and a smile crossed his face. *Interesting, wonder what will come of our meeting, I'm kind of excited,* he thought as he made his way into his apartment and set his groceries down.

The excitement he felt was good. There were no rape and murder fantasies dancing in his head, and he thought that to be kind of strange. Usually all he saw when he was close to women was mayhem. Today though, as with many days that passed, those desires and visions were becoming less frequent, and for that he was grateful. It is not to say that he didn't have fantasies. He often did, but he was training himself that is all that they were. Fantasies about murder and mayhem, after all those years of treatment as a patient at the Calimay Mental Hospital, were finally fading into darkness. Normalcy for him was outweighing the abnormality of his past. This, for him, was good.

Kali pulled into her driveway a few houses down and parked her car. Gathering the items that she bought at both the grocery store and the boutique she and Rachel visited, she entered her house. It was cool inside to a degree that she was forced to open her curtains to let the afternoon sun in to warm things up a bit. Her mind raced to the night that she and Rachel had spent together. It was a night she knew she'd never forget. Rachel was a beautiful woman and her body felt good when they lay beside each other and played. Everything about that evening was as dreamy as the new kid on the block, Shane. *I can't wait to get to know him some. Sure hope Sapphire hasn't got any dibs on him, I could teach him a thing or two,* Kali thought as she made her way to the swimming pool in her backyard. Stretching out on a lounging lawn chair she put her sunglasses on and reminisced about the meeting she had with Shane and the evening she spent with Rachel.

At 1:00 p.m. that Saturday out of the blue, Blain received a phone call. The voice on the other end was familiar.

"Blain, this is Trent, your brother."

Blain was taken aback and he stuttered a response. “I, I, umm, who is this again?” he asked as he slumped into a chair to catch his breath.

“It is me, Trent.”

“Trent has been dead for years. Who the Hell is this?”

“I understand your doubt. It has been many years. But it is me.”

“I don’t understand, how, how can you be alive?”

“I’ll explain it all as soon as I get to Calimay. I’ll be boarding a plane soon and it is scheduled to land at the Calimay International 3:00 p.m., Tuesday. Can you meet me there?”

“How do I know you are who you say you are?”

“Ask me a question that only I would know how to answer,” Trent responded.

Blain grew silent as he thought for a few brief moments on what he would ask.

“Alright, when is my birthday and how old is our mother?”

“Our mother as well as our father are both dead. They were killed in a car accident when you and I were teens. Your birthday is Feb 16th. You were born in Kandaly.”

Blain shook his head, “Anyone could have found that out. I’ll ask you another.”

“Sure, go ahead.”

“What could I have found in Mud Creek taped to the bottom of a table, and where is Mud Creek, and why would I have been there?”

“You and I own a cabin in Mud Creek. It is located near Yellow Lake in the Yukon, and what you found taped under a table would have been two 3.5 inch floppy disks. Chances are, you were there to do research for the K.A.T. Agency that you and I created back in 1993."

A tear rolled down Blain's cheek as he listened to the response from the other end. No one other than Trent could have known what it was he found at Mud Creek.

"Tell me exactly what was on those floppies; also my brother Trent had a scar on part of his body, where is that scar and how did he get it?"

"The floppies have pictures of you and me and a document with 'K-15' written across the top of the page in your handwriting. I have a scar on my left buttock from when you pushed me off a tree swing when we were kids. I landed on an old broken wine bottle. The bottle was green. Have I convinced you?"

"No. You have only convinced me that you may be someone who knows more than they should. I won't be convinced until I lay my eyes on you."

"Then meet me at the Calimay International on Tuesday at 3:00 p.m. I will prove to you then that I am Trent. I'll be wearing a white T-shirt and khaki pants; plus, I'll be wearing aviator sunglasses."

"I'll be there. If I don't see my brother Trent, I will do everything in my power to track you down and I will kill you."

Blain hung up the phone without even saying 'goodbye'." Immediately after that, he dialed Rob's number.

"Hello, Rob. It is me, Blain."

"I know. I see your number on the screen. What's up, Blain?"

"I just got off the phone with that caller of yours. He answered a few questions that only Trent would know. I'm almost convinced it is him. Hard to say though without doubt. The call came from another pay phone, so there was no number listed that I could have called back. He said his plane would be landing here on Tuesday. I'd like you to join me when I meet it at the airport. I may need backup."

"Sure, I can meet you there. What time Tuesday?"

"3:00 p.m."

"I'll be there, Blain."

"Good. Okay, that is all I wanted to pass by you. I appreciate it, Rob. Thanks."

"No problem, Blain. You still aren't convinced that it might be Trent."

"Not really. I mean, I want to believe but I can't until I see him. In three days we'll know the answer I guess."

"Yeah. We could find out if anybody named Trent Sweet boarded a plane, in Uganda, couldn't we?"

"Not really. This is Trent we are talking about. He would be using an alias. I wouldn't even be able to guess what he might look like. Thirteen years changes a person's look. It took me a couple of days to figure out who you were," Blain half chuckled.

"True, but I'm bald now."

"You sure are and maybe Trent is too. I think we'll just show up at the airport and see. That is about all we can honestly do. I don't even know what country or state the call came from. We're kind of at a loss at figuring anything out yet."

"You are probably right. Okay, I'll see you Tuesday at the Calimay airport. Should I be packing?"

"Not on your person, I wouldn't suggest. Maybe store your Glock in your car. I'll be packing mine in my car too. We have to remember this might all be a ruse. It could be someone playing a joke on us. If that is the case, then we'll have to figure out who it is and go from there. If he isn't an operative then we might have some serious problems."

"And if it is we'll have problems too."

"Yep, and we'll have to put a stop to him," Blain sighed. "We'll stick with what is we are doing now. I'll head to my office soon and see if I can't dig up that piece of paper. You might as well continue with your research too. No use worrying over something that isn't going to take place for a few more days."

"Agreed. Alright, I'll talk to you Tuesday, unless something significant comes about."

"Yeah, thanks again, Rob, I'll see you Tuesday," Blain said as he hung up the phone.

He took a few moments to sit in silence and think. If the caller was Trent and he did have a cure or antidote, things would certainly move along quickly, and the K-15 virus that was sweeping across Canada might soon be halted for good. While he sat there at the kitchen table, he realized he had left Havoc outside.

"Aw shit," he said as he stood up quickly and made his way to the backyard.

Surprisingly, Havoc hadn't moved from the spot he was lying when Blain scolded him for digging.

"Good boy, Havoc. I thought for sure you would have dug up the lawn again."

He crouched down and patted him.

"We're probably going to head to the office in a bit. Hope you are up to it."

Blain chuckled as Havoc shook his stubby tail.

"So you are up to it? Good. I'm going to finish my coffee and we'll be off."

Standing now, he opened the sliding glass door and they made their way inside. Havoc as usual jumped over the couch and skidded to a halt in the kitchen. Blain only shook his head and smiled. *Damn dog anyway,* he thought as he made his way to his cooling cup of coffee. Two hours later after ripping his office apart and digging through every old box, he had found nothing.

"Well, I guess that piece of paper I was looking for isn't here. Must have thrown it out I guess," Blain said to Havoc who was lying at his feet. "Hmm, that is too bad," he said as he began putting things away. "Once I get the last of this stuff packed away again, we'll head for home. Rachel is going to call today. It'll be good to hear from her. I hope her mom is recovering well."

Blain tucked the last box away, and sat down at his desk as he waited for his computer to boot up. Then he checked his office email.

"Nothing, of any interest today," he said as he leaned back and stretched. "Alright then," he started as he shut it down. "I guess we're out of here Havoc."

Shutting off his monitor, he rose from his chair and the two headed back home. At 6:00 p.m., Rachel called.

"Hello hon," Blain said as he answered the phone.

"Hey, how are you today? How is Havoc?" she emphasized.

"Which question do you want me to answer first?" Blain teased.

"I'm sorry, Blain," Rachel snickered. "I want to know how you are first."

"That's not how it sounded," he joked, "but, I'm okay. I miss you."

"Tell me about it. I miss you too."

"How is your mom?"

"I saw her today. She's doing well and is recuperating. She'll probably be coming home on Monday. I hope to get out of here by Tuesday or Wednesday at the latest."

"That is great. I'm glad she is doing well. I'm even more pleased that I won't have to eat take-out anymore after Tuesday, if you are home by then, that is."

"Don't count on that, Blain. I might demand you take me out to supper," Rachel chuckled. "I'd love a big thick steak and 'Revs Steakhouse' has the best."

"Revs it is. I'd love one of those too. So, should we make a date of it?"

"Yeah. Tuesday or Wednesday."

"Okay. Wine as well I'm assuming, or should we go all out and order champagne?"

"Either or works for me. I'm getting hungry just thinking about it. How has Havoc been behaving?"

"Well, he is a puppy after all. I had the lawn fixed yesterday and this morning when we went out, he dug another hole. I stopped him though, before he got too carried away."

"You didn't hurt him did you?"

"Not at all. I only scolded him. He did something else too."

"What?" Rachel asked with curiosity.

Blain began to chuckle. "Well, you know those nice long curtains you used to have in the living-room?" he started, "he tore them down and shredded them. Even the curtain rod is bent."

"No! Not the curtains. How the hell did he manage that? Those were a special order."

"I know. Costly too, from what I remember."

"They were. What happened?"

"I guess you could say I'm partly to blame. I left him alone while I went into town. When I got back he was staring through the window. The curtains were all wrapped around him. When he saw me pull in, he darted to the door and pulled the rod right off the wall. It was actually pretty funny. He was okay, but the curtains certainly weren't."

"I guess that is pretty funny. Poor puppy."

"We're the ones that are going to be poor if he keeps up with his antics," Blain chuckled. "Ah, they're just curtains, and to be honest, I really didn't like them that much."

"What do you mean you didn't like them? They were beautiful."

"Through your eyes maybe," he teased.

Rachel smiling on the other end shook her head.

"You even helped me pick them out."

"Did I?" Blain asked with surprise.

"Yes you did. You and mother both helped me pick them out."

"Oh it was during one of those crazy shopping sprees we went on while the house was being built. I probably only agreed to keep you two hens from pecking me."

Rachel rolled her eyes and chuckled. "Whatever." Conversing for a few minutes longer they finally said their "I love you's" and hung up.

"Well Havoc, sounds like Rachel's mom is going to be okay. That is good news, one less thing to worry about."

Feeling bored, Blain rose from the couch and meandered into the kitchen.

"Want to go for a walk, Havoc. We haven't done that yet. What do you say?"

Reaching for Havoc's leash he shook it, and the sound brought him running. So excited was he that he piddled all over the kitchen floor as he ran in circles. Blain watching this shook his head and began to laugh.

"What the heck is that all about? Geez, man, can't you hold it in for a few seconds? Now you are going to have to wait for that walk while I clean this mess up."

It took only a few minutes to do so, and soon afterwards they were on their way.

Havoc, although still a puppy, was strong, and he pulled Blain at first until finally settling down to a comfortable pace.

"Holy, you're a strong little fellow aren't you? I'm not sure where you and Rachel walk, so, carry on. You lead, I'll follow."

Havoc lead him through the Calimay park, past an ice cream shack, down a back alley, and onto 4th street which was two blocks from home, and back again to the front steps of Blain and Rachel's house. The walk in total took almost an hour.

"Wow, I'm out of shape. That walk took a lot out of me, Havoc," Blain said as he sat down on the front steps, Havoc at his side. "You guys walk that route all the time?" he asked as though Havoc would answer.

The truth was it wasn't even close to the route they walked. Havoc sensed that Blain didn't know where to go, so he simply led him around, never once losing the scent of home. His head now lay across Blain's lap as he panted while Blain caught his breath.

"I guess we'll do that route tomorrow too. Maybe next time we can have a break though. Have you ever had ice cream, Havoc? I'm guessing not. Tomorrow night, I'll get you some."

He sat in silence now as he petted Havoc and looked to the horizon. It was warm evening and so he was in no rush to go inside. Instead they went through the gate to the backyard and Blain rested on the deck. Havoc meanwhile played gleefully on the lawn, chewing on a ball and a few lawn ornaments, but not once did he do any digging. Blain watched him with a smile. As Rachel told him, Havoc was certainly growing on him and he would not deny that he was indeed enjoying his presence. *Maybe I do love the little bugger after all,* he thought as he continued to watch the dog play.

The evening grew cool as he sat on the deck, and he and Havoc made their way inside. Blain put food in Havoc's dish and gave him fresh water while he put together a few frozen hamburgers for himself. Sitting down on the couch with his food in his hands, he turned on the television knowing full well there was nothing on. It was more for the noise, and not due to anything he wanted to watch. His mind drifted to the past day's events, the visit from Rob, the phone call from possibly Trent, the conversation he had with Rachel, and even the walk he had with Havoc.

Everything that went on that day raced through his mind as he sat there eating his dull hamburger. He could hardly wait to eat at 'Revs'. He hadn't eaten a steak in a while, nor had he sat down with Rachel in a fancy restaurant for God knew how long, not since the last time they visited 'Revs'. *It has been a long time since she and I ate at a restaurant together. Man, I've really let things go to Hell in a hand basket,* he thought as he finished his last burger. By now Havoc was stretched out on the couch next to him as he sat there skimming through the channels.

Back in New Kootenay, Kali was stepping out of her shower. She was excited at meeting up with Shane and having a few friendly games of pool. There were other things on her mind too, but for now she would let those ideas rest and get to know him before she acted on them. Still, it made her feel moist. Looking in the mirror, she dressed up her face and blow-dried her hair. Adding a few sprays of perfume to her wrists and neck, she pulled on jeans and slipped into a tight shirt that enhanced her already ample breasts. *Nothing wrong with a little embellishment,* she thought, as she once more looked herself over. Satisfied, she locked up and headed for the Koffee House.

Shane was waiting for her in the parking lot as she pulled in. Making his way to her car, his mind raced with what might come from their rendezvous.

"Hey, Shane, how was your shift?" Kali asked as he opened the passenger door and slid in.

"Same as always, busy. I don't suppose you could swing me home so that I could shower?"

"I have a shower," she replied as she pulled out onto the street.

"I'd like to get some fresh clothes if I could."

"Sure, I'll drive you by your place so you can do that, or I could drop you off there and you could meet me back at my place. I'll show you my house when we drive by."

"Thanks."

"No problem, Shane. Was Sapphire on shift tonight?" she asked to start conversation.

"Not tonight. She'll be there Monday, though. I find it gets a bit confusing when she isn't there. I'm slowly learning the ins and outs though," Shane chuckled.

"That's good. It does take a while to learn a new job. Where else have you worked, Shane?"

"Other than with Nick, nowhere. I'm only starting out."

"Really?"

"Yep, I'm from Calimay. I grew up there."

"It is a nice town Calimay. My friend Rachel, who you met the other day, and her husband Blain live there. So you attended both schools in Calimay?" Kali questioned out of curiosity.

"I did, yes." Shane lied.

He didn't want to tell her the truth, and he hoped that would end the questioning. He was beginning to feel a bit uneasy.

Kali slowed down now as they passed her house and she pointed to it.

“That is my place; the blue house with a pool in the back.”

“You have a swimming pool too?”

“Yeah. You are welcome to use it whenever you like, if you want. You must have swum a lot growing up in Calimay. Everyone there swims.”

“I did, yes.” Shane responded as Kali now turned into his driveway.

“Here we are. Should I wait for you?”

“Nah, I’ll have a quick shower and walk down to your place. I’m looking forward to learning how to play pool. Hope it isn’t too late for you?”

“Nah, I’m a bit of a nighthawk myself. I’ll meet you back at my place in a bit. Just ring the front door bell.”

“Will do, thanks, Kali,” Shane said as he opened his door and stepped out.

He watched as Kali backed out and headed to her place. *Whew, that was a little bit personal. I hope I answered all her questions right,* he thought as he made his way to his front door and opened it. Taking off his shoes, he tossed his apartment key on the makeshift table, then grabbed a set of fresh clothes from his room and headed off to the shower. At 12:45 a.m., he was ringing Kali’s doorbell. It took a few brief moments before she answered.

“Hello, Shane, come on in.”

“Thank you,” he said as she stepped inside. “Wow, nice place you have here.”

Shane looked around briefly before taking off his shoes.

“Thanks, Shane, yeah it is a pretty nice place. I have cold pop in the fridge would you like one now?”

"Sure," he said as he followed her into her gourmet kitchen.

"I hope you like cola?"

"It is my favorite."

"Good. Grab a seat and have a sit down. I'll show you around once I get our drinks." Shane pulled up a stool at the island counter that jetted out of the wall, and watched Kali as she poured their drinks.

"So Shane, you are from Calimay?" Kali reaffirmed as she handed him his cola, and sat down opposite him.

"Yep."

Shane took a sip of his cola as he looked at her. His heart beat fast and he began to feel a bit nervous. How he hoped she wouldn't keep prying.

"I don't usually invite strange men into my home," Kali chuckled. "But, knowing that you know Sapphire and work at the Koffee House, I feel like I already know you. Besides, you are new to town and I don't mind showing you some good old New Kootenay hospitality," Kali once again began to chuckle. "I hope you don't think that is too strange."

"Not at all. I am quite pleased to have met you, actually."

Shane took another sip from his cola.

"It is a small world when you think about it. I've already met Nick and Sapphire both of whom are related to you, and oddly enough, your friend Rachel as well."

"I know it is a small world that is for sure. Rachel feels badly that she didn't give you a ride."

"I don't blame her. After all, she was alone on a deserted highway. I could have been anybody. She did the right thing. She must have family here, if that is the same Rachel you mentioned earlier that lives in Calimay."

"It is. Yes, she does have family here, her mother actually. When she was here the last time, when you met her on the road, she was just visiting. This time though, her mother has fallen ill. I should actually go see her soon, but I hate hospitals. I'll visit her I guess when she gets home. Rachel and I grew up here together in New Kootenay, we're bff's," Kali smiled.

"Bff's? What is that?" Shane asked innocently.

He had no idea what that meant.

"Best friends forever. You've never heard that before?"

Shane shook his head.

"No, never. I guess you learn something every day."

Shrugging his shoulders, he took the last swallow of his cola.

"Would you like another?" Kali asked referring to his empty glass.

"Nah, I'm fine."

"Alright. Well how about I show you around, and then we can shoot a game of pool," Kali said as she stood up and pushed her stool in.

"Sure. Thank you," Shane replied as he stood up and followed her.

She led him through a glass door and out to her backyard. "There is my pool. The towel house is there, and my little flower garden is there," she said as she pointed things out. "I even have a sauna, but that is in the basement, and we'll get to that soon enough. The pool table is down there too."

They walked side by side as Kali continued showing him around. He was in total awe. He had never seen such a nice place in his entire life, except from pictures in magazines.

"Undoubtedly, this is the nicest place I've ever seen. It must have cost a fortune."

"Yeah, I tend to spoil myself. But, I bought this place when the housing market was good and the prices were attainable and not outrageous as they are now. Otherwise, I probably wouldn't own it. It is a house that Rachel's dad designed and built back in the late 80's. I remember even back then how badly I wanted to own it. I guess you could say it was dream come true. When the opportunity rose, I pounced."

She continued showing Shane around and he continued to be in awe. Finally, with the tour over, she led him downstairs to her recreation room and a big black velvet pool table.

"There is my baby. I love playing pool. I probably spend more time racking up balls then I do swimming laps."

Shane was by now standing next to the rack of pool cues that were along one wall.

"You sure have a lot of pool sticks. Nice ones too," he commented as he pulled one out of the rack, "I've never really held one in my hand."

"For a beginner you'd probably like this one," Kali said as she reached for and pulled a 16 oz. one from the rack. "Check this one out," she said as she handed it to him.

Shane handed her the one he was holding and took the other from her.

"I don't know; it seems pretty light. I like the heavier one actually."

"Well then, here you go," she said as she handed it back to him.

"Would you like to give it a try? I'll rack up the balls."

"Yeah sure," Shane replied as he watched her gathering the balls and put them in the triangular rack at one end of the table. She rolled the white ball down to the other end.

"That is the ball we start with. You use it to smash the heck out of these ones. Hopefully, you'll get a nice clean break and sink a few."

Kali smiled as she removed the rack.

"I've seen it played, I just have never played," Shane commented as he walked to the other end of the table. "I can place this ball anywhere behind this line, right?"

"That is right. It is also a good idea to keep your chin directly in line with your stick."

Kali took a moment and showed him.

"Like this," she said as she lined up the cue ball.

"Okay, I think I can manage that," Shane smiled as he followed her instructions. Taking his time, he aimed the stick at the cue ball, and slammed it. It darted down the length of the table smashing into the balls at the other end, and with a loud crash, the balls went in all different directions. Three found pockets; the rest rolled this way and that until finally coming to a stop.

"That was a very nice break. You sunk two solid balls and a striped one. You can now decide which balls you want to sink, the solids or the stripes."

"Okay, I see. I guess mathematically a wise choice would be the solids."

"Yep, and as long as you keep sinking them you can continue to shoot until you miss. You can't move the white cue ball though. It has to stay where ever it stopped, so you have to be cautious when making your next shot. Go ahead, Shane, line up your next shot," she encouraged him. "Remember you are trying to sink the solid balls. The 8 ball is the last one we try to sink, so for now ignore it."

Kali smiled as she stood back and watched as Shane took his time again, and finally took his shot.

"Damn, missed that time. Your shot, Kali. This is pretty fun actually."

He stepped back and watched as Kali lined up her shot. Watching her bend over as she did, made his stomach churn and heart skip a beat, and for a brief moment, he felt a tinge of sexual arousal and excitement. His mind raced with the visuals he saw the night before as Kali and Rachel danced together and kissed. It was the sound of Kali's shot that brought him back to the here and now. Shaking his head to clear his mind, he watched as she sunk two of her own balls and lined up another shot.

"That was a nice shot."

"Thanks, Shane, I promise I'll go easy on you," she teased as she sunk another ball.

They played three games all together and Shane lost each time, but he was certainly having fun, both at shooting the balls and watching Kali, as his desire to bed down with her grew. He had never been alone with such a woman his entire life, and the more they played pool the more he felt the pangs of sexuality. It was quite evident to Kali that he was beginning to act as though he was indeed aroused. Her plan was working. There was no doubt about it, and she too began to have an urge. As the early hours of Sunday came marching in and they finished their last game of pool, they found themselves entwined in each other's arms, sprawled out on Kali's bed. She was surprised to learn that Shane was a virgin and so she took her time in pleasuring him and teaching him. She had never been with a virgin before and he had never been with a woman.

It was an incredible experience for both of them. The scent of her skin, the firmness of her breasts, and wetness of her womanhood, made Shane squirm with delight. He had never felt so good in his life as he slipped his manhood deep inside. She softly moaned in his ear as she moved her hips up and down, and his manhood grew harder with each thrust she made. Then, like a volcano, he erupted in her. Falling away from her warm body, he rolled onto his back, and inhaled deeply trying to catch his breath.

Kali lay there next to him, her own body quivering from the orgasm they shared.

"Oh my God, Shane, that was incredible. Are you sure you have never been with a woman before," she questioned with exasperation and satisfaction, as she looked over to him.

"Honestly no. That was my first time. I hope I didn't offend you in anyway."

"Offend me? No way. You pleasured me in a way I haven't been pleasured in a long time. Whew, that was awesome," Kali said as she wiped the sweat from her lip and brow.

They lay on her bed in silence for a few minutes as they caught their breath.

"You are no longer a virgin, Shane. How was it for you?" she questioned as she propped up a pillow behind her head.

"I've never felt that way before," he replied as he looked at her. "I can't believe we actually did that."

"Why not? We're both consenting adults. I didn't offend you, did I?" she asked, the same question he had asked of her.

"No, not at all. I know what I've been missing out on now," he chuckled as he ran his fingers through her hair and looked up at the ceiling fan that was blowing down on them. "I thought I would end up doing this wrong. I was a bit afraid at first, but you made it easy. Thanks," he said as continued to stare at the ceiling.

"It was new for me, too. I've never been with a man who has never experienced sex before. You did well, Shane, really, really well," she chuckled. "I'm thirsty, how about you? Would you like another cola?"

she asked as she rolled out of bed and draped a housecoat around her shoulders. She was a bit concerned that they hadn't used protection, but Shane was a virgin after all, and she was on birth control. She was pretty confident that all was well. Under normal circumstances, she would have requested he use a condom. This, however, wasn't a normal circumstance. It was a learning experience for both of them, and she felt good about that.

"Sure. I am a bit parched too," Shane replied as he pulled his clothes on and stood up.

He followed her back upstairs, his manhood still hard and taut. The smell of her wafted to his nostrils as he pulled up to the stool he was on earlier and waited for her to pour their drinks. His eyes never left her view and he stared at her. She was even more beautiful now than when he first arrived at her place. Perhaps it was due to the intimate moments they shared. Whatever it was, she was in his mind the sexiest women he ever laid eyes on. He was drawn to her, he wanted her again and again, but he knew their moment was past and they would likely never do it again. The experience he would take away from their little rendezvous would forever be a memory etched in his mind.

"Here you go," Kali said as she handed him a glass of cola and sat down beside him. "I hope you don't think I'm some kind of pervert. I don't jump into bed with just anybody. I really find you attractive though, and perhaps we went a little far, but I still enjoyed it. How about you?" Kali asked out of curiosity.

"I, umm, I certainly enjoyed it as well," he replied a little embarrassed but at the same time quite pleased at the fact. "I didn't know how that could make a person feel. It was all tingly."

Shane brought his glass to his lips and took a long swallow.

"I'm still tingly," Kali responded with a smile.

Her nipples were even hard and Shane noticed this, but turned his head in embarrassment as she caught him looking.

"That's okay, Shane. You don't have to shy away from looking at me like that."

She smiled as she brought her own glass to her lips. Setting it down after a long drink she looked into his eyes.

"You have beautiful eyes, do you know that?"

"I have been told that before, yes. And you have beautiful eyes too, not to mention a very attractive smile."

"Only my eyes and smile are attractive?" she questioned with a tease.

"No, everything is attractive about you," Shane responded as he smiled back at her, his face growing flush.

"Everything about you is attractive too. How is it that you have never been with a woman before. With the looks you have, it surprises me."

"I never found the time or felt the desire, I guess. I don't know."

He shrugged his shoulders.

"You've never had a girlfriend before?" Kali asked.

"Not really. I had a few friends who were girls, but I never had sex with them."

He lowered his head.

"You were the first."

"Well, being your first, I hope I didn't scare you. I know the first time I had sex, I was scared; not to mention that it hurt like hell."

Kali chuckled at the fact she said that.

He knew what she meant. He had been taught sex education while he was a patient. He wasn't completely ignorant to the difference between a male virgin and a female virgin. He looked over to the clock on her wall.

"Oh geez, it is 5:00 a.m. I should probably get back home."

"You sure you don't want to stay for breakfast? I can make us eggs."

"Thanks, but I should probably get. I had a great time with you, and I thank you for teaching me how to play pool and... well, you know."

Kali smirked.

"No worries, Shane. I'm glad we did what we did. Maybe we can get together again sometime. You still haven't beat me in pool," she teased.

"True, you are really good at that, along with other things too."

"Those things one learns as they go on. Pool though, takes a lot of practice."

She winked at him.

"As I said earlier, feel free to come by whenever you want. After all, we are neighbors. Don't be shy, Shane. Maybe you and Sapphire might want to come by and go for a swim some time. I'm usually home. Just keep what we did between us. I don't need Sapphire thinking I'm some kind of tramp," Kali joked as they stood up and she walked him to the door.

"No, I won't mention it to anybody. It is alright to let her know we played pool together though, isn't it?"

"Of course. You can let her know that we know each other. I don't see any harm in that; and honestly, I see no harm in what we did either."

"Well, I'll still keep that a secret."

Shane smiled as he put on his shoes.

"Thanks again for a great experience and good time Kali. You'll always be my first," he said as he opened the door and stepped out into the cool morning.

"See you later, Shane, and don't be a stranger, alright."

"I won't be. Bye for now," he said as he turned and walked in the direction of his apartment. Kali leaned against the doorframe as she watched him walk away.

Wow, that was quite an experience. She felt giddy at the fact that she was his first, and that he was her first virgin. Closing the door she skipped across her living-room floor grinning from ear to ear. *I had a great time with him. Too bad I'm not ten years younger, I'd scoop him up in a minute.* Making her way back to her room she slumped onto the bed and closed her eyes. Soon she was fast asleep.

It was a cool walk back to his apartment. The sun was only cresting the eastern horizon, and a pleasant summer breeze tousled his hair. *So, that is what sex is all about.* Shane thought as he made his way along the quiet street to his apartment.

Chapter 23

The sun was hot that Sunday when Blain rolled out of bed. Making his way into the bathroom, he cleaned up and brushed his teeth. Noting the whiskers that covered his face, he turned on the shower and stepped inside. His mind was drifting with the possibility that in only a few more days he may once again be reunited with Trent. He wasn't so sure, however, that the caller was indeed Trent. The voice he had heard on the other end was certainly familiar; he couldn't deny the possibility. *A couple more days before I'll know. I hate waiting games,* he thought as he rinsed his hair.

With a fresh coffee in his hand, he made his way outside to the back deck and let Havoc out to take care of business. He didn't bother sitting at the deck table and instead found himself walking around the backyard, checking on how the repairs to his lawn were managing. Where the new sod was laid out it seemed to be taking to the soil. There was only one brown patch and that was where Havoc had dug the last hole. Blain sipped his coffee as he inspected the small but bothersome blemish to his lawn. Kentucky Bluegrass wasn't cheap and if he were to add up all the money that they spent since Havoc came into their world, he knew it would only make him angry. *Ah, it'll come back. One little patch of brown isn't nearly as bad as a dozen, I'll get over it,* he thought as he now rose and made his way through the gate to get the Sunday paper.

A story of a missing youth did catch his eye, considering the area from where the young boy went missing. It was very close to the eastern corridor of British Columbia, in a small community called Black Hill, a coal mining community. Blain read the article. There did seem to be some discrepancy on where the youth was last spotted. Nonetheless, it was something he knew the Agency should look into. Perhaps the youth was a victim of a K-15 carrier, perhaps not, but it was his opinion that steps should be taken to prove or disprove any correlation between the last sighting and the assassination of a K-15 carrier who was discovered in the proximity of the eastern corridor. Setting the paper down on the back deck table, he made his way inside, leaving Havoc to have run of the backyard. Retrieving, his cell phone he dialed the agency's number. It was early and it was a Sunday. Chances were it would take Canbra a few minutes to answer. The phone rang a few times before she answered with a tired voice.

"Hello, Entity, how are you today?"

"Good morning, Canbra, you sound tired."

"I am, Entity. It has been a long and tiring week."

"Have you heard about the missing youth in Black Hill?"

"Yes. From what we know it doesn't sound like an attack, but more of an abduction. We're certain it is not the work of any carrier. We were able to gather information that the youth in question has been involved in a custody battle. It is possible his mother is the abductor. She has not been found, but her ex-husband has been. He claims the boy was taken by her."

"I see. So it is more of an Amber Alert?"

"Correct."

"That is good news, or at least better news than it could have been. I guess we'll leave it at that. Has there been any progress in other projects? Are all the operatives sent to the eastern corridor now settled?"

"Yes, they are all active. Nothing so far on any sightings, attacks, or otherwise. Gonsite is convinced the virus has petered out. We are far from being in the clear though. New research has been developed and we are almost certain the virus has once again morphed. The decline in attacks and sightings only proves this."

"Proves what exactly?" Blain asked.

"That we are on the verge of another outbreak of some sort. We can't say for sure at this stage, but it is quite likely K-15 has morphed to an STD. That's bad news, I know, but that is what we are trying to evaluate."

"We discussed this before. How much longer until we can say that is the case?"

"It might only be days, but Gonsite is leaning towards a month at the latest."

"A lot of people could be infected in a month. Is there anything else we can do? Can't we speed up the progress of this research?"

"Not unless you have come up with the history of the Brentwood family. Personally, I believe that is the key, but we have nothing on that as of today. The only Brentwoods we've been able to find have been the ones that we have already tested, and as you know, they were clean."

"There is obviously something we are missing, Canbra. I have an idea but we aren't going to be able to move on it until tomorrow."

"What idea is that, Entity?"

"Has the agency by chance tried to locate any Brentwoods that may be imprisoned or institutionalized?"

"Yes, provincial and federal prison data bases have been searched by our own computer hackers. Nothing on that name came up. This was done weeks ago, when you were in Mud Creek."

"Okay, so what about mental institutions?"

"Entity, you are bouncing around like a beach ball. Institutions cannot be searched simply because patients are not prisoners and therefore there is no documentation on names of people who have been institutionalized. Only admitting doctors, psychologists, lawyers, and judges have that information. We would spend a lifetime trying to track down any that might have that information, and even then, they are required by privacy laws not to share that information. In other words, it is definitely a roadblock. We would never have the resources or ability to do any kind of research on that possibility."

"Are you saying institutions can't be infiltrated?"

"I am saying there are too many to even consider an operation like that."

Blain fell silent for a moment as he thought about it. He knew Canbra was right, and for a brief second he felt foolish to have even considered the possibility. After all, really, where would they start?

"I see your point. I'm betting though that is a piece of this puzzle that we are missing."

"That may very well be the case, but it is irrelevant since there is no way we could find stuff out like that."

"Yeah, alright. I'll leave it at that. I don't suppose you have any word yet on securing a monkey for live testing?"

"Nothing. Professor Schuler hasn't responded yet to my request."

"Have you tried contacting him again?"

"Of course. He is a busy man. The last time I spoke to his office at the university, he was on an expedition to Iceland. He's expected back in a few months."

"A few months doesn't help our cause. Shit, things keep snowballing don't they?"

"It comes with the territory, Entity. We are an invisible agency that doesn't exist, remember?"

"I know. That might change someday, but someday doesn't help us today or tomorrow. I'll carry on in trying to find out more on the Brentwood name. I visited the archives of the Calimay Library last week. That too was a dead end. Perhaps I'll check the archives of local newspapers. The agency would have the capabilities of hacking into those, wouldn't it?"

"Again we'd be looking at thousands of newspapers. It is a task that could be done, but is there really a point? It could take months and resources that we don't have." Canbra sighed as she considered the possibility.

"I guess we just carry on then. It is evident we have put a dent in the K-15 carriers. We've slowed down its progress; there is no doubt about that."

"You got that right. Now though, we're going to see a new outbreak, and I fear it will be ten-fold to what we have been facing, especially if it has morphed to an STD."

"Indeed that is possible, but there isn't much else we can do but keep at it. So, there have been no new attacks that the agency is aware of at all, eh?" Blain asked with hope.

"Nothing. I tend to agree with Gonsite that it has petered out as we know it today. The next transition is going to be the worst we've ever seen, I think."

"Let's hope it never gets that far and the research Gonsite and his team are doing solves the issue once and for all."

"Exactly. Let's hope."

"Well, I guess that'll be all for now. I'm looking forward to the meeting I have scheduled for Thursday at the agency. All things are in place, correct?"

"Yep. I have the personnel folders you have requested ready to roll, plus a few names of very successful researchers working on Gonsite's team. They are looking forward to the meeting actually. So, you'll be here Thursday?"

"That is my plan. I might have a few surprises too."

"Like what?"

"I'd rather not discuss it on the plastic. I'll see you on Thursday, Canbra. Keep me in the loop on anything relevant, and I mean anything."

"Of course, alright, Entity, we'll see you then. Bye for now," Canbra said as she hung up the phone.

Blain turned his cell phone off and tossed it on the kitchen table, disappointed that there hadn't been any news Canbra had for him regarding attacks, sightings, or assassinations of K-15 carriers. It had been well over a month since anything substantial had happened, and it bothered him a great deal. Boredom wasn't one of his favorite states. But, there he was, bored out of his skull, waiting on this, that, and the other thing. It was always the same, whenever attacks were few and far between, the entire K.A.T. Agency suffered; he could hear it in Canbra's voice. She too was bothered at the recent decrease in attacks and slow progress in the research. Something had to give though, and usually when it did they would all be scampering. It wasn't that they were bothered at not being able to kill carriers as frequently as they had been, but rather, the unknown. That is what bothered all the operatives the most.

Blain decided that for now he would concentrate his efforts on finding out more on the Brentwood name, and most importantly Anvil Brentwood, to whom Trent had referred in his research and Rob had deciphered from the documentation he had. Pouring himself a coffee, an unorthodox thought came to mind. One of the things that hadn't been done as far as he knew was the Agency hiring a Private Investigator to search for any Brentwoods who hadn't yet been tested. He knew exactly who to call. The idea was so outrageous and simple that it only disappointed him more that it hadn't been done or even discussed.

Jesus Christ, why didn't we think of that, he thought as he took a drink from his coffee. *Damn, that is a solution, I think...yeah, I think that is what needs to be done. An investigator could get access to court records, psychologists' reports and the like. Only thing is how do I approach it?* He took another drink of his coffee as he contemplated. He knew he couldn't hire a PI under the Agency's name and that he would have to use his own name or one of his aliases.

The PI he was thinking about was Tyler O'Brien, and O'Brien knew him as Ben Todd. It would be that alias he used if he decided to follow through with it. It would certainly speed up the Agency's progress in trying to locate any Brentwood descendants that hadn't yet been found, and more importantly, finding the one named Anvil. He pulled up a chair and sat down at the kitchen table, the script he would use in contacting O'Brien playing over in his mind as he sat there. Picking up his cell phone, he once more dialed the Agency's number. On the second ring Canbra picked it up.

"Entity, how pleasant of you to call again so soon. What is up?"

"I need Ben Todd's accounts, cell phone number, and credit cards reactivated as soon as possible. I'm on to something here and I need an alias," Blain said in one breath.

"Hold on a second, Entity. Slow down a bit. Why?"

"I already told you why. I'm onto something and I need an alias."

"I can't turn all that stuff back on with a click of a button you know. It needs approval."

"I'm approving it right now, Canbra. I have no time to argue. Do it and do it fast."

"It is going to take a minimum of 24 hours, Entity. Can you explain why you need that?"

"I could but there is no need. You are going to have to trust me on this."

"Fine. I'm putting in the order to reactivate now. Geez, I hate it when you pull rank," Canbra teased.

"Don't get me started," Blain teased back.

Not often did he pull rank, but sometimes it was a necessity like now. If his plan was going to work, he needed Ben Todd activated and he needed it done yesterday.

"Will the activation take place by tomorrow?"

"I'm pushing it through as fast as I can, Entity. Under normal circumstances 'yes' I hope that answers your question."

"It does. Let me know if it goes through sooner."

"I will. Anything else, Entity?" Canbra asked as she continued to bypass the Agency's approval system by shooting Ben Todd's activation directly to the Agency's mainframe.

"For now, no, but if there are any activation problems before tomorrow, let me know a.s.a.p., alright?"

"You are the boss. I will, Entity." Canbra's hope was she would have it activated before the day ended. She could tell by his insistence that it was important.

"Entity, are you still there?"

"I am."

"Listen, I have bypassed the approval system and Ben Todd's activation is now processing, we might get lucky and have him up and running before the end of today. Does that help?"

“You are the best, Canbra, damn right that helps. Thank you very much. Let me know when he’s activated.”

“I will, Entity, you can count on it,” Canbra responded as she hung up the phone.

Three hours later she returned the call.

Blain picked up the phone immediately and answered, “Entity, here.”

“Ben Todd is fully activated in the Agency’s system, Entity. You will still have to manually activate, and your new PIN number is 2647.”

Blain quickly jotted the number down.

“Do you have time now to explain?” Canbra questioned.

“Nope. I’ll fill everyone in that it concerns on Thursday. Thank you, Canbra.”

Blain didn’t wait for a response before he hung up. Shutting his cell phone off, he retrieved Tyler O’Brien’s business card so that he had it in front of him. There were things he needed to do before he called, such as, for instance, gathering all of Ben Todd’s documents from his office and activating them. It was a quick process but tedious just the same. Rising from the table, he made his way outside and called Havoc, who came running around the corner with a bird in his mouth.

“What the heck have you got there?” Blain asked as Havoc dropped the bird at his feet. “I see, a bird. What are you a bird killer now?” he asked as though the dog would answer. “Good job, I guess. We have to head to the office, buddy. I’m not going to leave you here alone, so come on, let’s go.”

Opening the sliding glass door, the two entered the house.

“You might as well grab a drink and some food. It is already in your dish. I need to make a phone call.

Go on, go have a bite to eat and a drink," Blain said as he dialed Rob's number.

"Hello," Rob said as he answered.

"Hey, Rob, Blain here. How are you today?"

"Pretty good, how are you?"

"For a lazy Sunday, not bad. I've come up with an idea on how we can speed up the progress in searching for that Anvil Brentwood character. The Agency has hacked into all the provincial and federal prison mainframes and there is no one in any of them with the last name of Brentwood, which, I know sounds hokey, since there are probably hundreds of them. Obviously though, none are criminals. Anyway, I'm going to hire an investigator to help us out. Under the name Ben Todd, I'm going to hire Tyler O'Brien. He knows Ben Todd," Blain half chuckled. "We couldn't have very well hired him under the Agency's name, since it is invisible and doesn't exist. Couldn't have used my name either since he can identify me and knows me as Ben Todd."

"What a brilliant idea. Why was that never thought of before?"

"I don't know. Maybe we have all just gotten stupid over the years."

"Hey, speak for yourself," Rob razzed.

"Yeah, yeah. Anyway, since the prisons have been searched for that name and nothing has come of that, and the majority of Brentwoods that the Agency has been able to locate have all tested clean, I'm thinking we have been looking in the wrong places. One thing we can't search out are the mental hospitals, since only doctors, lawyers, and of course psychologists would have that information. I think that is where we need to focus on. A private investigator could obtain the information, but not plain old civilians like you and me. You see where I'm heading with this?"

"I do. It is a good move, I think. I have one question though. How do I fit into this?"

"I'm not sure yet. I only wanted to discuss the idea with someone. I didn't mention it to Canbra, only had her reactivate Ben Todd's accounts, credit cards and cell phone."

"That takes a couple of days, doesn't it?"

"I had her put a rush on it and he's activated in the Agency's system now. I only have to go through all manual activations. I'll have that done by the end of the day."

"You do know that it is quite likely Anvil is long dead, right? If he had Kuru, he may have lived for a year after being diagnosed with it."

"I realize that. The thing is there are no death certificates that the Agency has found. If he is dead, chances are he has been buried in a mental hospital's graveyard. If he had been buried in a prison's bone yard, there would be a paper trail, a death certificate, or something."

"Good point. That is true."

"So there you have it. It is possible that he may have had children too, even if they were born out of wedlock. I think a PI would have a greater chance at finding that out."

"Most definitely, I would agree. That is one of the things the K.A.T. Agency has always lacked, recognition. If we were a Government institution, the Agency would have access to such things."

"One day that might change, Rob."

"Possibly. Are you still going to be able to meet up with our caller on Tuesday at the Calimay airport?"

"Oh yeah, I'm not going anywhere. I'm only going to use Ben Todd's ID to hire Tyler O'Brien. Any meetings I'll need to have with him can take place at Henderson & Co PI Agency in Fruitmont."

“Indeed. In fact you could even use my address as your residence.”

“Good idea. See, I knew there was a place for you in this. Thanks,” Blain responded with sincerity.

“No need to thank me, Blain. I want to find out more about Anvil Brentwood as well. It’ll help my research too. In fact, it will benefit the Agency as a whole if we can come up with some answers. We’ve all been battling K-15 for years, and I would like to see it stopped, halted, or eradicated, as much as the next guy.”

“You are right on the money with that, Rob. We all want it to end. Gonsite and his team believe another major outbreak is going to start soon. They too are leaning more towards it spreading in the next onslaught as an STD.”

“I know. I believe the same. It morphs to something different every time after a calm like we’ve been having. One could say it is the ‘calm before the storm’.”

“We have a few things going for us, though. If our caller is Trent and he has an antidote we might be able to slow it that way. Although I don’t know how long it would take to duplicate, we would at the least have a starting point. Next, if we can locate a descendant of Anvil or Anvil himself, we might be that much further ahead.”

“All true. Let’s hope it turns out that way, and that we aren’t too late. K-15 as a STD would be most devastating. There are so many heterosexuals, bisexuals, and homosexuals in the world today that I think it would be virtually impossible to cure all of them that may end up infected. Not to mention how would we know? We have no idea what symptoms a K-15 STD carrier might have.”

“I know. I have been thinking about that since the first time the possibility was discussed. Hopefully, most people engaging in casual sex are using protection."

"I'm sure a lot are, but you can bet a lot aren't. Mankind is stupid that way. Think about it. Even after the discovery of AIDS, people continue to have unprotected sex. I'm guilty of that myself."

"I'd say that from now on until we figure this K-15 crap out, that you start doubling up," Blain half chuckled.

"No worries there, I have been."

"Good. I'm lucky that way I guess since I'm monogamous."

"Not everyone can be married, though," Rob pointed out. "I think we are going to need educational campaigns in the not so faraway future, especially if K-15 becomes a dreaded STD. Mind you, they did that with AIDS too and people are still being infected on a daily basis."

"AIDS doesn't spread only through sexual contact, though."

"It certainly doesn't and who is to say that K-15 won't spread the same way? We're not going to know that answer until we do more research."

"The more we talk about the 'ifs' and 'whatnots', the more I wish K-15 would remain as it is now. At least we have some control on curbing its spread," Blain sighed, "anyway, Rob, I think I'm going to get on with it. I'll probably make contact with that O'Brien fellow tomorrow morning. I'll fill you in once contact has been made."

"Sure thing, I'll keep my line open. Good luck."

"Thanks, talk to you later, Rob."

"Yep, see you later," Rob responded as he hung up the phone.

Blain sat in contemplation for a few minutes as he conjured up a world in his mind that was overrun by a K-15 STD. It was a world he knew that would never recover without an antidote or cure. He thought back to Rob's visit that Saturday and his prognosis of birth defects and neurological conundrums, which according to Rob, might include a greater desire for those infected to kill, rape, and cannibalize victims. The more he thought about it, the more he wished he hadn't. *I hope it never comes to that,* he thought as he stood up.

"Alright Havoc, are you ready to head to the office? Come on, let's go," Blain said as he made his way to the front door and slipped on a pair of shoes, Havoc trailing close behind.

By 2:00 p.m., Ben Todd was once more on the grid of life, and Blain was back home, finally able to rest. He spent a few hours lounging in his hammock, something he hadn't done in weeks if not months. Havoc lay on the ground beside him snapping at bees that came too close and every now and again, he would chase after birds that he thought he could catch. It was indeed a lazy Sunday, and Blain was grateful he had the time to enjoy it. It wasn't often in the past that he could, and so he took it all in stride. Whatever came of the day, came, whatever didn't, didn't.

Rachel was pouring herself another ice tea when the phone rang.

"Hello," she answered.

"Rachel, you are not going to believe what I did last night," Kali began.

"Let me guess you picked up the guy from the Koffee House?" Rachel replied with a smile as she shook her head.

"How did you know that?"

"An obvious guess."

"Yes, that is what I did. He was a stallion," Kali chuckled, "and a virgin at that."

"Oh my God. Are you serious?"

"I am or at least that is what he claimed. The way he wasn't sure about certain things makes me believe him."

"I can't believe you did that, Kali, shame on you," Rachel chuckled.

"I know, I feel I'm such a pervert, but it was consensual, so I guess it is okay."

Rachel took a sip of her ice tea and shook her head.

"Did you at least get his name?" she teased.

"Of course I did. It is Shane. I never did catch his last name though. At first we just played some pool and then one thing lead to another and before you know it, we were tangled up in each other's arms."

"My God, Kali, you are a perv."

Kali chuckled.

"Maybe, but it was a good time."

"How old is he?"

"That I don't know, but I'm guessing in his mid-twenties. He doesn't even drink. We had pop and friendly chit chat. I really enjoyed myself."

"Sounds like you did. What is on your agenda today?"

"I think I'll lounge around. He didn't leave here until early morning, 5:00 a.m., or something like that. I invited him and Sapphire by for a swim if they are interested in it. How about you, do you want to come over for a dip in the pool?"

"Not today. I'm getting mom's house ready for her return. Did you by chance find out if that girl you mentioned was looking for a live-in position?"

"Not yet, I will though, later on, after I rest up. I'll call her this evening when I know she is home."

"Okay." She sipped from her glass in her hand.

"I guess I'll let you get back at it, I'm totally tired," Kali yawned, "but I'll phone Jasmine later and let you know if she is interested in what you are offering. Does your mom even know yet?"

"No, I haven't mentioned it. I just think it would be a really good idea. I can't be here all the time. I honestly think she needs someone to help her out though. So, this girl's name is Jasmine?"

"Yep, Jasmine Birch. You might even know her. She used to hang out with my youngest sister."

"Who, Leanne?"

"Yeah, little Leanne?"

"Hmm nope, the name doesn't sound familiar. How old is she?"

"Late twenties. She's the same age as Leanne, I'm guessing."

"Alright. Well, let me know what she says when you talk to her."

"I will, Rachel. I'll talk to you later I guess."

"Yep, I'll be here. Talk to you then, Kali," she said as she hung up her phone.

Rachel couldn't believe that Kali had confided in her regarding her little escapade. Nonetheless, she was in a sense happy to know that Kali could at least talk to her about such intimate moments. *She is a crazy girl, that Kali is,* Rachel thought as she stood up and made her way to the back garden. Weeds had begun to take it over and so she took the time now to remove them by pulling out each one. It took her almost an hour to do, even with the gardening tools she used. When it was finished, it looked as good as her mom kept it. *There that looks better,* she thought as she put the gardening tools back in the shed.

Next, she moved on to the bed linen and did laundry. By 5:00 p.m., her mother's house was beginning to look as clean as a museum. Turning the outside BBQ on, she tossed a few chicken breasts onto the grill and made a salad. Noting there wasn't much food in the cupboards or for that matter in the fridge, she wrote out a grocery list and stuck it to the fridge. She'd get to that on Monday before she picked up her mother.

Back in Calimay, Blain was BBQing as well, except he was doing up a couple of steaks and with those he cooked up some frozen French fries. He poured himself a glass of chocolate milk and sat out on the deck with Havoc at his side while his steaks sizzled. The air was scented with the smell of them cooking and even Havoc licked his lips, as Blain turned them one last time. He had totally forgotten about the fries and when his steak were almost done, he heard the sound of the smoke alarm as it whined with unbearable shrieking, *God damn it, forgot about the fries,* he thought as he stood up quickly and entered the smoke-filled house.

Havoc remained outside not wanting to enter as the smoke billowed out. Blain by now had all the widows opened, and was fanning the oven with an oven mitt to clean the air before he removed the cookie sheet filled with charcoal burnt fries. *Looks as though it is only steak for me tonight. Oh well, that doesn't hurt my feelings at all,* he thought as he tossed the burnt mess into the sink.

"Should have been paying more attention, I guess. My bad," he said softly as he once more made his way outside to the back deck.

His mouth salivated at the tantalizing smell of the cooking meat.

"Sure smells good doesn't it, Havoc. I might give you a taste. Depends of course on how much I can eat, and now that there isn't anything to go with them, I might eat both," Blain chuckled as he stooped down and patted the dog. "I'm only kidding of course," he smiled, "you'll get a taste, boy. You've been good company and haven't dug any more holes so that is a plus for you in my book."

Havoc shook his stubby tail and rolled onto his back begging to be scratched on his tummy.

"Oh you want a belly rub do you?" Blain understood now as he rubbed Havoc's furry stomach. "You seem to be growing bigger every day. You're going to be a big fellow aren't you?"

Rising now, he flipped his steak one last time and tossed them on his plate.

"Man, these look good. Can hardly wait to bite into one."

He sat at the deck table and dug in, tossing a piece of the fat to Havoc.

"There, how does that taste? Pretty good, eh? I could live on steak without a problem. That and spuds. Too bad about those fries," he half chuckled as he finished his meat.

Leaving some meat on one of the T-bones, he set his now empty plate down on the deck and told Havoc to go ahead and finish. Grabbing the meatiest bone, the pup ran down the stairs and lay beneath a tree in the shade as he munched the bone. Blain rubbed his own stomach now in self-gratification. Full as he was, he wanted something else, just wasn't sure what it was. Making his way into the kitchen, he looked through the cupboards for that one thing he wanted, but he didn't find it, and instead settled on making a fresh pot of coffee. The phone rang as he poured his first cup and he answered.

"Hello."

"Hey, Blain it is me, Rachel. How are things going?"

"Hello sweetheart. Things are going good. I just finished eating. How about you? How are things going over there?"

"Pretty good, I suppose. Kali might have a friend that would be willing to live with mother and help her out. She is supposed to get back to me sometime this evening. How is Havoc? Is he behaving?" Rachel wanted to know.

"You gave him the name Havoc. What do you expect?" Blain chuckled. "Yeah, he's behaving. Getting big too, I noticed this evening. He's going to be a brute of a dog, I think."

"Well that is good. I wanted him to be big."

"And big he'll be. So, how is your mother coming along?"

"I get to bring her home tomorrow. I'll help her get settled in and I'll head for home on Tuesday. Can you live without me for a couple more days, Blain?" Rachel teased.

"Yeah, we'll be okay. I'll have to do some grocery shopping tomorrow. The cupboards are bare. You know how I hate shopping, but I'll survive. Is there anything special you'd like me to pick up?"

"Nope, not really. Just get what you need. I'll do grocery shopping when I get back home."

"Alright."

"Well, I guess I should let you go. I still have a ton of laundry to finish. Mom was really behind on that. Plus, I'm hoping to hear from Kali soon."

"Okay, well, I guess I'll talk to you tomorrow sometime. Let me know once your mom is home so that I know all is well."

"Will do, Blain. I love you."

"I love you, too. I'll see you on Tuesday," Blain said as he hung up the phone.

Bringing his fresh cup of coffee to his lips, he took a long swallow as he reminisced about the upcoming Tuesday and the fact that he was going to find out if the caller claiming to be Trent, really was Trent. He hoped for nothing more than to see his kid brother for the first time in almost 13 years. He wondered how much he might have changed, if he had changed at all. He knew that he, himself, had certainly changed over the years and it hadn't always been a change for the better. Time and years though and what he did for a living were to blame for his change.

He felt miserable most times and sometimes even suicidal, but Rachel kept him on the right track. God, he owed the world to her. If it wasn't for her he wasn't sure where his life as a K-15 Operative may have taken him. Likely, he would have swallowed a bullet by now. One couldn't kill people and not feel like that, but Blain knew what his mission was and that was to follow Trent's dream in cleansing the world of all K-15 carriers. Now though, as so many operatives speculated, things were once more changing for the worse. Not one sighting or one killing of any carrier had taken place in well over a month.

All the K.A.T. Agency people could do was wait it out and see what happened next. The good news was that there was a possible cure in the horizon, if the caller claiming to be Trent really was him, and he brought with him a sample of the antidote. The only problem Blain could see with that was the fact that the remedy was made for those suffering with K-15 as they knew it now, not the STD K-15 that the agency and its researchers were claiming to be what the next morph would be. He shuddered at the thought. There were teenagers and young adults that were experiencing sexual activity every day, and every day the K-15 STD if that is what it was now, had the potential of infecting hundreds of people a day. To Blain, that was the most devastating possibility. He inhaled deeply as he thought about it.

The only thing anyone could be sure of was that the virus either petered out completely or it had become a completely new strain of the deadly K-15 they were battling. Either way without confirmation and answers, everyone including the K.A.T. operatives, was in the dark. Every heterosexual, bisexual, or homosexual was in danger, and that didn't sit well with him. For now though, until some questions were answered, no one could be sure of what was going on except that something most definitely was.

The best case scenario was that K-15 was now in the past and like many super viruses it had dissipated and burned itself out. That was everyone's hope; chances were, though, it was only hope. Blain looked up at the clock on the wall. It was getting late and the late evening sun was slipping behind the western horizon as he looked now out his kitchen window. Tomorrow he had things to do, like contacting Tyler O'Brien PI extraordinaire. With luck he would be able to help him locate any surviving members of Anvil Brentwood's family or better yet, Anvil himself. It was a long shot, there was no doubt about it; nonetheless it was still a shot, and who better to locate a person other than a Private Investigator. Sunday evening now faded into the past and he made his way upstairs to bed, Havoc nipping at his heels.

Chapter 24

It was Monday morning when he put his call into Tyler O'Brien only to learn that O'Brien was away for the day. He was assured that once O'Brien returned to the office, he would call. Blain thanked the investigator he was talking with and hung up the phone. *Guess I wait for his return call,* he thought as he poured his second coffee of the day. Letting Havoc outside, he joined him on the deck and sat down.

"It's going to be another hot one today I think, and to think it isn't even July yet, close but not quite."

He slurped his coffee as he said that to Havoc, who simply rolled onto his back and looked up to the sky as though he was dead. It was Blain's cue to give him a belly rub, and so he did.

"I think I spoil you more than Rachel, but I'm starting to like you a bit more every day. I believe now that Rachel did well in picking you up. I have to tell you though I wasn't so sure at first, you cost us a lot of money in repairs and replacements in things you've either gnawed or torn up. Still," Blain stated as he nodded his head, "you are good company."

It was the frantic call from Rachel later that morning that tossed his Monday for a loop. Her best friend, Kali, had been found dead, lying face down on her living room floor. There were no signs of foul play and it appeared as though she had simply died from old age. Rachel was in total hysterics as she relayed the message to him. There was something else too and she wasn't even sure she should mention it to the police; the last thing she wanted to do was paint her friend as a sexual deviant, but she did tell Blain.

"I don't know if that would have any bearing on her death, Rachel," Blain tried to console her.

"But isn't it odd that she slept with a stranger and then was found dead?"

"If there is no reason to believe that foul play is involved, I don't see the correlation. It is up to you, Rachel, if you want to mention that to the police, I just can't see how her sleeping around had anything to do with it. Perhaps she was sick and didn't tell anyone. I think you should calm down as much as you can. I'll head to New Kootenay right away."

Rachel began sobbing over the phone.

"It is so sad, Blain. I saw her only on Friday and she was her usual self. There was nothing that made me wonder if she was ill in anyway."

"Sometimes these things can't be picked out; sometimes people keep illnesses to themselves. You are going to have to calm down, Rachel. As I said, I'll head to your mom's house right away, Havoc and me both. I'll see you in a couple of hours, okay?"

"Thank you, Blain. I'm so devastated right now I don't know what to do, I still have to pick up mother sometime today.... and... and," she started to bawl as the memory of Kali only days earlier danced in her head.

"Rachel, Rachel, listen to me, calm down. I'm on my way, alright?"

"Yes, yes, okay Blain. I'll see you in a few hours," Rachel replied as she hung up the phone.

"Well, Havoc, we have a road trip to go on. Damn! And my Monday was starting off the way I like it to, calm and cool and collected. Now this. Oh well, come on, I need to pack a few things and make some quick phone calls."

The two entered the house and Blain poured another coffee to keep with him while he packed and made the calls. He called Rob and filled him in that he might very well have to meet the mystery caller by himself. Rob didn't mind and said that he would.

Next, he called the Agency and told Canbra that he'd be off the grid, referring to his work, for a couple of days, but that he still had every intention in making the meeting that was scheduled for that Thursday. All things good at that end, he dialed O'Brien's number once more to leave a message that he might be out of cell phone range for a while that day but nonetheless would await his call later. Only thing was, O'Brien just happened to have stepped into the office for a quick review of some documents that pertained to a case he was working on, and so he answered the phone.

"Henderson & Co. Tyler O'Brien here, how can I help you?" he answered.

"Hey, ahh, yeah. Mr. O'Brien, this is Ben Todd."

"Ben Todd? Jesus, how are you? How are you feeling these days?"

"All healed up, feeling pretty good. I was wondering if you'd be able to help me out on locating somebody?"

"I don't do domestic cases, if you're asking me to investigate a cheating wife."

"No, no, no, nothing like that, I'm trying to locate an old friend," Blain lied.

"What avenues have you already tried?"

"Everything I could think of. Then one day, I found your card and thought why not give you a call and see if you'd be interested."

"I'm always interested in new cases. Missing persons though aren't really one of my specializations. Who are you looking for?"

He was totally taken aback when he heard the name Anvil Brentwood.

"You said Anvil Brentwood?" O'Brien wanted to clarify.

He was shocked at even hearing that name, considering his bullets had put Anvil to rest years ago.

"Yes, that is correct."

"Is this a hoax or what? I know exactly who Anvil Brentwood was. I killed him years ago, What did you want with him?" O'Brien asked with evasiveness.

"You shot him?"

There was as much evasiveness in Blain's voice as there had been in O'Brien's.

"Anvil was a murderer back in the late 90's early 2000. He suffered from some kind of disease that came and went like the diarrhea he was. Anyway, I've already said too much. What was it you wanted from him?"

It took Blain a few minutes to reply as he sat there dumbfounded. How likely was it that Tyler O'Brien knew and killed Anvil.

"I ummm. Whew, Ah, I think we should meet and discuss this. Is there any chance of that happening?"

"There isn't much to discuss. It was a long time ago. I am interested though in knowing why you'd be looking for a dead man."

"That is why we need to meet. I work for a private agency. We do research in disease control. The name Anvil Brentwood has been mentioned in earlier documentation regarding an unknown virus that has been widespread here in British Columbia. There really isn't much I can explain to you on the plastic, Mr. O'Brien, but I'd certainly like to meet with you. I will be able to explain our situation better in person."

"You can call me O'Brien; no need for that mister crap. I'm pretty busy today and right through until Wednesday, we can meet sometime then."

"I live in Calimay. I know that you have an office in Fruitmont. Any chance we can meet there?"

"I work out of our Ridgeville office and Fruitmont is a distance away, but I could meet you there. Not sure it would be Wednesday though."

"Can we make it for Friday?"

Blain was hoping it would give him more time to take care of a few things before they met. He wasn't sure how he would even approach him then, but he already let the cat out of the bag. It wasn't supposed to have happened that way, but it had, and now he needed to explain the entire thing to O'Brien. *How I hate when things go wrong like this,* he thought as he waited for O'Brien's response. He could hear the shuffling of a few papers as O'Brien obviously looked at his itinerary for Friday.

"Yep, looks like I can be there on Friday. What time is good for you, Ben?"

"Whatever works best for you."

"How does 2:00 p.m., sound?"

"Sure. That works for me," Blain replied.

"Alright then, I'll see you in Fruitmont on Friday at 2:00 p.m."

"Will so. Thanks O'Brien, looking forward to our meeting," Blain said as he hung up the phone.

He almost felt dizzy there was so much going on, the death of Kali, Rachel's mother, the meeting he was supposed to have with some mystery caller, the research regarding which direction the K-15 virus was heading, the meeting he had now with Tyler O'Brien who only by coincidence knew Anvil Brentwood and in fact had killed him. He didn't know all the details now, but it was safe to assume that it he was about to learn a lot about Anvil. Not only would he be learning about Anvil, but, he was going to have to explain to O'Brien exactly what the K.A.T. Agency stood for and what it was they did, or so he thought.

With his calls done, he headed out to his car and straight for New Kooteny. He was able to drive only a few miles to the outskirts when all of a sudden he had to pull off the road because his head was spinning. He sat in his car as traffic raced by, shaking his head at how things had gone from simple that day to utter disbelief and confusion. He looked over to Havoc who was sitting on the front seat with him, drooling slobber all over the place.

"My, my, this day has just turned into a piece of shit. I have a lot of explaining to do now. For almost fourteen years not a soul knew about the K.A.T. Agency and now because of one phone call, I'm in deep. I got a couple of days to figure it out I guess. Best to take it one day at a time, eh Havoc? All the worrying I do today isn't going to change tomorrow's outcome."

Blain looked through his rear view mirror and side mirror making sure it was clear before he turned back onto the highway and continued on towards New Kootenay. The drive went quickly and before he knew it, he was driving up Kali's street as he made his way to Rachel's mother's place. There were quite a few cars in Kali's driveway, as family members gathered to grieve. He thought he saw Rachel in the window, but continued past and pulled into the Dupree driveway a few blocks away. There was a note on the door that said Rachel was indeed over at Kali's house, and he was invited to meet her there.

Blain sighed. He wasn't in the mood for that. It was sad enough that Kali had died; he really didn't want to be saddened anymore by all the crying and talk that he knew was going on. Instead, he made his way into the backyard and sat down at the picnic table and waited. Luckily, Rachel had seen him as he drove by, and after waiting a few minutes for him to show up, decided that she'd head for her mom's place, telling everyone that she would return later. Blain heard Rachel's car pull up next to his and he and Havoc met her as she was making her way to them.

She ran up and tossed her arms around his shoulders and began to sob.

"I, I'm going to miss her so much Blain. We've been friends since high school. God this world can be cruel. She was so young and vibrant. Why, why did she have to die!"

Blain wrapped her up in his arms even tighter and ran his fingers through her hair trying to console her.

"It'll be okay, Rachel. Come on, take it easy. Has there been any other news on what happened?"

"Nothing. Just that her niece Sapphire found her. Sapphire said her body was all contorted and that her face looked as though she had aged ten years. I don't know what could have happened to her. No one does."

"She may have had a heart attack or something. It does happen to folks our age all the time nowadays."

"No, no, Blain she couldn't have had a heart attack. She swims and dances and did exercises every day. I was with her on Friday and she was fine. I even talked with her yesterday, and that is when they are saying she must have died. For Christ's sake, this is so out of the ordinary, I can't make heads or tails of it. What could have happened, Blain? What?"

She began to sob even more dramatically as she said all that.

"I don't know, Rachel. I don't know," Blain cooed as he helped her to the table and sat her down. "I'm sure there will be an autopsy performed. Until then we can only speculate."

"What if that guy she picked up did this to her? What if he poisoned her or something?"

The more Rachel talked, the less sense she made, but Blain sat there and listened, cooing her every chance he had to console her.

"If she was murdered, Rachel, the autopsy will show that, and the last person to see her alive will be questioned. Now this guy, do you know who he is?"

Blain wanted to know out of curiosity. “Or is it somebody you have never met?”

“He works at the Koffee House. I did see him before. The last time I came here, he was hitchhiking and then on Friday, Kali and I...,” she began to cry again, “Kali and I saw him at the Koffee House. He works there now. Kali picked him up to play pool or something and to show him some hospitality since he was new in town. She told me she had sex with him, yadda, yadda, that was about as far as that conversation went, and that was the last time I spoke with her. And, and, it’ll be the last time too. Oh my God, Kali, Kali!”

Rachel broke down and put her head in her hands as she cried hysterically for a few minutes. Finally, catching her breath, she looked over to Blain.

He reached across the table and wiped away the tears streaking her face.

“Does this person even know that Kali has died?”

“I have no idea, I haven’t seen him since Friday. This is so terrible, Blain. God, she was my best friend. I’m going to miss her so much.”

“I know, I know. Everyone who knew her is going to miss her. We have to go on, though, in life, Rachel. We can grieve and grieve for years, but it will never bring back those that we have lost.”

“It is so damn sad and confusing. I can’t understand why she died or what might have happened. I guess I shouldn’t be so selfish. I can’t imagine what her family is going through. I’m so sad for them.”

“All part of the grieving process I’m sure. We have to take some time and remember her for her life, not her death. It is indeed a sad day, though.”

They fell silent as they remembered Kali and her philosophy of life. She was a carefree soul, happy to be single, liked to travel, and enjoyed life in general. There was no doubt about it; New Kootenay, had lost one of its most charismatic residents.

"I haven't even told mother yet. I'm sure by now she has heard the news though. There is so much going on, I'm sure glad you are here with me, Blain. Thanks for putting your work off."

Blain shook his head.

"You don't have to thank me, Rachel. Kali was a friend of mine too, and I would drop a day of work anytime if you or any of my friends needed me. I am glad to be here, actually. I only wish it was under different circumstances."

Rachel inhaled deeply as she now accepted the fact that Kali was dead. There wasn't much she could do but wait for the funeral and be strong for Kali's family.

"Well, I guess I better get cleaned up. I have to get mother soon," Rachel said.

Blain could tell she wasn't ready for that and instead offered to pick her mother up himself.

"I'll do it, Rachel. I wouldn't want you driving until you are feeling better. I lost one friend today; I don't want to lose my wife, too. Come on, I'll help you inside and make you some tea."

Blain rose and helped her up. Walking with their arms around each other, they made their way inside. He pulled out a chair at the kitchen table for her.

"There, you sit and I'll put the kettle on."

A few minutes later he handed Rachel her tea and poured himself a coffee. Havoc sat at their feet feeling uneasy about the new place, but nonetheless realized they were all there for a reason. He knew this by the way Rachel had shown sadness. He may have been only a dog, but he knew his people.

"What time am I able to pick up your mom?"

"Anytime after 2:00 p.m. It is almost that time now," Rachel said as she looked across the table at Blain.

God she loved him, everything about him she loved. To see him grieving over the same thing, seemed odd, not usually was he so deep. Rachel reached across the table and put her hand over his.

"I have missed you, Blain, for a long time. I'm so sorry that I even considered a divorce that last time. I understand about your desire to be all you can be, and you know what, you are everything in the world to me. I really, really appreciate you being here. I only wish it was like this all the time. I know now though it can't always be, and I thank you for being who you are."

She said that with sincerity and commitment. Blain knew she meant every word of it. He too felt the same about her and he wasted no time in telling her.

By 4:00 p.m., Rachel and her mom and even Blain were finished with their sobbing over the loss of Kali. For the remainder of the evening they reminisced about her as they shared stories and enjoyed each other's company. It was both a sad and somber day, and things would never be the same, but in time even Kali's family would heal, as would they. Finally as the evening came to a close and flowers and cards were ordered for Kali's grieving family, Blain, Rachel and her mother bid each other good night and retreated to their rooms.

Blain had a hard time sleeping. His mind now at ease about Kali's death, warped into overdrive in regards to the possibility that the caller he was supposed to meet the next day at the Calimay Airport was indeed his brother Trent. He was grateful that Rob would be there and disappointed that he wouldn't be, but that was life. That was how things went sometimes. His first concern had to be the death of Kali and comforting Rachel. Everything else would have to come second. He wouldn't know the outcome of the airport meeting regardless until he contacted Rob and until then he'd have to wait. Coming to terms with that, he finally closed his own eyes, and alongside Rachel fell asleep.

The following day the three of them spent time with Kali's family, offering their condolences and joining in on friendly conversation with all those present at Kali's home. It was a quiet get together. More tears were shed and laughter was shared, as everyone reminisced about the Kali they had known. It was early evening when people began to leave. Her parents decided that there would be one last visit at Kali's house after her funeral, and all those attending the funeral were asked to come. After that, her house would be cleaned out and put up for sale.

By Wednesday afternoon, word came in that Kali had died due to blood clotting brought on by an undetermined cause. Her body showed no signs of disease whatsoever. She was free of all known viral infections that could cause clotting, all that is except one virus no one knew about; the virus known as K-15, which the K.A.T. and its researchers had speculated had morphed into a deadly STD. Her funeral was scheduled for the following Monday. It was that Wednesday evening that Blain headed back home, leaving Havoc with Rachel and her mother, who had become very attached to the pup.

There were important meetings he had to attend on Thursday and then another one on Friday, but he did promise to return for Kali's funeral. There wasn't much else he could do in New Kootenay. Rachel was feeling better and she wanted to help out as much as she could with Kali's funeral arrangements, so it was decided she would stay behind for now. There were other things she needed to take care of as well, such as bringing up the conversation with her mother regarding a live-in.

It was 9:00 p.m. when Blain pulled into their driveway in Calimay. The first thing he did was call Rob to find out about the airport meeting. He was totally speechless when Rob handed the phone over to Trent.

"Hello Blain. Yes it is me. Sorry to hear about your wife's friend."

There was a long silence as Blain computed in his mind that he was talking with Trent.

"I, I, can't believe this is you. What the Hell, Trent. Why couldn't you have filled me in on this years ago. What was the big idea leaving all of us here to think you were dead? Jesus Christ, holy crap, man. What the Hell."

He was elated at the fact it was Trent and at the same time angry as Hell that he thought him to be dead for all these years. He had no other way of expressing himself, and Trent listened with respect and intent as Blain went off this way and that.

"I know, I know. It is a long story, Blain and I can't wait to fill you in on the last thirteen years of my life. Just know that things are good. I have a cure for K-15 and all its derivatives."

"I fucking don't care about that right now, Trent. Jesus man, do you know what you put me and everyone else through? Fuck, fuck man, I'm your brother. For thirteen years I've cried on the anniversary of your death. For thirteen years I've carried the sadness of losing you on my fucking shoulders."

Again there was a long pause as Blain caught his breath and cooled down enough to be able to talk.

"I tell you, I'm glad to be talking to you, but am having a lot of trouble keeping my cool with you," he sighed, "you know what you got owing to you from me don't you?"

Trent began to chuckle. He knew exactly what Blain was referring to and that was a whister-poop upside the head.

"Yeah, I do and I will gladly take it."

Tears welled up in Trent's eyes now as he thought about how devastating his presumed death must have been for his older brother.

"There aren't any words I could say Blain to make this all better. I did what I did because I had to. I'll explain it to you as soon as we can meet."

"Sit your arse down right where you are. I'm on my way to Fruitmont right now."

"Excellent. I'll see you when you get here," Trent said as he waited for a response.

There was none though, only the sound of a dial tone. Blain had already hung up and was out the door and on his way, making sure he had all of Trent's old research that he knew he would have to hand over to the Agency on Thursday.

Trent chuckled as he hung up the phone on his end.

"Blain is on his way."

"Good. He should be here in an hour or so," Rob responded. "You guys have a lot to catch up on. I think I'll head into town and leave the two of you alone."

"Thanks Rob. That would be appreciated."

"No problem. I'd rather watch a strip show then watch Blain strip a piece off of you, and you can bet he will," Rob chuckled. "You guys go ahead and make yourselves at home. Help yourself to coffee or whatever. There is even some whiskey in the cabinet. I'll come back later this evening or I'll see the two of you tomorrow."

Grabbing his keys and slipping on a jacket, he headed into the great big town of Fruitmont and the only bar/hotel in the entire town. *Hope the two of them don't burn the place down. Damn, I don't know how I would react if I had a brother who vanished for thirteen years and was presumed dead. I think I'd go off the deep end. Glad we had our talk about that yesterday. Even after that though, I was still peeved at him. I imagine Blain is too. Poor Trent.* Rob smirked as he thought about that. He knew it would be both a happy reunion and an angry one too.

Blain's head was spinning as he drove. Thirteen years was a long time. The thought that Trent had been alive and well all this time ate at him like worms in compost. That wasn't the only thing though. Kali's death and everything else that was or had been going on ate at him until it felt like his head was going to explode. There were so many feelings he was having that he almost drove off the road on a couple of occasions because his mind was so befuddled with the utter shock that Trent was alive. Finally, he pulled off at a viewing area and flung opened his door in time to vomit. It helped him feel a bit better, and he wiped his mouth with his shirt sleeve as he caught his breath and focused on the here and now and tried to come to terms with everything. After a few minutes of realization, and feeling calm enough to carry on, he continued on his way.

The rest of the drive to Rob's house went lightning fast and before he knew it, he was pulling into the driveway. It was 10:30 p.m. He could see Trent sitting in the window and watched him as he stood up and opened the front door. Stepping out of his car, he darted towards him and gathered his younger brother up in his arms and squeezed him in a bear hug, then punched him square in the mouth.

"For thirteen years you've been dead to me, and I've been saddened by your death. You couldn't even find it in yourself to shoot me a fucking letter. What the Hell was the matter with you, Trent. Jesus Christ!"

"I know, I know, I'm sorry about that and yeah, I should have sent you a letter or something, but I wasn't free to do whatever I wanted. I was watched by the Uganda Government like a cat watching a mouse. I was kept in solitude and had no access to keeping in touch. At first, I was under the impression that I wouldn't be a prisoner, and so I agreed with what was offered. Once I arrived in Uganda, I was briskly taken away to the Uganda Disease Control Center and locked up like a common prisoner. They treated me well enough, but I was never given access to the outside world. For all those years I worked with a team of top notch researchers. It wasn't until the cure was found that I was given the opportunity to leave or stay. I chose to leave, and when I did, I managed to steal a small vial of the formulated cure, which we can duplicate here," Trent said in one breath as he wiped his bloody mouth.

"Why couldn't you have let me know before you left?"

"There was no time, and I thought you would have tried to convince me otherwise. I knew you'd continue on here and keep our dream alive of a K-15 free world. From what Rob has told me, that is exactly what you and the others have done."

"Of course it is, but we aren't even close to finding a cure, and it would seem that K-15 has morphed again. There haven't been any sightings or attacks in well over a month."

"What we need to do, Blain, is forget about the past and get busy with the cure and its replication. The cure we did find in Uganda will destroy all the derivatives of K-15 that are possible. In Uganda the virus morphed many times to different viruses, but every person that they brought to us who was suffering from each, recovered with no side effects. It will do the same here."

"Only thing is, here in the western world, we don't have access to human subjects. So how do we go about distributing it?"

"That is something we'll have to work on. Perhaps pharmaceutical companies will buy into it once we have it perfected and replicated."

"Where does that leave the K.A.T. Agency?"

"The K.A.T. can be noted as the developer. Once we have the cure perfected there is enough documentation of the disease that we'll be able to convince those in power of its existence. That is the biggest hurtle the Agency has had, convincing the scientific community. That will change now."

"How can you be sure of that?"

"Because I have one contact from Uganda who is willing to come forward with documentation and enough scientific evidence to prove what it is we are facing."

"Yeah, well you had all of that way back when and still no one bothered to listen."

"That is because the K.A.T. Agency remained anonymous. The Uganda Disease Control isn't and they have governmental access to the World Disease Control. In fact, my contact is already working on this. We have two weeks to replicate the cure and make it available. It is going to take him about that long to make contact with the WDC. He is actually risking his own life, because the Uganda government has no desire to treat the outside world. If they ever get wind about what my contact is doing, he'll be struck down and buried."

"Sounds like Uganda is a pleasant place. I guess we shouldn't waste time, then. What do we need to do to get this thing moving?"

“A few ingredients and some equipment. Rob already has most of the equipment set up in his lab. The ingredients aren’t going to be so easy to get though, since there aren’t any documented carriers as of late. This is where the trouble lies. Rob said you two have found the documents regarding Anvil Brentwood. He is the first carrier of this disease. We need to locate him or anyone who is related, a direct descendant would be best. Rob mentioned that you have been trying to do that.”

“Yep. I actually have a meeting with a Private Investigator here in Fruitmont on Friday who knows a little bit about Anvil. In fact he’s the one who reportedly killed him. He claimed that Anvil was a serial killer and he ended his life years ago. So, locating Anvil himself is out of the question. Our only hope is that he has children or living siblings.”

“I was afraid of that. Without a blood sample, things might be tough, but there is hope. I have enough serum to get us started.”

“How much is enough?”

“Enough for twenty-six vials. Each vial will produce enough antidote for five carriers.”

“One hundred and thirty antidotes might only scratch the surface.”

“I know. But once K-15 becomes public knowledge perhaps our Government will request any related Brentwoods to come forward voluntarily or they could reach out to them with legalities.”

“I don’t know about that. Would you admittedly come forward if you were related to a serial killer? I don’t think it’ll happen that way. Besides, people change their last names all the time. I think it’ll have to be enforced by the Government. That, however, could take years.”

"Yes, there are many issues we need to be aware of, but they shouldn't get in our way. They will only slow us down. I say we do what we can before it comes down to that. Your meeting with this PI might solve that issue altogether."

"It might not too."

"Let's hope that it does. Are you ready to come in now and have a sit down?" Trent gestured to the kitchen table.

"Yeah, I guess we can continue this inside. Where is Rob?"

"He figured it was best to leave for the evening and give you and me the chance to catch up. He's aware of all these issues too," Trent commented as the two of them made their way inside and sat down. "Quite the adventure the two of you had up in Mud Creek."

"He told you about that?"

"Yeah. I'm glad it worked out though, and the two of you made amends. He's as good a researcher as Gonsite."

"I think so, too. He's lucky I didn't shoot him. His character Hector was a complete asshole and there were many times I thought about wasting a bullet on him. I'm glad now that I didn't. Which brings me to my next question. Did he tell you that he was supposed to be dead, that Chase was supposed to have killed him years ago, because he murdered seventeen people?"

"Yes, he did. It was explained to me. Those he killed were trash anyway, and I have to salute him for experimenting with live subjects. Not just anybody could do that, I know, because that is what we did in Uganda and not every time was it pretty."

"I bet not. How about making us some coffee, Trent? I could use a cup."

"Sure thing. So, I hear you are married and everything," Trent commented as he stood up and went about making coffee.

"Yep. It has been a tough go but Rachel and I seem to always work things out. She was contemplating a divorce a few weeks ago. My life hasn't been all peachy, that is for sure. When this is all finally over and I come clean with her, I still might be facing a divorce. I've been lying to her since the beginning. Deceit is a terrible thing to have to use. But, the Agency requires that. I hope that will change in the very near future. I'm sick of it to be honest, and now that you are back with the living, I just might walk away from the K.A.T. You can take it over."

"I'm not sure how the Agency would react to that. After all, I am supposed to be dead."

"Yeah, well you're not. I have a meeting tomorrow with the Agency. Maybe you should come along and take the licking you have coming to you from those still working there who knew you when you were around."

"Not sure that would be the right thing to do at this stage. I'd rather hold off and wait until we get closer to duplicating the serum. We should keep it hush, hush, until then, in my opinion."

"You could be right about that. Both you and Rob need to be inducted again; there is no two ways about it. For now though, I'll agree with you. I won't say a word about your return or Rob's for that matter until we're further ahead with development of your antidote. Rest assured though, both of you are going to have to step up to the plate eventually."

"I know. But now isn't the time. Soon though."

"Yeah, two weeks," Blain said as Trent handed him a coffee.

For the rest of the evening the two brothers reacquainted themselves with each other again. They even got into the whiskey. It was around 2:00 a.m. when they both finally passed out, one on the floor the other on the couch.

Chapter 25

Hung over as he was, Blain managed to hit the road before Rob returned and before Trent woke up. Leaving a note behind, he told Trent that he would make his way back to Rob's later that day and the three of them could go over everything together. He wanted them to start trying to duplicate the serum for K-15. There was no point in putting it off. The sooner they got started, the sooner they might be able to go public.

Sighing, Blain looked out the window as the sun rose. He had a long drive ahead of him. From Fruitmont to Clarkston it was easily a four hour drive and that is if one was in good shape and not hung over as he was. It would take him anywhere from four to six hours, he estimated. He checked his watch. It was 7:00 a.m. That would put him in or near Clarkston at the latest 1:00 p.m. Making his way out to his car, he made himself as comfortable as he could and settled in for the long tiresome drive.

Stopping for gas and a coffee, he used the restroom and splashed water on his face to clear away the cobwebs. *Should probably pick up some deodorant and maybe a razor too. Could have a shave and slap some pit stick on before I have to meet everyone,* he thought as he looked at himself in the small restroom mirror. *Should never have gotten into the whiskey, I feel like a bucket of crap and I don't smell any better, damn.* Exiting the restroom, he made his way back to his car and headed in the direction of Clarkston. Again, everything seemed to be in turmoil. He was getting tired of it that was for sure. Every time he turned around it seemed as though something else popped up.

Normalcy, humph, what is that... he thought as he carried on. His mind raced thinking about the day when he would finally retire from all of this. Now that

Trent was back with the living, he knew it wouldn't be long, but even then and after that, what would his life be like? That was the question. For fourteen years, he had known one thing only and that was living a lie. It would end eventually, but then he'd be faced with questions, and some he knew he'd never be able to answer. He often asked himself if what it was he did was even worth it. The Agency had slowed the virus down but had never annihilated it completely. Even now as he drove, he doubted the virus would ever be defeated. Giving up was never one of his strong points. There was always hope, and sometimes that is all anyone ever had.

Trying to beat time on the other hand was impossible, because time would always win. He knew this. He and the Agency had fought time for years, and today they were running out of it. If they didn't get ahead in the time race they were all in, then the virus would undoubtedly win, and he didn't want that to happen; no one did. Two hours outside of Clarkston, he pulled off the road and dialed the Agency's number.

"Hello," Canbra answered.

"Right back at you, Canbra. I'm close to Clarkston. A couple more hours and I'll be there."

"Excellent. We're all looking forward to meeting with you."

"Who is 'we' and how many of you are there today?"

"I called in all the operatives except those who are in the eastern core."

"Good. Do you have the documents and personnel files I requested on hand?"

"I do. I have it all here with me."

"Alright. Freshen up the coffee pot."

"That has already been done."

"Geez, you are ahead of me. Good to know. Alright, I'll see you all soon."

"Looking forward to it, Entity; or can we call you Blain since this is a formal visit?"

"Either or."

"Fair enough, we'll see you soon."

"Yep," Blain responded as he turned his cell phone off.

He sat in contemplation for a few minutes before turning back onto the highway. It had been a long time since he had met up with everyone, a year at least. Under normal circumstances, he wouldn't have been on his way now. There were things however that needed to be addressed, such as the security breach, and it was relevant that he hand over the information and documentation that Trent worked on. Soon they would all have to be on the same page. For now though, what he, Rob, and Trent were about to work on would remain unknown to the Agency.

Two hours later Blain pulled into the industrial area of Clarkston and the warehouse that housed the K.A.T. Agency. Parking his car, he stepped out into the warm afternoon and reached back for his briefcase. Making his way inside, he was met by Canbra and Dwayne.

"Afternoon guys," he said as he walked up to them and shook Dwayne's hand, then hugged Canbra. "It has been a long time."

He looked around.

"Glad to see things haven't changed much."

"Some things have and some things haven't," Dwayne smiled. "You are looking good Blain, you haven't changed much. Still got all your hair even."

"It is in the genes," Blain chuckled.

"I've often wondered what else is in those jeans," Canbra teased. "Just kidding, Boss. Sure glad to see you though. It has been a long time."

"Yes it has. I'm here now though. So, is there an office available where we can sit down before we get started?"

"Sure is, right this way, Blain."

Dwayne led the way to an empty office that had a couple of chairs and an interview table.

"Would you like a coffee Blain?"

"That would be great, thanks Dwayne," Blain responded as he sat down and tossed his briefcase on the table.

Canbra pulled up next to him and smiled. "So, how have you been, Blain?" she asked.

"Surviving; yourself?" he asked as he opened his briefcase and waited for Dwayne to return and be seated.

"Me too, I guess; surviving. Things have sure slowed down, haven't they?"

"Yeah, they have. Seems mighty odd to me, too."

"It seems odd to all of us. Dwayne and a few of the researchers who work alongside him have come up with a few different reasons on why this is happening. The good news is that the carriers of K-15 as we know them may have very well been slowed. The bad news is his research has shown the decline of attacks to be related to a rise in temperatures."

"You mean like global warming?"

"Yep. I don't know all the details; he'll explain it, but I tend to agree. The average world temperature over a period of time has gone up ten degrees. Somehow this affects the virus as a whole."

"What is the bad news about that?"

"If summer temperatures have risen, it is possible that the fall and winter temperatures might fall below normal, in which case..."

Blain cut her off there. “In which case the attacks may only be in remission for a short time. Is that about the gist of it?”

“Basically.”

“That is bad news. What about the possibility of it being an STD now. Is that still being looked into?”

“Most definitely. As I said, the K-15 virus and its carriers as we know them today may have slowed down, but that doesn’t mean it has stopped. More research needs to be done on that before we can say for sure. I think though, that we are going to be faced with an onslaught of killings soon. This virus is constantly changing from one form to another. It always seems to get ahead of us.”

“Yeah, it does seem that way, doesn’t it?” Blain questioned as Dwayne finally made his way back to them with three coffees on a tray.

Blain and Canbra thanked him as he handed each of them a cup.

“I take it that Canbra has mentioned the few issues we’re having with this damn virus?” Dwayne asked as he pulled up a chair and sat down.

“Yeah, she has. Global warming, eh?”

“It seems to be that way, yes. Research has shown that at certain temperatures the virus goes to sleep. It isn’t able to withstand temperatures above thirty-two degrees, and as of late around here we’ve been having temperatures of thirty-five, give or take.”

“We’ve always known that after a carrier has been assassinated that our operatives have to burn their corpses. But, those temperatures are a hundred times hotter than thirty-two degrees. What you are saying is that at thirty-two degrees the virus goes dormant?” Blain wanted to confirm.

“That is what our research shows. It doesn’t mean that the virus can’t be spread. It is just that at those temperatures, the carriers lose their desire to mutilate victims. K-15 can still be spread, via sexual activity, which is what we believe is happening now. Once the temperatures drop, their killing sprees will continue," Dwayne replied as he took a drink from his coffee. "I know how all that sounds, Blain, but that is what we are faced with. Scientific research proves it."

"Wow, I thought we were making progress in stopping it completely. I guess not, now," Blain replied.

"Without a designer serum or antidote, K-15 will always be what it is. Without the backing of our Government or for that matter help from the World Disease Center (WDC), we're going to be battling this damn thing until the end of time," Canbra pointed out.

"I don't believe that. I think we have the means and ability to stop it. We only need a bit more time. The problem with that is that time isn't what we have. It won't be long before autumn hits, a couple of months at most. If Dwayne's research is correct, which I don't doubt is, then, we have bit of a grace period here. I say we put a few more researchers on it and go full tilt in coming up with a cure. If at all possible work 24/7. There are what, six of you working in research, Dwayne?"

"Yep."

"Canbra, how soon can you dig up 6 more?"

"It might take a week. It isn't like I can advertise the job publicly."

"I realize that, but the Agency does have connections. Plus I'm sure a couple of our field operatives have research abilities. With the attacks slowed down at this point, pull a few of them from the field. Dwayne could probably train a few of them, right?" Blain questioned as he looked at him.

"I probably could. If nothing else the extra help might be all that we need. I'm for that Blain, for sure."

"There we have it. Let's build up our research team and go from there."

"Who should I pull from the field?" Canbra asked as she took a drink of her coffee.

"I imagine the two of you could go through our field operative's personnel files and go from there. It might take a day or two, but I have faith that you will choose the best candidates. I really wouldn't know. That is why we have you guys," Blain chuckled. "Whoever you decide to pull from the field, replace with the next in line. That is best, I think."

With all three in agreement, Blain moved on to the second phase of his visit. They made their way into the meeting hall and were met by the stares of ten field operatives. Blain went to the front of the room and introduced himself. Most of the operatives knew him, but there were a few new faces amongst the crowd.

"I gathered all of you here today for a couple of reasons," he began. "One is that over a period of time a security breach to the Agency's mainframe has occurred. I cannot stress how important it is to follow protocol. The K.A.T. Agency has been in operation for fourteen years. Many of you have been with us since then, but I see that a few of you are new. Welcome to the K.A.T. Agency.

The protocol we have for this Agency is as simple as we care to make it. It is required that passwords, both public and personal ones, are changed every six months and whenever one of us leaves the Agency. This is for our protection and most importantly to keep the Agency as private as possible. A couple of these passwords were not changed for years and it was that part of the Agency's mainframe that was jeopardized. The issue has been corrected at this point and I am glad to say that not any relevant information has been leaked, none, that is, that couldn't be fixed. This, however, doesn't excuse the failure.

The person in charge of those passwords knows who he or she is and I'm not about to point a finger at him or her. It was a mistake, a procedure that was overlooked on their part and they know now how important it is to keep the passwords updated and changed. The rest of you who use our database will be expected to change your passwords by the end of the day. Canbra and Dwayne will enforce this.

Now that the password issue is out of the way, I want to move on to what we as an Agency as a whole is up against.

The K-15 virus that we are all familiar with, as you all know, has morphed again. It is because of this that the attacks have become sporadic. We are, however, far from the light at the end of the tunnel. Dwayne and his research team have discovered something that will, for the time being, benefit our field operatives. You all need to be aware that it is due to the temperatures we have been having this summer that has slowed the carriers attacks down. There is also a real possibility that the carriers continue to spread the virus, only now they are spreading it through sexual activity.

The Agency, as of today, will be on high alert for any and all rape victims, both genders, of course. Those having consensual sex aren't very likely going to know anything is even wrong until it is too late."

He paused for a moment as he paced and contemplated what else he could say about this new focus.

"Doctor so and so, from the local Hospital or free clinic isn't going to be looking for an STD that he or she doesn't know a thing about, and that, of course, would be the K-15 STD. The Agency will monitor all local hospitals and clinics in our immediate area, from

East to West, with our focus on those patients who are reporting genital irritations. Rape victims, of course, don't walk into clinics for checkups. They are whisked away to hospitals where rape kits are used. It is relevant that those field operatives that are selected to obtain the information be discreet and do not compromise Clinic or Hospital medical reports in this regard.

You get in and you get out. Any and all swab and blood samples including rape kit samples that you also may be required to retrieve, must be handed over to Dwayne and our research team. Do not take complete samples leaving the doctors and hospital with nothing. The key words here are 'samples only'. It will be a tough undertaking, but I have faith in each of you and know that all of you have the diligence and ability to do the job; otherwise you wouldn't be working for this Agency. You are all the best that there is, and this new focus of stealing medical reports and samples is no different than tracking down and assassinating K-15 carriers. Diligence and discretion on when to act and when not to act will all come into play. Are there any questions?"

There were a few and Blain answered them all. With the questions now out of the way, he excused the ten operatives and he, Dwayne and Canbra continued with their meeting.

"That turned out better than I was expecting." Blain commented. "I'm not very good at these types of things. We have a great bunch of folks working here."

"It is as you said. They are the best that there is. I was particularly impressed with some of the questions they asked. I took each of their names down. I think it should be those few that we put in the field to monitor the hospitals and clinics. The majority were senior operatives. The rookies are a little green, I think."

"I wouldn't disagree. Get them out there and give them the cover they will need."

Blain looked at his watch and noted it was getting on to 3:00 p.m.

"Well, I don't want to wear out my welcome. Everything I needed to say has been said and I have learned a few things too, so, I think I'll head out. I have a long drive ahead of me."

Rising he gathered up his briefcase opened it and handed Trent's research over to Dwayne.

"This, my friend, is all of what Trent worked on. I know by giving it to you it is in good hands. Let me know what you find out."

Dwayne took it from him and started thumbing through one of the folders.

"You bet Blain. This will certainly help us out. Good stuff," Dwayne said as closed the folder.

He and Canbra walked him to the door.

"Well, Blain, give me a hug," Canbra said as she wrapped her arms around him. "It was good seeing you. Do pop by once in a while, I'm always here."

"I know, and I just might come by again sooner than you think. You two take care," Blain responded as he hugged her back, and shook Dwayne's hand.

"Keep me in the loop on any findings and whatnots that might come from Trent's work."

"Of course."

"Alright then, I'm all set. I guess I'll see the two you again sometime. Take care, you guys," he said as he opened the door and stepped out.

Canbra and Dwayne waved to him as he pulled out onto the street and headed home.

"He hasn't changed one bit, has he?" Canbra mentioned as she and Dwayne made their way back into the office where they sat with him.

"Not one bit at all. But, that is Blain. It was good seeing him that is for sure," Dwayne replied as he and Canbra sat down at the table. "These folders of Trent's have a lot of good insight. He had a brilliant mind."

"Indeed," Canbra responded as she grabbed one of the folders and began thumbing through it.

The drive back to Fruitmont that Thursday evening went well and at 8:00 p.m. Blain pulled into Rob's driveway. He was tired from the day's travel, but in good spirits. Things went well at the Agency and he had a few new insights to share with both Rob and Trent. It took Rob a couple of minutes to answer the door when Blain knocked. He and Trent were fastidiously working on the serum and so at first they hadn't heard the knocking. Finally Rob answered and invited Blain in.

"We've made some progress today, Blain. We're only a few tests away from duplicating the serum. Still, we're in need of some blood samples, but I think our progress is going to surprise you. Trent may have been gone for thirteen years but he's as quick as a whip with this research stuff."

"Good to know. I hope you don't mind if I take a shower. It has been a long day and my own body odor is quite revolting," Blain chuckled.

"No go ahead, help yourself to whatever you want. Trent and I will just be upstairs."

"Thanks, Rob. After I clean up and shave we'll have to have a sit down. You guys will be able to break, won't you?"

"I don't see why not. We've been at it steadily since 9:00 this morning. I don't think we've taken a break in a few hours. The shower is right that way," Rob pointed.

“Thanks,” Blain replied as he took off his shoes and sauntered into the bathroom, while Rob headed back upstairs.

“Blain is back. He’s having a shower, should be with us in a few minutes,” Rob reported as he pulled up a stool next to Trent and continued with the work they were doing.

“Good. I wonder how things went at the Agency?” Trent replied as he continued looking through a microscope.

“I don’t know. He seems pretty happy so I guess it wasn’t that bad. He looks a little tired. That is about it.”

“Yeah, it’s quite the trip to Clarkston and back. I used to hate that drive. Boring as watching golf,” Trent chuckled.

“I hear you. I think I’d rather play golf.”

“Me too, probably.”

There was a pause as Trent magnified what he was looking at.

“I hadn’t noticed this anomaly before. It seems this sample is deteriorating. Better get it on ice. It looks as though we’re missing one crucial step with this sample. What the hell. Take a look, Rob. What do you think?”

Rob stood up and looked through the microscope.

“Looks like you are right. Hmmm, what did we miss?”

“I don’t know, but we are missing something. Luckily we were able produce a few samples before this happened. I wonder if it has to do with the temperature. We had a problem in Uganda like this once; lost an entire batch and had to start all over. We’re going to have to toss this in the fridge, I think. Might be able to save it,” Trent said as he took the slide and made his way to Rob's bar fridge. "There we'll leave that in there with the others, and have another gander at it later.

We should maybe take a break now and pick up where we left off tomorrow. I'm just glad we were able to save those other three vial samples. Good progress for a day, I'd say."

"I agree, yeah. Let's break and get some food and coffee into us. It is early enough to fire up the BBQ and toss some steaks on the grill. What do you say?"

"I'm all for that," Trent agreed as he and Rob made their way down to the kitchen.

"I'll get coffee started."

"Okay, I'll get the BBQ going. There are a few steaks in the fridge freezer. You might as well toss them into the microwave to thaw them for a few minutes."

"Will do," Trent replied as he got coffee going and pulled the steaks out. "These aren't beef steak are they?"

"Nope, elk. They're delicious too."

"Geez, I haven't eaten Elk in years. I bet they are good."

By now Blain was finished showering and met them at the kitchen table.

"Man I feel 100% better after that. I was getting ripe. So, how did things go today?"

"Progress, progress. We managed to duplicate and fill a couple of vials. Things went kind of weird a few minutes ago. I think we'll be okay, though. Thank God for Rob's bar fridge. I don't think the serum can handle prolonged room temperatures."

"That is one of the things that Dwayne mentioned today, not about the serum, of course, but K-15 in general. His research has shown that the virus' progression has slowed due to the high temperatures we've been having. Could be that is what you guys are faced with in duplicating the serum."

"Really? I guess that does make sense and relates to why we haven't had any new attacks. The temperatures have been really hot lately. I hadn't thought about that," Rob said as he poured a coffee.

"It makes sense though. We had trouble too in developing the serum a few times in Uganda, but it is always hot there. We did notice a change in viscosity and when we cranked the air conditioning, things progressed nicely. I should have clued into that then. So, what Dwayne is saying is that the K-15 virus isn't as aggressive under hot temperatures. That would explain the difference between what we call K-15 and what Uganda calls 'laughing disease'. Man, after all these years of research, we're only figuring that out now?" Trent asked with interest and annoyance.

"I don't know. There is obviously some reason why the attacks have slowed down. The problem is, it doesn't mean the carriers aren't continuing to spread the virus. It is just that now they are doing it by different means. The idea is now, as Rob proclaimed a few days ago, it is possible that the virus is being spread via an STD. They are still working on that at the Agency, and we're putting a few field operatives out there to monitor the hospitals and clinics. We'll have more insight on that in time. My meeting with Tyler O'Brien tomorrow regarding Anvil Brentwood might also shed some light. I don't know, I'm only speculating."

"There is no doubt that a blood sample from that fellow or a child of his or even a sibling would speed this entire process up," Trent said as he looked at both Rob and Blain. "I only wish we had managed to locate a descendant by now. If K-15 has morphed to an STD, we're going to be behind by a few months. Damn, I hate the thought of that."

"Not much we can do about it though. We'll just have to work our asses off and see what we can come up with," Rob replied. "I think we are going in the right direction and if Blain can come up with some answers on Anvil, we'll be that much closer to solving the entire K-15 issue, I think."

Blain nodded his agreement.

"We can't get blood from a dead man, but a direct descendant would certainly help. Only thing is, right now we haven't a clue if Anvil has any."

Silence filled the room as they thought about that.

"In which case we'll have to do all we can with what we have," he added as he brought his coffee to his lips and took a swallow.

The microwave dinged letting the trio know that the steaks were thawed.

"Excellent," Rob said as he stood up and pulled them out. "You guys are going to be in for a real treat, once these babies are done. I harvested this Elk a couple years ago. It is the best Elk I have ever eaten."

"I can hardly wait," Blain said as he licked his lips. "I haven't had a thing to eat all day."

"It won't be long," Rob replied as he gathered the barbequing condiments and headed outside to his deck. "You guys want to join me out here? There is a great view of the sunset. Grab a couple of those ciders, too."

"Yeah, I could use some air. Where are the ciders you are talking about?"

"Oh yeah, I put them in the kitchen fridge when we needed the bar fridge."

"Alright," Trent responded as he and Blain made their way outside.

The smell of the grilling Elk steak as they sat down tantalized their palates and their mouths watered. Trent handed each of them a cold cider.

"You weren't kidding about that sunset; what a beautiful view."

"One of the best in all of Fruitmont, I'd say," Rob responded as he cracked open the cider and took a long swallow. "I shot this Elk up there," he pointed to the mountain where the sun was slipping behind. "There are actually a few others up there too, and I'm hoping to put lead in one again this fall. Blain said he might even join me. What about you Trent? Would you like to go on a bit of a hunting expedition this fall?"

"I've never hunted game before. Might be fun. We'll see how it goes."

"That would be great to have the three of us up there in those mountains. I have a cabin up there too. It isn't nearly as posh as the one you guys have at Mud Creek, but it works."

Rob flipped the steaks and dosed them with his homemade BBQ sauce.

"I make my own BBQ sauce too and it is a might hot. I hope you guys don't mind."

"Not at all. It smells damn good already," Blain commented as he stood up and leaned against the deck railing.

"How much land do you own around here, Rob?"

"I got a deal on seventy-five acres, half of which my cabin sits on."

"You are one lucky bastard to have that much land. What are your plans with it?" Blain questioned to make conversation.

"I'll likely keep it as wild as it is. Someday I might log some of it off or maybe subdivide, I'm not sure yet. Once the money I have accumulated over the years runs out, I'll decide then."

"I know the Agency never paid you enough to buy all this," Blain started to smirk. "I'm thinking you won the lottery or you have a few hippie gardens up in those hills."

Rob looked at him and smiled.

"Hippie gardens? What do you mean hippie gardens?" he teased as he flipped the steak one last time. "You're not suggesting weed are you?"

Blain nodded and chuckled. "Nah I would never suggest that."

"Well, you'd be right Blain. I don't smoke the shit, never have and never will, but you wouldn't believe the money one can make with it. I made near one hundred and fifty thousand dollars my first time and almost double the next. After five great seasons, I was able to put away well over five hundred grand. Had to do something. The Agency thought I was dead," Rob chuckled. "So now you know."

"Yep, now I know."

Blain looked at him and smiled.

"Too bad you don't smoke it. I've often wondered what it would be like. I've heard there are a lot of medicinal properties, I think they should legalize the stuff myself and tax it. The government would make a ton of revenue. BC bud, I've heard, is the best there is."

"Legalizing it would certainly help our economy. Only thing is, it will never happen. Those in power claim it to be a gateway drug which in my opinion is a load of crap. It doesn't matter though. I haven't grown the stuff in a few years. Sure have been living the good life, though, with the money I made. I have no intentions on growing it again either. It's too damn risky. Not so much in prison time terms, but in being ripped off and maybe killed, which I really don't want to happen. I leave it now to the growers who have protection. I've made my money. No use risking my life anymore."

“Makes sense,” Blain replied as he took a swallow of his cider and once more averted his gaze to the mountains that surrounded Rob’s place.

By 11:00 p.m., they retired for the evening, their stomachs full of some of the best steak they had eaten and their thirsts quenched with a dozen apple ciders. Tomorrow was the big day they would have some answers on who Anvil Brentwood was and if he had any living descendants.

Chapter 26

On Friday, the meeting with Tyler O'Brien went well and he was pleased to help Ben Todd out as much as he could. He explained to Blain how Anvil's death went down, and that he wasn't sure if he had any kids of his own. However, he did know that Anvil also had a sister who since died from Kuru. That was all Blain needed to know. Now the name Brentwood meant something. Now he knew that there was indeed a correlation between the name and the K-15 virus.

Blain hired Tyler to search for any living descendants of the Brentwood name. O'Brien agreed and told him he'd be in touch in the next couple of days, by mid-week at the latest. With their meeting over, Blain headed back to Rob's to fill him and Trent in on the results of the meeting. He was relieved that Tyler didn't question him too much regarding the Agency he worked for, or for that matter what it did.

"So, there we have it. Anvil was diagnosed with Kuru, but he also somehow managed to survive for a few years and would likely be alive now hadn't Tyler put a bullet in him. He also said that Anvil had a sister who did die from Kuru a few years before Anvil ate lead. O'Brien is going to see what he can come up with in the next couple of days in regard to any living descendants of Anvil or his sister."

"You didn't tell him who you really are did you? Or, for that matter, about the K.A.T Agency?" Rob asked.

"Hell no. I went in as Ben Todd. I had to because that is who he knows me by. I told him nothing else. At first I thought I might have to come clean with him, but I managed to steer around that, thankfully."

Blain took a drink of his afternoon coffee.

"I guess for now you two should continue with what it is you are doing, and I'll head back to Calimay. I have a funeral to attend on Monday. Once I hear back from O'Brien, both of you should be ready to move in case there is a living relative somewhere."

"Do you honestly think that there is?" Trent questioned.

"It is hard to say. O'Brien was certain that Anvil himself didn't have any kids. Up until he was killed, he was a transient. That doesn't mean though, that he didn't have kids. It is that none were obvious; that is all that means. There is hope, I suppose. O'Brien will find that out one way or the other. Until we hear from him, we'll not know. He is also going to look into Anvil's sister's past. Maybe she had kids."

Blain shrugged his shoulders.

"We're pretty much at a standstill in that regard until he fills us in. I guess now we know why the Agency was having trouble in tracking down a Brentwood with that DNA string that seems to put K-15 at rest. Obviously, the Brentwoods that they were able to track down aren't in any way associated or related to Anvil and his sister. The two of them are key, I'd say."

"I would agree there." Trent added. "I know my earlier research came up with that name. Only thing was I was whisked away to Uganda before I could do any further investigation into it. One good thing came from that. Now at least we have a small amount of antidote. Rob and I will keep working on it until we can fill at least twenty-six vials. It could take some time though, but I'm confident with or without a blood sample from a Brentwood descendant, we should be able to manage that."

"I have faith that you will," Blain responded as he rose from the table. "I'm going to head back now to

Calimay. I'm not sure how I will ever explain your rise from the dead to Rachel."

"When we get everything else figured out, we'll deal with that then," Trent offered.

"Yeah, I suppose that is best. Still, Rachel is going to be some surprised, not to mention the rest of the crew at the Agency. I still don't condone what you did Trent, nor do I condemn you for it. I am glad to have you back in my life, but and I repeat, never ever do that again," Blain said as sternly as possible. "These past weeks I've seen Rob rise from the dead and you. I'm not sure I could handle anymore dead rising," Blain half chuckled. "Anyway, you two keep at it and I'll stay in contact with you. As soon as I hear from O'Brien, I'll fill you in. And if there is anything that comes up between now and then at your end, let me know. I'll do the same. Agreed?"

"Agreed," both Rob and Trent answered in unison.

"Good, alright then, I'll be in touch. I'll talk to you later," Blain said as he made his way to the door.

"Oh yeah, about that hunting trip this fall, Rob, I think I'm into it. Those Elk steak we had last night sold me on the idea."

"Excellent, it'll be awesome to have you tag along. What about you Trent?"

"If Blain goes, I'll go, for sure."

"Cool. So, once things settle down, each of you will have to take the C.O.R.E (Canadian Outdoor Recreation Education) program and get FACs as well."

"A Firearms Acquisition Card, you mean?"

"Yeah."

"Not sure I need that, I'm already authorized to carry a firearm," Blain mentioned.

"Small caliber, yes, and probably under an alias," Rob chuckled. "You need a FAC to carry large caliber long guns."

"Well, I guess we'll work on that at a later date. No use getting ahead of ourselves."

Blain opened the door and stepped outside, as Trent and Rob followed.

"Okay, I guess I'm off."

He nodded to them as he made his way to his car and slid inside. Waving he pulled out of the driveway and headed for Calimay.

Back in New Kootenay, a new autopsy was scheduled for Kali's remains. One of the ME's had identified a type of STD that likely contributed to her death. It was a strange STD and one that until now had never been discovered. It appeared to have been the cause for her blood to clot. The virus somehow managed to constrict her breathing as well and now there was speculation that asphyxiation was also a part of her sudden death. It would have gone unnoticed under different scrutiny, but luckily or unluckily, depending on how one looked at it, the truth was a STD of unknown origin was about to sweep across Canada.

The bad was that now the K.A.T. Agency would eventually, and sooner than predicted, have to come forward with what it was they discovered over the years of being in practice, something the Agency on the whole wasn't ready to disclose yet. The good was that there were no more carriers of the old K-15. They had all been eradicated. There was only one carrier left and it was the K-15 STD virus that he carried and not until the authorities began looking for him, did he even know.

Dr Fansworth had indeed identified a certain viral infection. It was one that she had never before come across. What it meant to the world in general was that a new STD had been discovered. Dr. Fansworth immediately called upon her colleagues to help identify the virus and work began in pursuing who Kali may have had consensual intercourse with as recently as a week prior to her death.

As the days progressed into weeks and then into months, the K.A.T. Agency came forward with its own research. Both Trent and Rob were reunited with the Agency and its operatives. Tyler O'Brien's investigation into finding a direct descendant of the Brentwood family came up with one name, Shane Brentwood. After running for a short time to avoid those looking for him, Shane came forward voluntarily and was whisked away to a Government Research Lab, where both the K.A.T Agency and medical community developed an antidote for K-15 STD. Immunization programs were started by the Canadian Government and by 2009, the virus was eradicated and no more attacks took place.

Blain came clean with Rachel and retired from the Agency. He and Rachel moved on with their lives and became joint owners of the King Royal Hotel. Their life was finally back on track.

The lies and deceit that Blain Sweet lived by for fourteen years ended, and he was forgiven by the only woman he loved. Rachel's mother recuperated and eventually agreed to having a live-in caregiver.

The K.A.T. Agency still operates today taking on Disease Control that no other Agency has the ability to confront.

The cabin in Mud Creek became a second home to Blain and Rachel. Although, while there, he was still known as Ben Todd, life was good for now at least.

Author Biography

Brian is a nine-time published author.

In September 1988 until December 1989, he attended Columbia Academy of Radio, Television & Recording Arts in Calgary, Alberta, where he majored in Broadcast Journalism. Following that, and ten years later, he attended Selkirk College in Castlegar, British Columbia from September 1999 until April 2001. He was enrolled in UT Courses – English History, Philosophy, Creative Writing, and Canadian Literature. He majored in Print Journalism.

He has been happily married for 27 years and counting. He has four children, two from previous relationships, and two with his current wife.

He grew up on a small hobby farm outside of Fruitvale British Columbia. In 2000, he wrote for The Source, a community newspaper in Fruitvale. Since then, he has done freelance writing of human interest for the Trail Daily Times.

His book titles include: Absolute Anger, Escape, Bloodlines, Red Rock Canyon, The Coalition of Purgatory, Chased by Shadows, Return to Red Rock and the forthcoming title The Missing Years- Part 1: (a Tyrell Sloan western).

He is also the co-author of the recently released title, A Bloodstained Hammer, a true crime story based on actual events.

William Jenkins, Publisher

This publishing house was established in 2015 for the purpose of self-publishing the stories by William Jenkins. These stories are intended to be supplementary reading for elementary school students (about Grade 5).

Brian and William have yet to meet, although they did communicate years ago when Brian was writing his first book, "Chased by Shadows".

When Brian's previous publisher decided not to handle new books, Brian and William got together to keep some of Brian's books available.

William Jenkins has published books by Brian Seifrit, Olive Caldwell Lee, Jackey Mukhawana and his own writing (mystery-adventure stories for kids between 9 and 90).

Any communications with the publisher can be emailed to:

williamhenryjenkins@gmail.com

Information on how to order these books is available at website:

http://www.williamjenkins.ca

or by searching on Amazon.com or Kindle websites for books by Brian T. Seifrit.

81069453R00232

Made in the USA
Middletown, DE
20 July 2018